The Ark

The Ark

by
André Arnyvelde

translated, annotated and introduced by
Brian Stableford

A Black Coat Press Book

Visit our website at www.blackcoatpress.com

ISBN 978-1-61227-432-4. First Printing. September 2015. Published by Black Coat Press, an imprint of Hollywood Comics.com, LLC, P.O. Box 17270, Encino, CA 91416. All rights reserved. Except for review purposes, no part of this book may be reproduced or transmitted in any form or by any means, electronic or mechanical, including photocopying, recording, or by any information storage and retrieval system, without permission in writing from the publisher. The stories and characters depicted in this novel are entirely fictional. Printed in the United States of America.

TABLE OF CONTENTS

Introduction

This is the first of two volumes containing translations of all four of the original novels that André Arnyvelde published during his lifetime. Although each of the four is complete in itself, the four narratives form a coherent sequence tracking a single theme, and they gain considerable interest from being read as a set, in the order of their composition. This first volume contains the first two, *Le Roi de Galade, conte bleu* (1910), here translated as "The King of Galade; a Fantastic Story" and *L'Arche* (1920), here translated as "The Ark." The second, entitled *The Mutilated Bacchus*,[1] contains the other two, *Le Bacchus mutilé* (1922), translated as "The Mutilated Bacchus," and *On demande un homme... ou L'Étrange tournoi d'amour* (1924), translated as "Man Wanted; or, The Strange Tournament of Love."

"André Arnyvelde" was the anagrammatic pseudonym of André Lévy, who was born in Paris in November 1881. He completed his education at the Collège Saint-Barbe, whose alumni included Gustave Eiffel, Alfred Dreyfus, the socialist leader Jean Jaurès and Louis Blériot. Already committed to literature before that completion, he then hung around with young writers of the Symbolist school, including Guillaume Apollinaire, and lived a conventionally unconventional Bohemian existence for a while, doing odd jobs, singing in Montmartre cafés, and writing for the radical press, as well as poetry, until he achieved a strange celebrity in 1902, at the age of twenty. Having written a comedy in verse, *La Courtisane* [The Courtesan], he submitted it to Jules Clarétie, the director of the Comédie Française—a gesture of bravado and seemingly-impossible ambition. Improbably, however, Clarétie accepted the play immediately after having read it, and the publicity

---

[1] Black Coat Press, ISBN 978-1-61227-433-1.

generated by that decision made Arnyvelde suddenly famous within the Parisian literary community.

The text of *L'Arche*—whose autobiographical sections are deliberately vague but undoubtedly accurate—describes what happened next in a harrowingly ironic fashion, as the author, entirely in the grip of the conviction of his own genius, was interrupted in his quest to express that genius by his compulsory military service, which rudely shattered many of the illusions that he had sustained at Sainte-Barbe and in Montmartre, but only enhanced his determination to produce a world-changing work, for which purpose he isolated himself in Ascain, in the far south-west of France, thinking that solitude would enable him to gather and organize his ideas. It did not—and time dragged by while he suffered a massive writer's block, which was brought to a deeply humiliating conclusion when Clarétie finally got around to staging *La Courtisane*, four years after accepting it. It turned out, in spite of all the pent-up expectation, to be a resounding flop, was assassinated by the critics, and closed after five performances.

Arnyvelde picked himself up from that disappointment, throwing himself ardently into a career in journalism, with enormous determination, and soon became enormously prolific, writing for a wide range of periodicals on every subject under the sun, including all the arts and sciences as well as politics and current events. His interviews are still a rich source for contemporary historians, his interviewees including Marcel Proust, Claude Monet, Filippo Marinetti, Edmond Rostand, Colette and Jean Giraudoux. The interview with Marinetti followed a futurist exhibition in Paris on which Arnyvelde reported enthusiastically, unsurprisingly, given that the ideas expressed in the 1909 Futurist Manifesto—translated into French a fortnight after its first appearance and published in *Le Figaro*, one of the many papers for which Arnyvelde worked—dovetailed reasonably well with his own ideas about the new ways of seeing permitted, and perhaps demanded, by modern knowledge and the dynamism of modern life.

Arnyvelde continued writing for the theater as a sideline, sometimes writing librettos for musical compositions by his younger brother Michel-Maurice Lévy (1883-1965), who used his own name on more serious works, including the opera *Psyché* (1910), but wrote more frivolous material, including operettas and comic songs, under the pseudonym Bétove. The most successful of Arnyvelde's later plays was the drama *L'Autre nuit* [The Other Night] (1921). Eventually, he was also to do a good deal of writing for the cinema, too, but that was never the principal focus of his literary endeavor, or at least the fraction of it in which he strove to develop his own philosophy of life and his own prospectus for the future. That quest, and its personal development, was committed to his four novels, which are partly an attempt to popularize his ideas and partly an attempt to work them out in more detail and weigh them more carefully. Their propagandist purpose is continually undermined by the difficulties he had in the latter task, which became more intense as the quest went on, not only because of the difficulty of the ideas themselves but because an interval of severe disenchantment suffered after he returned home from active service in the Great War seems to have temporarily obliterated his faith and conviction.

The ultimate result of that tangled agenda was to produce a unique document of personal hope, desire, anguish and desperation, in which the four texts form a somewhat tormented but deeply fascinating ensemble. There is a singular irony, perhaps extending to paradox, in the fact that such anguish—visible in the first and second texts, although it does not reach its crisis until the end of the third—was generated and fuelled by an obsession with joy, that being the central theme and analytical focus of the series.

In order to understand Arnyvelde's particular obsession with the idea of joy, it is useful to consider not only the kinship of his ideas with Marinetti's futurist manifesto but also the roots it has in the ideas of the philosophy of Friedrich Nietzsche. Although the novels only mention Nietzsche obliquely—*L'Arche* only refers to his notion of "the will to power" in

9

passing, and no comment is added to the fact that his portrait is one of the iconic in-ups in room where the protagonist of *Le Bacchus mutilé* reaches a key turning-point in his life—there are continual subtle echoes not only of Nietzsche's notion of the advent of the *übermensch* but also the arguments employed in his castigation of Christianity as an essentially "life-denying" philosophy.

As the passage in *L'Arche* points out, Nietzsche's notion of the "will to power" is a sequential development of Arthur Schopenhauer's notions of "will and idea," and Arnyvelde's vocabulary of joy is partly an attempt to substitute for awkward feature of the earlier terms that lent them, especially in translation, to misinterpretation. Put very crudely, Schopenhauer's argument is that the world is full of evils and misfortunes that make the success of all human endeavor highly improbable, but that humans are sustained in their struggle against the odds by a fundamental blind and unconscious "will to survive"—a phrase that is slightly unfortunate, in that "will" usually refers to conscious determination and its use thus tends to obscure the fact that Schopenhauer is referring to something that is essentially and by definition unconscious.

Schopenhauer observes that the blind urging of the "will to survive," which, by virtue of the calculus of probability, produces far more failures than successes as humans struggle against the vicissitudes of life, engenders numerous problems for consciousness, which inevitably finds the resultant anguish problematic and seeks a solution ardently. Schopenhauer's suggested solution is that humans ought to strive to substitute the force of a sighted conscious "idea" for that of the blind unconscious will, which can not only provide them with an objective in life but a reason to pursue it. His specification of that "idea" is vague, to say the least, but he is fairly certain that the best model of it that we have is the creative fervor at the heart of endeavor in the arts and sciences.

Nietzsche took up his predecessor's idea of "idea," attempting not only to make it more distinct but to make it much more positive, as a recreation of human being itself, and a

10

quest for a psychological transcendence of the essentially troubled human condition, and the anguish inflicted upon it by the probabilistic miscalculations of the unconscious "will." That quest he labeled "the will to power," thus further compounding the confusions inherent in Schopenhauer's stretching of the meaning of the term "will"—something to which the German language is presumably more hospitable than French or English.

The crusade that Arnyvelde found at the age of twenty and took up with such fervor was that same quest for psychological transcendence, but, being unsurprisingly unsympathetic—at least to begin with—to the terminology employed by his philosophical forbears, he found a new label for it, defining his notion of the quest to transcend the iniquities of the human condition as a quest for joy—or, rather, Joy, because what he means by the term is, by definition, a transcendent kind of joy ampler, nobler and more rewarding than the relatively trivial and petty things that we normally think of as "enjoyments": eating, drinking, playing and—most significantly and most problematically—sexual intercourse.

Nineteenth century philosophers were, of course, by no means the first thinkers to observe the iniquitous features of the human condition, or to seek psychological solutions to it. Religions had long been in the business of that supply, followed, usually in a docile fashion but sometimes in a spirit of opposition, by litterateurs. Some of the former, including Christianity, and most of the latter, had come up with a solution not dissimilar to Arnyvelde's, although they rarely called it joy or Joy, generally preferring love or Love, routinely emphasizing that what they meant by the latter was a kind of Love ampler and nobler than the everyday kinds of love—most significantly and most problematically, sexual love.

Arnyvelde, like many predecessors among philosophers, litterateurs and even religionists, thought that there was something direly askew, not to say perverted, about the attitudes of the Christian Churches to love (ideas arguably very far from those of Christ himself). That was one of the reasons why he thought that a new idea of Joy and the means of attaining it was direly needed. The other was that he was convinced that the new ways of seeing, experiencing and living permitted by modern science and modern life had opened up a path to the practical attainment of transcendent Joy, which had never been available before, but of which the vast majority of people were unaware, precisely because it had never been available before, and they were still stuck in the old ruts. In his four novels, he set out to post signposts to that pathway, and to explore it himself in experimental thought while doing so.

Le Roi de Galade follows in the great Voltairean tradition of French *contes philosophiques* by adopting a fantastic standpoint in order to look back at reality and see it more panoramically, more objectively and—hopefully—more clearly. It describes itself as a *conte bleu*—a label generally used in France to describe what are generally known in English as "fairy tales"—not because it is full of supernatural devices, but simply to avoid the bother of having issues of crude probability hamper the necessities of the narrative. With an unusual bluntness, the text actually cites that literary license on two of the occasions that it is employed. Like Samuel Johnson's Rasselas, the eponymous hero emerges from his idyllic homeland to explore the world and investigate its wonders and vicissitudes, but the "happy valley" of Galade is much more elaborately described than the one from which Rasselas came, being equipped with an elaborate history, and its happiness is carefully qualified, its limitations mapped out like the seemingly-insurmountable mountains that surround it. The world outside is not mapped so elaborately, partly because the reader is assumed to be familiar with it already, but mostly because it is so much more complex that a full elaboration would be impractical, but it is subjected to appropriately fervent analysis as the naïve king discovers its wonders first, and then—rather horribly—its iniquities.

The story is relatively straightforward until it reaches its climax, which is exceptional not only for the fervor that the author was able to put into its strident crescendo, but also the manner in which an abrupt sidestep permits that very fervor to be subjected to scrupulous skeptical criticism, weighed and, if not exactly found wanting, at least found in need of further thought. It is traditional for *contes bleus* to reach closure, whether the closure in question takes the form of "and they lived happily ever after" or "we have to go work in the garden," but Arnyvelde, while conscientiously making both suggestions, leaves no doubt that they can only be beginnings and not endings, and that the problems raised by the story have been deferred rather than solved.

The first to be published of the works in which he took up the theme again was composed in circumstances that might be considered the ultimate challenge to any philosophy of Joy, but that only made his attempt to take such a philosophy to its ultimate extreme more interesting, more heroic, and, as it turned out, more fervent. The text of *L'Arche* takes the trouble to make it abundantly clear that the novel was begun shortly after the author was conscripted during the Great War and was eventually finished—when the fragments composed during the war were collated, and perhaps smoothed over—after he was demobilized in 1919. It is not the Great Work that Arnyvelde had tried unsuccessfully to pen in the early years of the century, but it certainly attempts to substitute for it, and there is no doubt that, although it is a deliberately extravagant visionary fantasy, he took its fundamental arguments very seriously.

The substance of the vision experienced by the narrator of *L'Arche*—Arnyvelde himself, although the circumstances of the real Arnyvelde's own vision are simplified and stylized for the literary purposes of the novel—is a dramatic expansion of ideas introduced in *Le Roi de Galade*, repeating many of the same key images, sometimes placing them in the actual autobiographical context at which the earlier novel only hinted. The narrative is framed as a letter to the author's wife, whom he had married not long before the war began, the radical feminist and pacifist poet Henriette Sauret (1890-1976). Obviously, it is not an actual letter, although the first few pages might have begun that way, but he presumably did send her sections of the work as it progressed, and the text always retains an awareness that she is its first, though certainly not its only, addressee. The title of the work is derived from the notion that the writing of the text was planned to constitute a kind of psychological Ark to carry the author through the figurative Deluge of the war, permitting him—so long as he avoids being killed—to endure the devastation of his personal happy valley and the greater world constituted by the conflict.

It is worth noting in that context that the word *arche* has two meanings in French, signifying "arch" as well as "ark." Although the opening of the novel leaves no doubt that, as a title, it means Ark, the word is used at another point in the text in a context that makes it perfectly clear that it is there to be construed as "arch." That ambiguity extends much further when the central motif of the story is introduced, under the improvised label *arcandre*—a term that I have left as it appears in the original rather than subjecting it to any transcription. Its Greek roots encourage the term to be construed as "arch-human," or "superhuman," and there is some reason to suspect that the author intended it as a more accurate translation of the German *übermensch* than the *surhomme* used in the standard French translation of Nietzsche, but the arcandre is by no means a straightforward depiction of the new being to whose advent Nietzsche's Zarathustra looked forward. The name could, in fact, be construed as "arch-human" in all three of the common significances of the English "arch"—ultra-, over and bridge—and also, in a sense peculiar to the novel, as ark-human, in that it is the vision of the arcandre, rather than the original amorous ark that the narrator initially intended to construct, that actually helped to bring the author through the war. *L'Arche* was by no means the only novel written by a soldier on active duty during the Great War, nor was it the only one written partly as a psychological crutch to sustain the soldier in question through dark hours, but there is no other Ark of that sort as self-conscious or as far-reaching as Arnyvelde's.

L'Arche seems far more conclusive, in a purely literary sense, than *Le Roi de Galade*, but that is because the end of the Great War really did present itself—falsely—as one of history's great conclusions, which would have to be followed by a new world because the old one was dead: a new world, therefore, in which a general discovery of Arnyvelde's path to Joy, and a willingness to follow it, might be more feasible than it had been in 1910. With the aid of historical hindsight, we know that things did not turn out that way, and that the abject failure of the post-war world to escape the toils of the old one were tragic in every possible way. That same hindsight informs us of the rapid disillusionment of the people who had lived through the war and had come out of it hoping for a new beginning, and the most powerful information of that disillusionment is contained in novels written, especially but by no means exclusively in France, in the early 1920s. *Le Bacchus mutilé* turned out, perhaps expectably, to be one of the most extreme expressions of that anguished disillusionment, and perhaps the most anguished of them all, but that, too, was not the end of the story.

The story of that disillusionment and its aftermath will, inevitably, be taken up in the commentary attached to the second volume in this series, but it is worth noting here that Arnyvelde also continued to express and explore his notion of Joy in some of the articles he penned in the twenties and thirties, and that the metaphysical theses of the novel were eventually summarized in "Introduction à la métaphysique d'un deuxième univers" [Introduction to the Metaphysics of a Second Universe] (1939 in the *Mercure de France*), which was apparently based on previous non-fictional explorations, some dating all the way back to the early 1900s, which he had never managed to publish. Some of the many scientific articles he produced for periodicals had a futurological twist, and he published at least one further item of far-reaching *roman scientifique* once the sequence of four novels was complete in "Dix siècles de progrès médicaux, ou Le Triomphe du docteur Knock" [Ten Centuries of Medical Progress, or Dr. Knock's

Triumph"] in the special "Thirtieth Century" Christmas 1933 issue of *Le Revue Mondiale*.

Unfortunately, when the second world war came along, Arnyvelde had no material Ark to carry him through it, and he did not have the opportunity to construct another psychological Ark, although he was still writing to Henriette Sauret from the internment camp in Compiègne in which he was imprisoned by the Nazis—where he died of pneumonia in 1942 before he could be shipped off to Auschwitz along with the great majority of the camp's other Jewish inmates.

The translation of *Le Roi de Galade* was made from a copy of the 1910 edition published by the press associated with the periodical *Le Monde Illustré*, to whose editor, Jean-José Frappa, the book is dedicated. The copy I have (which had remained partly uncut for more than a hundred years before I released the text from its virginity) was given away free as a sweetener to subscribers to the periodical and is marked "not for sale," but I do not know whether the entire print run was circulated in that fashion; there is a price marked on the spine, which might suggest otherwise. The translation of *L'Arche* was made from a photocopy of the 1920 edition published by Societé Mutuelle d'Édition. The photocopy was made by Jean-Marc Lofficier from a copy of the book lent to him by Marc Madouraud, and I am very grateful to both of them for enabling me to make the translation of a text that I was particularly interested to see.

Brian Stableford

THE KING OF GALADE
A Fantastic Tale

Preliminaries

The Physical and Moral Constitution of Galade

I

It is from Emmanuel, who was the king of which this book is the history, from the king himself, during the time when he was living in Paris, that the existence of Galade was revealed to me. You will search in vain for that country in the atlas. To the east of Italy, to the west of Austria, bordered by Illyria, Neuria and Senestria, rocky mountains surround it, which render access to it impossible, and the Illyrians, the Neurians and Senestrians have believed, since the beginning of the world, that a great lake slumbers behind those mountains, by which they are limited.

Galade is a country of vast cultivable plains, forests abundant in game, mines of iron, copper and gold. Two watercourses, the Haint and the Jogne, sometimes parallel and sometimes drawing apart, wind sinuously across it. encircling villages, flowing alongside forests, and, emerging from two different points in the mountains, join up and escape into a gulf opening up behind the hamlet of Aldegonde, in the fearful din of an unfathomable fall, at the end of which they must continue their route—but God alone knows where.

At the foot of the mountains, numerous villages, one or two leagues apart at the most, raise their wooden houses with thatched roofs, and white stone houses with roofs of clay, forming, when seen from above, a kind of girdle of alabaster, agate and ruby, the buckle of which is Gyzir, the capital of Galade, where the palace of the king stands.

That palace, which overlooks the entire country with its crenellated towers, the slender steeple of its chapel and its proud fronton—a kind of broad terrace whose balustrade supports statues of the kings of Galade—backs up against the mountains, which, in times of war, render it attackable only from the front and the flanks.

The climate is, in general, agreeable and temperate. High winds are unknown there. The sun is very warm for half the year, and, in the other half, is often covered by clouds that burst in rain, and sometimes in snow. The Haint and the Jogne, swollen by the rain or the snow, then overflow somewhat, which only benefits the cultivated fields in their vicinity. There is scarcely any evidence, in the meteorological annals, of the two rivers ever having been entirely frozen. On the rare occasions when that happens, the Galadians indulge themselves in joyful glissades.

The routes that the instinct of the primitive inhabitants of Galade established through the forests and the plains to facilitate communications between their first groups, were never improved and are almost impracticable to pedestrians in times of ice or mud, but it does not matter, because the kings and aristocrats of Galade only go on foot inside their palaces. Elsewhere, they are only seen in carriages or on horseback.

II

Galade has retained to the present century the soul and the mores of the Europe of the Middle Ages. You will soon understand why.

Of the race itself, with regard to its origins, nothing can be presumed, except that which is presumed to be common to the origin of all human races, whether it resulted from the slow evolution of an animal kingdom or whether its forefather emerged, ready formed, from the mud of the earth, animated by the breath of a god.

As soon as the first-born of Galade had acquired, by a succession of victories over nature, the use of speech, fire and clothing, they formed tribes, hunted, built and pillaged one another.

They made invincible forces—lightning, sunlight and darkness, hunger, wars and death—into deities, malevolent or benevolent according to the weather and events. Above the gods and goddesses they placed Goho and Vzygine, capital powers, male and female together or separately, in such a number of cases, and so subtly, that it is better to pass over any attempt to enumerate them and refer the curious to the religious history of all primitive peoples, where they will assuredly find cases and subtleties of the same order, if not absolutely parallel, to those of Galadian hierology.

Under the reign of Harb, which corresponds approximately to the reign of Nebuchadnezzar the Great, lord of Chaldea, son of Nabopolassar,[2] in the history of the Hebrews, which is more familiar to us, great events took place in Galade: the union of the tribes under the scepter of Harb, the construction of the royal palace of Gyzir, and the piercing of the mountain behind the palace.

At the emergence from the earliest ages, as soon as they were able to obtain a little leisure from the rude struggles to eat, sleep and dress themselves, some of the Galadians became preoccupied with what we would call the geographical situation of their homeland. As a result of long labors they realized that Galade was completely enclosed by the mountains. A troubling problem rose up before them: were those the extrem-

---

[2] The son of Nabopolassar was Nebuchadnezzar II, who reigned from approximately 605 B.C. to 562 B.C., and is featured in the Biblical book of *Daniel*.

ities of the world, under a sky that seemed to extend far beyond those mountains, well above their summits, and not to curve over them?

How could they resolve that problem? To reach the sky, there seemed to be no conceivable way except death—and no dead person had yet descended again to narrate what he had seen. As for the audacity, it would have been too bold and perilous to go to present oneself, alive, before Goho, before Vzygine, of which it was the abode, even admitting that a means could be found.

With regard to ascension, the tops of the mountains were much closer than the sky.

Now, from generation to generation, until the reign of Harb the most knowledgeable Galadians built or designed machines made of rope, stone and piled up wood, by means of which they counted on raising themselves all the way to the mysterious summits—but none of them ever succeeded.

Only one managed to reach a height of seven thousand nine hundred and four feet above the ground, clinging, from the seven thousand eight hundred and seventy-ninth foot onwards, to pointed and cutting rocks; then, having turned his head, he was seized by vertigo and horror, let himself fall backwards, and was found in pieces.

With the aid of time, in accordance with the propensity that the mind has in all countries to form legends regarding what it cannot scale or penetrate, they imagined, behind the mountains, an entire abominable world only accessible to degraded souls. And in order that they might be dragged by the Haint and the Jogne into the accursed world, they threw the cadavers of miscreants into the bottom of the gulf of Aldegonde.

Then came the reign of the sage king Harb, who had the dead incinerated, and the climbing came to an end.

Harb and the Troglodytes

Harb, the son of a priest of Naul, the goddess of estival springs, lived a healthy life in Gyzir, under the tender gaze of his father. He was tall, handsome and obliging, ready to lend his assistance to anyone who asked. As he went hunting almost every day, he sometimes, while running after a deer or a wolf, missed the hour for the family meal. Then he went to the house of a peasant in the nearest village to the place where he had stopped, with the wolf or the deer over his shoulders, and asked to be given bread, water and a few cooked vegetables. Thus, he knew almost all the peasants in Galade, and they knew him. Many of them liked him, because he often abandoned his prey as thanks for the meal that he had been served, saying that, so far as he was concerned, the true pleasure of hunting was in running through the thickets, the clearings and the brambles, and that as soon as the animal was killed, it was no longer anything to him, only having been seduced by the living to the extent that it gave him a pretext to run, hope and vanquish.

The inhabitants of the area around Gyzir lamented that the other inhabitants of Galade often came to pillage them cruelly, because their region was the most fertile. Each of them had attempted, in the interests of self-defense, to exterminate the greatest possible number of marauders, but they arrived in bands, unexpectedly, and what could a lone peasant do, surprised by half a dozen united bandits, and who did not even have time to shout for help?

Those in the vicinity of Gyzir, therefore, having met together, decided to join forces, to arm themselves, select a leader and to resist the thieves *en masse*, if not attack them and reduce them to impotence and loyalty.

They fell into accord that no Galadian could lead them better in combat than Harb the hunter, the son of the priest of Naul. They pressed Harb, who accepted, placed himself at their head, marched against the pillagers and obliged them to beg for mercy and promise to content themselves henceforth with the profits of their own labor. He had twenty-four of them skinned alive, cut the ears off thirty-two, blinded in one eye fifty-six chosen from among the most redoubtable, and granted mercy to the rest, who proclaimed him magnificent.

From that combat he acquired a renown so great that he became ambitious to be the king of all the Galadians, and was, as soon as he manifested the desire publically.

The facility of his election stemmed from three causes: firstly, because those he called his friends, and who recognized that he was more skillful than they were in wielding the ax and the spear, and in leadership, felt glad and flattered to have a king for a friend, and they counted on him for certain favors that, difficult for them to acquire by themselves in isolation, would be achieved much more easily; secondly, the Galadians once pillaged thought that, under the protection of that strong individual, they would be sheltered from further invasions; and finally, the pillagers, quite frankly fearful of being skinned alive, having their ears cut off or losing an eye after a further battle, considered it an excellent idea to live in peace with their vanquisher. They even paid a tribute every year of virgins, minerals, pigs, lambs and cheeses.

Harb appointed his father the high priest of Naul, simple servant though he was, and the latter lived happy and honored until his hundred and seventy-third year, which was the normal age at which fortunate humans died in that epoch of Galade.

One day, Harb, then in the fullness of his strength and wisdom of mind, had gone out hunting capercaillie. He went alone, because he liked occasionally to recover in the forest his soul of a young man, and could not do it when his usual retinue accompanied him, who reminded him too much, at every moment and on every occasion, that he was His Serene Highness Harb, the Overlord, the wise King, His Majesty, and a hundred other resounding elevations.

After having pierced a large number of birds with his arrows, and put them in his belt and his game-bag, he felt tired, and lay down next to an oak tree, where he immediately fell asleep.

He was woken up by a murmur of voices, but he refrained from moving, for he was wise enough to be as prudent as he was courageous, and the opportunity seemed propitious to listen without being seen, in case he had been followed by conspirators intent on attacking him shamefully while he was alone and far from his court.

He raised his head silently, and through the foliage that concealed him he saw three old men, thin and wretchedly dressed.

Ah! said Harb to himself. *They must be there Wise Men of the Anaide Grotto. It was in that direction that the hazard of the hunt took me. The words of those men ought to be good to hear, because they're generally venerated.*

Against the wall of the mountain, at the back of a forest whose ultimate fir trees attempted to climb a few meters toward the summits, there was a grotto hollowed in the rocks, which was known as the Anaide Grotto. Three men lived there meagerly on forest roots, mushrooms and strawberries, and offerings that charitable Galadians made them. In return, they clarified certain complicated problems, such as the exchange between two peasants of a cow for a small field of carrots, counseled maidens on the subject of their marriages, and prophesied accurately what the weather would be like several weeks hence.

If any indiscreet person asked them why they isolated themselves as they did, and lived so precariously, refusing agricultural labor, they replied that commerce with people— apart from the two companions that each of them had—was not agreeable to them; that it pleased them to live thus, in an amity that nothing could dent, since they avoided all venoms by avoiding all agglomerations; that they did not ask anything of anyone; and that if they accepted the offerings that were made to them it was because they immediately gave in exchange the precious juice of their science and sagacity.

The peasants, occupied in working in the fields and the care of their own existence, did not take their inquisitions any further, and gradually, the solitaries became highly respected. They were admired for living so poorly, willingly depriving themselves of all the good things that the earth produced and the comforts that Galadian women so obligingly provided, even though no one felt inclined to imitate them.

They received visitors at the mouth of their grotto, and no one ever passed the threshold. Talkative and malicious adolescents fabricated fables about what the three men did in their grotto, but one bold child who penetrated into it one day when the Wise Men were gathering their harvest in some distant location saw nothing there but benches for sleeping on and iron pikes lined up against the wall. The back of the grotto was completely dark. It seemed that a strange grating sound was coming from it. He wanted to go closer but, having heard one of the Wise Men coming back, he fled in haste, slipping through the undergrowth.

"Some fox in a cage," his father said, when the scamp, having narrated his escapade, made allusion to the grating sound in the shadows.

Harb, who had heard mention of the sages, therefore listened to what they were saying, ready, in his soul open to all good seed, to profit from it if he could.

"Brothers," said one of them, "I assure you that I saw a blue-tinted light coming through the fissures. At the harder blows I struck then with my pike, full of pleasure, pieces of rock fell, which went into the fissures and caused darkness to be reborn."

"The labor had fatigued you, Brother," replied one of the others, "and when you saw the light it was a sort of illusion, as one has in sleep."

"Might it be possible that we're so far advanced already?" said the third.

The first one resumed: "I sense that each of you will, like me, keep a lookout for that light through the fissure—and both

24

of you think, internally, that it's possible that I saw it. But both of you want to be the first to reach the other side of the mountain, in order to announce your discovery with loud cries to Galade and reap all the honor, if not all the profit!"

"What could one of us do without the other two?" said the second. "Isn't our surest interest that all three of us should triumph? For, just as it's necessary to unite our efforts for the immense task, it will be necessary to unite our spirits for the immense benefits. How could only one of us take credit for the effort necessary for the discovery? And for the gifts that it will deliver to us, and the tributes that we'll demand for letting the curious in—in sum, the settlement of the offering and the enjoyment of the power—can one alone take on the burden?"

"As for the enjoyment," said the third, extending his arms in a broad gesture above his head, first to the left and then the right, "the capacity of a single man to support it is as extensive as the sky, whose limits we do not know."

"That's talking like a dog deprived of meat," said the first. "Having only ever had bones, you can't imagine that your stomach bursting with food and your belly with multiple delights. Believe me, three of us won't be too many to support our wealth!"

"To work," said the third, "To work! We've been piercing the rock for seventy-two years now. It takes more than a day's march to get to the point we've reached. Tomorrow, perhaps, under our pikes, the rock might split like a window! What shall the one of us who penetrates first into that unknown world find? And who knows whether he will ever come back?"

Well, said Harb, to himself, *there are some singular explorers!*

He waited until they had gone back into their grotto. He got up slowly, went back to Gyzir and returned home. The next day, he summoned the most ingenious builders and said to them:

"I want to make Gyzir the capital of Galade, because the man named king by the Galadians was born in that town, lives there and loves it. And I want to live in a palace worthy of the Galadians and their overlord, which I can leave to my successor, and in which the kings will live.

"All things considered, I have chosen as a location the part of the forest that surrounds the Anaide Grotto. You will fell some trees and leave others standing, which will make me a park. As for the Anaide Grotto, you will surround it with fountains, flowers and thick bushes, and everyone will refrain from going into it, if they want to live, because I know from a dream I have had that Goho sometimes haunts it."

The Glorification of Harb

When the Galadians learned that the king wanted a palace they applauded unanimously. Even peasants who would have refused a place in their barn to a vagabond—for there were some in Galade—sent their obol gladly, too dull-witted to explain to themselves the pride that they felt in thinking about the King of Galade in his royal palace. Undoubtedly, national sentiment was, albeit subconsciously, already profound in the soul of the people.

Work was begun without delay. But the person who was horrified when he saw the builders coming toward his grotto, making measurements and drawing up plans was the Wise Man on guard duty—for one of them always remained in guard while another went in quest of food and the third worked.

"Hey," he said, "what are you doing here?"

"We've come to establish the limits of Harb's palace," one of the builders replied.

"Can't you," he said, "go somewhere away from the grotto?"

"As to that," was the reply, "the king intends that it will be part of the palace."

The Wise Man collapsed heavily on the threshold, stammering incomprehensible words, as anguish gripped his throat, caused his teeth to chatter, compressed the air in his chest, twisted his muscles and paralyzed his tongue.

"The king is good," said a man who misinterpreted that great distress. "He'll lodge you worthily if he dislodges you from here."

But the Wise Man thought that he ought not, in such a grave circumstance, either say or attempt anything without the advice of his companions. He decided to await their return in order to discuss what they could do, and, sitting on the threshold, he folded his arms and watched the work without saying another word.

After having deliberated from the dusk that drove the builders away until the following morning as to what to do about the disastrous affair, the Wise Men decided that with the aid of irresistible speeches, vehement supplications, and even lies, they would strive to convince the king to take the location of his palace elsewhere.

Harb, however, was quick to interrupt them. He took the three of them to one side and, having made sure that no one could hear what was said between them, he made them a proposal.

"I know why you've come to implore me. I know the secret of your work, and no one apart from me can know it. In any case, if I'm the king, it's because certain virtues and prerogatives make me a man different from others. That explains to you sufficiently how I can know, naturally, many hidden things.

"If, therefore, you want to continue piercing the mountain, not only will I not hinder you in any way, but I'll do everything I can to help you—on the sole condition that you keep your endeavor as secret as before. As for the profit and glory for which you hope, have no fear that I'll spoil it. From this day on, I appoint all three of you High Priests of Goho. You'll live in the palace. The first apartments constructed will be for me, the king, and for you. Every night you'll go to pierce the rock. When you've reached the other side of the mountain, come and tell me, and Galade will know when the next day breaks what a marvelous discovery has been made, and by whom.

"Don't embrace my knees. What are all my exploits, compared with the silent and patient labor of your entire lives? It's me, if my heavy mantle didn't prevent me, who would bow down before you. Go. Don't talk about this to anyone, and come back tomorrow to find here the three linen robes and three golden crowns of the supreme priesthood."

Galade having accepted, without overmuch astonishment, the promotion to the pontificate that the king had given to the Wise Men, both because they respected them and because they had confidence in their king, no one worried any longer about the edification of the palace. Every Galadian contributed to it, and wanted to play some part in its elevation. It was marvelous to see, for forty-four years, sixteen days and nine hours, a people swarming delightedly, working, sweating and singing around enormous cubes that were ingeniously heaped on top of one another.

The workers in the porphyry quarries of Assanaan carved and transported themselves the blocks that would form the base of the peristyle and the foundations of the pillars. Singing hymns, the miners of Boudroude brought the masses of gold to make the external friezes. The vine-growers of Melydire, the market gardeners of Lunilon and the horticulturalists of Agrazzin, came laden with grapes, vegetables and flowers. Finally, the fishermen of the Blue Lake transported, in vast watertight tanks filled with fresh water, the most beautiful carp from their waters.

The fish from the Blue Lake were thrown into an immense pond that the king had established in his park, not far from the palace, a short distance from the Anaide grotto. For that pond it was necessary to dig out the soil to a depth of thirty meters, and such a quantity of earth was removed that a hill was made of it, still visible in the vicinity of Gyzir, in open country, which is known as Harb's Pond Hill. The Jogne was deflected to fill the pond, and then continued its course as if nothing had happened.

On the day when the king said: "By Goho, that's the royal palace finished!" there was such rejoicing throughout Galade that the Galadians, drunk and sated, exhausted by delight and festivity, slept thereafter, some for fourteen days and nights in succession, and others, more temperate, only for a week.

The three High Priests of Goho worked every night, in the deepest mystery, on the piercing of the mountain. In order to get the work done more rapidly, all three of them worked together.

People would have been very astonished to see their nocturnal accoutrement: thick clothing, masks over their eyes to protect them from splinters of rock, and iron spikes shining in their hands, after having seen them by day, sumptuously dressed in gold fabric in crowns studded with gems. But no one ever saw them like that. In fact, people rarely saw them at all, because they slept by day, exhausted by the labor of the night. "They're praying to Goho for the salvation of Galade," the king said—and the Galadians praised the fervor of the high priests with all their hearts.

"Most Serene Harb," one of the Wise Men said to the king, finally, "my brothers and I have reached the miraculous goal. Under one of our pikes, a kind of luminous hole was made in the rock. We fell upon the hole and toward its light, and we saw the earth and the sky that are on the other side of the mountains. Stars were shining in the sky, exactly like those we see in Galade when we raise our heads by night. The earth extended like a vast plain, and we were scarcely able to distinguish anything but an undulation similar to that of our fields of wheat under the breeze..."

"You shall be glorified forever in the history of Galade, my brothers," said the king, embracing them. "Have you enlarged the hole?"

"We thought it appropriate to enlarge it in the presence of our king," they replied. "Let him deign to accompany us this evening. In three days, before dawn, we will reach the end of the road. We will then administer the last blows of the pick...and the mystery will be vanquished!"

"Be glorified all the more for that respectful thought! I shall accompany you, Brothers. and I shall salute with you the light of the strange dawn."

On the night of his departure, the wise King Harb put on a corselet of fine steel mail under his royal tunic, because he feared, notwithstanding all the embraces, that the High Priests of Goho might have formed a plan to assassinate him at the portal to the new world, in order to claim all the glory of their discovery, utilize it for themselves alone, and to find, in order to explain the king's death, some clever invention that their pontifical situation would ender easy enough.

On the afternoon of the expedition, he summoned his most faithful servant, whom he had tested in many circumstances, and said to him: "Anaigal, the words that you are about to hear are the result of my gravest thoughts, and my political desires most profitable to Galade. Whatever happens, do not repeat them to anyone in the world—not to your wife, your sons, nor even your animals, while caring for them, for beasts have been known to be transformed into human brings by the power of magic. Nor should the order that I am about to give you be revealed to anyone.

"This is it: tonight I am going into the Anaide Grotto with the three High Priests of Goho. They and I are going to spend three days and nights in the grotto praying. After the third day, go to post yourself immediately outside, and keep a careful watch. When you see me come out with them, wait until a sudden and rapid stride has placed me ahead of them; then appear, run toward them and shove them with all your might into the pond that we'll be alongside. As for the rest, I'll indicate it to you then."

As soon as they had gone into the grotto the king made the three priests go ahead of him, saying to them: "As well as it being appropriate for me to walk behind you on a route that is unknown to me and which you know, I want you to be the first to go into the world that you have opened. If any danger threatens you, I shall throw myself before you, for all that is combat and struggle, where the strength of arms is necessary, is my concern. If not, although the first in Galade, I intend only to be the second with you."

They marched thus, the Wise Men in front and the king behind. They broke the rock, penetrated into the new earth, and saw an immense plain that seemed limitless. However, monuments of gigantic proportions appeared on the very horizon. When the Wise Men wanted to go toward them, the king remarked to them that their garments might be surprising to the inhabitants of the distant city, that it was prudent not to draw the attention of any stranger to the road that might permit, if known, an invasion of calm Galade, and that they would have plenty of time to return later. In addition, they were exhausted by three days and nights of walking, without sleep, and the great work was now accomplished, the triumph assured.

"So well assured," he added, "that I still want you to come back as the first in Galade, for it is elementary justice, on this occasion, that I should glorify you before all, and show myself humbly after you."

He also added: "Let us charge ourselves with a few fragments of these immortal rocks. I intend to make a triumphant heap of them, which will be raised in the middle of the square of Gyzir, with your name engraved at the base in golden letters, with the date of my reign, which saw such a great deed."

That was done. The company resumed marching, after having taken care to erect a pile of rocks in front of the great breach in the foot of the mountain, which would hide it from foreigners from beyond the mountain.

Scarcely had the three Wise Men crossed the threshold of the grotto than the faithful Anaigal hurled himself upon them as all three of them were marching in the lead and bustled them into the pond with a shove so unexpected and so prompt that they stumbled and fell into the deep water before even having time to be astonished.

As Anaigal, the faithful domestic, was braced on his robust legs, the upper part of his body leaning over, following his arms, which were shoving the last of the Wise Men, King Harb approached him, and with a violent thrust on the shoulders he sent him to join the high priests.

That was a fine splash!

Struggling in the water, each fighting the others in order to cling on to the most skilful swimmer, they sank abruptly, then reappeared and clustered together, blowing at their soaking hair, which had fallen over their eyes, in order to see more clearly, while they drew breath. The rocks that the high priests were carrying about their person dragged them irresistibly to the bottom of the pool. They finally drew apart for a moment, each of them going his own way, but Harb was on the bank, shoving them back with his foot, detaching their hands when they grabbed hold of roots, and soon, only funereal bubbles of air, bursting on the surface, testified that four human sighs had just been exhaled for the last time.

Then Harb, uttering loud cries, leapt into the water in his turn, dived, reappeared, raising his arms, streaming and clamoring, dived again for a few seconds, and then came up for air again just as the inhabitants of the palace were running toward the pool with great signs of hope, ladders and ropes.

"Alas," said Harb, when he had been pulled out of the water, "look in the depths of the lake, where, in spite of my efforts, the three High Priests of Goho and my faithful Anaigal have remained. Perhaps they're still alive. Alas, alas! Will I have tried to save them in vain?"

In the midst of sobs and exclamations of dolor, the four cadavers were brought up to the surface and deposited on the grass. But as Harb, the wise king, still dripping wet, started explaining how the catastrophe had occurred, voices rose up among the sobs, which soon became a unanimous concert. "Look," they said, "look how good king Harb did not hesitate to throw himself into the pool to rescue his valet and the high priests! Instead of simply calling for help, as anyone else would have done, the sage king tried, at the risk of his august person, to be a hero once again! Glory to Harb, the father of the Galadians!"

"Sire, go home quickly and take off those wet clothes," begged Xylis, the Master of Ceremonies. "Sire, you'll have time to tell us how the catastrophe happened another day. Go and get dry, in the name of the supreme god, sire, and for love of your people and your friends."

Thus spread the news of the mourning that struck at the same time the cult of Goho and the widow of Anaigal, and the new exploit of King Harb, who had thrown himself in the water to rescue his valet and the priests.

Thus Harb remained the sole master of the secret road that permitted travel through the mountain to the rest of the earth.

Summary of the History of Galade from the reign of Harb to the accession of Emmanuel

Harb, having created for his own usage the custom of Royal Retreats, which consisted of enclosing oneself for several weeks in the Anaide Grotto—which had become exceedingly holy since the death of the Wise Men—in order to meditate on all things and seek the advice of Goho, who took charge in the meantime of providing the king with sustenance, in order that no one should disturb the sublime conversation, dressed himself one day in an unostentatious costume, filled his pockets with gold coins, and set off across the world.

He was not overly amazed by what he saw there. The mores of the world contemporary with Harb were scarcely different from Galadian mores, except that the populations were more numerous, the cities more extensive and the edifices more ample. He brought back from that voyage the science of glassmaking, which he learned from the Phoenicians, and the ability to read in the stars, which was taught to him by the elders of Chaldea. Henceforth, people in Galade could drink from goblets and tankards, instead of coarse wooden bowls whose fibers always absorbed a part of the liquid that was poured into them.

He made several voyages of that sort and brought back practical and spiritual information every time, which his discernment alone indicated as the most useful for Galade of the inventions of other peoples.

He made a law by which all the dead, indifferently, had to be burned, for he feared privately that the Haint and the Jogne might carry cadavers out of the gulf of Aldegonde and cast them up in a neighboring nation, where they would surely cause astonishment, and a desire to know whence so many bodies came.

Harb died laden with age, wisdom and glory in his two hundred and fifth year—an age that no other Galatian had attained, and which was never attained thereafter.

Before he died he designated as his successor the first of his ministers, Galenide, a perfectly wise, upright and perspicacious man, to whom he revealed his secret route through the mountain, and then passed away peacefully in the great respectful silence of all Galade. That proved, better than lamentations and funeral pomp, that a single heart beat for the king throughout the nation, and that that national heart, broken by such a loss, no longer had strength for anything, except to be completely what it was—which is to say, broken, which implies the fact of silence and annihilation.

Galenide founded a sect of initiates, among whom he recruited missionaries, who were secretly sent abroad to learn important discoveries. When they returned, they represented themselves as the inventors of what they brought back from their travels, and thus obtained a great deal of profit and renown.

That sect functioned until the epoch that corresponds to the fourteenth century, or thereabouts, of our history: the epoch of the regency of Mahara, the prime minister of King Dinion, who was a bad king, incapable and stupid. Mahara was the veritable king. He was very intelligent. It was under his government and by his will that a wall was built in front of the Anaide Grotto, thus sealing forever the marvelous route. He took the great secret to his grave, and you shall see for what motives he acted in that fashion; but first, it is necessary to sketch briefly the fall of the cult of the gods and the establishment of Christianity in Galade.

A young initiate by the name of Balbun had traversed, in the course of his voyage, a large country known as Gaul, and there he had witnessed the persecution of a sect that made a profession of worshiping a god crucified in the previous century by the Jews. A holy man named Pothin, Bishop of Lyon,[3]

---

[3] Pothin, or Photin, allegedly the first Bishop of Lyon and the first Bishop of Gaul, is said to have lived in the second century A.D., the date of his death in prison during persecutions

traveled from city to city evangelizing the crowds for the glory of that god, the son of god. Great massacres bloodied all of Gaul and many other neighboring nations.

Balbun had it explained to him by the holy man himself that the religion was powerful because its members accepted dying as martyrs, and having seen with his own eyes the fervor of the martyrized he felt an enthusiastic faith in the new god awakening in his soul.

Undoubtedly, the extreme poetry of the religion, the delightful explanation it gave for the capital mysteries and the hope of a fortunate resurrection that it offered to the worst disfigured, touched the young voyager, for he decided to devote his life to the triumph of Jesus and returned to Galade ready for all persecutions, and also for all delights, in the case that the worshipers of Goho, Vzygine, Naul and the other divinities allowed themselves to be convinced of the reality of Christianity.

It was, alas, for reasons similar to those of all races whose gods are destroyed, persecutions that he encountered, and, along with him, all those enchanted by his words.

As he had made an oath not to reveal his voyage, to which he was loyal, he made up great fables to explain, firstly, that Goho, in the grotto, had introduced Jesus himself as his successor, and then that Christ had come to Galade, but a long time before the generations still alive, and that no trace remained of his coming; that he had descended from the sky by the omnipotent will of his Father, and that he had been born in the barn of a farm in Galade, of a maiden and a carpenter.

Balbun, and the persecutor kings, and the fervent worshipers of Goho, Vzygine and the Galadian Olympus, and many generations, passed away before Christianity was established in Galade as the national religion. That finally happened, however, as might be expected. Of Goho and all the false gods the only vestiges that remained were a few partly-

---

launched by Marcus Aurelius being recorded in a letter of dubious authenticity as 177, supposedly at the age of ninety.

collapsed monuments, and all the poetry, pathos and politics of the pagan religion were cleverly mixed with the teachings of the cult that was henceforth sacred.

That is how Galade became a Christian country.

Between the martyrdom of Balbun and the regency of Mahara, the travels of the initiates continued, and beautiful and good inventions were given to the Galadians. Prudent and far-sighted kings intercepted everything that they considered as harmful. And it was for that reason that neither fulminating powder nor printing were introduced into Galade, because they were deemed to be unnecessary to happiness and very dangerous to handle.[4]

One night, Mahara, the prime minister, went up to the top of the highest tower in the royal palace and gazed at Galade, extended at his feet, sleeping tranquilly beneath the twinkling stars.

"Those people," Mahara said to himself, after having meditated for some time, "know how to built, to weave and cultivate the earth. They live happily and die lightly, in the hope of another life full of bliss. A harmonious and far-sighted religion assists them to support a few irremediable infirmities. The arts are always vivacious in Galade; poets and musicians have enough to sing about in the beauty of honest labor, women, the fatherland, the sky and the god who inhabits it. Sculptors and painters have eternal subjects in the human body, the movement of animals, the play of light in nature and on faces; finally, architects can embellish indefinitely, and ameliorate, the houses and palaces of Galade, to which sculptors can add all the lovely ornaments they wish.

"God alone knows what the people of neighboring lands might invent, over time, given their passions, their ambitions and their malice. A perpetual and permanent danger is lurking in Galade, which is the possible treason, one day, of an initi-

---

[4] In fact, printing had not been invented when the grotto was sealed, and thus could not have been refused entry by the Galadian sectarians.

ate. Then would penetrate freely into this happy land, along with progress—which is, in any case, superfluous—the unknown poisons that engender passions, ambitions and malice.

"In my conscience, I assume the right to wall up the grotto and close the route. And I leave to God the judgment of the individual who will, if such are his designs, by some miracle, in the near or far future, demolish the wall and reopen the route to the world."

And it was thus that Galade retained, until the present century, the soul and the mores of the Europe of the Middle Ages.

And it is here that the history of Emmanuel begins.

Part One
THE VOW

The Land of Amour

In the year 1900 of the Christian Era, on the death of Georgis the Pious, the son of Harb the Eleventh, Georgis' son Emmanuel mounted the throne of Galade.

He was eighteen years old. I, a faithful narrator, who saw him in Paris when he was not yet twenty-five, can imagine, by virtue of his beauty then, the magnificent adolescent he must have been the first time he put the royal crown on his long curly hair.

Capable of all corporeal audacities, and imposing the evidence of that in each of his supple, free and decisive movement, he was the living expression of strength and sensuality. Three masterpieces can give in idea of that king: the Bacchus sculpted by Michelangelo, the Young Athlete of which a copy in bronze founded by the Kellers is in the great gallery of the Louvre Museum that leads to the Victor of Samothrace, and the portrait that Sustermans painted of the son of Frederick III of Denmark.[5]

---

[5] There is more than one statue titled *Jeune athlète* in the Louvre, including two replicas of bronze statues by Polykleitos from the fifth century B.C., one of which is presumably the intended reference. Prints of the painting by the Flemish baroque artist Justus Sustermans (1597-1681) of Valdemar, the son of Frederick III, King of Denmark were widely circulated in France in the late 19th century, but Arnyvelde might well have seen the original in the Galeria Palatina in Florence, the city in which Michelangelo's statue of Bacchus is also to be found, in the Bargello.

Around him, the air was suddenly lighter, the light brighter. Whoever approached him felt sadness and malignity dying within him, and the desire awakening to love, to be enthusiastic and good, and no longer to believe in anything but Joy.

Seeing him gave the certainty of Joy; contrary to those who said that suffering was glorious and the earth miserable and wicked, he was the ravishing proof that Joy, which is the supreme blossoming, was possible to creatures on the earth, and that it as glorious and holy.

He was adored as a man, as a king and as a symbol, and for himself, he adored being—which is to say that he was happy. As a divine image, above an altar, seems to be smiling through the incense, he laughed in the perpetual perfumes of life that extended through all its hours and all its forms, flowering.

His uncle Gasp, the brother of King Georgis, the Archbishop of Gyzir, Monseigneur Gohain, and his tutor, Mnektes, were the guides of his conscience.

Space, light, fêtes and amour were the guides of everything else.

Gasp, his uncle—tall, blond abundantly bearded, apoplectic and truculent, his speech brazen and his flesh scarlet, turning violet at the slightest impulsion of pleasure or anger, almost to blue—said to Emmanuel: "Handsome nephew, under the reign of your father Georgis the Pious, may God beatify him, I was terribly bored. Fortunately, you're here, when I'm still at the age of vigorous compensations! Piety, damn it, and fervor, processions, observances and fasting are damnably consuming and damnably tedious, damn it! I'll say no more. Watching me will conclude my sentence better than words and oaths! My legs, wearied by genuflections before the holy tables and the Our Ladies, will rest in genuflections before our ladies, and stretch out excellently on tables sanctified by good food and bright wines!

"Let's amuse ourselves, handsome nephew! Life is short. Have you ever thought, while holding the face of a woman against your cheek, that your two heads, in a few years, will be skeletons? What's sixty years, for example, in the vertiginous unfurling of the centuries? What you do, what you might do, what you want and what you dream, die with you. Let's drink, let's hunt, let's run after deer and dears, the breasts of young women, the swarm of joys; let's feast and enjoy ourselves, and live life to the full! Death will blow out the candles and fold up the tablecloth. There'll be time then to go to sleep. Until it comes, handsome nephew, the sun, the lamp of diurnal celebrations, and lamps, the suns of the night, will persuade us that it's light and that it's necessary to stay awake.

"Come, my sovereign, to the house of Ginginella the dancer. I've promised to bring you there today, and her costume is prepared, which is only composed of her hair..."

"Sire," said Monseigneur Gohain, Archbishop of Gyzir, to the king, "What delights can you expect in heaven if you take so many on earth? Divine justice keeps a record of affliction and rejoicing. To the one who endures, compensations will be given. What dispensation is there for one who lives without troubles? Are you unaware that it's in silence and the subjugations of the senses that one hears the counsels and the golden voice of the soul, in which God has his kingdom within us? He resides there, Sire; the soul is a tabernacle easily opened to one who possesses the keys. Have I not given them to you, those delightful keys, which are purity and meditation in peace?

"Sire, think that one day, soon, as you mount a horse or quit this room, misfortune might fall upon you. What consolations will you find, if you are suddenly deprived of your habitual pleasures? Too far distanced from God by your profane occupations, you will be exactly parallel to a blind man devoid of a staff and a dog. You will search, with your anxious soul, similar to a clutching hand, for a point of support in your darkness. There are roads, Sire, that no night can darken, where, without sun, stars and guides, one advances without stumbling. Sire, in the name of your salvation, weigh the luxuries of the earth against the invisible pomps of heaven. Reserve in yourself the part of God!"

And the philosopher Mnektes said to him: "To enjoy oneself is good, Majesty; learn, know, and meditate upon what is good. The peace of meditation is good, and the turbulence of making merry is also good. Everything is good for one who knows. It is necessary to know what is inferior and what is superior. To know that one is similar to the beasts when one feasts, and that one is near to the gods when one thinks, renders all hours profitable. God judges the beast at the end of the feast, the beast judges the god at the conclusion of meditation...

"Where are you going, my son? To the home of Ginginella the dancer? As a beast, enfever yourself in your body, in the flux and reflux of her loins. As a mind, exert yourself in penetrating thereby the mystery of forms, which leads to God. Remember that the dancer is born of the earth, and that she is, with her free and resurgent movements, the sister of inert rocks, plants enslaved to their roots, beasts to their curbed spines, and that the same force palpitates in rocks, plants, animals and human beings, which is the creative force of God. Become alarmed by the fact that the will in question animates those forms with increasingly free movements, Sense in your mind how much more rapid and brisk in its mobility that same mind is than the agile dancer. And rejoice in perceiving in that animation increasingly subtle forms, the execution of the divine plan, which is the ascension toward the Immaterial...

"If you like, I'll accompany you to the dancer's house, and I'll convince you fully of the presence of the eternal in the least of her gestures."

Galade followed the character of its kings. Religious under Georgis, it was amorous under Emmanuel. The general mores of a country are easily influenced by the behavior of its kings. By the agitations that the latter create around that which they cherish—the countryside, if they have a bucolic soul; cathedrals, if they are pious; luxury, with sumptuous escorts, carrousels and brilliant décor, if they like magnificence—they attract crowds there, and communicate to them a little of their own nature and their tastes. Besides which, as favors hardly ever fall on any but those who praise their person and their exploits, one always sees a large number of ambitious individuals adapting to the tendencies of courts, in order to penetrate into them and acquire consideration there. Finally, it is necessary to take account of the fact that the majority of people, having no particular tastes, swiftly slide into established tastes, like chicks behind a mother hen who has taken the trouble to dig out the ground beneath the portal of the farm and make a passage there for her offspring.

It goes without saying that this does not affect the profound roots of peoples, nor the natural inclination of all beings to satisfy their instincts to the extent that the brakes are loosened. For the faculty of amour, which is like an ever-ignited flame for which the slightest excitation is the worst of stimulating winds, the example of a amorous king cannot help but find prompts imitators in all of his subjects of both sexes.

Under Emmanuel, son of Georgis, Galade was all amour. Never had the fields, in the evening, seen so many excited couples, grave beneath the lovely stars, uniting in their long grass, their clover and sainfoin, and their unripe wheat. Never had so many husbands surprised their wives in sin, and, if one wants to narrate impartially, never had so many wives had to reproach their husbands for being monsters and fauns. In spite of all these intimate incidents, however, all the annoyances, disputes, ruptures, beatings and shattered crockery, a delightful perfume emanated from all Galade—for amour is a florescence. And in spite of all the handsome, rude, delicate and pleasing lovers who accorded themselves to women of all ages, one man alone was the true lover behind the lips that they kissed and the breasts on which they nestled: the king.

Noble ladies, like the daughters of tenant farmers, maid-servants in taverns and female employees in the Galadian industries, idolized the king, were his before he had even desired them. And he desired a great many, and encountered no obstacles to his prompt victories. There remained, for those he vanquished, a consecration of beauty and voluptuous virtues. As for the lords, the husbands of the noble ladies, who tried hard to keep them safe from the king, if, at the end of their struggles they met piteous defeat, after having lamentably or furiously suffered therefrom, they found in that execrable affair a consolation of sorts in the pride they felt in being the husband of a woman that the king had distinguished.

Now, this is what befell the king when he became smitten with a lady named Melidine.

The King and the Beautiful Melidine

Melidine was the widow of a lord whom her parents had made her marry because he was rich and in favor at court. She did not detest him and she did not love him. She was only grateful to him for the good position he had given her, by marrying her, among the noble ladies of the kingdom.

The lord died quite rapidly, and when she had mourned him for a while, she considered that she had the right to expect a few of the pleasures of life. She had no lack of suitors, but she loved the king and nothing preoccupied her more than seducing him. It happened that the king was conquered by two other beautiful ladies before having noticed her, and she was so chagrined and resentful that she swore to refuse the king as often as was possible for her and would be seemly.

One day she was mingling with the company of princes and ladies who were escorting the king on a boar-hunt. The beast suddenly burst out of a thicket and passed, at a hectic gallop of its short legs, directly through the middle of the company, throwing complete disarray thereinto. The horses reared up and collided with one another, rumps against rumps and noses, and during their kicking and recoiling the order of the escort was disturbed, with the result that while bucking and snorting noisily from its scarlet nostrils, Melidine's horse came very close to the king's, which reared up diabolically, bucking worse than all the rest, like the royal horse it was.

Emmanuel had soon reduced it to immobility, and was then able to see Melidine, haughty and smiling, retaining, while shaken by her crazed mount, all the delicate and sure nobility of her lineage, and not departing from her smile until the horse had calmed down. Then, in a fugitive crease of the lips, she manifested all the delights of the expected triumph. So must Omphale, Delilah and Cleopatra have smiled on seeing the Mighty fallen beneath their slender hands with gleaming fingernails.

It was thus that the king noticed her; and, bowing, he paid her a thousand compliments on her skill and her courage.

46

Then he resumed the head of the escort, and they ran after the tracks of the boar.

The latter was at bay against a tree, and as the dogs held it in thrall, Emmanuel, having looked Melidine full in the face, leapt from his horse drew his dagger from its sheath, advanced toward the boar and, chasing the ardent dogs away with great thrusts of his boots, gave the animal time to recover its breath, to see its adversary, and to charge him.

A cry of anguish from the escort…an arm raised, then falling…the beast on the ground….

The king turned round and smiled at Melidine.

She had not foreseen that he would smile at her like that, immediately after having been so brave. She only remembered her oath after a quiver of pride and pleasure, which was prolonged outside herself and ran in little burning ripples all the way to the king. She pulled herself together, and responded to the king's smile with an inclination of the head full of deferential grace.

But the king was smitten with Melidine. And as soon as they had returned to the palace he went to her and said: "Melidine, it required the hazard of a hunt to make me see how beautiful you are!"

Then he tried to seize Melidine's hand—but with the smiling deference that she had shown a little while before, Melidine drew her hand away.

A slight astonishment turned the king's cheeks pink.

Trembling with profound contentment, Melidine weighed upon her heart with all the will-power she still felt. If she had parted her lips to respond, she would have fainted into the king's arms before saying a word. She did not reply, and her withdrawn hand, while all that agitation was concealed beneath a smile, caused the king to think what a woman's smile ordinarily makes all men think—that he was, in spite of his victories and his science of amour, like an infant stammering before the flame, the light or the great mute dark. And that silence on Melidine's part troubled him so greatly that he spoke again, quickly, in order that she should not sense his disturbance.

"Melidine, I understand now, by my remorse, how unworthy I am of your sweet benevolence. Unworthy—and perhaps forever—of the most precious of pardons...

"Allow, O Melidine, that *perhaps* to be as a hopeful gaze in the somber face of the frightful *forever*. Speak to me, dear Melidine. Must I hear, through that malevolent silence, that it is necessary for me to reject that *perhaps*, as a king throws his crown over his shoulder on to the ground of the battlefield where he has been defeated?"

At that moment, the palace bells rang, which announced the prayers before the meal. The king took possession imperiously of the hand that had been refused, pressed it between his own hands, approached it to his lips, and said:

"Melidine, this evening, at the hour when Galade goes to sleep, a reliable domestic will watch for you to come to the palace gates. You will come and you will follow him. And there, where he will take you, alone, simultaneously anxious and radiant, humble, fervent, as emotional as a priest at prayer, and as joyful as the earth at dawn, the king will be waiting for you, who will be dead tomorrow of lamentable ennui, Melidine, if you do not come..."

I will not go, said Melidine to herself proudly, as she returned to her house.

There was an isolated pavilion in the park, where the king sometimes received his intimates, sometimes had a snack on returning from a hunt, and above all, spent his beautiful nights of love.

There was a room therein with flagstones of red marble, finished with large chairs and divans covered with animal skins. The light there descended softly from a crystal window framed at the top of a cupola. When the door was open, one could see the park outside, with a bright fountain surrounded by flower-beds. In the distance, the other parts of the palace appeared between the branches of trees. No noise reached it to trouble the lovers, except for the joyful splash of the nearby fountain.

Statues, plants and soft fabrics ornamented the room, and among the statues, in a niche hollowed out in the wall, illuminated by a lamp that never went out, was the statue of the Virgin Mary. That was due to Monseigneur Gohain. Having no fear on her behalf of profane spectacles and speech, so far above all the games of humans was she, he wanted her there as a refuge ever open to the king.

Behind that room was the bedroom.

A soldier was placed every evening on sentry-duty at the door of the pavilion, whose orders were to patrol the surroundings, to drive away the malevolent, the indiscreet or furious husbands, and to run to take the king's orders if the latter summoned him.

The king and his lover remained alone, enclosed, as if separated from time and the rest of the world. The domestic charged with amorous offices, equipped with a key to the pavilion, waited wherever the king told him to for the person he was to escort there; then he withdrew, locked the door behind him, and only came back at dawn.

Words spoken in the streets of Gyzir, on the day when the king gave a rendezvous to the beautiful Melidine.

"Here's your milk, Mother Minette. It's very fresh and warm. Very fresh milk ought to be warm; seeming altogether as if it's scarcely emerged from the pink nipple, still steaming, with the scent of the stable."

"Thank you, friend; here's your money. Beautiful day. It will be a pleasure to wash this morning. The water in the bowl will be the color of the sky, and the soap will make golden streaks in the blue water."

"Ho! Who wants to buy my cabbages, my beets, my lettuces? Freshly picked, freshly cut, a charm for the eyes, a delight for the nose, and a feast for the belly!"

"Bonjour, neighbor. What's new?"

"The morning's scarcely begun. I'm still asleep. Life will be cheerful today, in the sunlight."

"It's spring. How is your daughter?"

"Still in bed."

"If she'd got up sooner she'd have seen the hunt go by. The king passed this way, followed by the princes."

"Bonjour, Father. Bonjour, neighbor. I saw the king's cortege. The gallop of the horses woke me up. I went to the window. I saw the king. Then I went back to sleep."

"Couldn't you stay up, get dressed, and get moving? Idler!"

"I went back to sleep for a little while, in order that the king wouldn't vanish..."

"What does that mean?"

"What a beautiful dream I had, Father!"

"A drink, custodian of the Blessed Wine! A moment's truce in toil. Serve quickly, and full. Where's your daughter?"

"Gone to fetch the wine."

"Bonjour, young woman! Come closer. Are you coming this evening?"

"Shut up! Shut up! My father is watching. Have you enough of this wine?"

"Another glass. Will you come this evening, to the meadow?"

"I'll let you know...."

"Soldier! Hey, soldier of my heart, are your duties so urgent?"

"I'm going back to barracks, taking an order to the captain."

"Kiss me."

"I'm chagrined."

"What's the matter, my dear?"

"I'm jealous."

"That's stupid!"

"Gillin's boating that you love him!"

"He's not ugly."

"Do you love him?"

"Come and find me tonight; you'll see which of the two of you I love."

"Tonight, you say?"

"Tonight."

"Alas! Alas! Poor me! Tonight I'm on guard outside the king's pavilion."

"Get someone to take your place."

"I'll try, I'll find someone..."

"Find him, my love."

"If I can't find anyone, swear to me that Gillin..."

"Find him, my love."

"Comrade, will you stand guard this evening in my place outside the king's pavilion? I'll give you this piece of silver...these two coins...these three...."

"I couldn't do it for a hundred. The flower-seller Galanelle has promised herself to me this evening."

...

Hey, Comrade, my good friend! Do you want to stand guard for me..."

"Of course. When?"

"This evening."

"This evening!"

"I'll give you three pieces of silver to send to your old father."

"Bad luck, Comrade. I have a rendezvous tonight with Menna, the chambermaid. Another time, if you like. Any time you like...except this one..."

...

"Captain?"

"What do you want?"

"Someone to replace me on guard duty outside the king's pavilion."

"Are you ill?"

"I'm jealous."

"All right. If one of your comrades..."

"There isn't any."

"Then what do you expect me to do? Stand your guard, my friend."

"But Captain...!"

"Isn't that Selice going by, over there, in her blue carriage? Cheer up, friend. Orders might come at any minute that will take me to Selice's house..."

"Alas, alas."

"Bonsoir, custodian of the Blessed Wine. Another glass before going home... Bonsoir, young woman...see you soon?"

"I'll let you know."

...

"Well, neighbor, what did I tell you? It's spring. Is business good?"

When the weather's as nice as today, people come out of their houses. They stop at the stalls. I've sold a lot. The curfew! Bonsoir, neighbor..."

"Bonsoir, neighbor. Goodnight to your daughter..."

The Consequence of Monseigneur Gohain's Pious Intentions

When the last chimes of the Gyzir curfew, repeated by all the villages on Galade, had died away, the king went into the pavilion with his servant and asked him whether the bedroom had been prepared as he had prescribed.

"Sire," said the domestic, "it only remains for me to throw the incense on the red coals, and strew the flowers from this basket throughout the room."

"Go," said Emmanuel, "and do it quickly, and then run to the palace gates.

Having detached a lighted torch from the walls of the main room, the domestic went into the bedroom next door. He blew on the coals, threw odorant gum on to them, used his torch to light a little lamp suspended from the vault by a long chain, the light of which passed through silvery gauze, and smoothed the harmonious gaps in the wall-hangings and heavy curtains with a few strokes of his hand. Then, fixing his torch into a ring in the wall, he spread the flowers on the floor and all the furniture. After that, he went back to join the king, bent his knees before him, and left the room, closing the door behind him.

"Good guard!" he said to the soldier on sentry duty.

The latter responded with a vague gesture, sufficient to show that he had heard. The soldier was leaning his head on the two hands that held the shaft of a halberd. He seemed to be sleeping, thinking, or even weeping. If the domestic had had the time to look harder at the man, he would have seen, under the cloak that covered him, his torso and shoulders agitated by involuntary jerky movements, like those of a man ready to run, who changes his mind, contains himself, then launches himself forward again, and changes his mind again.

Left alone, the king knelt down in front of the statue of the Virgin, and said a short prayer, for he had acquired a certain piety from his father Georgis, and also considered himself as quits with Heaven for having thought about it sincerely before surrendering himself to profane joys.

Then, lying down on a divan, he closed his eyes and allowed the image of Melidine to come to him. He evoked her proud smile and the suave contours of her body. He laughed at the little hand that had drawn away...and the suspicion crossed his mind, rapid and fluid, that perhaps Melidine might not come. Sure of himself, however, because of all his gallant victories, he laughed again and thought about the lovely combat in which he was soon about to engage.

So the king was dreaming pleasantly, his eyes half-closed, on the amicable divan...

A strange odor offended his nostrils. He sat up. He looked around, and saw nothing for a moment. Suddenly, he saw black smoke gliding between the wall and the pleats of the thick curtain that separated the bedroom from the main room.

He ran to it.

There was a fire.

Because of the inattention or carelessness of the servant, foolish or criminal, the torch had sent fire to the wall-hangings.

The king tried to go into the room but at the first step the smoke stopped him. It was, however, necessary to reach one of the items of furniture in order to get the key to the door...

The soldier!

He struck the main door with his fists, and called for the soldier on guard—but the latter did not come.

He tried to unseal the lock; he seized it, shook the lock and the door with all his might...but it did not open.

He was dazed. The idea of anger did not take possession of him at first. That soldier who had abandoned his post! That lover who was not yet here! And the fire extended into the room, having devoured the curtain between the two rooms, already licking gluttonously at the soft fabrics along the walls!

The only action possible was to flee. The king hammered on the door with his fists, his feet and his shoulder. Grabbing chairs, he made use of them as battering rams—but the doors behind which kings shelter are made of resistant wood. There are no doors stronger, except in the houses of bankers

The smoke, still relatively light, gradually filled the room. The king coughed; his eyes were pricked by little sharp points. Surprise and the instinct of survival had given way to anger: anger against the culpable servant; anger that he had not come back, against that proud Melidine, who, late in coming, was retaining the domestic at the palace gates; ferocious anger against the sentry who had deserted; bitter anger against himself, whom Melidine had disdained.

But the anger soon gave way, in its turn, to horror. In sum, if no miracle occurred, if Melidine really was not coming, the king was going to be quite simply roasted. That baroque, abominable end, appeared around him in the grimacing swirls of the smoke, now becoming heavy, like the links of a chain was slowly tightening about his chest.

It would give way, that door! It was not possible that it would remain firm! Was the smoke not going to escape through the interstices of the battens, was the heat not going to shatter the crystal of the cupola, in order to let the smoke and flame out and reveal the fire to the palace? But could the king, until then, resist the atrocious heat, the invasive vapor?

"Help! Help me!" he cried, deliriously, stubbornly attacking the unbreakable door.

"Dear God, have pity on me!" he said, suddenly staggering with a dolorous lassitude.

Then he straightened up again. In that instant, he perceived, shining feebly through the smoke, the Virgin Mary's lamp.

He ran to the statue, threw himself on his knees, and clenched his hands on the stone robe overflowing the niche.

"Virgin Mary! Our Lady of all succor! Get me out of this great peril! Save me from an ugly death! A miracle, Mother of men! Or let Melidine come..."

He stopped. Terror did not prevent him from hearing himself ask the exceedingly pure Virgin that she save him by making herself, so to speak, the accomplice of a consequence, in sum, of his profane amours. Was it not, on the contrary, her, the Saintly One, who wanted to punish him here?

"Mother! Mother! Before your sacred image, I've committed numerous sins. I've given, before you, too great a part to the delights of the earth. Monseigneur Gohain predicted it. Am I going to die burned, Eternal Mother? Is there no possible redemption? What do you want of your son full of terror, Blessed Virgin? A cathedral with a golden dome? A thousand perpetual candles, and before their tremulous light, relentless masses, so long as I live? Alas, don't you see that my garments are already catching fire? If I must expiate, is it necessary for me to renounce my dearest joys...hunts, feasts, rides through the forest, excursions in the city, inconstant amours? Is it my death, in sum, that you want? Alas, in what state will my soul present itself before you? Immaculate! Still full of Melidine, and all those who come here...I understand! And this is my greatest fault! You wanted this amour to punish me for my amours...you have charged that proud woman..."

He collapsed. His eyes closed.

...

And when he awoke, the door was open. The air was coming into the wrecked room in delicious waves. The domestic was sobbing at his feet. His ministers and his courtiers— the entire court—were waiting for his first sigh.

"The soldier?" asked the king.

"Caught with a mistress," someone replied, "arrested, perhaps punished already."

"And you?" he said, turning toward the distressed servant.

"Alas," the latter relied, "an execrable haste on my part must have caused the disaster!"

"And why that haste, curse you?"

"A girl I love...whom I was to meet as soon as my task was over...as soon as I had conducted to Your Majesty the..."

"Shut up," said the king. A laceration occurred in his mind. Amorous, the felonious soldier; amorous, the valet; and himself...

He got up painfully. He went to hide his face in the robe of the Virgin, which the fire had only partially spared. And he said: "The miracle occurred, O Savioress! My soul is enlightened in my breast, into which, thanks to you, the air of life still penetrates! You have uncovered for me the perilous path in which I was marching blindly, dragging the entire country with me. In gratitude for your tutelary aid, I shall make a vow to renounce..."

"What, my son?" asked Monseigneur Gohain, who had approached the king and received that confession at the same time as the Virgin, by the right conferred upon him by his pontifical dignity.

"Amour, Father," said the king.

"Oh! Stop!" said the bishop. "You're young, my son. The ways of nature are almost as mysterious as those of the Most Holy Virgin. I declare to you that making a vow to renounce it for the present year is sufficient. Such a vow will be, for the Virgin, a sufficiently intense mark of your profound devotion."

"For the entirety of the present year, O most Glorious," said the king. "I will not love any woman carnally."

And it was at that moment, breathless, disheveled, her strength exhausted, that Melidine came into the room and saw the king. "He's alive" she said, and fell down in a faint.

The king, having concluded his prayers, still shining with fervor, returned to the divan where he had miraculously awakened from death, and there he perceived Melidine. She opened her eyes.

She got up slowly, and approached the kind, murmuring: "Forgive me!" and extending her lips to him, offering herself to him as if the crowd were not there.

The king, seeing those red lips extended toward him, swollen with fever and passion, that beautiful body quivering with remorse and hope, leaned instinctively toward Melidine, but then straightened up and said, gravely: "I forgive you, Melidine; go in peace."

And, leaving her stupefied and distressed, he drew away, his eyes filled with an interior light.

THE SECRET OF THE ANAIDE GROTTO

The Land of Ennui

Avenues of Gyzir, where the populace rushed to see royal escorts pass by, woods of Galade where sleek foxes, unquiet wolves and great svelte deer with stupid eyes, grazed the moss, broke the branches, crushed the mauve flower-heads and decapitated the heather, songs, clash of weapons, outbursts of perpetual delight in the staircases of the palace, rustles of silks brushing past one another in the corridors, clanking of vast cooking-pots in the ardent kitchen, concerts of mingled music escaping at dusk from boats undulating on the pond, pathways of the park where the laughter of ladies climbed the rays of sunlight descending between the branches of the elms, and fusing with them—what is usurping you, enveloping you, rendering you furtive, muffling you, paralyzing you, extinguishing you?

The King of Galade is suffering from ennui.

At first, no one perceived that the king was no longer the same. He has hunted boar and foxes; he has given fêtes, and the inhabitants of Gyzir have danced under the illuminated windows through which passed, as if in gushing drops, the music of the royal salons; he has maintained his high place at table during the usual feasts; he has shown himself the most agile and the strongest in all the tourneys in Galade... But one day, he summoned Monseigneur Gohain, the archbishop, and threw himself at his knees, crying:

"Save me, Father, for I no longer know the joy of living since I must not make love to any woman! Father, their conquest was the involuntary goal of all my movements. The beasts killed while hunting, with great difficulty and great audacity, the victories of the spear and the dagger, chariot races and horse races, my cheerful voice, my limpid laughter, was

59

for them, had for its impulse and its goal women, the pretty, laughing, nonchalant ladies...

"Alas! I have separated myself from them, Father. They are not wicked, but malevolent nature has loaded me with the gift of seducing them; before me, I see them attentive, wide open from the outset, hopeful and desirous, and I, who know what florescence emerges from them, and who senses the same florescence blossoming in me, must cruelly wither all that benediction! In an instant, the fresh fountain where they came to drink, where they were about to drink, already advancing their avid lips, is covered over with sheets of ice, opaque and hard, as only old and funereal winter clothes all fountains.

" Father! Father! If you could see their large, plaintive eyes then, and sense beyond their astonished lips the lamentable depression of their hearts! Father, I no longer know how it is possible to live! So I go forth, weary of every hour, as if sated, devoid of desires, worse than dead!"

Monseigneur Gohain, Uncle Gasp and the sage Mnektes attempted to revivify the king.

"Damnation!" said the uncle. "We're going to start again, what! Coming out of the redoubtable religiosities, you'll give me Pleasure for a traveling companion. I'll go forth with you, gamboling like a young man, unfolding my legs, gone soft with kneeling, with a leap, and finding myself, when I come down again, at least twenty years younger. I'll laugh at every tree, every thicket, every blade of grass—which are all the pretty girls in Galade that one dared not take by the chin or pat on the cheek without rolling grave eyes and saying to them: 'Follow virtuous paths, my children; such is the commandment of the king, which transmit to his worthy people the commandments of have!' My hands trembling, under the aforementioned chins, and the tips of my fingers dancing through my sentences like sparrows chirping and hopping among the cypresses of a cemetery! Ha! Nephew, you're not going to bury us again under piety, the lid of the saucepan in which the holy and natural spices of our blood are simmering, seething and bubbling no matter what one does!

"Because you must not, due to your respectable vow, let yourself go to some honeyed brush with your neighbors left right and center, does it follow that there ought not to be any merriment at feasts? Double damn it, Majesty! And the sweet contemplation of joy? Are you not an artist, and the most artistic of artists, as you are the most of anyone and anything whatsoever, by the imperious right of sovereignty? Have you not seen how artists look at all things and pursue their idea through all forms? If, for the rest of us, a beautiful body is good and full flesh, it is for them transparent to their whim, as much as a window through which one considers the sun and the stars. They take their contentment in imagining rather than seeing, and creating, in accordance with what, something even more magnificent to see. For that man, therefore, feasts, harmonious grouping, the clink of crystal cups, pleasant discussions, the reflections of light on the flowers of the tablecloth..."

"Uncle Gasp," said the king, "although I'm the king, I'm not an artist, for the forms that I can imagine are no more beautiful than those I see, and through which I can't pursue anything else, if they're agreeable women, than the idea of the contentment I'd have in cherishing them and enjoying them...

"As for feasts, it's necessary for me to tell you bluntly that I presently find their pleasures paltry and crude, because they're always the same. Not being able, like you, to numb myself or intoxicate myself, the dishes, wines or light, which dispose one to caresses that are forbidden to me, my eyes, neither blurred nor vacillating, soon let me see their limitations. And then I feel ashamed of having attached so many attractions to a joy that is nothing more than noise and guzzling, if one takes away the amorous games. Meanwhile, I feel a tremendous power of joy ever present, and suffer from not knowing where to staunch or satisfy it, among all those guests drunk on alcohol and kisses."

"It's necessary," put in Monseigneur Gohain, "to staunch that beautiful river in nobler feasts. All your potencies of joy would be satisfied by the supreme joy that is the adoration of God. Understand that state of incomparable grace that consists of felling as if one were molten, bathed, dissolved and incorporated in his Light. The efforts indispensable to attain it, which are the disdain for terrestrial delights, drawing away from everything that one has cherished as a man born of humankind, the sacred expectation—taking possession of all other thirsts—of the hour when, in the cleansed soul, the blissful irruption of light is produced, are the only efforts, my son, sufficient to absorb and satisfy the forces that you dispense, like everyone else, in perpetual desires, and to annihilate the suffering that results from those unslaked desires. Such are, by mortification, renunciation and the substitution of divine objects for ordinary human ends, the substantial agapes to which I want to take you."

"If I understand you correctly, Father," the king replied, "and if I dare make a comparison, like a sack in which one taken new-born kittens to drown in a nearby pond, it would be necessary to extract from myself that adoration and that faith like a big sheet in which I would wrap all the attractions of the world, in which I would gradually heap them up one by one, tie them up with string, and when the package is duly secured by the four folded-over corners of the sheet, hurl them into forgetfulness...and it's then, completely miserable and naked, in relation to the earth, that I would be sumptuously inhabited by the glorious Light and warmed by the Heat of God...

"Alas! Is it possible, when one has clear eyesight, a sturdy and palpitating heart, and legs avid to go to all the places that seduce us, to close oneself off to all the pleasures of the earth? Is it possible not to sense the perpetual excitation of all the beautiful forms that artists have sung, magnified or created? And if one retrenches oneself, as you have said, from all the constructions of nature and humans, does one not end up retrenching oneself from oneself? I mean from everything that makes one feel that one exists, by knowledge of and contrast with everything that exists outside oneself, which is the world and all its forms and all its creatures. And thus, losing all notion of oneself, the visible world, time and space, and no longer having anything in oneself, since one has gradually expelled all the images, in order to aid one to comprehend God more broadly, to worship him and exalt in the power of adoration, one would be nothing before Him but a kind of nothingness, a stupid animal devoid of thought and soul, a very holy individual...such, therefore, that he would turn his Light away from you, because one no longer has anything in oneself worthy of receiving it worthily. Father, Father! Can you not give me a simpler consolation, and indicate to me where to expend the forces of my youth, elsewhere than in the love of women or the tyrannical adoration of God?"

"Those forces, permanent in humans," concluded the sage Mnektes, "and which have no innate desire except to dispense themselves, heading in all directions in disorder, like a blaze whose flames, pushed, dragged, jostled and pestered by the wind, sometimes go toward the forest, sometimes the city, sometimes the sky, sometimes curve over and lick the ground...let a wise man come along and construct an oven over that hearth, and set a chimney over it...the imprisoned flames will only have one direction left to go, drawn by the air current up into the chimney. Let our man throw between the flames and the air good pottery for firing, good kneaded dough for baking, and the good flames will cook a fine vessel or a gilded loaf.

"Call your mind the attractive air, my son, and consider your body as the clever construction in which the flames, which are your forces, are imprisoned. Learn to channel them in the direction your will decides, and by that means you will be their master rather than their plaything, and a great joyous miracle will follow. Doors that you have brushed many times in passing, behind which, because they were closed, you paid no heed to their contents, will open wide to you, and a thousand unsuspected treasures, will shine beyond them: a thousand beautiful and mysterious secrets by which the common run of humans are blindly tossed, will appear to you in their quasi-divine light, and communicate their power to you.

"Talking to you at present will not convince you. Only remember this: the act of meditation, which has appeared to you thus far tedious and flat, will then become an indescribable sensuality, and by its means, you will be transported to the top of the highest mountain, bathing your forehead in a sky rutilant with lightning, dazzling with fiery stars, while angels beating their wings fill up your fresh head and exquisitely limpid eyes.

"You will no longer suffer because you will have command over your entire body, and all the desires if your body. No particle of yourself will be agitated without your wishing it: the charm of women, the splendor of forms, the attractions of life...no influence will have the power to move you outside the circle in which it pleases you to enclose yourself.

"And as God directs the weather, the lightning and the sun at his whim, in the direction of the force that is yours, and from which your arms, legs, respiration, speech and all your desires obtain movement, you will find the joy that you demand—equal, perhaps, to the adoration of God, and certainly superior to the possession of women."

"Alas, Father Mnektes," said the king, "I will reply to you that being so wise and so sure of the obedience of my limbs, I would never again have any joy in hunting or fighting in tourneys, since I would, in my wisdom, choose the adversary and the beast to the measure of the power of my limbs, and would thus always be sure of victory, and would very quickly become blasé.

"I will also tell you that, fundamentally ignorant of what there is behind the smallest of clouds passing over the mountains, ignorant of what there is a thousand feet beneath me in the earth, ignorant as to how far the sky extends, reduced to impotence in my entire being in the time that the most benign of fevers last—in sum, not knowing any more profoundly than anyone else why I find myself alive on the earth, if not by the mysterious will of God—I would consider it as foolish presumption to decide with my petty will all that I ought or ought not to allow to act upon me or to enter into me, and patiently to control every impression that I receive, in order to decree whether it is good or bad for me.

"For, my dear Mnektes, that interior flame if which you speak so honestly, I believe that it is not in me alone, but that it is largely made of all the exterior warmths that touch me, impress me, excite me and penetrate me: the smiles of women, the grace of forms, the fervors and mischief of my people, and all the incompatible effluvia of nature and life—with the result that by regulating, in the name of my feeble human will, its ordinary nourishment, so complicated, universal and delicate, I would fear, my dear Mnektes, to bar the route to some mysteriously beneficial invasion, to the profit of some maleficent invasion more-or-less well-masked, and thus, far from stimulating, as is done so congruently outside my will, life and all that it encloses and carries, colliding with it, troubling it, diminishing it, and soon annihilating it, and eventually finding myself as paralyzed, my teeth chattering, only rich in that inefficacious will alone, a scepter without an arm, a sovereign without a realm.

"And so, after having hard all three of you, there is nothing, alas, but the contemplation of joys in which I cannot partake, the adoration of God and the adoration of the will, that can be offered to me in place of amour!"

Thus, in spite of Monseigneur Gohain, Uncle Gasp and the subtle Mnektes, the poor King of Galade supported very dolorously the consequences of his vow, and the court, and Gyzir, and all of Galade, supported its extending repercussions.

The Discontentment of Two Women

One day, in a quiet pathway in the park, the king encountered Melidine. He was emerging from a long conversation with his tutor Mnektes. The latter, to divert his sad disciple, was inclining his mind toward study, mingling therein, as sagaciously as possible, material demonstrations and their philosophical deductions, counting on the virtue of the latter to attract the king away from a reality in which everything excited his suffering and his ennui.

After having taken him to various factories in Galade, where glassware, garments, money and housing bricks were made, and interesting him in the most ingenious manipulations, transformations and constructions, Mnektes was developing in him the thought, which was dear to him, that in spite of the multiplicity of materials, all of them were combinations if one unique substance, which the senses could not attain, immaterial, and hence spiritual. He had taken pleasure, that day, in informing him how, in accordance with that principle, it was possible to reduce all compositions to the most extreme simplicity, in the same way that Numbers, no matter how high they might be, were always merely the repetition of the number One.

To captivate his slightly weary attention, Mnektes had made him, with the aid of drawing, notice that the figuration of the ten first numbers, which could themselves be assembled and multiplied infinitely, could be resolved into the sole components of the straight line and the circle...and that the straight line and the circle were, after the point that gave them birth, the simplest images that one could conceive...and that the mystical meaning of those images was admirable, and would serve as the subject for an imminent conversation.

Left alone, the king was following the path where he perceived Melidine sitting on a bench. A lady of the palace who was walking with her had left her there for a moment in order to acquit a duty with which she was charged. While waiting, Melidine was amusing herself with the sunlight.

Dusk was approaching. A slender beam fell upon the bench between the leaves, obliquely caressing Melidine's arm, which emerged bare from her sleeve from the neck down. As the sun descended toward the night, the slender beam was displaced, as if gliding along and trembling gently toward the ground. With her hand splayed on the bench. Melidine was watching it dance over her bare arm and her dress; then, as it drew away gradually and shone some distance from the bench, the ground and the hem of her dress, she advanced her foot into the thread of light, catching the sunlight on the tip of her shoe.

She saw the king approaching, and that he had seen her.

They each seemed to the other to be extremely troubled—for the king had not encountered Melidine since the blaze, and strove not to think about her, and Melidine, having learned about the king's inexplicable ennui, had no doubt that, firstly, he bore a grudge against her because she had not come that evening when he was waiting for her, secondly, that he had sworn never to see her again, thirdly, that he was observing his oath out of pride, and fourthly, that he was suffering very much because he loved her—and therefore, that all of his great ennui could only stem from that.

She made a movement to get up, curtsy to the king and go away, but the king said to her: "Bonjour, Melidine," and kissed her hand.

Then she thought that she too loved him dearly, and that she was suffering as much as he was, out of pride, like him, that she had been unable decorously to anticipate the silent desires of the king, but that perhaps, now, nothing any longer prevented them from being the two happiest lovers in all Galade.

And her pleasure was such that her bosom heaved, inflating her pale cleavage, reddening her face and closing her eyes momentarily before she responded to the king: "I salute Your Majesty."

He asked her permission to sit down beside her, and began talking to her. He enquired as to what she was doing in the park, and was informed that she was waiting for a lady, one of her friends. Melidine thought that those words were merely preliminary, and that he would soon talk to her about matters touching the two of them more particularly—and also that perhaps the king would not want to make any allusion to the sad night and would bring their long-tested hearts face to face, as if new and beating toward one another for the first time. She waited.

"This hour," said the king, "is the most noble of the festivals of the earth. The moments, Melidine are as if charged with enchantments. The sun, above the mountains, raises its last rays as the conductor of an orchestra raises his arms. A real symphony bursts forth, which has the changing light for its chords. They give birth, rippling and leaping from the ground to the sky, to flowers in the trees. Everything is transformed. The pond is golden, the grass crimson. Fragments of light hang on here and there, applying a swift note to the bark and disappearing, then reappearing, buoyantly on the shivering tips of the leaves. Every individual, at this moment is a king if he stands upright in the dying daylight. The humblest garments are brocade, rutilant and gleaming. The feverish sky deploys its oriflammes, constructs strong castles, and groups together squadrons of clouds to repel the assault of the great adversary: the Night. It comes. It rises. It enlaces the Day, and both are confused. The sun sinks. The voracious night absorbs the last scarlet bands, and pricks, as a sign of triumph, the shepherd's star in the forehead of the conquered sky."

Utterly astonished by that speech, Melidine replied: "It's beautiful, Sire, and you paint it pleasantly!" And she trembled a little, for it seemed to her that the king had brushed her arm. But if the king had brushed Melidine's arm, it was by chance, for he feared more than anything brushing anything whatever of Melidine, even the hem of her dress.

She said then: "One would love to be fluid and melt into the light. The colors that seem to you to be music are also caresses. One would sense them posing upon one, violent and soft, all rapid. The languid mauve and the penetrating and burning violet..."

"My tutor Mnektes," said the king, "who knows many astonishing things, claims that it is possible to escape the body and identify oneself with water, air, light, even flame. He has that information from science as old as the earth, which ancient manuscripts, rediscovered and deciphered with great difficulty, have revealed to him. Those manuscripts were dictated by the spirits—which no longer manifest themselves in our epoch—of the primitive Galadians, long before the coming of Christ, when innumerable gods were worshipped: Goho, Vzygine...

"All that is extremely remote from us. Those primitive Galadians possessed, it appears, the secret of scaling the mountains, and nothing of what might be beyond them, and throughout the sky, was unknown to them. There is a part of legends there, and a part of mystery, in which profound intelligences—like that of my tutor Mnektes—specialized in those arduous studies can distinguish certain marvelous verities."

"Ah!" said Melidine. She was quite astounded by the turn that the conversation was taking. Perhaps the king was playing with her, and deliberately talking about anything except what preoccupied him so forcefully. He was avenging himself and wanted to appear to have never had the slightest inclination for her. It suddenly seemed to her that his brain, which had imagined all that, was driving a clawed hand inside her, all the way to her heart, gripping it, squeezing it and scratching it.

"If you like, Melidine, "I can sent you one of those beautiful conversations."

For since the king had sat down next to Melidine, a strange warmth had flowed through his entire being, and it appeared to him that he could no longer live apart from her— that merely sensing her close to him was the most delicate of joys, intimate and sweet, as if it were changing all the blood in his veins to honey. Obviously, he would respect his vow and forbid himself any unchaste attraction toward Melidine. He would only kiss her hand and her forehead, as a fraternal friend...

She replied: "Sire, whatever Your Majesty would like me to hear, or that it would please him to send me, the honor of being close to Your Majesty would cause me to follow it swiftly. Sire, I will listen to the sage words of your tutor, and that which I cannot hear very well with my poor ears, I shall understand in your eyes and the light in your eyes. And if I see you enthusiastic, I shall immediately be filled with the surest intoxication."

She finished, and waited again. She was waiting for the king to pick up her hand and murmur: "The honor alone? Nothing but the honor, dear Melidine?" Then she would have confessed that another sentiment, less solemn and more august than honor, attached her to His Majesty. She was entirely ready. She would have made that confession.

The king did not take the hand at all, and he said: "Only the honor, dear Melidine? I would have liked it also to be the pleasure of learning beautiful and brilliant things."

It would not have taken much, at that moment, for him to declare that no fêtes were worth as much as Mnektes' lessons—as much because the thought of having Melidine with him troubled him delightfully, as because it appeared that the presence in question would give an extreme glamour to the information of philosophy.

"Since I've been listening attentively to Mnektes," he continued, "I see marvelously that there are many things among those which we pass over indifferently that are precious to know. In the songs of birds, the colors of foliage, the perfume of flowers, the sound of springs, the character of people... Like a sculptor with his chisel, carving, hollowing, lashing, mutilating and lacerating a block of stone, in order to extract a ravishing form, Mnektes cuts up, decompose, digs and renders nature transparent, in order to form a divine architecture. Imagine, Melidine, what joy there would be for us, after having listened to Mnektes' beautiful descriptions, after having gone, together from marvel to marvel, the heart more lively, the gaze widened, and the mind ardent, to attain, as the ballets of the court succeed one another with increasingly perfect dances, the terminal apotheosis…to attain for the apotheosis…"

"I understand, Sire!" said Melidine, who could no longer contain herself. "The kiss! The kiss of our impatient lips, the worthy and unique apotheosis of such rare transports!"

"I meant joy," stammered the poor king. "The glorious joy of knowing a little more…" He stood up. "Adieu, Melidine. Here comes your friend." And he quit her, immediately, almost weeping inside himself.

As for Melidine, she cut her walk short, replied feverishly and at random to her friend, and went home exceedingly upset, wounded, ashamed, furious, sobbing, and asking herself: *Is that the king who is said to have such great prowess in amour? Is he disdaining me? But he invited me to accompany him. Is he making fun of me? But I did not see him tremble as he left me. Has he judged me stupid, and that I did not understand what he was saying to me, or is renown a liar and that handsome king does not know that such a pretty woman ought to be offered more than speeches and declamations?*

Sobbing more forcefully, she added: *Alas, I think that I hate him, and that I'm the most unfortunate of women.*

It happened, on another day, that the king was standing at the window of the great hall of the palace, gazing distractedly at what was on the other side of the glass.

The window of the great hall overlooked the square of Gyzir, and it was market day. The people of Gyzir were going, baskets in hand, past the stalls and displays, the piles of cabbages, apples, and all the usual fruits and vegetables of Galade. That swarm, in the sunlight, was very pleasant to see. Men were tugging the bridles of horses or donkeys that they had come to buy or brought to sell; women were proclaiming the merits of their merchandise at the top of their voice.

"My people! My good people!" said the king. He thought that it had been a long time since he had made contact with his good people. The day opened before him like the mouth of an ogress. With irremediable ennui it would devour him, conscientiously and voluptuously, until the hour of sleep, and grind his twelve hours with pointed teeth...as well that distraction as another.

He sent for his high chamberlain and said to him: "Announce that the palace gates will soon be wide open, and that the king will listen to complaints from anyone, and will receive the good people of Galade with joy."

And the news immediately spread through the town.

There was a market gardener in one of the outlying districts of Gyzir named Fanoche, who was reputed to be the prettiest market gardener in the environs of Gyzir, and even of all Galade. She had many admirers among the gardeners. She was ardently courted, and she was not—as many Galadian women in the vicinity of Gyzir maliciously said—insensible to the covetousness of her courtiers.

When she heard that the king was receiving his people, she blushed, went pale, dropped her baskets, left the market, ran home and began to dress herself pompously. In love with the king, like all Galadian women , the thought—which she had not dared to formulate previously—of being distinguished by him among all others invaded and excited her. She made up her face and put golden pins in her hair. She put on her Sunday dress, which was silk with a low neckline.

Beneath her neck, gilded somewhat by the customary open air, the top of her bosom was a trifle rosy, because she sometimes loosened her corsage while working on her crops. The gilt gradually faded into the pink, and a little beneath the pink, her flesh was a white as pure as that of any noble lady rich in powders, pastes, paints, unguents and milky lotions. Her beautiful dominical costume displayed her gilded neck boldly, left her pink bosom visible and permitted a glimpse of her white breasts.

Thus prepared, she headed for the palace.

Every Galadian woman had done as much as Fanoche, but not all of them were as agreeable.

The crowd went into the hall, murmuring and intimidated, everyone shoving everyone else as hard as they could, because everyone wanted to get to the front rank-but they shoved slyly and in silence, because of the gold on the walls and the beautiful fabrics and the noble furniture. A few toes were crushed underfoot without evoking a sound, and a few ribs jabbed. But when Fanoche came in and wanted to fray a passage, an accentuated eddy was produced. The men made way for her, smiling; the women amplified and stiffened the triangles formed by their shoulders, their bent elbows and the hands resting on their hips, in order to prevent her from getting past. But the men were heavier and stronger than the women, and their smiling movement of recoil obliged the latter to recoil too, cursing. And Fanoche was in the front rank when the king appeared.

Acclamations burst forth. The king darted an amicable glance over his people, went up the steps of the throne and made a little well-turned speech about the peace of Galade, the good understanding of its citizens, the honesty of its mores—which had been represented to him, he said, as a trifle free—and in which respect everyone ought to remember that one could not, even in the name of amour, trample underfoot in any way whatsoever piety, duty, decency and respect for the law.

Then he descended from the throne and approached the people. Fanoche, trembling, tried to stiffen herself and not to let her keen desire to be noticed show, but, involuntarily, she shuddered, and went pale, and blushed as the king came closer. That he was going to see her, among the entire crowd, look at her, speak to her...it would be too much...

He looked at her. He stopped in front of her. He spoke to her. She fainted.

"There, exactly," he said, "with regard to decency, is an exceedingly low-cut dress." And he said it in an ill-humored tone that touched her horribly.

The king passed on. If she did not collapse entirely, it was because the crowd was pressing to the point that no movement was possible for anyone. A large tear ran down her cheek. She did not know whether she was furious or in despair. She was deeply wounded. And it is necessary that the reader should not forget that, because it was to have considerable consequences.

Archeological Studies

The last day of the year, which would mark the completion of the king's vow—all the more sacred because he experienced so much pain in consequence—was not approaching very rapidly. In the meantime, he distracted himself as best he could, and almost always without effusion, as if with nonchalance, lassitude and making do. He devoted himself, for a time, to collecting old coins, and then antique weapons found by digging in the soil in the country and under ruined monuments. He took slight interest in the cultivation of flowers and the breeding of hunting dogs and horses. He only hosted feasts when forced.

His usual poets no longer dared sing or compose pleasant ballets or light comedies, because no subject was tolerated that might darken the king's mood, and so nothing remained but those that had no need of svelte dancers and their thin veils, such as miracles or sententious proverbs cut into scenes for the theater. The king having withdrawn his august favor from a painter who had depicted a bather in the nude, sculpture and painting gradually engaged in dry, tedious and mystical representations.

The Yawn was the master of ceremonies at the court of Galade. Like the proud standards flapping in the wind that are covered and paralyzed by crepe in times of mourning, amours, once blossoming, hymns and freely luminous, hid under severe attitudes and serious discussions, and, once buoyant, whispered, as if furtively.

Uncle Gasp no longer set foot in the court, having acquired a little house a long way from the palace, where he made merry at his ease, and reassumed, when he went out, the pious appearances he had put on under Georgis. Monseigneur Gohain approved of the funereal atmosphere, because the obstacles and dissimulations thrown in the path of amour gave it a disagreeable taste of transgression, rendered present in the mind the bitter dread of sin and put the brake on certain unquiet souls—and, by the same token, brought a great number back, as constraints and apprehensions increased, toward the celestial liberties.

Along with the coins and the weapons, the king had discovered and collected undatable and indecipherable manuscripts, as yellow and dry as iron, in which the ink had gradually eroded the paper underneath in places, designing capricious grooves therein. He had handed the greater number over to Mnektes, but had kept a few of them to riffle through, because he had seen illuminations and designs therein, incomprehensible at first glance.

After hard labor, Mnektes, having succeeded in reading several of the manuscripts, taught the king to read, and the latter strove in idle moments to penetrate, by means of the text that accompanied or surrounded them, the meaning of the illustrations and designs.

One of them, in particular, intrigued him. It depicted a kind of grossly-formed leg, the ankle of which was swelled by a short spur, and the heel of which was elongated to form a point, curved back at the extremity toward the foot, which was divided into two, as if the big toe, swollen and tumefied, were trying to catch up with the others, separated from it, if one could admit as toes a compact mass that seemed rather to be an entire foot, designed even more crudely than the leg. At the top of the singular limb, a line sketched something like the hem of a dancer's skirt, becoming blurred some distance from the line and soon dissipated, made a variously and vaguely colored fabrics. One searched in vain for a second leg, nowhere indicated. On each of the differently colored patches of fabric forming the sketch of the skirt a name was written: Iberia, France, Germany. On the leg was another name: Italy.

The king did not understand any of it.

After long and dogged effort, he read, more astonished as he pieced the phrase together: *Disposition of the countries north of the Mediterranean Sea...*

Further along in the same manuscript he read: *Report of the humble and zealous missionary Zahun, son of Aharg, to*

His Excellency Mahara, regent minister of Galade, on his voyage through the three worlds.

That same evening, he asked Mnektes what the significance was of the names Germany, Iberia and France, but without showing him the image. Mnektes made him repeat them, and affirmed that they did not correspond to anything know to him.

"Are they not the ancient names of Galadian hamlets, deformed by time?"

But the savant Mnektes assured him once again that he had never read or heard those names. "Where did you get them from, my son?" he asked.

"One of the old manuscripts," said the king, and added: "I count on determining their meaning by more ample reading."

And the following day, he plunged into the report of Zahun, son of Aharg. He learned therefrom that three immense worlds, each of which would have contained the entirety of Galade ten thousand times over, surrounded the sea called Mediterranean, as flower-beds and trees surrounded the pond in the park, and that that sea was so vast that, in order to begin to imagine it, it was necessary to know that a ship at least a thousand times larger than the largest skiff on the pond in the park, would have to go straight ahead without stopping for more than forty days and forty nights to reach the shore opposite the one from which it had started. Those three immense worlds were Europe, Asia and Africa, the first inhabited by people with white faces, the second by yellow people and the third by black ones! The last was almost completely unexplored, with the absence of Arabia, which occupied its edge.

Zahun, having left Gyzir aged twenty-five, had returned at the age of forty-eight, and said that he had not seen everything, but felt too old and weary to remain far from Galade without having reported on his mission. In the manuscript, which was torn in places and lacked numerous pages, there were extraordinary narrations. An incalculable people, beyond the extreme limits of Europe, uncountable days' march therefrom, possessed a magical substance, one pinch of which, in exploding, could reckon with the hardest rocks. He had brought some back, in fact, and presented it under the name of fulminating powder. A few European princes also knew how to make it, but they utilized it in combats. He described the magnificent monuments elevated to the glory of the different gods of the lands traversed, including the cathedral of Notre-Dame de Paris in France and the temple of Kayraha in India.[6]

A second part of the report began thus:

After the great voyage in which I was able to see for my-self and then condense what my predecessors had seen and related in the course of multiple generations, I have attempted to represent for Your Excellency, as succinctly as possible, the state of the world in the year of grace 1320...

Following the names of emperors, kings, caliphs and princes, the story of incessant battles that transformed the political situation of each continent in a few years, giving Africa and Iberia to the Arabs, part of Germany to the French, part of France to the Germans, and many other perpetual upheavals, Zahun had divided the world into three castes: the emperors, the priests and the peoples. The first were always engaged in battles, the second in prayers and the third in labor. He glorified calm Galade in the midst of that incessantly bloodied world, tortured by a thousand ambitions and the thousand scourges. He also recorded the names and works of the great scientists and artists that he had met in France, Germany and the Orient, and wrote about the profundity of the knowledge of some men and the ignorance of others, the splendor of palaces, the indescribable pullulation of human beings, the diversity of races and the unanimity of suffering, villainies and dreams.

The king, his eyes wide and his brain buzzing, read on and on... He was searching now for a page that might inform him of the route that Zahun had taken to get out of Galade. There was no mention of scaling the mountains. He knew from Galadian history that all attempts of that sort had stopped

---

[6] The Khajuraho temples in Madhya Pradesh.

in the reign of Harb. Had there been mysterious procedures in Zahun's time? Could one escape from one's body, as Mnektes had given him to believe?

He was about to run to his tutor, when he felt so happy, having recovering his appetite for life, in having such a marvelous problem to solve, that he preferred to keep everything to himself, burning with curiosity, and he continued to turn the pages with his quivering fingers.

After having marched for three days in the darkness of the Grotto, I reached a plain dazzling with light. At the extremity of the plain, large edifices loomed up. I soon arrived there, and found myself in a city called Traese, capital of Senestria...[7]

At present, the pages were consecutive. They were marked with various dates. The oldest was a report addressed to His Serene Highness Galenide, successor of Harb, the second king of Galade.

The king tidied away the manuscripts and ran to the Anaide Grotto, which opened in the wall of the mountain at the back of the park. It was dusk; shadows were rising around things. For centuries, no one had gone into the grotto, whose entrance was obstructed by thick ivy. The king cleared a passage and penetrated cautiously.

The grotto was dark and the king could scarcely make out anything except the stalactites in the vault. In any case, a disturbance so new, anguishing and charming at the same time had invaded him that he did not want to know immediately whether it really was the route that had taken the Galadian missionaries to the rest of the world.

He went back to the palace, had supper as usual, and went to bed, putting off all exploration until the following day.

---

[7] In our history, Trieste—the equivalent of the story's Traese—was under the rule of the Patriarchy of Aquileia during the early fourteenth century, and there was no such place as Senestria.

He could not sleep. He got up in the middle of the night. He went into a room nearby where weapons were arranged. He picked up a steel pike and emerged from the room.

An astonished guard saw him pass by; he expected the king to ask him to accompany him, but the latter, as if hallucinated, continued on his way, went into the gardens and reached the grotto.

There, in the heavy and mute obscurity, he was gripped by a great apprehension. He knelt down and prayed to the Virgin. Then he began striking the walls of the grotto with his pike. One place resounded under the steel in a fashion different from the others. He struck it with the point. He braced himself on his young, strong limbs and struck with all his vigor, increasing his effort from moment to moment. Soon, under a more brutal thrust, a block came away. The pike went through into empty space, and the king felt so excited that his knees wobbled; he closed his eyes and stood there, holding his breath.

Then he recovered his senses and continued his work. The wall built by Mahara crumbled beneath his pike. The old cement fell as dust to the ground; the breach was large enough to allow the king to pass through. He went through.

The darkness and the silence were absolute. He opened his arms, and his hands encountered the walls of the corridor.

He knew enough. He left the pike behind and returned to his bedroom. He meditated.

Eventually, this is what he did:

He filled his pockets with all the gold that he found in his apartments, and left a letter he had written visible on a table:

In consequence of a vow, I, the king, have decided to enclose myself until the end of the present year in an abbey in Galade, and to lead and austere and reclusive life there in the company of monks. I do not want anyone to search for me, or anyone to attempt to trouble my retreat. For all the time of my absence I declare my Uncle Gasp, the brother of my venerated

father King Georguis, regent of Galade, and my tutor Mnektes
as his privy councilor.

    Written in the royal palace of Gyzir on the night preced-
ing the twentieth Sunday of the present year, the fifth of my
reign, and the nineteen hundred and fifth of the Christian Era.

Emmanuel.

He placed his seal at the bottom of that fine lie, went past
the soldier on guard, went down to the gardens, made sure that
no one had followed him, went back to the grotto and the
breach, went into it, and set out along the corridor.

Part Two
ASTONISHMENTS

The Orient Express

He arrived on the other side of the mountain two days later, at dawn, exhausted. He traversed the plain. He went into Traese. He was very hungry. His costume caused a passer-by to turn his head. A child taking cows to pasture burst out laughing. He continued on his way. The early hour helped him not to attract too much attention. He went into a clothing merchant's shop, threw a gold coin on the counter and said: "A suit of clothes."

The merchant picked up the coin, turned it over, looked at his customer suspiciously, and then, having weighed the coin and having turned it between his fingers again, toward the window, put it in his pocket, asked the king to follow him, and dressed him.

Thus, Emmanuel was able to go, without attracting attention, to look around with all the thirst of his gaze. He went into an inn and ate. Nothing seemed very astonishing to him: the form of the plates, the nourishment, the faces of the diners, the innkeeper and his daughter did not appear very different from those he had seen in Galade.

Having eaten, he emerged from the inn and wandered through the streets. Suddenly, behind him, a violent rumble nailed him to the spot. He turned around to confront the unexpected, and saw a carriage coming toward him that was moving on its own.

Amazed, he stepped back a few paces and found himself on a sidewalk. The carriage was far away by the time he recovered his senses. Finally, he decided to make sure. He followed its direction, trying to catch up with it. He perceived it in the distance. He hastened his pace. A strident whistle rang out behind him. He turned his head swiftly and stepped aside just in time to let a young man go by who was moving without putting his feet on the ground, sitting down, balanced over two narrow wheels placed one in front of the other, moved by a chain that the equilibrist was activating by moving his legs up and down in a regular rhythm.

The king smiled and said to himself: *It's baroque, but convenient*. Then he resumed his pursuit of the strange vehicle. He perceived it, stopped in front of a monument of stone and iron, around which a busy crowd was coming and going. He went into the monument. He was in a large hall, filed by a similarly agitated crowd. Blasts of whistles, the ringing of bells and strange roars dominated the hubbub of the crowd. In the middle of the room a glazed door was open. He went through it.

An extraordinary spectacle was before his eyes.

It seemed to him as if someone had cut his palace in Galade into several rooms, with their furniture, their fabrics and the gold on their walls, and, with their walls and the façade, their floor, their windows, had transported them here and set them on massive low wheels. Those rooms followed one another in a file, and in front to the sequence of rooms, puffing and smoking, rumbling and shaking its entire being, as if racked by formidable coughs, was an enormous thing composed of two huge cauldrons inverted and fixed on a colossal tube, lying on a large platform supported by wheels. There was a long tapering pipe at one extremity of the tube and a kind of cage at the other extremity, where two black, sweating men were moving precipitately, turning copper levers, and in which a little low door suddenly opened, behind which the king saw a dazzling blaze, which could only be burning in the very entrails of the Thing.

Two huge wheels under its breast were offered, smooth and shiny, to the wind and the open air, resembling the deployment of the knees of a large beast lowering itself down and turning its back. Beneath it and in front of it, and under all the beautiful rooms, stretched steel bars.

The king went up a few steps and penetrated audaciously into one of the rooms.

Several people were installed there, sitting down, who paid no attention to the newcomer. He traversed a corridor, went into another room, and was amusing himself contemplating the fabrics and the furniture when he suddenly heard and felt, almost simultaneously, the sound of a bell, a furious whistling, cries of adieu, and a great shaking throughout his being.

The roaring Thing drew the rooms behind it, with their windows, their hangings, their armchairs and their occupants; in an instant, the stone monument and its crowd disappeared, and an inextricable tangle of large thin wooden stakes, ornamented at their summit by little porcelain bells from which wires escaped, and iron stalks at the top of which huge arms of glass or painted iron agitated, brushed the glass of the room where the king was.

He threw himself backwards, instinctively, and then he felt himself carried away: carried away by an irresistible force; carried away at high speed, through he knew not what, toward he knew not what, his haggard and bulging eyes, dazzled, seeing nothing but grassy banks, trees, and then villages, and then forests, racing , it seemed, toward the windows, like night-birds toward a lighted window—but in reality, disappearing as quickly as they appeared, without even having touched anything, giving way to others, and yet others, in a vertiginous cortege...

None of the king's companions seemed astonished, and the king, tottering, let himself fall into an armchair, shut his eyes and fainted, with the final sensation of having been snatched from the ground, snatched out of himself, and dragged away, without any possible resistance, like a dead leaf along a highway over which a winter wind is blowing.

Paris

Grindings, stops, somersaults of the gasping machine, further leaps into the unknown, immense cities glimpsed in the hectic course, with their domes, their steeples and their towers, the multicolored vagueness of their roofs, their swarming crowds... At every stop, the desire to get down and flee, and the desire to know what there might be at the end of that race... A dolorous turbulence, and then confusion, a kind of semi-dream; then a veritable awakening, audacity and youth gripping the reins again, a bewildered curiosity, the acceptance of a temporarily ineluctable destiny... The king of Galade, standing at the window, hanging on to the curtain rail, watches the landscapes fly past and feels ablaze with life.

Spoken words extracted him from his daze. Two travelers chatting some distance away from the armchair into which he had fallen exchanged a few banal remarks.

"I'm going all the way to Paris," one said.

"Of course," said the other. "You can't go any further."

The king inferred that the name signified the destination. Unconscious effort took place in his still-torpid mind.

Paris...where he had heard that name before? Paris...a monument...ah! It was in Zahun's manuscript...the cathedral of Notre-Dame...

Then he let himself slide again into a kind of nonchalance.

Eventually, standing up, alive and lucid, he waited for the unforeseeable and unimaginable future.

He dined with a hearty appetite in one of the rooms, brightly lit, furnished with little florid tables; night had arrived, rendering the roaring of the machine more frightful; the calm of his companions gave him confidence. Like them, he had gone to sleep, work up, still moving; a day went by, he arrived at the destination.

A man dressed in a uniform had asked him where he came from. "Traese," he replied, and took gold out of his pocket. The man had taken his gold and given him several silver coins. And then he had arrived; he was able to go forth and march as he pleased through the unknown city.

He emerged from the vast edifice in which the train had immobilized and, finding himself on a sidewalk, in a vague light, divined houses in the shadow facing him, distinguishing their forms poorly, and was soon surrounded by valets, who hastened to offer him shelter. He decided that he would wait for daylight to see what was there. He followed one of the valets to a nearby house, brilliantly lit, high, vast and sumptuous.

He was taken to the foot of a staircase. He got ready to go up...a grille opened in front of him. The man escorting him stood aside to let him pass. Ready for anything, moving into the accepted Unknown, the king went into a kind of cage fitted with mirrors. The valet followed him, pressed lightly on a copper button, and the king felt himself uprooted from the ground again, irresistibly...

The cage soon stopped. The valet opened it. The king came out and looked around, over the ramp. The staircase had been climbed without him making a movement. A steel arm, round and smooth, had lifted him up, along with the valet— the arm of some unknown giant hidden under the staircase, whom a mysterious signal had alerted.

Preceding the king, the valet stopped in front of a door in a corridor, and opened it; the king penetrated into a dark room. Suddenly, without him having heard any sound or seeing and porter of light come in, the chamber was inundated with brightness. A lamp hanging from the ceiling had lit up of its own accord.

"Ho!" said the king, anxiously. "How did that lamp light up?"

The valet shivered; he looked the king up and down, anxiously, from head to toe, and then said: "Has Monsieur come far?"

Parenthesis

You will doubtless be astonished that the king is presumed to be able to understand and speak the language of the lands through which he is passing and will pass. You should not be astonished. In truth, if nothing were to be astonishing in this book, there would have been no need to subtitle it a fantastic tale.

Furthermore, illustrious examples inform us that certain voyagers understand and speak the language of countries that are most strange and unexpected to them. Thus, Ulysses saved himself from the cyclops Polyphemus by means of an unforgettable pun; hence, we must admit that the son of Laertes, in a single day, had succeeded in penetrating the linguistic subtleties appropriate to the sons of Neptune. Also, there are innumerable historical narratives, accounts of voyages, epics and beautiful tragedies in which you have read or heard the dialogue: "Be welcome to our shores, stranger. Sit down and tell us your name, your race and your beliefs," and the stranger replies, immediately, without any mention ever being made even of any difficulty of pronunciation: "Very hospitable men, the gods that have permitted me to land on your shores enabled me to be born under other skies. I come from a distant land..." Etc.

Let us therefore go back as soon as possible to the king and the nonplussed bellboy, who has just asked him whether he had come far.

"Very far," replied the king.

The bellboy went to the door, took between his fingers a little wooden bulb suspended on a thread that was attached to the wall, went along the ceiling and connected with the lamp. He said: "Like this...," pressed the bottom of the bulb with his finger, and everything went dark. An instant later, the lamp was shining again.

The king looked at the valet, abruptly. He was correctly dressed; gilded braid even circled his cap and his sleeves and ran down the sides of his trousers, but his face was merely vulgar. His eyes, rather sharp were more like those of a cunning man fond of petty profits, on the lookout for them and provoking them, than a magician producing and suppressing light at a distance. One sensed, beneath his beautiful costume, his body, although straight and robust, was elastic in the spine, ever ready for bows and hasty servitudes.

"Thank you," said the king. "You can go."

"If Monsieur needs me," said the man, after a curt bow, "press on that other button." And he went.

Left alone, the king played with the button in the wooden bulb, making the light go on and off several times in succession. He opened the door suddenly, and saw no one. He closed it again, and wondered whether there might be someone in the ceiling. It was absolutely impossible for him to explain by what mysterious mechanism a simple pressure of the finger had been able, a little while ago, to hoist a cage and its occupants to the top of a staircase, without any shocks, and now another simple pressure could create, annihilate and recreate light.

He told himself that many other stupefactions undoubtedly awaited him, that six hundred years had gone by between Zahun's voyage and his own—six hundred years in which cloistered Galade, having neither known anything about nor received anything from the external world, had lived the same life of nourishing labor, corporeal, sentimental and religious joys—and that many other amazing things certainly lay in store for him. The people he was going to see must, although they were not made any differently than the Galadians, have very different mores, activities and sentiments...

He went to bed. Before sleep rolled him up in its thick padding, incoherent dreams laid siege to him, from which two images were detached, entangled in horrific enlacements, and dominating him alternately: the immense machine with the fiery entrails that had brought him from Traese to Paris in a few hours, and the valet with the vulgar face and servile spine, who toyed with light and weight.

Finally, he fell asleep.

When he woke up, he strove to recall his impressions and organize them. He decided that he was unable as yet to think or deduce, or even imagine, anything. He went to the window, opened it, and gazed at the city. It was still very early, and yet a crowd was thronging the streets, going back and forth along them in haste. The sole preoccupation of getting to where they were going was legible in their faces.

The king conjectured that they were artisans, employees and scribes going to work. The houses facing him, although much higher than Galadian habitations, were commonplace in appearance: doors, plaster walls on the façades, windows, roofs, no decoration except for some poor moldings and a few painted signs...but between them, and beyond the roofs, he perceived the tips of steeples, towers and brilliant cupolas.

He was about to close the window, feeling a great desire to go and mingle with that crowd, to wander at hazard, with his eyes wide open, and therefore to hasten getting dressed, when and inexplicable noise sent the air above him, like the buzz of a giant dragonfly. He leaned out, looked up, and saw an immense, inassimilable form pass over, a kind of giant fish without gills, fins or a head, which, for a tail, had a great wing rotting under the body at a prodigious speed, and which held suspended, sat the end of slanting cables departing from the two extremities of its belly, a long and frail walkway on which two men were standing.

It was so excessive and fantastic that he was afraid, sensing his chest tighten, and he put his hand over his eyes. The immense form drew away, advancing serenely through the air perhaps fifty meters above the roofs; then, at a certain moment, it swerved in the air and turned right.

Into what world had the king fallen? How could he ever comprehend it? How was it possible that the pedestrians in the street, who had looked up like him, were continuing their bleak and hasty route, not uttering cries of terror on seeing men in the claws of that apocalyptic bird, which was slowly disappearing in the gray sky?

He needed to see a face, to hear a voice. He remembered the signal that summoned the valet. He pressed the button on the wall and waited.

The valet came in. He saw the distressed face of the king. The latter drew the valet to the window and asked him: "What passed over...up there is the air...above the roofs...and disappeared in the sky?"

The bellboy scrutinized the horizon. "Monsieur is doubtless talking about the dirigible? But Monsieur seems to be feeling poorly..."

"Tell me, tell me what it is..."

"But Monsieur...a balloon...which travels at the will of the two men who were in the nacelle."

The king did not understand at all. He opened his eyes wide and asked, again: "It was the two men who were underneath...who were directing it?"

"Undoubtedly, Monsieur. They're the ones who built it. A long time ago now...at least two years.[8] There are bigger ones. Many have been made since. And there are airplanes..."

---

[8] The first of the dirigible airships constructed by the Lebaudy brothers and Henri Julliot, nicknamed *Le Jaune*, was launched in 1903, but by 1905 it would have been replaced by the third model in the series.

The king knew enough. He knew that he could not understand. He could not ask that man—for he could see in daylight his stupid, coarse and unenlightened face—by what succession of ages and events humans had succeeded in directing the thing that hung in the air and moved there freely...

He became calm again. He told himself that he would give himself time to understand, and would no longer be frightened by anything, and would be ready for anything, even to see the valet in front of him suddenly dissolve into the atmosphere...

"Is Monsieur not hungry?" the bellboy asked. "Would Monsieur like a cup of tea?"

"Yes," the king replied.

The bellboy went to a shiny little wooden box attached to the wall, which had two steel handles, to which two items of apparatus were attached, each made of a wooden stem surmounted by a round flat head. He unhooked one of the stems, but the box to his lips and said; "Hello?" He waited for a moment, and then added: "A cup of tea to room fifty."

"Have you put me to sleep next to the kitchens?" the king asked, frowning.

"Monsieur?"

"Is this room next to the kitchens?" the king repeated.

"But Monsieur," said the confused bellboy, "the kitchens are in the basement, two feet underground, at least fifteen meters in distance and depths from the room where Monsieur has slept."

"Why, in that case, did you approach the wall to make yourself heard there, as if they were on the other side?"

"But Monsieur, I communicated with the kitchens by means of the apparatus." Slightly fearful, the bellboy added: "Has Monsieur never seen a telephone?"

"I've told you that I've come from far away," said the king, striving to remain impassive

At that moment, someone knocked on the door. The valet opened it. A chambermaid brought in the king's breakfast.

"Does Monsieur need anything else?" asked the valet.

"No."

The valet and the maid withdrew.

The king advanced toward the little box, but he did not dare to touch it, because he did not know how one made use of it, and what might be inside, behind and around it...

He was full of trouble, and pleasure.

He ate, got dressed, and went down into the lobby of the hotel.

There was a great movement of people, travelers and valets, in a vast gallery with brightly-colored walls at which the stairways and corridors ended. People were going out into the street or coming into the hotel, going up and down the stairs, busy and in haste; other, calmer, were moving back and forth, chatting; others still were sitting in armchairs, reading or smoking. He recognized among the travelers a group of three people he had seen in the carriage that he had boarded in Traese and had made the journey with him. He sat down some distance away.

At one moment, a young servant clad in a tight red waistcoat with golden buttons, with black leather gaiters, coifed with a round cap as red as the waistcoat, with a gilded chinstrap, received a piece of blue paper from a dignified man sitting behind a counter and brought it to the group near to whom the king had sat down. There were two men and a woman. One of the men took the piece of paper and said: "Here's news from Traese!" The king heard.

The man opened the piece of paper, unfolded it and said again, with a deep happy sigh. "God be praised! Our daughter gave birth this morning to a healthy boy!"

"Praise God!" said the other two.

The king, amazed, wondered whether he had misunderstood, but the exact phrase was still running in his ears.

Go on! These travelers had, like him, and in his sight, spent two days coming from Traese without stopping, or very nearly, behind the fulgurant machine, and now they were informed this morning of something that had happened in Traese that same morning? By what extraordinary route had the messenger...or the message...come? What must its speed have been if it covered in a few hours what had taken the king, bewildered by the inconceivable velocity, two days?

He was on the point of going to the travelers to question them, but he thought, recalling the bellboy's alarm the previous evening, of the emotion he might cause by asking a question about a matter entirely natural to those people, only insoluble for a man arriving in the world after an interval of six centuries.

He got up and went out into the street. A beautiful ray of sunlight enveloped him entirely as soon as he crossed the threshold. He paused momentarily in the lovely gilded caress, and then set forth, at random, straight ahead.

At first he was only struck by the inextricable swarm of people and things on the roads. Vehicles of every form, men of the people carrying burdens, shouting at each other in loud voices; other enormous vehicles filled with passengers, moving without horses, powered by an invisible mechanism, passing by with a noise that made the ground shake, making the ground shiver under their wheels, filling the ears with a diabolical racket, absorbing all other sounds; ambulant vendors pushing barrows in front of them full of vegetables and fruits, shouting, proclaiming the excellence of their merchandise, very similar to Galadian market gardeners.

He succeeded, not without a certain jostling here and there, in reaching a wider road, just as inextricably pullulating. He wondered vaguely what could be occupying so many people in such a hurry, but, to tell the truth, he was not wondering anything very precisely, gazing with all his attention.

He perceived, a few paces away, a small light wrought iron balustrade surrounding three quarters of an opening in the ground, into which a stairway plunged. A crowd was plunging into the opening and going down the stairs, which he followed curiously and which led him into a strange and picturesque corridor illuminated by a hundred little lamps fairly similar to the one in his room, which the white porcelain titles of the vaults reflected innumerably. At the two extremities of the corridor in which where the crowd accumulated two mouths opened, full of darkness, as if swallowing four slender lines of steel that ran along the ground beneath the two sidewalks.

He was unable to see any more because, in a shower of pink-tinted sparks and with a frightful din, a long file of carriages, similar but less ornamented that those that had brought him from Traese to Paris, passed in front of him, causing him to leap backwards.

In front of these, however, there was no monstrous directive machine, merely a young man dressed in blue sitting placidly in front of a thick iron box, his fingers placed on two or three short copper levers, who appeared to be the conductor and animator of the noisy cortege.

The crowd precipitated forward, jostling one another, into the carriages, and as the king had noticed that the majority were dressed in such a way that one could not imagine that they were departing for a long voyage, he allowed himself to be pushed and guided by the jostling and his present destiny into one of the carriages, and, fearlessly this time, felt himself dragged toward the somber mouth, which swallowed him up with all the travelers and all the carriages.

He was in a long and spacious corridor illuminated here and there by little lamps. Wires ran and snaked along the walls. After a short interval the cortege stopped. Some people got out, others came aboard. The king waited. Only a few minutes had gone by, and several short stops had take place, when, at a new stop, a man dressed in a uniform shouted in an imperious voice: "All change!"

Everyone got out, the king doing what everyone else did. He went up a staircase and found himself in daylight. He was at the gates of a wood: a very neatly divided wood, trimmed and cut through by wide avenues, furrowed with placid strollers, children playing and shiny carriages. A wood or a park? It was hard to imagine that deer and wolves could be residing in those well-ordered thickets, but the absence of flowers and the extent was hardly that of a park.

The king went along one of the beautiful avenues, breathing delightedly, quite satisfied by no longer being underground. Even though he had been very astonished and amused to go at his ease, comfortably seated and in bright light through a part of the world reserved in Galade for moles and roots.

He had turned into a quiet path where he intended to put a little method into his reflections when he came upon another lateral path where men and women were running, their faces ardent, toward a goal that he could not see, toward which he ran with the crowd as gaily as anything in the world, wondering what extraordinary event awaited him.

The whole movement stopped at the edge of an immense lawn, in the middle of which a black group surrounded a kind of large white palpitation spread on the ground, which could only be glimpsed through the gestures of the group.

He was about to advance when a prodigious spectacle nailed him to the spot.

The black group had abruptly divided and dispersed, drawing away from the while palpitation, and that, which was a vast and svelte canvas bird, in the middle of which two men were sitting, had risen from the ground, and without beating its wings, simply, nobly, without jerks, as if breathed in by the sunlight, climbed into the air toward the blue sky, went forward, turned right, the left, then around, and then descended again toward the ground, and climbed back toward the sky with the most perfect and surest ease, in the midst of the applause of the group and the enthusiastic clamors of the crowd.

It was not the enormous and monstrous birds that the king had seen that morning passing over the roofs; it was a frail and charming construction, which a gust of wind, one might have thought, would have knocked over, torn apart and destroyed, but which, gracefully, went at the caprice of its conductors, purring softly in the bright light.

After a time, it came to settle slowly on to the lawn, and one of the travelers descended, so that another could replace him. It rose up again then, recommenced its supple flights, came directly over the crowd, whose heads were tilted back and eyes bulging with pleasure, and as a thousand voices acclaimed the wingers voyagers, one of them saluted the crowd with a casual hand gesture, as calm and smiling, suspended and moving freely in the void, as if he had been standing on his feet on the customary ground.[9]

When the king was sated with that vision, and as the bird has descended near a hangar, the doors of which were opened for it, he resumed his stroll, and soon found himself mingling with the crowd again, in the place where he had returned to the sunlight emerging from his subterranean voyage.

He was hungry. He ate lunch. Then, once again, setting forth at hazard and spotting one of the enormous vehicles he had seen that morning going past with hellish din, half full of passengers, he went into it and allowed it to carry him away.

Sitting facing him in the large vehicle was a young man with clear and regular features, whose gaze seduced him. That gaze, as if indifferent to the surrounding forms, seemed to be contemplating, fixed upon and caressing a delightful spectacle. And as the king, having turned round, had seen that the vehicle was moving too quickly for the young man to be looking at anything through the windows with such fixity, he was convinced that it was a happy thought from which the latter was extracting al the illumination of his gaze. The serenity of the visage affirmed the nobility of the reverie.

The king envied the young man. How many subjects of meditation might be offered to a thinking being in a world in which he, having only been in it for a few hours, had seen so many astonishing things: the obedient light, distance annihilated, the winged men, the earth penetrated...! Howe many other domains, inaccessible or even unknown in Galade, were

---

[9] The craft described is presumably one of Ferdinand Ferber's powered gliders; it was in May 1905 that Ferber first achieved free flight in Europe in a powered aircraft.

doubtless wide open realms to men here, freely accessible, with their edifices, their secrets and their florescences...?

The vehicle had stopped, and the young man with the beautiful gaze had stood up and was preparing to get off. The king imitated him and followed him. They were a short distance from a tall monument of stone, before which were assembled numerous young men, chatting to one another tranquilly; others were climbing the steps of the monument and going in. His traveling companion joined one of the groups.

The clock of a nearby church having gravely sounded several strokes, the crowd headed toward the monument, and the king mingled with them

After having traversed a vast antechamber of stone and marble, and a rather dark corridor, in which several small doors opened, the king suddenly found himself in an immense hall, filled with terraces covered with spectators, facing a platform on which there was nothing but a table, a chair and a large screen of white canvas.

The king compared that hall with his stage in the festival hall of the palace of Gyzir, and the stage where the svelte ballerinas danced. What ballet, or what comedy, was going to be performed before these spectators?

A man appeared on the platform. Complete silence fell in the audience, which had been abuzz a moment before.

"Messieurs," said the man, standing up, rather small on the large empty stage, to the silent audience. "Before speaking to you about the movement of atoms, I can offer you the cinematographic vision of an ordinary drop of water. No one is now unaware of the quantity of living and singularly constituted beings that a drop of water can contain; the spectacle of that phenomenon, magnified and animated, will be a pleasant preamble to what I want to demonstrate to you."[10]

---

[10] Given the combination of topics, the lecturer might be Jean-Baptiste Perrin (1870-1942), who combined studied of Brownian motion in liquids with a strong interest in atomic theory; in 1905 he was a lecturer in physical chemistry at the Sorbonne.

He finished. The hall was suddenly plunged into darkness. No sound was audible, except for a kind of little sizzling, which soon became a luminous beam, departing from an apparatus placed on the upper steps, opposite the stage, and ending, enlarged, on the canvas screen. On that screen a circle was designed, in which a host of terrifying forms were swarming.

"This is the drop of water," the little man repeated, whose hand alone was visible in the jet of light. "Soon," he added, "I hope to be able to isolate on that screen one of the infinitesimal members of that populace, and show you, as visible as at present, its modes of irritability and nutrition."

The bewildered king looked at the moving image. Stupefied by the forms that were agitating there, he was even more so by the thought that, if he had understood correctly, he was no looking at a pond, a puddle or a sea but a drop of water. A drop of water? Water that he was accustomed to drink? What! Was he swallowing at the same time those monsters with complicated tentacles, arms without bodies, prolonged by a kind of feather, the extremity of which strand formed a living mouth, aspiring and sucking...? The most insane imagination could not have created anything approaching it...

Everything vanished. The light surged forth again. The screen was as blank and clear as it had been before. No trace of the movement of the beasts in their liquid abode. What was all this phantasmagoria? Had the streak of light transported it, deposited it on the canvas and then returned, once again to enclose that fantastic world in its fluid rays within the little sizzling apparatus?

But darkness fell again within the hall, and a sphere appeared on the screen, the surface of which was a strange mass of blisters and ravines, which one might have thought a cluster of pustule.

"A part of the Moon," said the orator, "the Mare Tenebrosum, surrounded by mountains and valleys, and"— another image followed that one on the screen—"the planet Mars, with what are believed to be its canals and its pains."

The images dissipated. Light filled the hall again and the crowd. The orator, imperturbable, his back turned to the inert screen, continued:

"The drop of water, the heavenly body, the star…what a universe! The gilded dot shining in the sky, a world a hundred thousand times larger than the entire earth...the imperceptible drop of water, an empire in which an innumerable population lives!

"The drop of water and the star, Messieurs! What infinities! But the time is already far behind us when humans learned, for the first time, about their immensities!

"At present, it is before the atom, the ultimate constituent of all forms, that humans are directing their vanquishing apparatus. We are penetrating the ultimate secret of matter, grasping it in its ultimate mode.

"The pavement on which our feet tread, the air that our throats breathe in, plants, animals and humans, everything has delivered its ultimate basis, behind which nothing any longer lies but the immaterial unknown.

"The infinitely small is a positive center around which negative corpuscles gravitate. Every molecule of a substance palpitates and lives in the fashion of the stars, moves like the Earth in space, like the entire solar system around the sun, in the infinite..."

Here the orator employed terms absolutely incomprehensible to the poor king: electric bulb, cathode, electrode, ion, electron...

So many extravagant thoughts were colliding in his head that he was no longer listening, no longer able to hear, would have liked to get out of the hall in order to breathe in a good mouthful of air and walk, with long strides.

The orator finally stopped speaking; the audience stood up; the hall emptied. The king found himself outside again.

Some of the young people dispersed, others, remaining together in two or threes, turned the corner of the street in which the monument was situated, and followed a broad road that slanted slightly upwards.

The king walked behind them. The road was quite different from the pullulating streets through which he had passed that morning on emerging from the hotel. The majority of faces he passed were not men of the people weighed down by burdens, but young men with keen and enthusiastic gazes, and joyful women. At the end of the wide street was a garden whose gates were open. He went in and was charmed by the grace of the flowers, the majesty of the pathways, and the healthy joy that rose into the air, of running children, attentive mothers, and numerous seated or slowly strolling groups of young men and women with faces animated by the pleasure of conversation.

The king sat down on a bench, replete with the suave harmony of the garden, the beautiful disposition of its flights of steps, its stone balustrade, its low basin surrounded by vivid flowers, and its great trees, and he remained immobile, gently breathing the perfumed dusk.

"Now," he said to himself, "let's put some order into our judgment. Here, then, men fly, penetrate the stars, go from one point of the earth to another without moving their limbs, cross mountains, rivers and torrents, traverse forests, cities, the countryside—those, at least, that separate Traese from Paris—in scarcely more time than it takes to blink…like the messenger who brought news to my traveling companions this morning. Certainly, strange privileges have been acquired by the people of this world. Nevertheless, I see them before me, in this very place, walking, sitting down and gesticulating just as Galadians do. And all the others, it seems to me—thus far, for what magic des the next minute have in store or me?—are similar to Galadians, two legs beneath the torso, a head above it, and a nose in the middle of the face…

"Yes indeed…but inside that torso…yes…inside, with what palpitations must their hearts beat? Behind their forehead, what light must their mind recreate? And of what emotions, what passions, what desires, what joys are those palpitations and that light made? In Gyzir, eating well, being rich, well-dressed, decorated…in Gyzir, health, glory, Paradise, the love of women, were the only immutable goals, the source and summit of dreams, desires and delights...

"Certainly, also for those rare individuals who attained the elevation of a Mnektes, the possession of Wisdom...

"But what am I saying? In Gyzir, were there so many goals? If I can judge by myself, and my cruel ordeal, and the vow that followed it, nothing soon existed for me any longer that was worth being loved, as soon as the love of women was forbidden to me! And it was as if all other goals and other joys immediately dried up for me...and desubstantiated one by one into distractions!"

Feeling as if his soul were spreading out within him, he went on: "Oh, blessed be that ordeal! And blessed be my vow, which, truly inspired by heaven, led me via ennui and the privation of joy to discover the secret route to the world!

"Nevertheless, if by privation of amour, all other joys and distractions came to dry up within me, how thin, it must be said, were Galadian joys and distractions!

"Ah, for those of this world, I would swear...

"My God, how pitiful would the people of this world judge such a case to be!

"Even though very new among them, I would swear, that those who have, I sense, more distractions than a great bear of our forests has hairs on its entire body, those not only have an extend of the earth to come and go, all garnished with forests flowers, monuments, cities, domestic machines—compared with which my homeland is like a little heap of sand—but have all the roads of that earth open before them, and also roads above the earth and similarly below it, doubtless having what is necessary for prodigious distraction from amour, either do not accord it the importance that I accorded it, or, being humans and similar to the humans of Galade, they make it the sum of all joys, what an astonishing amour, containing them all and surpassing them all, their amour must be!

"Oh, assuredly blessed was my vow, and very useful at this moment. How could I approach a woman here? What a figure I would cut, and how could I avoid her laughing in my

face? What pale words and what poor little fêtes could I offer—me, a narrow Galadian—to her, who knows what there is
in the stars, can doubtless be given the moon, other than in
songs, and who must enjoy all the natural prodigies as much
as my beautiful lady-friends in Gyzir enjoy the adornments
and precious stones that they take out of their golden caskets,
and caused to jump between their fingers from one hand to
another...

"Oh, how can I think of loving? First...first...to learn...

"That's it, Sire of Galade, my good friend! Of course!
The wherewithal to love, and without betraying the vow....
Open your eyes, Sire de Galade, Emmanuel, and with all the
force of your young heart... Work, Sire, work to know what
humans have become...men, women and amour...in the six
hundred years that you have been sleeping the great sleep of
Galade!"

At that moment, music rose up in the beautiful garden,
some distance away, and the king, extracted from his reflections, immediately looked in the direction from which the
sounds were coming—but at first he only saw a compact
crowd circling slowly around a little pavilion. Soon, through
the rare and narrow gaps in that crowd, he perceived musicians dressed in military costumes sitting in the pavilion and
playing instruments of gleaming brass.

A young man went past the bench were the king was sitting, holding a brightly-dressed young woman by the arm. The
couple were chatting gaily, At the first sounds, the young man
said to his companion: "Beethoven." They sat down nearby on
iron chairs.

The king looked at the musicians again, while an astonishing emotion took hold of him, which came from musical
chords rising up from the group of instruments, with such an
amplitude and power that they were, so to speak, fixed in his
soul, and obliged him to listen, as an idle stroller along the
shore of the ocean can be suddenly nailed to the spot by the
sight of an immense wave springing from the midst of the
calm waves, which submerges the shore in an instant, and eve-

rything, in front of that stupefied, anguished passer-by, simultaneously struck with admiration.

Far from spreading out and slowly being absorbed, like a wave, however, the chords were further amplified, and continued rising, extending above the crowd surrounding the pavilion, above the crowd scattered about the garden, above the statues and the trees, beyond the clouds, reaching the sky, clothing it, developing something akin to another sky, tumultuous and multicolored; they espoused the air, the light, becoming confused with them, substituted for them, making gazes, hands and nostrils of dazzled ears.

Gripped by an ineffable vertigo, the king allowed himself to be lifted from the earth, balanced by the subtle waves, feeling his heart turbulent with the rhythm of the impetuous movement, his blood rushing like lava through his veins, confusedly recovering the sensation of being snatched away that he had experienced during the departure from Traese, but with as much superb and veritable voluptuous emotion as he had then felt dolor and fear.

The king did not know of any music other than the popular songs of the villages of Galade, which shepherds, washerwomen and drunkards sang, the plainsong of the churches, transmitted by the priests, and a few joyful operas to which the ballerinas of the court had danced before his vow, which lords invented between an amorous night and a hunting party. Instruments were not very numerous in Galade: sistrums, cistoles, mandoras, cymbals, rebecs, flutes, trumpets and horns. The musical emotions of the king had scarcely ever been anything but melancholy in church, playful in ballets. What was this music, which, abruptly and imperiously penetrated his soul and his heart, kneading them, as if juggling with them, invading the sky, usurping the light: that formidable tide by which all realities were submerged, and whose flux created a hundred others?

But it became slow and murmurous, that music, then brisk and cheerful, soon descending once again toward the earth. It hung on to the flowers, rippled the water in the basin, slid between the trees and rose up again into the sky: gallop, charge, cascade, zephyr, cries of infants playing in the flower-beds, clamors of the crowd, sobs, prayers....something strange occurred. All the intimacy of the king was exhaled, adapted itself to, modeled itself on, the music; all the confusion, all the chaos of his mind since the departure from Traese, the marvels of an unsuspected world, and his still-unresolved problems, and the profundities of him, of his former being and his present being, of the child, the young man, his games and amours, his joys and his chagrins…all of it issued from him in a living population, of which the music was the palpitating blood and sap…

Yes, it was really thus that he had run and played in the flowery paths of the royal park, that he had ridden through the woods of Galade, and those cries of passion and joy, he had uttered them…but how much fainter, scarcely whimper-ing…how many cries and infantile games there had been in six hundred years! That music evoked, but it immensified… Of what joy, of what sobs, was it the expression? Oh, if it was with that force and that magnificence, that the beings of this world loved, suffered, dreamed, their life must truly be what he had sensed!

Yes, it really was that. The music affirmed it. It resolved problems. If these beings dreamed and suffered, and if they still loved, the music affirmed, and measured, there were gi-ants and kings in this world…

Silence fell. He rediscovered the enchanted garden in the blond dusk. He got up from the bench, and moved his numb body. And as the music resumed, he was afraid… He knew enough… He felt happy, but weary, as if exhausted.

Without hearing any more, he went out of the garden.

Incident

For me, a very truthful storyteller, it is not easy to describe in detail the actions and emotions of the king between that first day and a singular event that happened to him after he had visited Paris for a long time, and the principal capitals of Europe. About that singular event I shall be able to say everything I know, as you will see, in any case, in the following chapter—but before then, I would have liked to show you the king in the streets of Paris, on the great boulevards, at the theater, at concerts, and then on the shore of the Mediterranean, in Venice, in Florence, in Rome, and then in Berlin, at Bayreuth, and also in London...

Except that I was not with him. I only know what he has told me orally. It was in accordance with his account that I have been able to reconstruct the intoxication of his Beethovian contact, and the idea he formed of our complex humanity on emerging from that contact.

When I was his friend, he was a laborer—to be more precise, a laborer employed in working on the excavations for the Métropolitain railway in the Place Saint-Michel[11]—so I can only say, about his adventures in Paris, his travels in Italy, Germany and England, what he told me in retracing the course of his memories. In detail, that would require a volume double or triple the size of this one. Assuredly, in substance, I prefer humbly to let everyone imagine what the impressions of a young traveler twenty years old before Notre-Dame de Paris and the panorama that extends to the left and the right of the

---

[11] The excavations in the Place Saint-Michel for the construction of the Metro tunnel that had to be extended under the Seine were carried out between 1905 and 1907; they attracted tremendous interest, by virtue of being in the very heart of Paris, and because of the impressive system of caissons used to construct the tunnel under the river. The iconic motif crops up again in *Le Bacchus mutilé*, when the protagonist of that novel is twenty years old in 1907.

Pont Royal, in the morning, in the vaporous dawn, and the evening, when the reddening sun sprinkles, like a magical powder-puff, a gilded dust over the Tuileries, the Cours-la-Reine and the hills of Passy; before Santa Maria della Salute in Venice; before Donatello's Saint George that stands in the very street in a niche in the Orsanmichele church in Florence; before…before…never mind! I'm not Baedeker and my recitation of his enthusiasms would be tedious for you, who are reading me and who know as well as I do what can be said about that, by virtue of having read all the poets and all the estheticians, or by virtue of having contemplated it yourself.

Undoubtedly, I would amuse you if I reported that the king, having gone into a music hall on the grand boulevards of Paris, was even more impressed by the play of the lights and machinery than by the songs, the dances and the acrobatics. The beauty of the dances touched him by virtue of the generous harmony to which the slimness and beauty of each dancer contributed. Having heard one of his neighbors manifest to a companion the pleasure that he would have in holding one of those dancers in his arms, he did not think for a moment that it could be for one of the embraces to which he was accustomed himself with the ballerinas if Gyzir, but certainly for a reason of an order superior to anything he could imagine.

Shall I tell you how the king left Paris for the first time? One morning, when the sky was gray and the air cold, while he was going along the boulevard, his attention was attracted by a painted image stuck to a wooden panel, which represented a brightly sunlit country on the edge of an azure sea. He looked at the dull sky, and then the establishment, which, on the window of its door announced in large colored letters: *Travel Agency*. He opened the promising door, went in, and said that he wanted to go to that beautiful sunlight.

A man clad in a somber uniform brightened by gilded buttons, coiffed in a cap with the name of the company inscribed in gold thread, got him to give some money to a man seated in a cage, and asked him to follow him. He had the king climb into a little automobile stationed outside the door. The vehicle conveyed the king and his companion to a nearby railway station in the blink of an eye. The uniformed man took the king to a train whose machine was puffing out dense spirals of black smoke, handed him a small piece of paper, bowed respectfully and went away as the train departed.

A few hours later the king was on the shore of the blue sea, beneath the bright sun, in the middle of flowery summer.

It was from there, after having stayed there for a week or two, that the king went to visit Italy...but as I say, a great many pages would be necessary to describe his journeys in detail. It is decidedly necessary to pass over them, and to permit myself to show you the moment when, full of contemplation, having acquired a little more certainty every day of the size of the world and the beauty of living, he found himself in Paris without a sou in his pocket, having spent in the course of his travels all the gold that he had brought from Galade.

On the advice of the old lady who managed the hotel where he had stayed in the first days after his arrival, he had confided all his gold to a bank, which had given him in exchange for the gold a little booklet made up of pages with stubs, on which he only had to write, in accordance with his caprice, the sum of which he had need, in order to receive it immediately from any bank in the country he was traversing.

One Sunday afternoon he perceived while making a purchase in the street that he had come out without any money. It was necessary for him to return to his current hotel and ask for a few coins in exchange for one of the pages in his booklet, because the banks were closed on Sundays. Mechanically, he took the booklet out of his pocket and opened it, His attention was vaguely alerted, although he was thinking about something else, by the fact that there was only one page left in the booklet, and that on the stub of the penultimate page, above a very small number, was written "funds remaining."

What? he said to himself, without losing his customary good humor. *Don't I have any more money?*

He reflected, standing still, suddenly gripped by the circumstance, full of unforeseen consequences. He went through the stubs in the booklet, back to the beginning, and saw that he really had exhausted, except for the minimal sum marked as "funds remaining," the entire sum indicated on the first leaf.

Uh oh! he thought, a trifle anguished. *Am I going to find myself a prisoner in Paris, without even having the means to go back to Galade if I want to?*

Return to Galade...I've scarcely thought about it. Have I not come back to Paris to learn, in this great city, the thousand profound things that I still need to know before telling my dear people, judiciously, about all the splendors of a world ignored for too long?

...

Of course!

He had remembered an episode in Galadian history. Toward 1500, his ancestor Georgis the Headstrong, after a violent war in which all Galade had been at odds, had been obliged to flee Gyzir and take refuge for some time, hiding his sovereign dignity, among the miners of Boudroude, sharing their life and their mores, and giving not the slightest indication, even during his worst labors, that he was King Georgis.

Of course! He was strong, young, hardy and self-confident. He too would work with his hands—his vigorous hands—and his strong shoulders...

He went back to his hotel, changed the last page of the booklet, summoned the bellboy who normally served him to his room, and asked him: "Tell me, what can a man without money do, in Paris?"

"With all due respect, Monsieur," the bellboy replied. "die of starvation."

Another Parenthesis

One day, in Rome, the king was leaving the little church of San Pietro in Vincoli, where he had just spent a long time before Michelangelo's Moses, when a drunkard collided rudely with him. The latter had come away from the wall that he normally used as a point of support for his vacillating march, and was desperately trying to get back to it—which is to say that he was extending his arms in one direction, and then the other, and zigzagging in the direction of his extended arms. The king, happening to be between the arms and the wall, had received the man's impetus. He pushed him away, his mind elsewhere; the drunkard fell, and the king, taking pity on him, helped him to get up again—but the drunkard's rubicund face, stupid gaze and foaming lips left him for a few moments with an image that superimposed itself over the warm memory of Michelangelo's statue.

"Beside that, this!" he murmured.

As one can imagine, the king had encountered drunkards many a time: men of the people with gross gestures, individuals clad in rags, workers with black hands. How could he not be astonished that in a world of which he had the certainty that it was a liberated, magnificent world, a world of kings and giants, brutes, wretches and slaves still existed...?

Fundamentally, the king's mind was that of a Medieval king. A Christian, he readily admitted that all men were brothers, that the unshakable justice of God and the infinite mercy of his Son made them equal in Paradise—but not on earth. As soon as he arrived in Paris, he had felt a assurance forming within him that life on earth, as it was presented to him there, was not a vale of tears, as Monseigneur Gohain had preached to him in little Galade, and that the beings of this earth were great and inflated by superior amours; he had not taken into consideration the poor, who were as poor here as they were in Galade and everywhere else.

The stoker of the locomotive that had drawn him toward the Mediterranean, such as he saw him walking idly alongside the train during a halt, was evidently not a man who took his place in the category of those he considered to be the men of this astonishing world. Certainly, that stoker traversed the earth without moving his legs; he profited naturally, from the benefits of an enlarged life, but he had remained—black, sweaty, bent down before the furnace on the narrow iron platform—among the number of all those men of all times and places whose function is to serve other men.

Forgive me. I do not know how to put it any other way.

The king, entirely gripped by unassimilable emotions, by the contemplation of beautiful works of art, picturesque or grandiose panoramas, by the edification of his esthetic sensibilities, and a consciousness that had leapt over six centuries, had scarcely had time, thus far, to study the regimes of the countries through which he passed, or their democratic systems. Men were greater in this world than Galade, that was certain; but the others—the slaves, the workers, the peasants, the poor—were still the slaves, the workers, the peasants, the poor...the others...

The Laborers

"There must be métiers," said the king, mildly, "in which a man can be used who has a strong back and robust muscles?"

"Métiers of beasts of burden, undoubtedly, Monsieur," aid the bellboy. "There are market porters, coal-heavers on the quays, ditch-diggers...all those who have no need to reflect much on their work, to whom one puts a sack or basket on their back, a pick or a spade in their hand, and to whom one says: *This is what you have to do*..."

Excellent, thought the king. *So, while the hands and the arms exert themselves, the mind is free to devote itself to memories and reflections, not to mention profound meditations*. "And how, my friend," he asked, aloud, "can one become a digger?"

"By going to get oneself hired by an entrepreneur, or simply in a workplace. There's no shortage of them at present. One strolls through Paris; one sees a construction site; one goes to it and asks a man: 'Comrade, is there work here?'" The bellboy added: "At least. I think that's how it's done; for myself, I've never had the slightest desire to be a digger. Nor has Monsieur...?"

The king turned his back on the bellboy and arranged a few books on the table.

"Then again, if Monsieur presented himself dressed as he is now, people would think he was joking. I suppose Monsieur has the intention of studying the workers...Monsieur ought to put on a corduroy costume with a red belt, and above all, never call anyone 'Monsieur' but always 'Comrade' or 'Citizen.'"

"Thank you, my friend," said the king. "You can go now."

With the few dozen francs he had left the king paid the hotel bill, bought a corduroy jacket and trousers, strong boots, a red belt and a flannel shirt, and went in search of a workplace.

"Bonjour, Comrade," he said to a man who was pushing a wheelbarrow full of sand. "Where is it necessary to address oneself in order to be hired?"

The other continued on his way as if he had not heard, went to empty his wheelbarrow, and came back slowly and placidly toward the king. He looked at him, spat on the ground, wiped his mouth with the back of his hand and looked at him again before replying.

"You want to be hired?" he said, finally. "Are you in the union?"

"Pardon?" said the king.

"I asked if you're in the union."

"What's that?"

"Where have you come from?"

"But....," said the king, a trifle embarrassed.

"If you aren't in the union there's nothing for you here; it's not worth the trouble of trying." He spat on his hands, picked up his wheelbarrow and drew away from the king.

Very perplexed, the king waited for a moment to see whether the man was coming back. Another man emerged from the work site carrying a sack of chalk, which he went to place beside the sand that the first man had poured out of the wheelbarrow. As he went past the king, the latter stopped him.

"Comrade," he said, "listen: I had money; I don't have any more. I want to earn my living and work with you. What is it necessary to do?"

"Right!" said the worker. "You've had bad luck...you can't look for another trade? It's hard here...you have white hands...you'll soon be worn out."

"Look," said the king. He picked up the sack of chalk that the man had been carrying under his arm with some difficulty. He gripped it by the edges and carried it for a few moments with his arms at full length, without a quiver."

"Well, if you like," said the man. "It's a funny idea, but when one has to eat...I'll try to arrange it. You're not in the union? No, since you had money, you said. Right...we'll see. Wait here."

He came back with a man similar to himself in his costume, but who had something curt and authoritarian in his manner.

"Come with me," said the newcomer to the king. They went into the work-site. "Pick up a shovel. Empty this hole for me."

The king leapt into the hole, his feet sinking a little into the soft earth. He began to pick up earth and throw it out of the hole. When he had removed all the earth, he emerged from the hole. The foreman saw him and said: "Follow the comrades."

A few men went to take hold of a heavy beam, lift it up and move it. The king joined them and helped them.

Break time arrived. The men sat down on piles of stones, wheelbarrows or beams. They took bread, meat and a bottle of wine out of a sack. They placed the bread on their thumb, the meat on the bread, and carved large slices with their knives.

"I still have a little money," said the king. "Would you like wine?"

They stared at him. Mastications stopped. The man to whom he owed having been hired, his cheek inflated by a mouthful that he had crammed in, said: "Do you need to ask? There's a bistro behind the fence."

The king got up, left the site, went to buy the wine and brought it back to the laborers.

"So, you've been a monsieur?" said one.

"Me, I told him not to persist, seeing as he's not in the union," said another, "but he hadn't explained…need to eat…but need to be in the union…"

"To your health, Comrades!" said the king, raising his glass, his voice cheerful and his eyes bright.

"To yours," replied weary, hoarse, lax voices, which contrasted with his.

They drank.

Soon, they resumed work.

In the middle of the day, during a brief rest, one of the laborers went to the king.

"My name's Lobre, Joséphin," he said. "What's yours?"

"Emmanuel," said the king.

"Just Emmanuel?"

"Just," said the king.

"Where are you from?"

"Paris," said the king.

"Me, Ollinges in Savoy. Where do you live?"

"Nowhere, at least until this evening."

"If you buy me a drink when we go, I'll find you a bed, not dear, and good."

"Agreed."

Lobre, Joséphin, drew away. He was a young fellow, heavily built, with a broad and short torso on firm stout legs. He had big hands, a squashed nose, yellow teeth, a little moustache, and when he took off his hat one could see his square, massive, shiny forehead, reminiscent of a closed fist.

The king was delighted and thought that everything was going smoothly. The work did not frighten him. While plying the heavy shovel, he edified his life-plan. He would stay with these men who had given him a good welcome. He would accept everything that happened to him, with regard to subsistence, lodging and contact with the humble. The form of the bed did not matter to him, as long as he could sleep in it, nor the room, provided that he could reflect a little and rediscover himself before going to sleep, nor the food, provided that it maintained his muscles.

Nothing mattered to him much, since he felt full of life, free to feel, to gaze and to think, and he knew that a time would come when everything would sort itself out, either because he had enough money to return to Galade or because some unexpected opportunity would crop up. Hope was within him, like the regular flow of his blood, like the play of his strong, agile limbs, and just as certain. He would be capable, just like the others, of the work that was demanded of him; and in any case, whatever he did, doing it with good humor would multiply his strength tenfold.

114

Thus, as soon as he had adapted to the material conditions of his new existence, he would organize himself to safeguard, nourish and satisfy his spiritual necessities, spending a part of his wages in on quotidian necessities, while saving the rest for his return to Galade, and employing a little of it for whatever might serve to further his education: a book, a fête, a concert on days of rest...

Night came, the site emptied

"Do you have a bed?" his first protector asked the king.

"Yes," said the king. "Comrade Lobre is going to show me where I can get one."

"Until tomorrow, then," said the other.

The king left with Lobre, Joséphin, who took him through narrow and increasingly poorer streets, soon sordid, to a frightful house.

The Rooming-House

Its façade was bleeding its plaster from a hundred crevices. A lantern in the center announced in white letters on blue glass that lodgings for the night were available from fifty centimes. On the ground floor, a wine-merchant's shop was illuminated by a tremulous gas-lamp, where a quantity of men and women dressed in rags was heaped up, eating, drinking and, most of all, sleeping, their heads buried in their folded arms.

Lobre opened the door of the shop, greeted the proprietor standing behind a narrow wooden counter, and crossed the room. A complex stink grabbed the king by the throat. He resisted it and followed Lobre. The latter sat down at a half-empty table and said: "A drink before bed."

"I'm very tired now," said the king. "The first day, you understand. Have me shown to me room..."

"Right!" said Lobre. "A drink will help you sleep." He rapped the table. A bottle was brought, and two glasses. They drank.

Finally, Lobre got up and preceded the king. Behind the shop there was a little door, which opened on to a long corridor at the end of which was a staircase, impenetrably obscure. At the bottom of the staircase, in the wall, there was an alcove, a glass cage, and a man asleep in the cage.

"Hey! A room for the comrade!" said Lobre to the man.

The latter, lighting the stairway, took them to all the way up to the top floor. In the angle of a corridor, on a landing, he opened a door and said: "In here," to the king.

"I sleep there," said Lobre, indicating another door. "You're lucky that there's a room free directly facing mine. Bonsoir."

But the king, who had taken a step into the room, recoiled, nauseated and suffocated.

"It's a trifle lacking in air," he said, striving to smile. "The window can't be opened often..."

"There's no point," replied the clerk. "It opens into a corridor."

"There isn't another room...?" said the king, but he saw Lobre so astonished, and the indignant reaction of the clerk, looking him up and down as if the king had just overturned all normal notions of life and the world, that he dared not go on.

"What!" said Lobre. "Monsieur would perhaps like the Élysée for ten sous. And he added: "It's the odors that offend you. It's no worse than barracks in summer. Haven't you ever been a soldier?"

"Bonsoir, Lobre," said the king. He held out his hand, took the candlestick from the clerk, went resolutely into the room, closed the door and considered his lodging.

An iron bed and a rickety table, on which was set a half-full jug of water, a basin the size of a soup-bowl and a kind of dish-cloth, formed the entire furniture. The flower-patterned wallpaper was sweating, blistering and peeling off in long shreds. The window was closed. The king opened it and saw, facing him, by the light of his candle, several doors like his own, and heard, coming through some of those doors, copious snores mingling without harmony.

He closed the window again and, in spite of all his determined endurance, in spite of all he had promised to take to account of forms and places, and merely to parade an amused glance and curious around them, without allowing them to affect or afflict his mind, he could not help shivering a little. He let himself fall on to the bed, vacillating under the envelopment of heavy odors.

There was no way out for him but temporary acceptance of this precarious life. He was good for nothing, unable to do anything, except contemplate and love. However, he had confidence...he had confidence...

He began to undress, when a terrible snore made him start. It was Lobre, who had fallen asleep. That snoring was extremely disagreeable: imposing, imperious, inevitable, shaking there walls. It seemed, on escaping the sleeper's mouth, to hang on before emerging therefrom, to some sort of nasal ridge, to lift up a noisy valve, close it again, then continue on its way, furiously...and then resume.

The king made a gesture of chagrin. He counted, as soon as he was in bed, on closing his eyes, liberating himself from the surrounding ugliness, meditating a little on recent events, and on himself among the events. The snoring precipitated itself through his reveries, shoving the fragmentary thoughts left and right, carried them away into its rugged undulations as soon as they were born, falling silent for a moment, and re-commenced its glutinous course.

He sighed, and slid beneath the cold sheets. A hammering noise caused him to start again. It was a tenant coming up the stairs, legs and boots leaden, complaining, in a drunken voice, that he had been refused a drink on credit, and that he would settle the boss's hash, and that it was a shameful way to treat his clients, and that he would show him, the boss, whether he was a thief that it was necessary to mistrust, that he had always been an honest man, that he father had been an old soldier, that he had served his time himself without punishments...and then a door slammed, shaking all the partition walls of the landing, interrupting the monologue with a clap of thunder...which resumed, some distance away from the king's room, perceptible through the walls.

"Everything," said the king. "I shall accept everything...but I need to sleep..." He felt weary after the day's work. The effort of will that he made to forget the stifling atmosphere and abstract himself from the sounds of the rooming-house, and not to let himself fall into depression, made him slightly feverish. His eyelids refused to remain closed. He tried to fix his thoughts, in order to numb himself gradually. He tried to create the illusion that he was lying in a comfortable bed in a silent room; he evoked images, imagined himself in Florence, strove to contemplate Benvenuto Cellini's Perseus, which was in the Loggia on the Piazza della Signoria; songs hovered on the edge of his lips...he resisted with all his strength the obsession of the snoring and the unarrested monologue of his neighbor; he whistled tunes with the residues of his respiration... the Moonlight Sonata, which he remembered having heard in Germany, with its evocation of perfumed quietude, confusedly silvered light, sylvan calm, floated around him...and he fell asleep.

A bright light struck his eyes, lingering upon his eyelids. He opened them, and voices near his head completed his awakening. Beyond the window, in the corridor, a group was chatting outside a door while a key was inserted into a lock. He heard the clerk receive the money, close the door again and go away, hammering the stairs, which groaned beneath his steps, without any concern for the sleeping tenants.

The light had disappeared. The king tried to go back to sleep. A conversation in the room that had just been occupied reached him, even though he pulled the sheet over his ears, clenched his eyelids shut, assembled all his forces in order not to hear, and to go to sleep. But he heard! He heard the bargaining of a young woman and a man—and what he heard made his heart leap in his chest and waves of nausea rise into his throat.

"Bah!" said the man, at the end of a harsh and revolting discussion, "I don't amuse myself every day. You'll have what you desire."

"Oh, my darling," replied a hoarse, withered, thick voice, which was the young woman's; it had been insulting and harsh a moment before.

The noise of a kiss transpierced the wall and reached the king. He made a dolorous grimace. He could not avoid picturing the horrible couple: her, bareheaded, clad in a skirt muddy at the hem, a mantle of threadbare wool with frayed edges, flabby, shiny, soiled, her face striated by little red vessels, her eyes vitreous, her hair loose, sticky, dirty; and the man, doubtless similar to all those he had seen in the tavern downstairs or had passed in the sordid streets, with troubled eyes through which yellow gleams of desire were passing, and trembling hands, waiting for the moment to grip, opening and closing in the darkness, all ready...

And the kiss that he had heard...the kiss...the kiss...

119

He felt that he was on the point of bursting into sobs. The kiss! The kiss! He evoked the divine music of the pure Beethoven, as if to roll in it, to drown himself in it, to let it drag him away...far, far away...from that ignoble hotel, and far away, above all, from the sacrilegious act, the bought and sold intercourse of those two monsters...

And suddenly...!

Suddenly, a phrase emerged from his heart, took form in his mind, before he had deliberately thought it, before he had expressed it with his trembling lips:

Poor people!

What strange ensemble of sensations, what unconscious connection between the music he had summoned to his aid, and the hideous conversation...?

Poor people, thought the king, his eyes wide open, his heard skipping a beat. *What! I dare to feel sorry for myself and suffer on my own behalf! For me, who knows the noble joy of living, for me, still all ablaze with brilliant contemplations!*

Oh, poor people, who take such joys amid the paradise of life! For whom frightful kisses and stinking wine are delicious dew, because they don't know that there are a thousand noble sensualities in the world...

Oh, if I have to suffer, let it be for them and not for me!

For him, happy, rich in himself, the horrors, the ugliness, the bestiality that for all these wretches were joys, could only be horrible, ugly, bestial, the privation of nobler joys, and lack of light—and not only ought he to traverse the ordeal without weakness, without nausea, but he felt, in his heart swollen by an infinite pain, which now prevented him from hearing the filthy noise, the raucous snores, the hiccups of the drunkard and kisses of the couple, that the ordeal would be august, and that he ought to go saturated with love and compassion...he, who Knew...among these brothers of the shadows into which hazard had led him...

The Discovery of Equality

The king sang as he worked. He whistled tunes, brought his actions into accord with his song, passed mechanically from whistling to murmuring, and finally let his voice go— and his companions labored to the rhythm of his song. They liked Emmanuel. He liked them...

One day in summer, when he had allowed himself to be carried away by the exaltation of the joy of laboring and moving his body in the limpid light and the caressant air, he had noticed that as he was further uplifted, his companions became anxious, wearier and heavier, and then envious, and their gazes hostile. He had lowered his voice. He thought he had understood. He was weary, of course, but no more so than on days when he had hunted deer or wolves all day long in the woods of Galade. And after all, he retained the power of thought. He had a thousand beautiful consolations within him when he was tired. They, quick to grumble, always peevish, curing their shovels and picks as they manipulated them, always cursing the hardness of the labor, and the difficulty of living...they *did not know anything else...*

On some evenings they got him to sing in the tavern where the laborers met after work. One evening, one of them said to him: "Tomorrow's my wife's birthday. Would you like to come to eat with us? There'll be a few friends, and Koutzeff, an old Russian anarchist who talks like a book. It's not beautiful, at home, but we'll replace the carpet and sofas with good stories and the pleasure of knowing that we're among friends. You can sing us things, after dessert."

"Gladly," said the king.

He went the next day, and saw a sad spectacle. Far away from the city center, where the monuments and lights were, in a quarter in which every house sweated misery, at the top of a narrow and worm-eaten staircase in one of the houses, he went into a room where the laborer's family was crowded. It was there that they lived. Two iron beds and two mattresses on the tiled floor; between the beds a little red-hot stove filed the room with an odor of drying linen, burnt linen, cooking fat, amplifying, exasperating, overheating and mingling with damp, confused respirations, poorly-washed flesh—and, in that stinking cauldron, a wife and three children...

On a slightly rickety table, places had been set. Several rude fellows, entering with the king and the host, accumulated therein. Old Koutzeff was already there, waiting for them. He had big blue child-like eyes, disdainful lips, a long white beard and dirty clothes.

And the meal commenced.

The host apologized for the narrowness of the lodgings and the lack of air. "Bah—one's among friends!" a guest replied.

"To be sure, that's worth as much as the Doge's palace!" said another.

"Have you seen the Doge's palace?" asked the king.

"I've seen pictures," said the companion "Ha ha! Say, to take a tour like that...to go to stroll like a bourgeois, for a fortnight, without worrying about earning one's bread, this rotten life! But those things are too beautiful—best not to think about them!"

"Hey, aristo," said another to the king, "you who take pleasure in Paris, on the site, when a ray of sunlight strikes your back, what would you say out there?"

"Yes, yes," said the king, softly, "but those pleasures aren't for everyone..."

"Oh," said old Koutzeff, "it's coming, the time when everyone can have his ray of sunlight. And we'll see, this time! A little more patience. Then, it'll no longer be some who have the light, the facile voyages in beautiful lands, and all the luxury, and all the pleasure, while all the others work themselves to death building their monuments, their railways, their light. It really will be everyone..."

"We're not there yet," said the host's wife.

"It will be everyone," Koutzeff repeated, his fork upright in his firm fist, hammering the table. "It will be all individuals, equal in pleasure as they're equal in nature."

"Bravo!" said one of the men, his mouth full.

"Claptrap," said another.

"But men aren't equal...," the king began.

"Who's that?" demanded Koutzeff, immediately, squinting and passing his hand beneath his long beard.

"A comrade who's been rich, and has come to work with us to earn his bread. A good fellow. You'll hear him sing after dessert."

"You've been rich, eh?" said Koutzeff. "Raised in the old traditions, eh? And they hold good, in spite of your poverty? There are still a lot, among you, in spite of your Revolution, in spite of everything, the great poets, the great painters, who believe in the divine right, the eternal privilege of castes. Ha ha!"

He stood up, and placed his hands heavily on the king's shoulders. "Listen," he said, "listen, young man, I don't know where you come from, or where you were brought up. You're not a coward, since you've come to work with your hands, in order to eat, among the people. And yet, perhaps you'll return to the side of the tyrants on the day of the great battle. Listen, and remember that they're blind, criminal and deprived of the flame of love, those who refuse to admit that all men are sons of the earth, and that there is an original, ineffaceable injustice, in the fact that two naked infants born at the same hour, one in the home of a poor man and one in the home of a rich man, one of whom will have all the roads of life opened to him, smoothed before him, from his very first sigh, and the other poverty, the incessant and mortal combat merely to eat, to clothe himself...

"Listen! To eat, to clothe himself, to struggle again to protect himself from hunger, from cold, to acquire bread, a roof, clothing, when there's so much to do simply to discern what one is capable of doing, if one's true self has blossomed, when there are so many things to learn, so many secret problems to penetrate, when a new hour has sounded for men, when only intellectual conquests, the only ones worthy of men, will appear as the only important and—then—the only necessary goal!

"Look at me, with my sordid clothes, a man who is only eating this evening thanks to the charity of a neighbor, a man who is telling you these things among men who, at dawn tomorrow, after heavy sleep, will resume their bestial labor!

"I'm a man. They're men. They have a brain and a heart to comprehend beauty, to love and to bloom. Now, they're reduced to hatred, to darkness, and they go, deaf and imprisoned, through the luminous life that surrounds them, among the noble and the liberated, like primitives tracked by all fatalities in forest full of wild beasts...by all the fatalities that one finds behind all actions throughout the ages: hunger, cold, darkness, carnal thirsts. The elements grinding humans down, making them ignorant, making them hate one another and tear one another apart, making them beg, shivering and stupid, for the help of omnipotent gods, divine crutches.

"Understand the crime of those of your caste, the crime of the masters and the priests!

"It's not beneath those fatalities that those humans are crushed; it's beneath the egotism of the rich and the lies of religions! For those fatalities *no longer exist*, and all human beings could be *human*.

"Oh, the supreme fatality, the one that you can understand, young man, the one that you must combat, you who have lived among us—the supreme fatality of human being is not to be able to be human! To be the bearer of intelligence, of consciousness and thought; to be able to admire and love, and enjoy the elevated delight of life; and then to expend one's energy in base struggles, to be enslaved to the grossest needs, to exhaust the best of oneself therein, to imprison one's consciousness therein!

"And that in a world where human beings, relieved of material care, cleansed of the defects, deformities and vices that it engenders, could allow all their human possibilities—which is to say, intelligence, consciousness, thought and love—to blossom worthily.

"For it exists, that world! It exists. The fatalities are no more. Death itself is retreating. In a healthy society, humans will be able to live physically for a hundred and fifty years. For food, clothing and the primary necessities, humans, with their machines, without suffering, without struggles, without hecatombs, while smiling, can produce, in sufficient quantity for everyone, bread, roofs, clothing and light.

"Diseases? Listen: ten years ago, an infant I cherished died of diphtheria in an hour. Yesterday, my neighbor's son was afflicted by the same malady. The doctor came, gave him an injection of serum, and an instant, saved him. He saved him. The disease is not, therefore incurable? Ten years ago, however, I was made to believe so. I bowed down to it; I resigned myself to it.

"Resign oneself! If a hunchback knew that his deformity could be cured, the blind man that he could see clearly, the invalid that he could walk and breathe in the sunlight—tell me, do you believe that they would resign themselves to be deformed, blind and bedridden?

"Now, what proves to me that they can't be cured?

"I won't resign myself to suffering, for I see great scientists everywhere, only paralyzed by lack of money—the money that is spent on vices and wars!

"I won't resign myself to poverty, when I see the possibility of a world liberated from the base charges under which human nobility and curbed and debased.

"Religion, which tells me to resign myself, shows me the earth fatal and the heavens benevolent...I see the earth happy and its fatalities vanquished!

"And like me, all those down below have seen, all those who are exploited and crushed—and they're no longer unaware that life is beautiful. They seek it; they're organizing, uniting, for the revolt, for all the revolts. United, they'll force the doors that the powerful keep bolted; they'll take possession of the new world; they'll enter the promised land.

"You'll be crushed too, if you put yourself across their path. Be with us; our cause is holy. Bless, with us, all those who, by means of speech, by means of arms, and even by means of crimes, are undermining the ramparts of the old world, in order to hasten the coming of the worthy city of human beings!"

Old Koutzeff shut up, and the guests remained silent, and the food went cold, while none of the men were thinking any longer about eating, and the woman too—and the pupils were dilated, and the faces had suddenly been stripped of all lassitude and all darkness, and the hands were trembling slightly on the waxed tablecloth.

Chaos

The king underwent a singular crisis.

They Know, he thought. *They're like me. They have as much right as I do to a joy... a joy so elevated that for having known it, I, a king, feel far more than a rich and powerful king, and inexhaustibly rich. A joy such that, in thinking them unaware of it, I pitied them, and I loved them with all the might of my love and compassion. But they know, they want it, and no one can wither their desire without immediately becoming criminal.*

He looked within himself. It was true that he had done nothing except to be born the son of a king, to find the scented roads of life open before him, ready smoothed. And as a king, what he he done? He had left his ministers, Gasp, Gohain and Mnektes, the care of directing the people, of remedying their misfortunes, while he hunted, feasted and made love. It was true too, that he had, at first doubted and then privately denied the teachings of Gohain; that he had seen the earth fertile and beautiful, and humans standing tall, not debilitated and pitiful on a spiteful planet, victims of the capricious will of an impenetrable God.

He talked often to Koutzeff; he read the books that the latter gave him; he swallowed voraciously, his soul seething, the revolutionary works of the previous century; he agitated anxiously among the great mystical hopes, the ingenious economic theories and the sparkling utopias the manipulated humanity as an infant carries a doll from the house into the garden.

Koutzeff was right. It was true! For century after century, one fraction of humankind had played, sung, danced over the other fraction, crushed, dimmed and bloodied. Kings, priests and noblemen passed before his eyes during his sleepless nights in a long cortege laughing joyfully, and treading waist-deep in a bloody mire made of the bodies, hearts and the dreams of oppressed plebeians.

And he, the King of Galade, was among the cortege. Oh, if, like him, now, the powerful men of the world had mingled with the plebeians, opened their hearts and understood that resident within every man was a marvelous flower ready to bloom, instead of withering, in darkness and devoid of warmth, how quickly they would water it with all their love, with all their might, in order that a healthy, and harmonious humankind would soon bloom in its entirety, rich in all is worth!

For even the powerful, the fortunate, had not savored fully the immense joy permissible to humankind—so many forces were spoiled, so many souls annihilated, so much possible genius extinguished, perhaps, in all those who were dying at present of hunger and cold on the roadside and in hovels!

And then, the highest were interlinked with the lowest, who constructed their edifices and their railways, who prepared their food, the lowest filled with hatred and revolt. The human spirit was paralyzed by all that human matter; the greatest, the freest, were dragging the redoubtable weight of all the enslaved, all the obscured.

Oh, if everyone could understand, rapidly, that the evil was now remediable, and that a superior joy was possible for all, that no one would any longer be resigned to it and, having organized, would soon agitate—those at the bottom by means of incessant revolt, those at the top by love and commiseration—to realize the great Reform, now possible!

Sometimes, the king dreamed of returning to Galade, creating an elite people, informing the Galadians of the upheaval of the world, the fall of fatalities, the end of dogmas of sadness, the reality of joy and power, and going at their head to announce all over the world the era of human Liberty—and of reducing by force all those, armored with dread, prejudiced or ignorance, the deaf, voluntary or otherwise, whom love could not convince, those who doubted, obstacles retarding the forward march of those who knew, those who wanted...

Taken by Koutzeff into milieux in perpetual agitation, mingled by the life of his companions with all the miseries and all the filth of hovels and garrets, the king suffered all human suffering, sang all the ideals of revolt and love, lamented, and became exasperated. Sometimes, in the midst of simple souls, he simplified the world and human beings, turned the planet over with a gesture of his hand; at other times he stopped, breathless and frightened, before the complexity of the obstacles.

And he no longer had any respite.

The evil was no longer fatal...the evil was remediable...every unfortunate, every invalid, every ugly or stupid visage stimulated his excitement. Quickly, before anything else, let there be an end to *that!* Every passer-by that he saw laughing, every individual he saw enjoying some petty pleasure, exasperated him, setting his entire being aquiver. He considered them as obstacles.

Don't laugh, passer-by, be serous; there's so much to do! You'll have time to laugh—oh, how you'll laugh!—when it's done. You, you're contenting yourself with your ridiculous petty joy at the gates of a realm of unsuspectable sensualities, unimaginable delights! That petty joy, in satisfying you, is turning you away from the urgent action. The splendid tomorrow has need of all revolts for its aurora, and sees because of those who laugh, who content themselves, and resign themselves, eternalizing its eve, while all the wretched are croaking!

And it was saturated with similar ideas that he stopped, on the evening of the fourteenth of July, in Paris, in front of a dace hall in the Boulevard Saint-Michel, in the little crossroads formed by the Sorbonne, and, with his back against the statue of Auguste Comte, while watching the dancing and the joyful crowd, was seized by a strange delirium.

The Reappearance of a Philosopher

He had not been working that day, because it was the great feast-day of France. All the work-sites in Paris were closed. He had been strolling through the city, had been to see a few beloved works at the Musée du Louvre, and at dusk had gone to sit down in the Jardin de Luxembourg. The beauty of the light and the memory of contemplations urged him toward a gentle and charming reverie, but he was full of bitterness. The more reasons he had to be joyful, the more replete with bitterness he was, always, by virtue of the singular fact that in sensing how joyful he might be, he saw how it was possible to be joyful, and how lamentable it was that so many people like him were deprived of a similar joy.

Thus, all his hours were spoiled, and he veiled the brilliant light, and dulled himself to all beauty, froze all effusion within him.

In the evening, he was following the boulevard, amid the illuminations, the songs and the cries, when he stopped outside that little dance-hall, and without thinking about anything else, at first, but distracting his eyes, placed himself in a shadowy corner with his back to the pedestal of the statue.

Domestics, chambermaids with white aprons, soldiers in garish costumes, your clerks with thick faces, awkwardly holding or coarsely squeezing their dancing partners, intoxicated by dancing, red-faced and sweating, laughing in bursts at nothing at all...the confused whirl of bright colors and heavy forms gave him a sort of vertigo. He would have liked to move away from the vulgar and ugly spectacle, but he savored a bitter pleasure in suffering so much ugliness and vulgarity, which might be, or could have been, so much beauty, grace, expansion, genius...

The musicians leading the dance, with the grotesque chords of two cornets and a trombone, were sitting on a little platform decked with flags and paper flowers, piecing his ears and his heart, and, combined with the whirling of the dances, they completed his daze.

Gradually, the real spectacle was effaced, the couples, the musicians, the illuminations and the banners all fusing together; there was nothing any longer before his eyes but a formless, leaping, howling, spinning mass of soft flesh that Tomorrow would petrify, trample and crush...

"Dance! Dance, idiots!" he murmured. "Tomorrow, you resume your stupid labors. Laugh, cry with pleasure as you spin, rub one another's dirty epidermis, consent to these poor joys...around you, over you, beneath you, flourishing and reaching out to you, are sublime delights, ineffable orchestras—but content yourselves with the cacophony of those three loud-mouthed musicians and your leaden tournaments..."

The sight of a red-faced soldier, his mouth immeasurably open, in a laugh that lacked twenty-five teeth and was disgraced by the yellow and black survivors, his violet-tinted hands plastered on the back of a fat scarlet-clad woman whose hair was dangling down over her face, stiff and shiny, pricking the nose and fluttering around the nostrils, cut his monologue short and caused him to put his clenched fist to his heart.

"True pigs," he murmured—and his soul vacillated. "They don't give a damn about sublime delights and ineffable orchestras. And yet, it's necessary for them, too, to join forces with those of us who know and want Joy...the immense movement of human beings stamping their feet outside the closed doors of Happiness, because there are thousand more like those..."

The hallucinating vision passed before him of the slow, gradual comprehension of the necessary revolt, of a superior love, which would unite all humankind for the splendid Aurora. How many hours had gone by that might have been fecund! Poets sang about the smiles of women, painters represented pools and trees... Oh, there would be plenty of time to dance, to sing, to paint... When curable misery was howling from all directions, the hatred and the mediocrity of which the age was replete, and a realized paradise could be glimpsed!

No more dancing! Sop dancing! Make that abominable orchestra shut up! If you knew! If you only knew!

He had come away from the statue; he advanced among the indifferent dancers, who jostled whim with their shoulders, and went, with eyes dilated, extending his joined hands, imploring, between couples, above heads.

The worker with the demented gaze was noticed, but what he was saying was inaudible; the musicians carried on playing but the dancers paused.

"He's drunk," said some.

"What is he saying?"

"Bah! Today, the people celebrate their victory!

"A little glass on such a day..."

"Watch my dress, if he vomits!" said one young woman.

People laughed; the king's lips moved; he lost his footing; all the faces, alarmed or sniggering, leaned toward him—so far from him, all those gazes, placid in their drunkenness, in which he searched in vain for the reflection of his dream...

He staggered, he buckled, and fell to the ground as if pole-axed, amid the loud bursts of laughter.

"Bonne nuit!"

"Call a cop!"

"Get him away from here—he'll get in the way of the waltz."

"Hey, comrade, get up.

"Such a state! It's shameful!"

People had bent over him, turned him over, lifted him up, and looked at him while they carried him a little further away.

"He's a handsome fellow," said one woman. "He must have been drinking to forget...a faithless mistress...I'd gladly replace her...if I didn't love you, my beau," she added, hanging on to the arm of a man.

"Divine bounty," said someone in the chattering crowd.

And someone advanced toward the king, who had been placed on a bench. "I know him," he said to the crowd. "Don't worry—I'll take care of him."

It was an old man with a slender face and bright, serious eyes. He did not have the appearance of a malevolent man.

The drunkard could be confided to him, since he knew him, and they could go back to dancing.

"Divine bounty!" repeated the old man, loosening the king's collar—and he looked at him passionately, and rubbed his temples gently.

Gradually, the king opened his yes, and, recovering consciousness, recognized Mnektes.

Just as there was no reason for Mnektes—you shall see in due course how he was able to leave Galade—to be looking for the king, in complete ignorance of the five continents of the world, all of the cities of the five continents of the world, and all of the places in any of those cities, to be in any of those cities and any place within one of those cities, rather than any other, there was no reason why he should not have been in the very city and the very place where the king was, and where he found him. There are as many reasons to be astonished by the fact that he was there as there would have been to for him to be anywhere else. And so, if the slightest reason comes between their equal astonishments, the party that can supply the slightest reason will necessarily hold sway over the other. Now, that slight reason, which ought to appease any overly prolonged astonishment, is that this is a fantastic story.

But let us listen to Mnektes speak.

"In your haste to depart," he said to the king, "you had forgotten to tidy away the manuscripts that you and I were the only people in Galade capable of deciphering. It was thus, after a certain amount of effort, that I was able, always having doubts regarding your supposed monastic retreat, to discover the existence of the transgaladian world, comprehend that it had attracted you, learn about the road of the Grotto, and depart after you by the same route.

"I went straight on and traversed Traese. The express train that must have taken you away took me. I was very frightened but soon reassured, because I saw that my companions were tranquil. I arrived in Paris. I commended myself piously to Hazard to bring us together in all that pullulation.

Both to find you and—shall I confess it?—stupefied, disorientated and dazzled by s many new spectacles, in order to learn, to know, and to bring marvelous information back from such a voyage to Galade—I traveled the world.

"Why have I finally found you? And this evening? And in this state? Blessed be Hazard, friend of philosophers. Furthermore, having admired the ability of a dog to find its master or a friend by sniffing a trail, I can also admit—and admire even more—that there is in the human soul a sense even more penetrating than that in a dog's nose. At any rate, here you are. Sire, it's really you that I'm holding in my arms…forgive the unworthy weakness that I owe to too much weeping…"

The king was also weeping in warm and delicious contentment.

"Now, it's necessary for us to return. Strange events must have happened in Galade. When I left, certain singular whims had appeared among the people. I don't know what you can have done to excite them, but something about you must have discontented them, and their fine docility, their virtuous respect for laws and customs seemed to be beginning to break down. Gasp was not much liked, because he liked young women too much. He was accused of having got rid of you. Your welcome return will return good order to that slight disturbance.

"Yes, let's go," said the king. "And blessed be any effervescence that might be observable in my people. Into then, I shall throw the seeds of new florescences, the foundations of new palaces. Can my people have revolted? Those who revolt are right. The world in which we live is iniquitous. Joy exists for all, and no one profits from it fully. The powerful drag the heavy weight of the oppressed, and all the wretched are victims. Come—I shall organize Happiness.

"Uh oh!" said Mnektes. "Can you get up, my child. Lean on my old shoulder and take a few steps. Let's find a peaceful street and get out of this festival crowd. Tell me, what is this costume?"

134

"I ran out of money. I wanted to work with my hands, like Georgis the Headstrong, and I became a laborer, as he became a miner. I had no means of returning to Galade or of informing anyone there. I had to eat. I've experienced a great pride in sensing my vigorous and capable body serving me faithfully. Then I discovered human distress, after I had contemplated the splendor of the earth and human greatness."

"Instead of 'human,'" said Mnektes, softly, "it's necessary to say 'humans.' Humans are innumerable, and no two are alike..."

"Father!" said the king, his face red. "Don't go on. You've come from a world six centuries old. I'll teach you the laws that have edified modern times."

"Do you think that I haven't seen them?" replied Mnektes. "And that I haven't perceived the great rebellion of the masses? What are they, the laws of modern times? The equality of men, the right to happiness...... Admirable laws. Do you take me for a wolf, my son?

"If I haven't lost all clear-sightedness, it appears to me that you're suffering, and I believe I'm able to deduce the cause of your distress. At first, my king, I imagine that after a too-sudden vision of a world that is, indeed, transformed in many aspects, and being of a nature to persuade yourself of great joys promised to human beings and unsuspected in Galade, you found yourself, without having had time to learn by how many centuries of perpetual and permanent effort, that world had been edified, suddenly cast into its underside, which is the eternal misery of the wretched..."

"Eternal!" said the king. "Father..."

But they were walking under the bright stars through the silent streets that surround the Panthéon. Mnektes had taken the king's arm in his turn, and he squeezed it gently, both like an old man seeking support and a rider restraining his horse...

"And there," Mneketes continued, "you were obliged to stay. Unconsciously, all the delicacy and refinement of your being, desperately sought a refuge from the dirty promiscuities and animal habits of the milieu in which you were imprisoned.

Having no external viewpoint, in the base, nauseating or lamentable spectacles, it searched internally, and found, vivacious and fresh, the idea of Joy that you have just affirmed. It recreated it, amplified it and exaggerated it for the needs of its existence—because, my dear king, without a refuge, you would have ended up falling into the gutter, no longer being my handsome king! You would have become one of those brutes! It aggrandized your idea of joy and light, in proportion to the distress and darkness in which you were living. And your great suffering comes from the fact that, all your strength being necessary to withstand the perpetual siege of your ideative refuge, gradually, it nourished itself on your entire being, aspired the blood of your heart, drew life therefrom, and became vibrant...and then, what was only an Idea, nourished with blood, became Reality!

"Sire, there is for humans a mysterious world, of which all heavens and all hells are merely dull reflections. No one can enter into it, without deadly peril, who has not slowly climbed, one by one the ardent steps that lead to it. That is the realm of Ideas. For the man who can move freely there, it is heaven, and no voluptuousness, no sensation of power, is comparable to their contact. For those whom it directs and possesses, it is the death that humans call Madness.

"Sire, you have been the slave of Ideas.

"Once, you went among them cheerful and nimble. They were merely passing subtleties, sparkling veils, that one caressed while brushing pat them. A thousand beautiful attractions appealed to you then, and the gallop of a good horse in the forest, and the last beams of the sun at dusk, and tournaments with the sword, and charming ballets, were much more real than they were.

"They were only ideas. The idea of love, the idea of feasting, the idea of labor—they were simply evocative.

"Now, whoever gives the blood of his heart to an Idea penetrates into the realm of Ideas, and his entire being is transposed. He sees them rushing upon him, alive, sovereigns of men and their actions.

"It sometimes happens on the shore of the ocean that one is struck violently by the rotating beam of a lighthouse, and that light, having paused momentarily in confrontation with the gaze, leaves behind as it moves on a kind of dazzlement, which renders al nearby images shadows, phantoms and silhouettes. In the same way, the afflicted man will only any longer see there world through the ideas by which he is obsessed. Nothing exists any more outside of them. He can no longer perceive reality except as they allow him to perceive it. He will only take from all the facts he encounters that which belongs to the ideas that grip him, and worse than that, he will soon only encounter the facts that belong to his ideas.

"Thus, the world and everything it contains will gradually be modeled on the imaginary world that the ideas have created for him. He will carry within him a universe compared with which the real universe is only apparent. And depending on whether he is the master or slave of ideas, he will be like a god who floats over the actions of human beings, and who sometimes, seduced by one of their objects, ravishes and divinizes it—as Jupiter did to Leda—or he will be like a pig marching indifferently through odorous herbs, only able to scent the cherished truffles.

"My son, you have enclosed the world, and all its realities, within two ideas, which are Distress and Joy, and there is nothing, no fact, no intermediary, that you do not immediately cram inside one of your two universes.

"Add that you were plunged up to your eyes in a milieu strangely strewn with discourses simplifying all things for simple minds, and simple minds supersimplifying the simplifications of the said simplifiers, where Humanity, Justice, Happiness and Equality emerge as easily from mouths and souls as soap-bubbles blown by infants, round, brilliant and colored but no more durable and solid than is demandable from bubbles obtained by thinning down soap with water and blowing for a few seconds into the end of a fragile pipe: a milieu assuredly ill-equipped for discussing with the critical sensibility so useful in such circumstances, those exceedingly complex and perfidious entities—and agree that you, too rapidly informed about everything, in sum, and also being at odds with yourself in a horrific combat, no longer had your common sense or your sage equilibrium.

"Sire, let us return to Galade, and along the way, we shall discuss, if you please, various complexities. Among others, it will be necessary for us take some account of the propensity that one has to transfer one's personal fashions of sensibility on to all beings, and ask ourselves whether the suffering of the wretched or their aspiration to joy are, for them, what you imagine them to be, with your ardent nature and the richness of your soul. And by that means, we shall strive to perceive whether there might be an innumerable quantity of humanities in the bosom of what you call Humanity.

"And by that means we can examine, again, if it pleases you, whether it is really just or sensible—and worthy—for every man to consider all others as his brothers and equals, and then to weigh up whether every man is not, in a sense, what you call a humanity, in himself alone, bearing within himself the powerful and the plebeian, the noble and the vile, the oppressed and the tyrannical, miseries and joys, revolts and hopes...and thus, whether every man ought to demand of himself, and expect from himself alone, what he wants in the world, or to expect the help of others...whether, if the anarchist who wants to overturn all established things, the man who has to complain of an injustice, and the one who wants to be better, looked to themselves first, sought, reformed, overturned internally, they might not find that the world has changed, that the injustice was just and is repaired, that the reform is accomplished...

"Let us return to Galade, my son.

"But as it is possible that we shall find some change in that country, and that it is the only place on earth where modern humans have not been, with their automobiles, their airplanes, their locomotives, their telescopes, their cinematographs and other powers with names as acidic as the juice of the lemons of the Mediterranean coast, and as the Galadians are the one ones for whom it is impossible to conceive of any other idea than eating well, drinking well, sleeping well, embracing well and merited heaven as well, it is necessary to reveal to them as sagely as possible the existence of a transgaladian universe, and the power that certain humans have attained there.

"And then, it is necessary to let them do as they wish. Some among the Galadians will prefer their customary joys, others will strive to attain a more ample blossoming.

"Those who will have raised themselves above all the others, it will be necessary to allow to go into the world. That will be the supreme proof, in which the weak will be vanquished, for they will remain prisoners of the base attractions of this world, and in which the strong will come back more elevated, and bring back the beautiful acquisitions that they will have made, and which they will complete amid Galadian peace.

"Then the flower of their efforts will spread through society. For to render to humans what one has received from them, amplified, is the duty of human beings..."

And, discussing in that fashion, Mnektes developing all these notions for the king, they returned to Galade.

Part Three
THE RETURN OF THE KING

The Revolution in Galade

Perhaps you have not forgotten the great bitterness of the market-gardener named Fanoche, who had put on her beautiful dress in order to be noticed by the king, and whom the king reproached for the indecency of her neckline. It was from the bitterness of Fanoche that the first tremors issued that were soon to agitate the entire populace of Galade.

"That king!" she said to her courtiers—you will remember that she had many among the market gardeners. "We're too insignificant for him. Look how he treated the person that you're courting! He only has eyes for his beautiful ladies of the court. Well, if, instead of digging the soil that gives them their nourishment—him and them—I only had to laugh, sing and spout nonsense, and dress in silk, he would have looked at me too... It's necessary to believe that you have no taste, since you find amiable and pretty a woman that the king disdained... Or, rather," she went on, "that you have to fall back on her because the ladies of the court are not for your clumsy hands..."

And she persisted stubbornly, no longer wanting to let it go, and the courtiers found themselves rejected. "No! You're only talking to me like that because you can't court the others.

"What! What's that?" they said to her. "Hark at Fanoche! Does she think that there aren't well-built, handsome and gentle fellows among us who couldn't see some great lady and their knees?"

"Sixty years old and toothless, the great lady who'd choose you!"

"Beautiful and fresh, and full of attractions!

"Not for any of you to have!"

She had among her gallants a strapping fellow named Mysil, who was then working in the orchards of an estate belonging to the noble Lady Koraine, who, having taken a walk in her gardens and kitchen-gardens in the company of her chief steward, noticed Mysil, whose gilded arms were glistening in the sunlight.

The latter, remembering Fanoche's words, had wanted to try the experiment, and, as cleverly as possible, had done everything he could to be noticed—among other stratagems, that of making it appear that one does not fervently desire to be noticed. Lady Koraine was suffering from considerable ennui at that moment, and could not find, in the inspection of her apple trees, gooseberry bushes and strawberry bushes, a distraction adequate to compensate her for the absence of her husband, who had been sent by the Gyzir Academy of Sciences on a geological mission to the far side of Galade. The strapping Mysil was not effaced rapidly enough from her memory, to the extent that, having returned home, she was unable to think about her apple trees, strawberry bushes and gooseberry bushes without seeing the sun-bronzed face of Mysil appearing insidiously between their branches, leaves and stems.

Some time afterwards, Fanoche's adorers said to her: "Well, stubborn girl, do you still claim that we're courting you as a matter of making do? Look at Mysil, who's loved by a great lady!"

"What fine lie are you telling me?"

"It's no secret for anyone, although it's only spoken in whispers, that Mysil has touched the heart of the noble Lady Koraine."

"Mysil?"

"Mysil."

They added: "You see, Fanoche, that it's no longer necessary to reject us."

Full of chagrin, however, she said: "Isn't it shameful that these ladies of the court come to take our gallants!"

And as her chagrin was augmented by the thought that, if she had wanted, Mysil would presently be with her and not with Lady Koraine, she spoke very audaciously to her courtiers: "These great ladies and princesses, who are great ladies and princesses by the privilege of heaven, hide beneath their brilliant attire vices of which we cannot even think. And there are those among them who preach, or set us an example!"

She also said: "Are the noble lords no longer sufficient, then, to content the great ladies, they have to go as far as lowering themselves to the gallants of the women of the people?"

And: "They can lower themselves to our level, but we cannot raise ourselves at all!"

And then: "If ever Monseigneur Gasp pinches my chin as he passes along the road, I shall say to him, forthrightly: 'Monseigneur Gasp, go pinch the chins of the great ladies, your equals!'"

And again: "Equals! In knavery and dissimulation!"

And besides: "Those who know that they can do whatever they want without peril, protected by their rank, their wealth and the privilege of the good Lord are much worse than us, whom they criticize for the slightest peccadilloes!"

And furthermore: "Save for being born the sons and daughters of princes, how are they different from us, in the visage? Do they not have arms, legs and maladies like ours? And if they have vices worse than ours, which of us are the least noble, the nobles or the people?"

And even: "Look at Seigneur Mingrelis going by. Is he not ugly, meager and paltry, and could not one of you, market gardeners and lime-burners, put him in the pocket of your blouse? And yet, there he goes, idle while you toil, under the sun and in the snow. And he profits without effort from all the pleasures of the court, by your efforts, and all the good things of the earth, and he is well seated at tournaments while you carne your necks to see and remain standing, crowded together..."

Now, it happened that some among those before whom she talked in that fashion, after she had calmed down, went home and thought: *She's not wrong...*

If one adds to that the ennui that was hanging over the country, in the early days following the king's vow; and then the abrupt disappearance of the king, followed by that of Mnektes; and Gasp's excesses; and the great difficulty the government had in explaining the king's retreat to the Galadians, given that even the government did not know in which abbey he had gone to enclose himself; and that, when the year had expired—for it had been a long time, more than a year, that the king had spent traveling the world and finding himself a prisoner in Paris—one can understand the facility with which the people credited the opinion that Gasp had made the king and Mnektes disappear (no one dared say worse) in order to take power...

And in the meantime, gradually influenced by the words of Fanoche, repeated and deformed, a great many men and women of the people asked monks, clerics and deacons, then priests, and eventually the archbishop himself, troubling questions about the divine reason for differences in caste; and demanded certainty from the archbishop, priests, deacons, clerics, monks, that justice would be rendered in heaven, where God would make princes and common people equal, and proofs in support of that certainty...

In sum, if you consent to have a glance at all the history books of all lands that narrate the multiple origins and the ordinary phases of all revolutions, you will have no difficulty in imagining in what state the king found his peaceful Galade on his return with Mnektes.

Various Facts

The government was in chaos. Gasp had fled. The nobles were barricaded in their homes. Monseigneur Gohain and the priests, after having preached in increasingly empty churches, no longer dared preach, nor even go out in the streets, for they were treated as liars and stoned, and some of them thought, as at the commencement of a vocation, about adding their names to Christian martyrology. The people, about to overthrow the government, were determined to enjoy in their turn everything that the princes had enjoyed, and to proclaim itself sovereign, owner of the land, tools and edifice, legislator and great pontiff.

The king secretly summoned his ministers, who were amazed by his reappearance, forbade them to reveal it, and had the state of things explained to him accurately. But Monseigneur Gohain, from whom it had been impossible to conceal the providential return, came running, and, seeing him, raised his arms to the heavens, as high as his deltoids permitted.

The deltoids are the muscles articulating the shoulder, which the Monseigneur had exhausted by the exercise to which he had submitted them in raising his arms to the heavens so many times since the revolution began, so that he now only had languid arms, which dangled by his sides, scarcely capable of allowing the hands to be interlinked over the abdomen—but such a surprising events suddenly reanimated those exhausted deltoids. He exclaimed "Alas, my son!" and then added: "If I had known what abominable consequences the vow I made you make—the vow I let you make—might have, it would not have been a year but a day to which I would have limited you!"

"Want vow, Father?" the king asked.

The archbishop opened his eyes wide.

"In fact, I do remember the vow of which you speak, Father," said the king. "To tell the truth, I had completely forgotten it. Since my disappearance, I've scarcely had time to think about it, I was so entirely absorbed by other objects, and all my living forces were expended to such an extent in contemplations, and then in suffering..."

Mnektes looked at the prelate, and made a sign to him that a calmer hour would sound when he would have the leisure to give him a few explanations.

In spite of the precautions, the news ran throughout Galade that the king was safe and sound, and was about to be seen again.

And he reappeared one morning among all the people, assembled in great agitation in the public square of Gyzir.

In spite of their anger, the members of the audience were glad to see the son of Georgis again, the amorous king with the harmonious features. And when he had spoken, saying that great power resides within every human being, preaching the virtue of pride, which impels everyone to want to draw his own help from within himself, painting in symbolic terms a being that he and Mnektes had seen, whose existence they affirmed, and which everyone could know, which played with material objects, extended itself as far as the stars in heaven and could shrink so far as to penetrate the ultimate retreat of all form, bearing in its intelligence inexhaustible reserves of joy, and for which there was only voluntary suffering, that each Galadian there present could approach, whether noble or of the people, if they sought it first within themselves...and a thousand other things that cannot be the object of this story...the crowd flowed away, reserving the possibility of resuming the revolution after having seen the king at work for a while.

In the meantime, the king went back into his palace, and then perceived a woman who was waiting for him, and whose face lit up as soon as he appeared.

It was Melidine.

The King and Melidine

"Sire," she said, "I was waiting for you. Until today, I have not ceased to suffer, and now it seems to me that I have never been unhappy, and that I am before you for the first time. Have you not forgotten me? Am I not a stranger to you?"

The king took her hand, and went, squeezing it gently, into the path in the park where they had once separated so unfortunately. He contemplated Melidine, and saw that she was different. Her features had been hollowed out, modeled by chagrin, suffering and uncertainty. Her eyes were larger. She was more beautiful, and less pretty.

And the king felt his heart beating with a fever that he had not experienced for a long time.

But as Melidine waited mutely for him to speak, he was in great perplexity and he wondered whether, now, with all that he had seen, suffered and loved, he would be able to find in Melidine a vast and comprehensive soul, something other than a mere lover...

Softly, with precaution, he began to confess to her that he had lied to all of Galade, and then he explained, vaguely, that he had been beyond the mountains, and he gradually became excited, and he told Melidine about the masterpieces and great prodigies, and when he had finished, as the shadows of nonchalant leaves danced at their feet, he saw that Melidine's gaze was fixed, as if lost in a distant dream, and he could not help thinking: *Doubtless the sound of my voice is not disagreeable to her, but she must soon have wearied of following my descriptions. The expectation of the kiss, the concern for the act of love, absorbs her entirely, and it's purely out of politeness that she isn't yawning...*

And he said to himself, again: *Alas!*

Then he resumed, aloud: "I see from your immobile eyes, Melidine, that you are in some reverie, and that I must have bored you with these unknown things..." And he would have liked to have dared to express what he was thinking, by which he was very annoyed and full of pain: *She has not understood.*

Now, a fairy—the fairy that every fantastic tale has, and which this one does not lack—emerged from the anguish of his soul, invisible to Melidine, and said this to him:

"What do you expect? Those immobile eyes are her beautiful response. Through all the marvels you describe, her eyes have pursued their indescribable dream. And beyond all those prodigies, that immutable dream, the flower of all female gazes, is like the perpetual expectation of even greater prodigies. Whatever you see and do, that mute dream will gaze further, and higher...

"And as her heart, agitated by all that you say, which is like the stage of a journey between what she knows and what she senses at the extremity of her dream, which is infinite, can no longer beat as present for any hero inferior to the one that you have come to be, here you are before the impossibility of forfeiture, if you want to keep her love, and before greater prodigies to accomplish, if you want to make it greater..."

Around the king and Melidine the light was vaporous, and over their heads, the songs of the birds in the trees were like a crystal cupola. Melidine's eyes closed slowly, for she felt that she was dying of knowing that the king had come back to her, after such a long time...

And he gently tilted Melidine's head toward him, feeling himself enveloped by the same suave warmth—as if his blood were changing into honey—that he had felt before, on that same bench, in the dusk.

And Melidine's forehead brushed the king's face.

And then, for the first time, their lips met.

THE ARK

1

Aux Armées, *1914*

Since it is necessary for us, my love, to submit along with the entire world to the cruel moment of the world's destiny, in the universal enslavement of people and things to martial force, would you like us to attempt the madness of declaring ourselves to be free—and saying it so forcefully that we succeed in believing it?

For myself, I will dispense in that victory of pride all my resources on conviction; and I sense in myself such vigor in that endeavor, my love, and such faith, that I am almost ready, in spite if my pain, to consider it with joy. I shall enumerate our still-vivacious capabilities and accumulate the reasons that we have, thanks to them, to declare ourselves happy in spite of the harshness of circumstances. I shall retrace with the eloquence that will give me the most tender and most moving of memories, the pleasures and beauties of the amorous hours that we lived before the war. I shall evoke the sumptuous garden of dreams that we formulated and the hopes that it was permissible to raise.

Doubtless you have experienced and know as well as I do everything that I shall have to say about that, but when we savored those pleasures and hose hopes, their warmth was so soft and so evident that we had no need to give them a name. They were the elements of our happiness, and we respired them naturally with the air and the daylight. We did not stand them up before us to estimate their size. No more would it have come to our minds to scrutinize and measure the quantity

149

that each of us was taking from our enjoyment, nor whether the quality was exactly the same in the balances of our sensations. That is why there might be a new value, a more resplendent appearance for each of us, if I express them as generally as they merit.

And I intend that, far from aggravating your sadness with the spectacle of forbidden felicities, the sparkle and the music of those felicities will excite in you the sentiment of the happiness that we possessed. And before you weep for that happiness, the least that can happen is that you will first savor them again, that you will live them for a second time. That feast of the imagination, shall I suppose, shall I say that it will last long enough for the war to be over before you find yourself confronted by the bare table? If it is not, I believe that it will leave you so much light that a consciousness of it will burst forth within you, a consciousness that you doubtless possess, but which is wandering vagabond along interior paths, and that you have not yet grasped—grasped as it seems to us that a cloudless sky grasps the midday sun in summer.

Yes, I think that you will then discover such a richness that sadness will appear to you to be a weakness that ought to be left to those who have nothing.

And this will be the Ark that I shall construct, and which will protect us through the second deluge, unleashed by the entire earth. Already, many houses, and the bodies of their residents, entire cities and the pride of their scattered stones, have gone, submerged by the great red tide. Thus, we have both thought until now that our dreams and our desires, the fiefs, cities and souls of our happiness, would be smashed and crushed by the tempest...no, no. Standing, my love! I shall reassemble our goods, adapt the timbers of our Ark. And if powder and iron do not interrupt my labor, oh, I affirm that after the work is done, Noah running aground on the dry summit of Ararat did not extend his hands toward Adonai with a greater gratitude and a more ardent intoxication, and the branch did not gleam with a fresher green in the beak of the dove, than the joy, youth and voluptuousness we shall have, my beloved, in obtaining consciousness of our liberty.

2

But your confidence which always accompanies me, is holding back, anxiously. Ah, I understand! Whether delightful illusion, or even conviction, what charm could ever replace the inexhaustible delights of veritable presence? Do I not grasp sufficiently that the sadness I need to vanquish is that of our separation? When we are together, what adversity do we fear? Whatever they were, the proofs that once afflicted us were still joys. Each of them brought to one of us a pretext to seek in the other's eyes for courage, security or the certainty of victory...

Well, let your confidence be serene. Follow me. Whatever might be the apparent disorder and discontinuity of this endeavor, it is the certitude of our liberty, I tell you; it is our inviolate happiness that ought to be resuscitated therein. Follow me my beloved. Wherever I go, whatever detours the vicissitudes of the war, the gusts of my memory and the train of my thoughts might impose upon us, it is toward you, with no relapse, that all my effusions will go. In spite of time, distance and circumstances, how can the fervor and force with which I sense you close to me not communicate the vivid impression of my thought to you too? For me, whose distress will have no other refuge, whose pride will have no other throne, than this message, I say, I know, that my will and my passion will attract, bring and fix here, real, your distant substance, your eyes, your soul and your passion.

What dear images shall I commence by evoking. First of all, I want to cause to reflourish on these leaves that you are holding a few of the ornaments of our hours, the pleasures of our household, pleasures such that a perpetual spring blossoms around us.

As soon as our threshold was crossed, everything foggy or irritating that either one of us dragged outside was suddenly chased away, dissipated like the dust that, as soon as our door was open, would have been caught and, in a sense, set away by a current of joyful air. At home! Here I am. Here is the cheerful garden, the banal staircase, our door...

Our door, which I am about to open....

Oh, let us hold back the advent of that moment slightly. My heart has suddenly swollen and its beating is becoming more precipitate. I would like to impose on myself here the bitter and delicious voluptuousness of expectation, and savor my emotion first. I sense myself joyous, impatient and solemn. O slowness of my pen...I cannot retain myself...

I go in...

You have heard me. Here you are, and you are holding out your arms, and have thrown them around my neck.

Bonjour my love, my darling, bonjour my little queen, my beautiful bird, my golden lamp...

This evening you're wearing the blue muslin dress with the light green and red Greek embroidery around the sleeves, the belt and the collar. A little of your bare shoulders and your neck rise from the fluid fabric with the supple majesty that the movements of lionesses have, and the glitter of those movements...loosen your arms, let's interrupt our kiss so that I can look at you...but you, impatient, are waiting for the moment...come...

I walk in front of you, and yet I sense the murmur of your eyes. Every evening it is the same, and that moment for which you wait, my little one, is the one where I hold you against me and tell you the slightest minutes of my day.

Here is the room where I work. The divan appeals to us with all the yellow arabesques of its Persian fabric, and I would not change anything in the disorders of the multicolored cushions that are slightly reminiscent of a band of intoxicated goblins. I can see from their hollows that you were lying here a little while ago...and the one that conserves the imprint of your arm seems to be gazing with a superiority full of indolence, at the one at the very end, kneaded by your fidgeting heels. I let myself fall into the middle of that soft little people,

152

and all the fumes of the day are exhaled in my sigh of quietude and pleasure.

It's necessary that I clear a space within myself before holding you, abandoned against my breast. In an instant, I disencumber myself. Until tomorrow, people external affairs, sentiments, words for your usage...outside words and sentiments, my weavers, my forgers, creatures of the outskirts of my hearth, go away and rest until tomorrow.

You are huddled against me, and it's a calm evening of customary life. In the other rooms we can hear the great confused and heavy rumor of our populous street. Its noises arrive here, filtered by the garden, like the purr of a distant machine, like the grave rhythmic chant of the chambers of seashells.

Let's not light the lamp yet. Above our heads, on the wall, the old frame garlanded with gilded wood of the Arab mirror is still vaguely radiant, and the prestigious blue background of the *image d'Épinal*, the glory of the wall, is not entirely extinct—the image of I'm as proud, almost, and as content as if it were a Ghirlandaio![12] It has the naïve splendor of a work by that primitive.

It's a crucified Christ, at whose feet the Saintly Women are weeping. I brought it to you marvelously one day, with a hundred other *images* that I had just bought from the factory itself, during the voyage we made to Épinal. They weren't the illustrations, so widespread, recalling in miniature the misadventures of lazy Gilbert or the prowesses of Prince Cornalin, but those posters by Georgin[13] that the colporteurs once sold

---

[12] The Italian Renaissance painter Domenico Ghirlandaio (1449-1494), the guiding light of a large workshop in which many of his relatives collaborated and in which Michelangelo was once apprenticed.

[13] The popular engraver François Georgin (1801-1863) was largely responsible for the distinctive style acquired in the early 19th century by *images d'Épinal*—brightly-colored pictures, often with rhymed captions, hawked by colporteurs [itinerant pedlars] in the days when they were the only decora-

in the villages and were fixed on brown walls not far from the holy water stoup or the hunting rifles. Beautiful religious fables, Napoléonic adventures...

Do you remember the joyful cry of enthusiasm with which I threw the roll of those images on to the bed in our hotel room? You abandoned whatever you were doing and we pored over the dazzling sheets, laughing and emotional, soon spread out on the eiderdown and the pillows, on the tables, the chairs and the floor. They soon filled the sullen room with an extraordinary host of the Grande Armée's battles and biblical scenes in costumes from the Thousand-and-One Nights! Oh, my darling, before those images, costing a few sous, we were delighted, and clapped our hands like children taken for the first time to see a fairy play...

Who, having read in the first lines of this message the sentences in which I spoke to pompously of our pleasures, would not smile on hearing me declare our puerile admiration for those humble images, and think that it is very easy to say that one is happy when one is so easily enchanted! But that is what it will be necessary for me to do when I enumerate my joys, is it not, my beloved? It will be necessary for me to count the smallest grain of the sand of the beaches, the ripple of light over a leaf, as well as the rude scaling of summits, as well as the nuptial contemplations of the great works of art, the earth and time. It will be necessary for me to describe the perpetual fête that the unfolding of the world was for us, in particles and in number...

To describe, in sum, that which was the truth, the meaning, the very substance of our being, that which we had no need to name, and which I shall be able, in this era of horror, to signify: the instinct, the will and the force of joy...

---

tions that poor people could afford. Most were postcard sized, but they could be poster-sized, especially when bought direct from the factory in Épinal.

3

But it's necessary that I interrupt myself and tell you about a certain prodigy...

I suddenly experience the sentiment, since I began to write *The Ark*, of having vanquished, with my little pencil and notebook—with regard to what concerns me, of course—the war, the Great War. But dare I pursue my confession?

To escape, or merely to seek to disintegrate, by intellect and the sentiments, and for whatever reason, such a formidable event, is it not an abominable egotism, at the same time as a stupid blindness? Does not this immense affair in which we are the actors and the witnesses require all our activities and all our intelligence to be employed in considering it in its most ardent appearances, passionate in studying its causes, conjecturing as to its consequences?

On the other hand, is it possible that a human sensibility can refuse to be moved, can succeed in remaining estranged from the terrible and lamentable spectacles that are continually inflicted upon it? What response can I give myself? When I write that I experience the impression of having, for my part, vanquished the War with my pencil and my notebook, it's doubtless necessary to understand by it that I believe I have a resource, a passion that is stronger, more pressing and more absorbing for me than the War and all its episodes...

That active resource and that passion are, I imagine, the voluptuousness that I savor in evoking our days of love, and also the light that flows within me, since I have been writing *The Ark*, in sensing your body in all my gestures, your heart in all my emotions...but are those the same elements of what I call my Victory? No. They are only the effects of a certain state of mind.

If I can write this, evoke you so substantially, superimposing, full of life, the images of cherished memories upon rude realities...it is, as I said , because some strangely efficacious and powerful force gives me the means, and it is also because there must be in me and irresistible, an inviolable non-acceptance of the martial adventure...

These sentiments, issuing from the depths, become precise as my pencil obliges them to deliver themselves. Where can I find the reason, the source, the mechanism for that strange force, that non-acceptance of the most positive and most imperious of evidence? A word that I wrote a little while ago brings my soul before my consciousness.

4

In a beautiful oriental fable, a poor man goes to sleep and has an absurd and magnificent dream. In the bosom of a palace, of which he is the prince, all delights surround him, and as soon as he experiences a desire, perfumes, sensualities, ineffable dishes, gold, adornments and music fly to him. The sleeper, who senses himself dissolving in blissful satisfaction, utters in his sleep an exclamation of joy, and the sound of his exclamation wakes him up.

Now, he is certainly awake; he has propped himself up on his bed, his eyelids flutter, his fingers clench on the sheet, but his dream follows him. The craziest hallucination has him in its grip. It is not the familiar rickety table that is in the middle of his room, but the one resplendent with crystal, scarlet and glided victuals and the fruits of Canaan; his scarred plaster walls have retreated strangely; he perceives in their stead the tapestries, the hangings and the trophies of the magnificent hall of his dream; his window with dirty panes has become the vast bay behind which his gardens and his forests extend...

He is fearful and wonderstruck at the same time. He knows full well that he is a poor man in his attic and yet he reaches out his hand toward the table, and the fruit and honey that he takes and chews convinces him that he is no longer dreaming...

Such is my hallucination.

When I wrote above "instinct, will and the force of joy," it was at that moment only a detail of my evocation. Now, that

156

phrase, and most particularly the word "Joy" was, for me, the exclamation that woke the sleeper. As soon as I had written that line the word Joy came to collide with my soul as the sun suddenly strikes the rose-window of a cathedral and causes it to blossom in a thousand petals of flame. Since I have fixed that word, a vertiginous emotion has possessed me. I no longer know whether it is the reality I see that is real, or whether the prodigy that vivifies and multiplies every pulsation of my vertigo is real.

I am no longer in the sweet and languid half-light of memory. I sense myself positively in my limbs, my heart and my mind as entirely as I did before the war. I gaze, I breathe and I move in a spacious lightness. As the globe rings, and from its crypts rise the world's strength at the summons of Antaeus' heel, at the word Joy the foundations of my consciousness trembled, and my certainly rose up. It has risen in confrontation with the verity of the moment, in confrontation with the reality of mourning and massacre.

What is this certainty? What is it that snatches me thus from the tumultuous and bloody event? What is it that now gives the rhythm of a hosanna to the palpitations of my heart and regenerates my blood within the song of death?

My voice became the one that attained one day the clear certainty that Joy was the human verity...the clear certainty that in spite of the immense and millenary edifice of contrary evidence, Joy was, physically, mystically and spiritually, the sum of human verity...

I had slowly and arduously conquered that certainty once. For days and years I had marched, sensing it in advance, toward the verity of Joy. And I had found it, a Princess in the dormant wood, in the depths of the dense forest of ancient terrestrial, obsolete anankés;[14] a black forest of dead trees, rigid phantoms, still terrible but empty of heartwood...

---

[14] Ananké is the Greek mythological personification of ultimate destiny, to which even the gods are subject. Employed as a trivial noun, when it can be pluralized, the word usually re-

As soon as I had stolen my certainty, it was incorporated into my being; my blood carried it in my veins; it was alloyed with fluid saps flowing through the network of my nerves. And now it is awakening, unpolluted and unobscured.

I dare to admit it now. My eyes can see but I shall be like a blind man. My heart senses the hour but my mind has placed itself beyond emotion. My will is no longer participating in the War. My will is entirely contained in my certainty, which is a prisoner of facts but is not their slave.

But you...you, my love, my wife, are listening to me, following me, and are astonished. A confused jealousy is born in you. What? It is not, it is not, therefore, uniquely in your body, in our kisses, in our thoughts, in our memories, not absolutely within us and in our love that all grandeur and all liberty rises for me...?

My beloved, my beloved, listen again, because it must be apparent to you that our love is the miracle of my faith, the crown of my certainty.

5

I will tell you right away about my discovery of the truth of Joy and the foundations of my certainty. I have made too much use of the future tense. "I shall invoke our sumptuous dreams, I shall enumerate our powers..." What debts underwritten to time! In a few hours, this evening, tomorrow, one of those conjuring tricks of machine-gun fire into which my service continually takes me will perhaps have delegated some incontrovertible lead through all my whimsies. If that happens, my love, what will I have bequeathed you? Here, I have said nothing yet; I have not detached a seed from one of the thousand clusters in our orchards. In our home are my books, my pictures, a hundred incomplete manuscripts...

---

fers to the literary contrivance that simulates the workings of fate in a story, especially a tragedy; it recurs within the present text with that special significance.

Doubtless, to that poor heritage, the memory of our embraces, our laughter and our reveries will give some value, some warmth...but that memory, alas...

I imagine, my love, if I perish, our beautiful memories, similar for you to those meadows in maritime regions that are terminated by a cliff...you are before the field where the grass is trembling, amid the ardent sweetness of hyacinths and primroses, and you go through that living multicolored velvet...you go, and suddenly, there is the ridge, the void and the mysterious waves...

What! Will it be thus for our memories, stopped dead and gaping at the edge of my death? No, no, it is necessary that that should not be. I wrote that, so far as I am concerned, I had vanquished the war. So far as you are concerned, I shall be able to vanquish death. Welcome the best of my possessions. I want to give you a heritage that will leave me alive for you in spite of all appearances, which will be my body present in all your movements, my heart beating in all your passions. My legacy, beyond me, will give you the will and power to live, will give you, as if I were there, joy, pride and the voluptuousness of being.

That legacy, that philter, that treasure is the science of Joy. My beloved, open your bright hands, hold out the cup of your spirit. Your hands and your spirit are just, my beloved, and you are ready to receive the philter and the treasure. That which I name science, you possess in instinct. Both the elect of Joy, we come from two races and our minds emerge from dissimilar crucibles. One single sign has coupled us. Joy is in you as flight is in a wing; Joy is in me as the Fleece was in Jason, Galatea in Pygmalion.

I am no longer different. That is the legacy that prolongs me, that duplicates me, and will allow our Ark its constructor and its pilot even if I am broken by the war and my body in drowned in its red waters.

6

Are you ready to follow me immediately into the heart of enchantment? You must be, for my dictation of Joy cannot work without the strangest of contexts, for my very positive adventure is surrounded by an adventure that is all enchantments and prodigies...

One day when, solitary and meditating in a clearing in a beloved forest, I combined, with the ardent lists of my mind, the abstract intelligence of the truth of Joy, it came about that a miraculous being rose up from the waves of my exaltation and appeared to me...

Here commences the phantasmagoria, if it is befitting to call by that name a sum of events assuredly most improbable and extraordinary, but in which there is not the slightest detail that does not correspond to a reality and cannot be certified and "evidenced by numbers, the balance or the meter"—to employ the same words that were employed at the beginning of our relationship, as you shall see, by the miraculous being himself.

The apparition had a completely human form. He could have been some stroller in the forest passing through the clearing at that moment. I would probably have mistaken the individual for a stroller, in fact, if he—a person I have not seen coming—had not assumed before me the casual attitude of a comrade who had been there for a long time, and with whom I was in the process of conversing with the greatest familiarity in the world. His costume was not very different from the one I was wearing. It seemed to me that his height was not superior to mine.

As I looked at him, I had the confused impression of finding some resemblance in his features to an image sometimes sent back to me by mirrors unexpectedly encountered by my eyes at singular moments: those when, after feverish internal debates on some beautiful philosophical problem I emerged from the debates triumphantly joyful with some great evidence attained. Such celebrations came to me sometimes when I was wandering at random through the streets of the city, and the mirrors that my eyes encountered were simply those in shops... Then, I saw myself, going along, my torso taut with proud strength, me head held high and radiant, and I sensed my thoughts above me like an awning...

It really was a sort of image of my own face in those regal minutes that the visage of my unusual companion evoked.

But he began talking and introduced himself. He acquitted that ritual in a language sibylline at first, very solemn and declamatory, to tell the truth. Subsequently, his language became familiar. The bizarre—to say the least—impression that I had experienced since the newcomer had been beside me increased singularly as soon as he spoke...but the best way for you to judge the nature of my astonishment is to transcribe right away what I heard, moreover, with the most serious courtesy.

"To the man," the apparition said to me, "who follows the road of Passion, and who, rich at the outset in the Will to knowledge, conserves his wealth intact during the journey, to the point that he could show it at any moment in his travels as brilliant and resonant as it was when he set forth—and yet, without having ceased to spend that wealth throughout the journey—to the man following the road of Passion, both lavishing and keeping intact the treasure of the Will to knowledge, it is perhaps accorded to know me and to listen to me.

"If you had not gone," he continued, "by that road of Passion, both lavishing and keeping intact the treasure of the Will to knowledge, you would never have known me in my veritable person, for I am similar to another man in appearance; and I have perhaps been your nearest neighbor a thousand times without your ever suspecting who your neighbor really was. And it is thus that I am continually among humans, but they do not know me, and as if I did not exist, and yet you can see, in seeing me, that I am real.

"I say that I am similar to a man in appearance, because my body is similar to that of a man. And yet...but what will follow will give you an initial notion of my character, and it will also be the enunciation of my privileges and the table of my excellences.

"My body is like that of a man, and yet my movements and my liberty are to the movements and liberty of a man as the course of a spring is to the compact waters that lie dormant between calcareous subterrains, and only succeed in flowing in slow serpentine fashion through the fissures of internal silicas. My rich possessions are of this world. My delectations are deployed over the treasures and the virtues of my very being, and all the concrete and spiritual treasures of human creatures, works and constructions, and over all the visible and occult treasures of space and time, of the land, the air and the sea, and are not limited to this universe, extending to the treasures of the stars.

"I shall not enumerate the countenance of these words, for it is not possible to state the number and the diversity of the outside and the inside of creation. And it is that number and that diversity which my words signify, because there is not one single being or object in creation that does not enclose for me a treasure or a virtue. And these words, therefore, signify that everything there is in earth and in heaven, in the present as in the upstream and the downstream of the ages, is offered to my dilection, and that I have the license, in order to attain it, to go into all universal regions, to traverse periods, souls, elements and substances.

"It follows that if I undertake to summon in detail the names of the places, objects and beings, and the names of the interior of the places, objects and beings that are for me as many cups of Joy from which I can drink, and if, calling by name one after another, I spoke for such a long time that the most majestic forests would have time to die and decompose, and their plants and their trees would have reentered the soil and melted into the surrounding humus, and the most abundant rivers would have time to dry up and the rocks over which they flow would be dissolves and all their particles dissolved into the dust of the air—all the names of the places,

162

objects and beings that I would have summoned until the moment when I chose to stop, no matter how far away that moment might be in the centuries, and every second having contained the name of a place, an object or a being, all those names would still be no more than dust on the roads that I have the leisure to tread, feeble splinters of my privilege, hamlets in the empire in which I can frolic as I please, traveling, pausing, contemplating, embracing and bringing further forward in consciousness every treasure among my treasures,"

7

He continued:

"And that infinite opulence is, however, only a first degree of richness, the carving and metalwork of my coffers, the envelope of a second opulence that surpasses everything that is conceivable of the most furious and vast covetousness.

"For there, where each of you, ordinarily, can only perceive and savor an object, a spectacle, a gesture, be it a fruit, a gem, a perfume, a festival, a music, an arrangement of nature, a caress, an idea, the charm of a being, the grace of a soul, and whatever it is, in sum, that is savored or admired, that pleases or rejoices, that is eaten or sniffed, that shines or sings—in sum, whatever it is that confers pleasure, emotion, pride, sensuality or happiness—in the same spectacle, the same object, the same gesture, I can, thanks to my nature, perceive and savor tastes, clarities and graces perpetually nascent, perpetually new, incessantly sweeter, brighter and more subtle, without it being possible to set a limit to that torrential multiplication of treasures and virtues in each object, each spectacle and each gesture.

"Thus, whatever might be the pleasure or the beauty that I take, always new to me, some new beauty denounces itself to be discovered within that beauty, and after that, in the same way, a thousand others, some unexpected delight within that delight, and a thousand others after that. Thus, wherever I go, no matter how far, how excellent, how high, once I have at-

163

tained the limit of a world, the sum of a science, the plenitude of a possession, I see that limit opening up in a thousand new and unsuspected paths, more attractive than all those I have followed to reach what appeared to be the terminus; the sum of the science is no more than the sprig of moss at the foot of the tree of science, each branch of which and each leaf of each branch and each vein of each leaf is a new mystery offered to my curiosity; the plenitude is no more than a threshold before the seductions that shine through the hours to come.

"Have you never heard an individual rich in possessions or adventures say: 'I have done everything; I have seen everything; I am sated.'? What petty appetites such a man must have!

"For me, since I possess the certainty of the unlimited opulence of the world, with the sentiment of my unlimited privileges over that opulence, and the sentiment that after each fortune achieved, there will still remain thousands upon thousands of others yet to grasp and savor, dispensers of felicities always new and keener—whether I steal the fire of lust from lips more beautiful than Cleopatra's, or roam the realms that Orpheus and Dante made, or discover a continent like Columbus, or one of the arcana of heaven like Newton—I could only then declare, in all honesty: 'What is what I have done compared with what I have yet to do? What have I seen compared to what I have yet to see?'

"And it follows that in all places, in all circumstances, I am like a lord of the manor in the home of one of his tenant farmers; while he delights in looking at his flocks and his fields, he increases his pleasure by thinking at the same time of his nearby forests where game abounds, his ponds, his blooming gardens. I am also like a child on the first day of his vacation, when a long period of games and sunshine opens up before him. Every minute of my hours, everywhere and in all circumstances, is similar to the first day of the vacation for the child, similarly engendering in me both the enthusiasm and the delight of the present and the marvelous impatience for recreations to come.

"I shall not enumerate my privileges or my excellences, because it is not possible to state the number and the diversity of the outside and the inside of creation, and because it is that number and that diversity that are my excellences, and on one and the other that my privileges are exercised. However, as much is possible, I want to make you know the materials of my being and the nature of my joy.

"But first, do not omit to suspend from my words any reminiscence of fable or fantasy, for none of the names that will come to your mind in my regard will be appropriate to me. Might they be names like demon, spirit, archangel or certain others, more singular, that one finds in religion and sorcery? Those names, issues of faith, poetry and wonderment, and all the exaltations of sentiment likewise, correspond to ideas or suppositions rather than to facts; no scientist in a laboratory had ever weighed or measured a god, a demon, an angel, or analyzed the least of the elements of their personal substance. Now, everything that constitutes my being, my person and my substance, and the substance of my powers and my possessions, is in the domain of reality, of human reason and positive knowledge, can be held and scrutinized, evidenced by numbers, the balance and the meter.

"Do not expect your memory, either, to find in bibles or in history, figures, feats and ostentations, no matter how vast or prestigious they might be, that offer anything comparable to me. For however prestigious and vast those ostentations, feats and figures might be, I insist that they correspond to me in the measure in which the reflection of a ray of sunlight from a shard of crystal corresponds to light itself."

8

The apparition went on…and here, because I am in haste to come to the narrative of the unusual adventures into which I was drawn, I shall summarize the peroration…

The human appearance of the strange individual permitted him to come and go among us without anyone being able to suspect the secret of his authentic nature. As soon as there was any risk of the mystery being detected, as the chameleon takes on the color of the branch that bear it, this individual melted into the surrounding people or things. Thus, what he would enable me to see were merely metamorphoses that he could accomplish. If I expressed the desire, he could immediately be the tiny creature running through the moss at our feet, the eglantine trembling above my head, a shimmer of light or the buzz of a wasp.

He added that he was going to saturate me with marvels, with positive marvels, all emerging from the brilliant verity of Joy, with which, by virtue of my research alone, I had been able to illuminate my consciousness—marvels, finally, that would bring me the indestructible confirmation of my certainty. And furthermore, when, by the exercise to certain of the admirable privileges that he had—and which I would have myself, thanks to his presence—privileges also emerging from the same verity of Joy, he had definitely dispensed sufficient proofs of that verity, then, for the more excellent profit of my consciousness and the completion of my faith, he would confess his identity to me...

"I am," he said, "an *arcandre*, but that appellation is merely a kind of temporary pseudonym." He also assured me that: "It would not serve any purpose if I told you my real name immediately, for that one, in your present understanding, would not represent anything that it ought to signify. The term *arcandre* has no other reason than to mark a distinction between the enigmatic name that I reserve for myself and the one that all humans apply to me inconsiderately...which is the same name, given that I too am...a man. But the enigma subsists in its entirety. For what sort of man am I, then, who can amuse himself with the games of which you shall be the spectator?"

9

He took me gently by the hand; I had no sensation of passing from one state to another. I perceived perfectly that the man I normally was remained as he was the instant before, sitting with his back to the same tree; and yet, I suddenly sensed that I had also become that tree in its entirety, and all the trees in the vicinity, and also each of the birds hopping and whistling in the foliage of those trees, and also the wind agitating the leaves and slightly stirring the plumage, and also the air, striated and stung by the flight of insects, charged with aromas, and also each of those insects and every swirl of those aromas, and also the ambient light that the verdure, the wings, the antennae and the carapaces scattered, juggled and launched forth in pearls, darts, sparks and reflections as supple as loosened ribbons.

"Would you care to accompany me?" asked the arcandre. "You can designate the being, the place and the game yourself. Would you like, along with me, to be the grass, the bird or the dew? Would you like to leave this forest by vaporizing yourself and traveling space with the wind, or, as light, mingle with the luminous flux and dance on the crest of vibrations with the damsel-flies and golden gnats? Would you like to move lightly in the ground, become for a moment one of the subterranean stones scattered in the strata?" Without letting go of my hand, he added: "But come. As soon as it suits you to change form and domain, as soon as your desire is formulated, you will be what you want to be, here or wherever you want to go."

Instantly, I found myself inside the ground. No hindrance in my new being. I circulated amid the dense, amid the opaque, with as much ease as if I had been on a highway on the surface. But in what manner was I circulating? It seemed to me, as a perfectly simple evidence, that I was, successively, all the substances through which I traveled...

Nevertheless, I conserved sensibility and consciousness, and I was perfectly sure that I was not dreaming. Thus, my human reason was still functioning, even in that extravagant moment. I possessed, intact, in my new state, the same reason that registers, examines, deduces...

I stopped for a moment. My person then presented itself to my reasoning faculty in the aspect of layers of friable humus, dented in places by very ordinary stones, furrowed by ferociously contorted roots. The arcandre was beside me, but the term "beside" only expresses arbitrarily his situation in relation to mine, since he was, like me, momentarily incorporated in that inferior extent of the earth, the same earth on which we had been standing a little while before.

What I observed first of all in my surroundings was, therefore, humus, stones and roots. The latter were occupied in drawing sustenance. To the fluid serosity issuing from their pores, which, in extending, narrowly coated their nodes and meanders with a syrupy swathe, agglutinated the juices and alcohols sweating from the proximal silicates and peat, hydromels with which the earth surrounding their hunger kept an open cellar, profusely, elixirs slowly distilled from the ambient minerals and vegetables by time, moisture and the seasons.

"Would you like to see these roots hunting?" asked the arcandre, unexpectedly.

"Hunting?" I said.

"What else can one call," he said, "their search for pasture through the earth, the gymnastics of their tentacles searching the compact extent avidly, as cephalopods uncoil their voracious thongs in the waters?"

"Indeed, Monsieur," I replied. "Can you give me a sight piercing enough to seize the molecular movement of these roots, although I would be obliged to wait for a long time to see them elongate and run. In my understanding, everything has its own time, and these roots cannot grow before our eyes as colts gallop on the stud-farm, or glass swells up at the end of the blower's pipe..."

"Friend," said the arcandre, familiarly, "my advantages would be poor if, being able to play with matter, traverse it and confound myself with it, I had to be stopped by duration! Time is, for my whim, like a kind of infinitely elastic tissue, with neither front nor back, which I can unwind to infinite length or roll up so tightly that it can be contained entirely within an ant's egg. Thus, I can, as a matter of mere child's play, contract into one or two minutes for you the ten or twelve dozen months that would be necessary for these roots to extend half a meter, and draw my carpet an honest million years backwards, before any one of these little stones, which would resuscitate what had happened around it since the age of the stegosaurus and the triceratops."

"Let's see," I replied.

There was a kind of unctuous click in our conglomerate of humus. Immediately, the roots swelled up, gibbosities were displaced, nodosities flattened out, a thousand vegetal snakes advanced, encountering one another and crossing one another's paths in blind reptations. At the same time, innumerable rootlets emerged from every part of the body of each snake; every filament groped the extent anxiously, inserting itself thereinto and sucking from the peat itself the juices pearling on the walls of the route that it was tunneling. As for the roots, each drawing its swarming fringes, they similarly sought their pittance, but gluttonously, darting their ever-new extremities into the midst of the tellurian magma.

On contact with reefs of chalk or flint barring their path, they reared up, raising their points, and beating the surroundings with a furious and awkward coming-and-going, until the obstacle was avoided. Before the insurmountable they stopped suddenly, as if to reflect, folding back their antennae, inflating their mass, to the point that one thought them ready to explode with indignation, and then, in prudent curves and gentle zig-zags, they went to search the depths beneath them for a feast less rigorously defended.

But what were those gesticulations, singular as they were, by comparison with the hallucinatory melee of other roots, which, having collided on the same route, struggled in order to conquer passage. It seemed that each of them knew that it was responsible to the tree, the lord that loomed up on high, in the world of light...

It seemed...but the impressions I experienced in watching the combatants wrestle and writhe, strangling one another in frenetic duels, transposing themselves....

The arcandre, who was reading within me, doubtless guided that sorcery; I became one of those roots, and the one that was me suddenly acquired the virtue of intelligence and sentiment. Now, I made war among the obscure purveyors of saps. Around me the more agile roots, disdaining the skirmish, slid through the ephemeral gaps, perpetually enlarged or diminished, that were designed in the hand-to-hand conflict; others, slyly twining around the victorious, grew in an instant in their direction, and profiting from their weariness after the battle that the fortunate jousters had fought some distance away, detached themselves at a given moment, overtook them and filled in the path ahead of them.

Entangled in the conflagration, I fought rudely. In my turn, I was responsible to the tree. The branches, the leaves and the fruits delegated me to search in the profound bunkers for the coarse nourishment of the framework and the flesh. They charged themselves with finding, in their world, the subtle aliments of color, sheen and sculpture. An apocalyptic being, simultaneously animal, vegetable and human, I made use of that which was my head, perpetually elongated by continual birth, stiffening it like a pike, piercing the strata, hollowing out the clay, or, becoming elastic, like a trunk, taking gluttonous possession in passage of eggs, animalcules, seeds, or again, like a whip, flagellating and repelling any aggressive enterprises.

Careless of the terrible tourney, my radicles were insatiably active in pumping the liquids that the earth bled incessantly around their piercing. And while I strove doggedly, driving myself slowly into the solid space, in my consciousness that was simultaneously observing my martial furies and my fierce hunt for nourishment, sensed their passion, and at the same time recorded every detail and every vicissitude of the exterminating riot, retaining in that vaporously glittering consciousness the image of the tree...

Now, I was also that gracious and conceited prince, anointed by daylight, adorned with reflections and plumage, upstanding in the palace of the air, at the center of the farandoles of the wind, embalmed by all their perfumes, caressed by all their robes...

I worked tenaciously in the densities on order to be resplendent on high, swaying indolently amid the crowd of the other trees, stretching al my odorous branches proudly. I was the forge and the jewel, the gehenna and the seraph, the soldier rushing to pillage and murder, and the advantageous captain, the black and grunting people of my royalty. I sensed absolutely that unusual duplication. A joyous will to conquer, coming from my arboreal consciousness, made my radical consciousness more ardent.

A fever of delight and strength, a warm burst of laughter, shook the third consciousness, that of the man that I still was, the marvelous holder of those three simultaneous states...

I laughed! And I found myself once again sitting on my bank of moss in the heart of the forest; the arcandre was before me.

He said to me, graciously: "Would it suit you to change realms and society, root that crawled; would you like to be an eagle, a flame, the sun?"

10

I believe that I replied, mechanically: "Thank you..."

I was extremely emotional after the subterranean adventure. I experienced a need to catch my breath for a moment and put a little clarity into a hundred questions that were passing in disorder through my mind. I breathed in a few lungfuls of the gilded air that filed the clearing, voluptuously, as if I were drinking a cordial wine from a nobly sculpted cup.

There was a prodigy that I could not explain in any manner: that of having well and truly passed into the soil, of having become earth, root and tree, consubstantially, if I might put it like that, and without having sensed the slightest corporeal tickle. On the other hand, I feared squandering in interrogations the moments that it had been offered to me to fill with marvelous adventures...

The arcandre's offer to make me the sun, a flame, an eagle—what do I know?—authorized me to suppose that he was now about to produce surprising things compared with which our subterranean voyage would only be, according to my companion's expression, mere child's play...

That decided me to continue the enchantment and postpone the leisure of philosophizing.

Before quitting my bank of moss in order to change into a bird or a star, however, I had a slight twinge of regret at only having been a tree for such a short time. By prolonging the hypostasis I could doubtless have seen and sensed by sap, my bark and got to know the thousand tiny kisses of lichen and ivy...

"And to be the lichen and the ivy," the arcandre put in.

My petty cerebral labor must have been as visible to him, I suppose, as the work of lacemaker weaving her florets and traceries is to us.

"To be the lichen and the ivy," said the arcandre, "and the caterpillar and the beetle in that vagabond ivy; and to witness, as a caterpillar, in singularly propitious conditions of experience, the diversion of seeing yourself become a butterfly; and, as a butterfly, to flutter over nearby corollas; and, as a corolla, to observe something of the ingenious mechanisms by which the plundering insect is obliged to carry away on its wings or feet the pollen that can, no less ingeniously, and to the great profit of their pistils, be unloaded by the corollas of the neighborhood...and—why not?—as the pollen, know...but what's the point of even making lists? Assuredly, you can, since everything that is in the world, for as long as I am with you, offers itself to your whim."

He advanced his hand toward mine.

172

"I think," I observed, "that at the beginning of our association, you proposed to me to resuscitate by means of one of the little stones down there, what was happening around it several million years ago..."

"Did I say millions?" replied the arcandre. "A few billions as well. I'd forgotten the little stone, but it's sufficient for you to express the desire. Come."

11

We found ourselves underground again, in the same place as before. The same stones were studding the soil. I considered one among them in particular.

"That pebble," said the arcandre. "So be it."

And immediately, everything collapsed.

At any rate, there was no longer anything for me, or of me. I was lost. For a time whose duration I could not perceive, my self was completely obliterated. There was not even a void or darkness, for I would have been able to sense a void or darkness, but a condition devoid of character and devoid of extent, which only the word "nothing" can express...

From that nothing awoke, still numb, the notion that I had begun once again to exist, if perceiving oneself confusedly in the absence of any kind of form or place can be called "existence."

To describe that moment as appropriately as possible, I was I-know-not-what, having the impression of being I-know-not-where...

Arcandre! How difficult, among all the extraordinary excursions that I owe to you, this one is to narrate!

Scarcely had the notion formed that the I-know-not-what had begun to "exist" again, I-know-not-where, than I experienced what must have been that nowhere suddenly cracking, and that it was me that had begun to dilate, to grow, without encountering anything that braked the dilation. I grew, I unfolded, beyond all discernible measure, and, still growing and unfolding, I began to rotate immeasurably, my incessantly vaster extent, my incessantly increasing quantity...

I sought in vain for a comparison. I cannot imagine what could have given me the idea of that phenomenon of immense rotation and that unlimited expansion, save for naming the phenomenon itself...which would be an unfortunate anticipation of the stages of the event, it being sufficiently incredible for it to be necessary to take the relation of it slowly...

I interrupted myself as I was still merely rotating and dilating continuously, having not the slightest consciousness of what my new state of being represented. To the double and coincident sensation that I experienced then, no vertigo was added, because of a singular mildness and almost voluptuous sway... Would it be possible for those who are not physically familiar with a certain kind of hyperestheia that the Brahmins of India regard as an ecstatic state, and to which they attribute a divine character under the name of Yoga, to imagine the order of that sway, that kind of vaporous oscillation in an indefinite space...?

I was, therefore, for the moment, that strange swaying, that rotation and that immeasurable unfolding, which were, as I say, accomplished in an extent that, for my precarious perceptions, could only correspond to the notion of "nowhere." Were not those three sensations enough? Now, at the same time and as if interior to what I was already experiencing, a sudden and amazing reversal occurred: somewhere in that immense, still rotating me, a part of me contracted, shrank, while it too was spinning, running, dancing and still shrinking, incessantly diminishing, until it seemed to me that it had attained the supreme smallness at which it could still be something, the final dimension after which the something would have had to become immaterial, dissolving into infinity...

When that other me had reached that infinitesimal, then my consciousness was triggered, and I could see.

I was a particle of a gigantic tangle of light, and that very tangle, the total extent of which was rotating on its axis and also describing incommensurable ellipses in a black and icy ether. Simultaneously an atom and the whole of the most enormous blaze, I was in addition that which could gaze at the conflagration, containing its measure and sustaining its glare.

I say that I contained its measure...I mean that a consciousness of mine, situated outside the immense rutilance, embraced the whole of it, but that was without being able to relate any of the proportions of the phenomenon to anything that had be terrestrially knowable, or even imaginable, previously. No idea formed in my terrified mind of grandeur, of the possibility of calculating some dimension in accordance with anything I had been able to conceive of the most spacious and the most enormous in my ordinary life. I observed that my gaze embraced the totality of that incomparable flamboyance, and that is all that I can say.

As for the flamboyance itself, its glare...what words are available to me that would not be utterly exhausted as soon as I attempted to describe it?

I saw a kind of spasmodic chaos of incandescence, a block of clouds of fire perpetually changing shape, extent and density. Tresses, bristles and manes of flame elongated in every direction, and their furious flux, on encountering the cold of space, volatilized, or fell back as ardent rains. At the points where those rains fell, ephemeral whirlpools formed, darkening with brown pools the resplendence of the mass; but those whirlpools immediately fell back, dislocated and devoured by the perpetual convulsions of the whole. Here, blisters as vast as suns burst in a spray of adamantine geysers and left in their place crevasses so profound that they seemed to traverse the entire thickness of the formidable furnace. That which was central, immensely flooding away, became peripheral. Seas of gold and emerald shrank and rose up as mountains. Capes and gulfs melted in a tidal wave of fulgurance. Brewed into enormous squalls, it seemed that the light was bounding, boiling, unfurling...

And before my mind, gradually, the irrevocable and insane certainty asserted itself that I had been, thanks to the arcandre, transported to the primordial fire: that it had been

175

sufficient for me to observe for an instant the most banal of pebbles in the subsoil of a forest, to go back through the history of that crumb of flint, for it have resuscitated the adventure of the earth itself...

That light was the light of a fire that had just been born in the surf of stellar dust...in the silent fields of time its particles has assembled. From their duels and their alliances, the shock of their gyrations, the innumerable labor of electricities, fire, the first visible face of forces, had surged...

That light was the light of the primal fire, the robe of the period when fire and cold had kneaded the atoms and condensed the fluids of the billows of their blind embraces, engendering the vapors of mercury and iron and solidifying the gases into the pure metals, which oxidized and diversified relentlessly in deluges of new vapors, re-engendering cosmic maelstroms without pause. Like as many cries, clamored by as many myriads of beings, every combination, every fusion of molecules, every elementary substance, all the alchemies of the furnace, darted forth their flames, and that light was the host of all those colors and all those flames, the hymn of those cries, the hosanna of the primal birth of a universe.

That which would one day be a world, in aggregating, would retain those flames buried in the flint of its mines. Time would crystallize their virgin refractions, matrices of sapphires, rubies and opals, and those stones would always testify, beyond the metamorphoses of all substances, to that hosanna of the primal fire...

And me, I was one of the particles of that light, and that light in its entirety, and the conscious spectator of such a splendor! Intoxicated and unlimited, juggled in that tide of fire, juggling, s light, with that tempest of stones, I felt myself streaming, flamboyant, resplendent, in a demiurgical orgy of radiance, color and space...

And yet, in the fullness of the enchantment, what was it, I thought, that enchantment, that left me conscious of being still the same, master, if it pleased me, of recovering my bank of moss at the foot of the tree...and better yet, of still being on that bank of moss, while I was rolling in fire in infinity?

12

So, I delighted in that cosmic celebration and intoxicated myself ineffably in its light. But in the end, and in truth, what was that resurrection of the commencement of a world, of our world, but that of the little stone, of our world, in its physical mode, in the concrete play of its forces, and in dimensions so formidable that I had to ask myself what place remained for the real earth, the one on which I found myself before the adventure, the one in which the arcandre had come to surprise me—in sum, the one that circled in its orbit in our old solar system? And how could the latter, differentiated into planets, coexist with its own nebular commencement?

I affirm, in spite of my emotion and voluptuousness in contemplation and knowledge being exalted to paroxysm, that I sensed in myself a perfect state of intelligence, in possession of all my positive resources of reason, and rigorously awake.

"Arcandre!" I cried. "Friend, what power is yours and what name is given to it that no book records, since what I see here, which surpasses in brilliance the marvelous spectacles painted by the poets and the most inspired mystics, is not the supernatural of a Saint John or that of a Dante, but the world itself, such as it must have appeared in the remotest times. There is nothing supernatural here but my presence...my presence in what must be millions of centuries ago, and which has, from age to age and hour to hour, been transformed to the point that I know it in my ordinary life. What power is yours that abolishes for me extent, duration and my own substance, and causes the world to revert to its age of fire?

"However, at this moment, and in this same world, where no life palpitates as yet, where no form will be sketched for thousands of millennia, beings are coming and going on earth, living their customary existence. History has been. From the men of the caverns to my contemporaries, my planet has

177

lived. Charlemagne... Attila... Galileo... Robespierre... What have you done with real time?"

He said to me: "Would you like, at this instant, to be that Attila, that Robespierre, with their living epoch around you? Would you like to follow the Huns, to go on horseback to attack the Gauls? Would you like to mingle with the crowd that read Marat's newspaper on the street-corner one day?"

My human consciousness saw the arcandre confounded with me in the immense Sabbat of flames

"But are you sated with the cosmos?" he continued. "It's a beautiful diversion, however...again, very easy to obtain. Would you like to see the first rocks spring up in the first seas, the first plants being born in the new land, the first animal, still half-plant, crawling, bewildered to have broken its stem?"

Whereupon I cried out: "Yes, I want to! Whatever you can take me to see and live, no drama of human history can equal the great mystery of origins!"

I seemed to perceive the arcandre laughing ironically.

Then I said: "Yes, I want to see and live those times which were only filled with the terrible duels of elements, in the opaque silence of a world without consciousness. What is there now that can astonish me, under your aegis? You offer me the supreme impossible, which seems to deny itself in expressing itself, knowing and sensing what it was when nothing existed of that which can be known and sensed! Yes, I want to be that gaze, that ear and that passion of time before life and before sight. Go. Order. Realize."

13

Another face appeared of the astral work of time. It was the earth in the age of the universal waters. I saw, from I don't know what point in the ether, the entire sphere rotating on its axis, while tracing its giant ellipses through space. The planet, glaucous, like a globe of jade, on the hemisphere it offered to the sun, reverberated the light of the major star with a dazzling violence.

Now, as I thought of approaching it, in order to contemplate at closer range the polished gleam due to its distance, what monstrous effervescences, what vertiginous eruptions were accomplished on its surface! Suddenly, I saw a thin white circle rising up around it, like a halo of nacre, from which the sunlight was refracted. Soon, that circle enlarged, thickened, and was soon a great ring the color of iron, soon denser and broader, a kind of shell enclosing all the sumptuous scintillations of jade and nacre like a mantle of heavy gray velvet thrown over a lily-white shoulder. The orb's prison was still becoming denser, the color of lead. In vain the generous waves of sunlight rolled over it. No refraction, no more light...it seemed that the planet was hooded with scarves of shadow. And gradually, like scarves, in effect, lifted and whipped by the wind of the course of the star's rotation, mists deployed around the earth, extending, hirsute and compact, climbing the field of sunlight, staining the golden extent with immense rivers of soot.

Curiosity gripped me, and transported me, at the same moment that it lit up, beneath the carapace of mists. Then, I rolled with the turbulence of the seething expanses. The young oceans, bitten by the solar effluvia, exhaled themselves in vapors, and the liquid universe was enveloped by a cocoon of cloud.

Above the tumultuous waters ran hordes of clouds, swollen with deluges. Many waves bounded through the fumes of the sky, and their crests, like battering rams, cut into the black caravans. Enormous flakes were detaches, falling into the waves, their swellings trailing momentarily, as if stupid, limp at the level of the angry waves, which took possession of them, disemboweled them, and ripped them into errant wisps, quickly engulfed in the voracious hollows of the surf. Sky and waves mingled in a seething sweat-bath fog, blue-tinted at intervals by the angular fire of lightning-bolts. Outside of those flashes of electric color, the light of the world was almost black, striped with bands of earthy red and living green.

The distant splendor of the sun arrived here thus, diffused by mists saturated by sulfur.

A frightful despair emanated from those sordid gleams. The lugubriousness that the painters of Hell have tried to depict in the most tormented of Malebolges, I saw there, intensified by the frightful grandeur of things. But I had no terror of it, and I contemplated that grim chaos of water and darkness, of which I was not the prisoner but the prodigious guest, with a bitter exaltation.

Meanwhile, as if to test my fantastic liberty, I said: "Would you care, Arcandre, to accelerate the ages here, in order that I can see, delivered from the matrix of the clouds, the beautiful terrestrial jewel shining once again in the sunlight."

Then, in the depths of the sky, a trenchant luminosity was designed within the funereal ensemble, a sort of vast lake of fleecy cloud, pale at first and then yellow-tinted, which the light enlivened, attained the brilliance of brass. Uncertain reflections undulated in the ambient blackness; pathways of gilded light lit up, and lengthened, tremulously, through the mourning of the cloud-mass. Tufts of pink vapor ran lightly over the new clarities. The darkness thinned out. An imminent light quivered behind it, like youth shining through the crepes of young windows. The atmosphere was opalized. Ringlets of coral rimmed the ridges of the clouds nearest to the celestial lake, incessantly growing vaster and more brilliant. The oceans, previously inky, in which all the adventures of the sky were mirrored, rolled waves of topaz and crimson through the smoke.

Suddenly, the course of the clouds opened up; the contours of the lake blurred, naked light entered through the fissure in the mists. An immense sheaf of vapors flowed toward the sun, as if aspired by an irresistible appeal of space. It received the first contact of the light. It was invested with it, all the way to its ultimate atoms. Each of its innumerable droplets sparkled with seven fires. Around it, the air was iridescent and the waves were constellated. Then the glory of the day imposed itself. The diaphanous clouds glided as if nonchalant amid the ardent azure, and the marine vapors rose up in silvery tufts from the calm waters. The profound blue of the sky gave the waves the grave color of amethyst.

But scarcely had I savored that sumptuous serenity...

14

It seemed to me that anguish passed through the air, in the mild solemnity of the light, over the surface of the oceans. Broad frissons creased the liquid extents. The beautiful violet waves were covered in places by foam, spread like white surplices over archbishops' aventails...

What genesis was being accomplished in the depths? Whirlpools hollowed out, stirring up the gracious ascent of vapors, curving their fine evolutions, attracting them and tearing apart their spirals. The waves rose up, bounding and swelling, setting off in a galloping cavalcade of blisters, incessantly growing larger and more furious. Suddenly, the waters burst under the pressure of lava-flows. The parturition of worlds twisted the surface of the oceans. Blocks of fuming rocks springing from submarine craters perforated space, shaking it with hoarse whining, peppering the skies momentarily with a heavy flocks of fantastic black birds, with white wings of vapor escaping from them, which battered the reflux of the wind and fell back into the waves with innumerable explosive splashes.

Dense fogs rose up from abyssal evolutions. They accumulated and thickened, stifling the light again. Like a creature attacked from all sides, striking out desperately with all its limbs to defend itself, the air was flagellated everywhere by new eruptions, unleashing squalls that rolled in all directions through the vapors, entangling them, confounding them with one another and whirling in a hectic saraband. At the hazard of those crazed currents, mists, lifted up from below, flew away, detached from the waters. Then the ocean reappeared through those ephemeral ventilation-shafts. Here and there, russet masses extended, motionless, in exasperated unfurlings. The waves, as if insurgent, rushed against their invariable contours. The primary substances of continents, immense, were like the backs of monstrous beasts within the swell, grazing the bottom of the sea.

While the fumes licked them, clinging to their peaks, scattering on their jagged ridges, losing themselves in the darkness of their fissures, the spasms of the crust must have died down on the sea-bed. Calm was inserted into the rhythm of the surface. The great cavalcade of the waves relaxed. Streaks of light infiltrated the fog, less compact, needles of sunlight sewing the pearls of the prism to the hemp of smoke. The waves, black, dappled with golden patches at points where the light pierced the mists and attained the placed ripples, coiled around the contours of the reefs. As the eddies died down, the lowering of the level revealed the gigantic extent of the red rocks. Then, it seemed that they rose up, and that the pulsation of the ocean was giving rise to the elevation of the land; for the majestic swaying of the waters in the fogs, still rising, was cadenced like breathing; ultimately from each palpitation of that species of immense respiration, incessantly vaster, more terrible and more grandiose, the mineral stays of the world emerged.

At that moment, a new prodigy intervened in the succession of prodigies of that entire resurrection of commencements: vast and tragic, as if modeled on the very effort of matter, a musical theme burst forth! Or rather, it seemed to well up from the feats of the genesis, inflating and palpitating through the atmosphere and unrolling, prolonging in sounds in space the lines and episodes of the sea. And in that theme, from which I could believe that he had taken the very elements of his organs, his bows and his harps, I recognized one of the treasures of my memory, the prelude of Richard Wagner's *Das Rheingold.*

15

Once, in normal times, whenever I heard that prelude, I had always been gripped, half-idea and half-image, by a confused impression of genesis; and, as concretely as a similar impression could be translated, I sensed in the kind of hypnosis into which all great music plunges the fervent listener, the slow rise of those great chords heavy with mystery and menace was loosed before my sensibility like an ascensional movement of great nebular waves.

Those waves affirmed for me the image of those that emerged from some crypts of the original darkness, fog and fluid and forces, prior to Number and Form, before and through the initial space, carrying in their orbs all the fatality of the future universe...

Once, in normal times, in the gray light of dreams, those phantasms had rolled before me, growing and swaying as the theme of the *Ring* was amplified. An obscure certainty, come from I don't know what seemingly fraternal affirmation of my instinct, imposed the authenticity of that cosmic image on my consciousness, numbed by the pathetic voluptuousness of sound...

Certainly, many commentators on the Wagnerian work, and many pious listeners to the tetralogy must have discerned or felt the esotericism of the Prelude, as I did then, and I make no claim at all as to the exclusivity of my sensation, but that does not matter. Here, I was alone in being occupied with the prodigy of that extravagant upheaval, in which it that moment, it was no longer the music that was provoking the hallucination of genesis, but genesis itself that was causing the hallucination of music to surge forth.

Was it truly a hallucination? In evoking that sudden assumption of sound, it is easy for me to say that it was certainly not from things that the song was emanating but from me, from my emotion, and that, at the time, I transferred to things, by virtue of a kind of mirage, that singular musical explosion of my overexcited sensibility. Exalted without respite in the course of the epic of fire, of waves, of mists, of rocks, my emotion must gradually have attained a point of extreme intensity. The heart and gaze of that epic, I had, while reopening the archives of creation for myself, burned, shone, undulated and unfurled. A living arena of primordial activities, their consciousness and their passion, I had just felt myself, by turns, bound with the wind in the vapors, had been the irruption of light triumphant over mists, and, as those mists, the voice of light. When the rocks rose from the waters and the fogs, I was, as it were, immersed in the triple parental rhythm of the new face of the world...

It was at that moment that the prodigy was accomplished. In the same way that energy can be transformed from heat into light, my exaltation was sublimated and suddenly passed into a state that only music could express. My entire being became song. And from my memory rose the theme that adapted itself imperiously to the immense spectacle and the immense sensation.

Now, so many dear and noble recreations of my soul were linked to that music in my memory. I owed so many profound flames to the tetralogy that, in spite of the physical enchantment, my vertigo of contemplation, and my infinite curiosity regarding the next scene in the planetary tragedy, a certain familiar image was ignited within me and began to shine in the most intimate depths of my heart. Its light expanded, gently, but with an irresistible movement, throughout my being, overflowing me, it seemed, growing, its colors and contours affirming, interposing itself between the new creation and my disconcerted gaze. And while a supremely unexpected décor condensed around me, becoming more and more precise, the rocks, the mists and the oceans blurred, dissolving into vaporous silhouettes, soon indistinct and soon effaced under new forms. Thus in a screen, by virtue of the artifice of a magic lantern operator, two images are momentarily superimposed, and the older one is discolored and disappears, as if diluted, beneath the new arrival...

The rocks, oceans and mists vanished, or were reabsorbed, into the four walls of a small drawing room. There, I found myself in an old armchair, simulation Louis XV, in wood stripped of its gilt by age—and that small drawing room belonged to my father and mother. My brother, sitting at the piano, was just finishing playing the Prelude to *Das Rheingold*, and soon the clear voices of the Daughters of the Rhine resonated blithely through the little room...

16

My three dearest friends, habitual companions of our quiet family celebrations, were sprawled in armchairs similar to mine, listening. My mother, seated next to my brother, her attentive and grave gaze going from the score to the face of the beloved musician, was turning the pages. My brother was singing and playing. His voice frolicked in the music as a slender jet of sparkling water rises and dances among the flowers of a garden in August. And my brother's soul was, at that moment, similar to his song, joyous and radiant and in full bloom, because the people who were in that drawing room meant more to the singer than the most numerous or most ostentatious audience, and because, equally charmed and tremulous, the sensibility of the listeners and that of the musician were united in the same holy enthusiasm.

Oh, how delectable still, today, in my memory, those hours in that small drawing room are, as warm and sweet as bites of ripe fruits, balsamic and spacious too, like excursions to bright mountains...those penetrating hours in which my brother, with his robust and tender fingers, and his simultaneously skillful and passionate voice, delivered to us, quivering, the spirit, the blood and the flesh of works by Wagner, Beethoven and César Franck...

And it was into the décor of one of those precious evenings that the arcandre threw me. And everything there appeared as was customary, my father, stretched out on the sofa near the white fireplace, somnolent and weary, as usual, after the day's bleak and bitter labor. He alone seemed estranged from the noble emotion painted on the fraternal audience. The countless wrinkles of his bony face were like the visible grillage of his soul, infinitely imprisoned by material cares.

All day long he went from shop to shop, the establishments of his clients, petty tailors to whom he praised the fabrics he sold on behalf of manufacturers in the Nord or Alsace. He was a humble broker, such as one sees in thousands or hundreds of thousands, clever in earning money, shrewd in spending it. His mind scarcely had the leisure to aim beyond the dull and despotic adventures that the placement of his fabrics renewed for him every day. His samples, his clients, their demands or their delayed payments, the problems by which one and the other were incessantly afflicted, the settlements due at the end of the month, the domestic expenses, implacably took over all his activity and all his reflection. Only a miserly psychic territory remained to him.

My father obtained his happiness from very simple things: an advantageous business deal; the marks of esteem of the weavers for whom he worked; the compliments that people might pay him regarding his sons…and he rejoiced with all his heart in the fact that my mother still retained something of her youth and character, and—thank God!—was able, thanks to him, still to be unaware of the rude labor that that is finding money for rent, for clothing, for food, and for light. In any case, good quality food, two seats for the comedy in vogue on Saturday evening, a lunch in the country in summer, Sunday with his wife and children, fulfilled all his needs for diversion and pleasure.

One of his greatest sources of pride was the affectionate consideration that the majority of his old clients showed him. They judged him cunning in commercial complexities, often asking his advice, and they liked him because, in the forty or forty-five years that he had been "running the beat" his thin and lively silhouette had become familiar to them. They called him, simply, "Monsieur Bernard."

"Oh, Monsieur Bernard," they said, on seeing him, "what are you going to stick us with today?" They meant by that verb that my father would once again have sufficient persuasion and artifice to make them buy a bolt or half a bolt of cloth, in spite of their stock being full and business being slow...

"No, no, Monsieur Bernard, we don't need anything at present!" cried the tailors' wives from the back of the shop, precipitately. Tailors' wives are terrible; if one listened to them, one would never need to buy any cloth. However, people wear clothes, and from time to time they need new clothes! The tailors bought, notwithstanding the aggressiveness or jeremiads of their wives, but my poor father had to use a hundred times more cunning and eloquence when they were there than was necessary when the tailors were alone in their shops, or bachelors.

Every day he carted around his thick wads of samples, enveloped in paper, crudely bound with string. Once—before, as a humble Lear, he was obliged to butcher himself to aid his children—when he was a proprietor, buying and selling on his own account, he had carried his little rectangles of cheviot or frieze in a large leather case that gave him the appearance of an advocate with a portfolio bulging with briefs. When the case was worn out, times becoming harder and harder, it had not been replaced, and parceling in paper was considered adequate. So, with his wretched package under his arm, my father, short and stiff, fragile in appearance but nevertheless animated by a continuous energy and a steely vitality, trotted around Paris from morning to evening, in all temperatures and the worst kinds of weather, trying with an unfailing tenacity to extract from his fragments of cloth, in addition to his own substance and my mother's, the resources that would permit my brother and me to spend our primary adolescence free of the black coercions of earning a crust, giving us license to discover and climb the miraculous routes that lead the artist to the emotion and intelligence of Beauty...

As tragic in his way as the ananké of some illustrious drama was the unmerited fatality that fell upon that laborious and modest man on the day when my brother and I were seized by the gusts of that emotion. As a student, I dabbled in poetry; at the same time, my brother was studying music in order to become a teacher. In my poetry, and the compositions that he sketched insouciantly, our parents and the petit bourgeois milieu in which we lived saw nothing but puerile prettiness, drawing room amusements, qualities in the same category as elegance in square-dancing or an aptitude for charades. But profound forces of instinct were doubtless quivering behind those amiable talents, since contact with a few artists of our own age, the warmth of a few excursions to museums with them, and a few enthusiasms in their cenacles, caused an irresistible light suddenly to dazzle us, a spell to intoxicate us, which, awakening us to our destiny, made of our games a devoted and sacred passion, and raised within us the inexorable and marvelous determination to be, or to attempt to be, creators.

And at a stroke, at the same moment, the same light caused all the shadows to appear to us of our house and our milieu, of all that we had been taught to esteem and respect, and business, and the conquest of money, and the effort that is good and beautiful in proportion to the price that is paid for it…a breath of wind struck us that revealed the atmosphere in which we had lived as the most paltry and stifling of prisons.

And then commenced a time when, wolf-cubs running toward the ideal and biting all the branches of the vast forest of human genius, we lacerated with our pointed teeth the toils of our bourgeois upbringing, its prejudices and its rituals, and bounded through the humble laws that regulate petty cloth salesmen. And everything that gradually became, so far as we were concerned, good and fine, adorable and true, worthy of enterprise and worthy of veneration, all the charms of art, all the rejoicings of the soul, all the feasts of sensibility and intelligence, our new feats, labors and goals, became increasingly distant from what my father was able to understand and enjoy...

And as we were too young—too frenetic, in truth—to double ourselves, and to be able to translate our gods for him, and to be able to retain the sarcasms that we often uttered in the course of collisions between the immense problems that burned our marrow and his anecdotes about tailors...and as my mother followed us, amazed, and radiant in the sunlight that we cast untiringly into her wan destiny, my father was left alone, without a wife and without children, with whom to mourn his monotonous pains, with whom to share his excessively mediocre joys...

And he, because he loved us, as the patriarchs must have loved in the Biblical times of Reuben and Levi, because, after all, we were of his tribe, because we were his sons, although born a second time of all the fathers of the soul, who shine from Moses to Plato and from Leonard to Beethoven, he wanted to sustain us, being unable to bear the thought that we might suffer the base poverty of debuts, which might perhaps have corroded our impetus...the impetus that signified nothing to him, because it did not emerge from money...

Money...

As the wave is to the fish the universe entire and fatality entire, so, by the force of circumstance, money was to my father the basis of life and the essential element of all happiness, the ultimate goal of all effort and the proof of all merit. "Earning a living" and paying for life in order that one should remain capable of earning, always and incessantly, and to spend one's entire life earning, in truth, and doing that, passing, curbed by the iron halter, through the perfumes, songs and laughter of the world, and its harmonious forms and subtle hatching of passions, and the nacreous glide of dreams...

Money: my father, pledged to the gehenna of money, knowing the damnation of extracting it every day from circumstance, gave, for those unproductive ideals and those inaccessible joys, his money, which was the fire of his body and his muscles, and his innumerable paces, and his late nights, and his white hair, and his multiple wrinkles: that money, every coin of which ought, in his eyes, to merit a joy and a tenderness, and in return for which he received nothing...nothing that he could welcome...

Father, in helping us to be free and to breathe deeply, you were the bearer of a flag that you could not see, fluttering in the ardent waves of a wind that you could not feel; and you did not even know what its colors were, nor of what fabric the flag was woven...and yet, you fought for it, doggedly, until your last breath. Father, you were the martyr and the cup-bearer of an idol of which you never knew the name or meaning, and never contemplated the face, and served it nevertheless until the moment that you died before its altar.

In realizing ourselves in accordance with the hungers of our instinct, my brother and I, unconsciously, Father, allowed ourselves to dry up the blood in your veins, to dry up, without being able to staunch it, the sweat of your brow, and to exhaust the pulses of your heart; and we stripped you of all your simple pleasures, without putting anything in their place that could satisfy you...

Be vainly praised. Father, and be vainly blessed for the blood of your veins that flowed for us until it dried up, for the sweat of your brow that we were unable to wipe away, for all the pulses of your blind, magnificent and perpetually constrained heart...

17

And so, conducted by a sweet musical memory, I found myself in my parents' little drawing room, and my eyes, still full of miracles, posed feverishly on the objects and the people. And I was about to interrupt that dear concert, to proclaim to my friends the unparalleled spectacles from which I had arrived, paying no heed to all to what that implausible substance might make of the reality of that décor and those individuals...

From what crystallizations of time had the appeal of my memory drawn them? I saw them before me, the individuals living and the ambience identical, in spite of the fact that I knew that ambience to be dispersed now and the moment of the concert and the assembly disappeared forever into the past.

I did not think about that at all. My heart bounded, uniquely, with the marvelous tale that I was about to tell, and I had already opened my mouth.

At that moment, my gaze, which was still wandering, passed over the mirror that hung over the white fireplace. Then the glass sent back my reflection, and, although my hands remained clenched, I was sure, upon the armchair, my reflection raised an arm, put a finger to its lips, and, slowly emerging from the mirror, came toward me, as if gliding through the air. And it said to me, in the now-familiar voice of the arcandre, and in the most natural tone: "Have I not chosen well, and the most beloved among the images that the Theme awoke in you?"

In my amazement, I nevertheless retained the wit to ask, stammering slightly: "Then this…is an image?"

But the arcandre went on "If you would have preferred Bayreuth, there would have been no more difficulty, either in bringing Bayreuth to you or in taking you there. You would have found yourself instantly in a seat in the theater stalls, at the moment when the orchestra finished the prelude, and soon, for you, the curtain would have gone up on the concoction of muslin, gold paper and green light whose combined prestige opens to the spectator the fabulous haven of the Rheingold."

Although my father, my mother, my friends and the singer were real, it seemed evident that I was alone in being able to hear the arcandre, for no gesture of those surrounding me revealed that they were aware of our conversation, or anything abnormal.

"Friend," I asked the arcandre, "where are we, at present?"

He smiled and replied: "In your parents' drawing room, of course. Don't you recognize its slightest details?"

"But what is the year and the day of this gathering?" I persisted.

"Well," said my magical companion, "interrogate your memory. It's one of your evenings some years ago, if you relate it to the day on which I came to surprise you by the tree...which is to say, the day that since this morning and until now you have naturally called today. But the evening of the concert is really and truly today, for you, if you have retreated in time to the minute of its occurrence..."

He was still smiling. "Furthermore," he added, "I can similarly assure you that you are presently, simultaneously, at the foot of your tree, in the forest, and in this drawing room, just as, at the same time, today is the day of the evening of the concert, and the day that, since this morning and until now, you have naturally named 'today.'"

My reason was beginning to overheat.

"And them?" I said.

"They are in their present: that of the minute in which you see them. The question does not arise for them. It is you who have been transported to them in retreating, as I said, through time, to this moment in which you could encounter them as they are here; or else, while remaining immobile in your normal today, you have turned back time until what extends before you, provoked by your emotion, is this moment, containing all that you ought to see within it.

Like a pile of leaves abruptly dispersed by a gust of wind, it seemed to me that my intelligence suddenly began to flutter in dilemmas, ludicrous hypotheses and irreconcilable suggestions.

As one runs after scattered leaves, I caught up with a few scraps of reason.

"So much ease! In short, it's too many enigmas! The effort of comprehension is squeezing me hard...even more than seeing your finest enchantment! Let's put a little order into it first. And then clarity! First, how would you have brought me the theater of Bayreuth? In the fashion in which a genie in some tale in the Thousand-and-One Nights removes and dis-

192

places in space a palace, not to mention an entire city and its inhabitants? How would you have taken me to that theater, at the very moment of my desire? By taking me on your wings the like devil of old legends? But what are these simple translations of my body or a theater for you, who have taken me to the realm of the roots to live through...their future?

"Well, yes, what are these voyages, in sum, of beings and things that exist...compared with free excursions into vanished minutes, or phenomena that have not yet been born? And that faculty you confer upon me of maneuvering time at my whim? Time...which is pure abstraction...which only exists, in the final analysis, in the conceptual realm...time which is only...metaphysically...a notion obtained by the mind in considering the evolution of things, their changes, their disappearances...an entirely subjective convention that ingeniously permits events and the states of substance to be enumerated...

"But no! Now, time, in listening to you, has become, like earth or water, a kind of element in which I can stroll at whim, without even needing, like some famous character of the novelist Wells, a time machine, or is, instead, a kind of docile monster, charged with containing its centuries like an elephant is some court of Asia, clad in brocade and pearls...and which, if I lift a finger, will walk backwards or forwards, or lie down without budging at my feet, until I give it the signal to start moving again!"

I was still running after a few flying scraps of lucidity.

"And even if you were to reveal to me the mechanisms of this frightful mobility of things and minutes in regard to me, and those of my own mobility in regard to them, it would still, if the guests of this little drawing room are, as they are, in their present, and if it is me who has retreated to the moment when he concert occurred...it would still remain to be explained how that exact moment, that ambience, those individuals, their gestures, could be conserved intact. In what space, in what location, in what fashion, does that conservation take place...?"

I fell silent momentarily because I was choking and because I hoped for a response from the arcandre. He was listening to me nonchalantly. My reason exasperated itself in the impossibilities that it was accumulating.

I went on, with a kind of hostility: "Where is that assembly conserved intact? Where are the minutes conserved of the times of Attila, Galileo and Robespierre, which you offered to revive for me a little while ago? In what antechambers of the real are the millennia retained of the terrestrial genesis from which we have come?"

A baroque image crossed my mind.

"If I can provoke at will, in the past as in the future, any moment of time, and better still, any of the circumstances, absolutely innumerable, that are produced throughout the universe in a single moment of time, whether it is a matter of one of these petty Wagnerian concerts of my adolescence, or the growth of roots, the first ages of creation, the theater of Bayreuth, or a street in Paris under Robespierre, it therefore follows necessarily..."

My imagination resumed its gallop.

"In truth, it makes one think that, just as in a dark room into which a ray of sunlight filters, the luminous line, as it moves, illuminates the particles of dust and returns to shadow those that it caused to scintillate a moment before...so...under the projection and displacement of my emotion or my desire, events, individuals and things are illuminated and extinguished..."

I stopped, vaguely fearful, instinctively glimpsing where the logic of my comparison was going to take me. But I went on.

"If it is the projection of desire that causes events, individuals and things to appear, as the beam of light striking them causes the particles of dust to light up...in the same way that those in the shadow of the atmosphere are present but invisible until the moment that the fiery streak reveals...it therefore follows necessarily that things and individuals, and all the events of time and space, although invisible, are present—in

194

what zone and what shadow?—ready to surge forth at my appeal?"

The arcandre did not blink. Resolutely, I argued:

"Thus can be conceived—without being any better explained—my presence in all sorts of places and ages at the same time. I would be, in some sense, at the center of a kind of total universal coexistence. Distance, duration, rigid laws of nature and substance would be as many scales over the eyes of those poor people who do not have the good fortune to possess the amity of an arcandre. Things might be dissolved in the past or not yet be, events might have occurred, effaced, but those events, those things, would nevertheless exist integrally for me. I could dart upon them, in every direction, at any velocity that my fantasy might dictate, the ray of my desire, or merely my curiosity. I could illuminate things in any of their states, in those yet as easily as in the reverse direction, if I might put it like that...

"I can see the cake baked while the pastry-cook is kneading the dough, and before the constructed house I can see the day when its bricks were clay, and its beams and floor-tiles leafy trees. All simply because the baked cake coexists with its flour still in powder form and the tree with the beam that it has become. Because all the states elapsed or to come of the cake or the house coexist around the flour and the visible edifice...in another reality absolutely indifferent to normal evolution and necessarily successive...

"An embryo become a child, that child having become a man, and that man having grown old, coexist in each of their own developments...the child having become an old man lurks, as a child, in the shadow of his own decrepitude, ready to appear in his concrete infant form, if I invite him to!"

"That's exactly right," said the arcandre, tranquilly. He endorsed the crazy hypothesis!

"In consequence, the nebula to which you took me once coexisted with the earth in the liquid state that we haunted subsequently, and that liquid earth with the earth that I believe myself able to call contemporary...and those three states coexist with all the states, and the successive aspects, and the events and forms of all the other ages, and all the minutes of that same and unique earth."

It appeared to me that he nodded his head. And I burst forth: "Well then, name it! Name that fantastic shadow in which, in an immutable present, the gigantic totality of the past the present and the future of the universe coexist!"

I had run out of breath and disorderly reasoning. I fell silent at last.

"The candles on the piano are ready to go out," said the arcandre. "The first scene of the *Rheingold* only has a few measures to go. Your friends are about to take their leave of your parents. You will not have savored anything of that concert. And then, what a rage of ratiocination!"

He went on, with forbearance: "Admit that the moment and the place are not made for such debate. What do you want from me? That I explain the nature and the functioning of that authentic coexistence? But that is far from summarizing, in itself, as you seem to think, all the enigmas posed by the privilege of instantaneously provoking the one that you wish to savor and to live, of identifying yourself with it completely. Even if that coexistence were out of the way, the marvelous elasticity of time to your caprice would remain, the plasticity of things to your appeal, that of your body toward things...and within them...

"All those singular properties of extension and consubstantiation are independent. Each has a different mechanism. It would be necessary for me to analyze all those mechanisms for you. That is a great many explanations in prospect, many mechanisms to take apart...."

I sensed an ungraspable irony in his words.

He paused thoughtfully. Then, in a charming voice, he said: "Trust me, my friend. Let me guide you."

His voice became even more enveloping: "As rockets assembled on a framework suddenly burst forth in a firework display, designing golden limbs in sparkling lines and some beautiful subject of the celebration in flame, all my phantas-

196

magorias, will illuminate a certain word, which will suddenly be their key, their sum and their capital light. Trust me, my friend, until the hour to which I am leading you. And know that the tricks with which I have gratified you thus far, those whose splendor you have experienced, and of which you have made use without yet understanding them, only represent— and will for as long as I am with you, however long that might be—a few meager impulsions of your absolute sovereignty over fiefs that are nothing less than the universe and eternity.

"And that being settled, would it not please you to vary the atmosphere slightly?"

18

He had spoken. I prepared myself immediately to see my parents' little drawing room vanish, along with its guests, like the flame of a candle that one blows out. Nothing happened. The arcandre appeared to reflect.

"I will give you a trinket," he said, "as a concrete memory of the concert of which you were unable to take advantage."

He extended his hands, wide open, palms up.

My brother was still playing and singing, and the appearance of the audience remained the same. Suddenly, the sounds that were rising simultaneously from the musician's throat and the instrument seemed to deviate, designing a kind of trajectory a plume of vibrations whose extremity curved back toward one of the arcandre's extended hands.

At the same time, the drawing room, its walls, the furniture, my friends and my parents all began to tremble, to blink, to shiver, and as that kind of general flutter became more rapid, the forms were fused and interpenetrated, gradually becoming a confused dance of fluid lines and bizarrely mingled colors, a brilliant and convulsive mist, which steered and precipitated toward the arcandre's other open hand, as if it had constituted a kind of aerial summons; and that variegated mist thinned out, narrowing as it approached the hand.

The ensemble had the approximate form of a cone of sparkling smoke, the base being that which still seemed vaguely consistent with the décor, the tip being so vaporous that it seemed to vanish on contact with the hand.

And while the sounds and forms were engulfed, so to speak, in the two hands, a strange russet secretion appeared in the center of the palms; I did not know whether it was emerging from the arcandre's hands or whether it was being deposited there in passing, on the one hand by the musical flux and on the other by the course of the cloudy substance. The mysterious matter was augmented in proportion to the fading away of the sounds and the diminution of the vaporous mass.

The moment came when the things and the songs were completely consumed. There was silence, and a wan light emanating from the arcandre, insufficient for me to see beyond him, or where we were, now that the drawing room had disappeared.

The arcandre closed his hands again; kneaded and rolled between his fingers the substance that had amassed there, into the form of two minuscule balls, two pills that seemed to be made of wax, and he offered them to me.

"Take them," he said. "This is the concert, its ambience, its audience and its music."

I received the singular gift. The pills were as hard as balls of agate, but they did not have the coldness of stone; they seemed to me to be smooth and silky, like ebonite. I turned them around in my fingers, stupidly.

"Keep them in the depths one of your pockets, or simply in your fob-pocket," said the arcandre. "At any time whatsoever, when you no longer have me, and any moment you are able to do so, hold those pills in the warmth of your hands momentarily. They will soon evaporate, in a sense contrary to the coagulation you have just seen. There will be a brief interval, a bewildering phase, during which the objects and individuals will reconstitute, returning from the cloudy to the solid state, and the sounds will go backwards to the beginning of the theme...but the cacophony and the solidification will cease, and whatever the place, the people and the sounds might be that surround you, even if you are at the ends of the earth, that drawing room, your parents, your friends, your brother and the Prelude will be rendered to you in their entirety."

I pocketed the décor and music in pill form, and began to look around me, trying to make out where we were. My eyes, becoming accustomed, recognized the tree, and then the bank of moss, and I felt the light cool breeze of the clearing.

It was dark, and I naturally thought that it was the evening of that improbable day. My adventures, well nourished as they had been, could well have been realized between the moment of the afternoon when I was meditating innocently, still alone, and whatever time of night it was now. However, in the company of an individual like the arcandre, could the slightest relationship exist between a succession of events and the progress of the hands of a watch? Since I had not quit my bank of moss for an instant—I recalled my companion's affirmation during our recent discussion of my simultaneous presence in several todays, and in the small drawing room as well as the foot of the tree—even when I was floating over the boiling oceans, it was logical that the hours of the forest…the normal hours of the me who remained in the forest…had elapsed regularly. In that case, the fact that I might find that night had followed day could only seem perfectly natural.

The night was quite dark and rather cold, an uncertain October night, meagerly constellated. A slight wind was teasing the foliage. I was lying down on the mossy bank. My hands were damp, from the moist vegetation. A twig fell from the tree and brushed my cheek. I rubbed my eyes and one of my hands, returned to the vegetation, fell upon some viscous creature.

"Friend," I said, "it's cold and I can hardly see…"

"Indeed," the arcandre replied. "Well then, we'll summon the light and go to summer."

19

He raised an arm, and extended the hand, keeping the fingers slightly folded, as if to collect an apple from a tree. A long red spark crackled and flashed between the thumb and the four fingers.

"There exists," said the arcandre, "in addition to the familiar sun of the diurnal sky, a second sun, the virtue of which circulates, invisible, in the very weft of the night. Its light is extracted from space as one takes water from a river or collects grapes from vine. A sun, moreover, that is the most docile and supple...you shall see..."

He pointed his finger at my tree. A streak of light as slender as a needle struck the bark and illuminated a minuscule surface. An ant foraging there beat a hasty retreat.

"The most docile and supple of suns, I was saying, as slender as a thread...as broad as a road...as vast as all of space. At my whim, or yours..."

For a second time, the fingers were rounded. Within their curve, a luminous ball appeared, which the arcandre pressed as if it were an orange or an apricot. Suddenly, a trickle of pink light flowed from the raised hand, snaking along the arm, illuminated the face in passing, and then the upper body, and the legs, and designed a sparkling pool at the arcandre's feet.

The rivulet became a torrent, setting my companion's body ablaze, inflated around his body, extended in all directions, filled the clearing, reached the horizon, climbed into the air, and seemed to reach the sky, absorbing there the feeble light of the moon; and in spite of the fact that the hour was its own and its empire, the night, like the old women in folktales who, when their mantles and crutches vanish, suddenly appear as fresh and ornamented as young queens, lit up like the day.

The birds woke up; some of them began to sing immediately; some fled in a great racket of startled wings, beating the foliage chaotically; insects swarmed; one might have thought that the very vegetation was frightened by that sudden morning, without any preliminary dawn tickling the corollas and the stems gently, devoid of the zephyr and the dew. Bewildered and dazzled, I closed my eyes, half swooning.

When I opened them again, everything was black again; the light had vanished.

Only the arcandre was shining, with the slightly phosphorescent gleam that had emanated from him a little while ago when my parents' little drawing room had become...pills.

Ah! I could not help making a gesture, as if to some rude joker...

My companion's laughter sounded, clear and cordial.

"I wanted," he said, "by means of those petty exercises, to assure myself of the presence of that discreet light..." He went on: "You're complaining, then, of being unable to see. I'll lend your eyes a little privilege of mine..."

He struck the air gently with his hand, as if he were knocking on an invisible door. The daylight reappeared—or, at least, an immense pink light inundated the forest, and the expanse, as far as the eye could see...

20

If it is only possible, with the aid of image or comparison, to render more penetrating and more communally understandable certain phenomena that are not ordinarily glimpsed because of their rarity or their complexity, to a small number of initiates or doctors, what a task must it be to describe clearly one that was positively inconceivable prior to the moment of its manifestation, never perceived by any gaze until that moment—absolutely original, in sum—and such that no correspondences, relative or fragmentary, in its regard can be found in our knowledge of the world?

I want to do my best to get over the difficulty that I encounter at this point in my story, which is to succeed in depicting what I saw with the sole resource of approximate images and words. As for the latter, which are the sign and, as it were, the robe and the color of determinate things, they inevitably become narrow, dull and sullen when it is necessary to make use of them to express objects so extraordinary and unexpected that the language cannot prepare any figure for them, much less tailor a garment.

Indulgence, therefore, for the teller, dear distant reader for whom I am telling the tale!

It commenced with a transfiguration of the forest, of the light, of the air, of my own body and the arcandre's. No object was displaced; no mist troubled the mysterious clarity of space; the wind did not blow any more bitterly through the air. The tree at the foot of which I was lying remained upright, and the ground was not subject to the slightest tremor. In sum, I was still seated on the moss without perceiving any other movement on my own part except for the seemingly-hectic acceleration of my blood; and the arcandre was standing a few paces away, in the same cordial and slightly nonchalant pose that he had assumed a moment ago.

No object was displaced. It happened in the very structure of things. That corner of nature, with everything that was within it, beings and species, offered to my eyes in its entirety the spectacle offered by a molecule considered under a microscope.

Everything cracked, substances subdivided, their constitutive elements disintegrating; the air was swarming, the light was decomposed into prismatic waves. The different aspects under which the characteristics of matter are manifest were abolished; organic, mineral, liquid and fluid were reduced to a common molecular state. From the smallest sprig of moss to the tallest tree, so far as I could count, the birds, the insects dig in the bark or in the soil, and my body with its clothing, and the arcandre in front of me, were no more than a swarm of rotating corpuscles, colliding and mingling; and the ground, as profoundly as my gaze could penetrate it, with its creases and its stones, was no longer anything but a dust of indefinite particles, slowly oscillating toward one another.

There was no more opacity, no planes, no more exterior and interior, properly speaking. The internal organs of tiny creatures, birds and vegetables, the insides of pebbles and the humus, all, like the blood, the juices, the bones and the viscera in the arcandre and myself, became equally visible, as crowds of particles bathing and moving in the multicolored flood of decomposed light.

Forms, and the details of each form, conserved their shape, which became a kind of shadowy contour, standing out against the light, a kind of gaseous sheath, indescribably tenuous, enveloping the displacements and gyrations of each specific agglomeration. The smallest particles of the air, incessantly drawn by the wind, traversed those crowds in all directions in their dancing courses.

That hallucinatory spectacle only lasted for a moment. Molecules and particles subdivided again. Everything that was matter was disassociated to the point of disappearance. The atom, which is merely a knot of electricities, was undone and reabsorbed into the ambient influences. Air, light and substance were no longer anything but a kind of complex glittering, in which, if some infinitesimal grain, some clot of matter still lingered here and there, that grain resembled diamond dust, refracting a light that was itself all refractions.

21

The swimmer who amuses himself by diving, if he suddenly opens his eyes under water, sees himself at first as if imprisoned in a dense glaucous space, and it is only after an interval of time that he recovers, along with a sense of distance, the perception of an above, a below and an around. Then his gaze adapts; he begins to sense the crystalline luminosity of the surface; he soon sees the troubled masses of algae and rocks standing out. Finally, in order for him to be able to remain in the element, he succeeds in discerning the detail of things with increasing accuracy.

Thus I found myself, at first, in the prodigious atmosphere of the denatured forest like the swimmer in the first phase of a dive, perceiving neither surface nor bottom, nor limits—deprived, in sum, of any reference-point, and I felt as if I, along with the air and fluids, the earth and forms, densities, volumes and currents, was absolutely dissolved in the universal glitter.

By means of what eyes, however, was I seeing that light? And above all, by means of what cerebral apparatus was I continuing to reason and to be conscious of my existence? The persistence of the self in that total dilution seemed to me to be even more extraordinary than the most stupefying modalities of the phenomenon. By what incomprehensible mechanism, by the coagulation of what ungraspable substance, had the supports of my sensibility and my reason remained aggregated?

Ha! The enigma had scarcely commenced! As, in the land of the hobgoblins, brambles and crevasses succeed one another before the traveler who has gone astray, the mystery multiplied before my stumbling mind.

In the same way that the diver recovers the perception of distance, I suddenly sensed the luminous sheet shifting. Tidally—the bore of what gigantic electrical river?—that sheet flowed in an uninterrupted surge, in what direction? I was unable then to tell East from West or South from North. That immensity, devoid of a surface, devoid of a bed and devoid of borders, went as the waters of a river go, and by virtue of that, what had been the forest, the tree, my body, and the supports of my sensibility and my consciousness, were dissolved in that river, going too, drawing away, dragged by that strange current.

Now—may words pursue me with their effort here!— notwithstanding that derivation and the continuing course of what had been my body, the tree and the forest, I did not cease to sense myself at a fixed point, still against the tree, immobile in the forest, still in its place. The elements of what had been the tree, the forest, my body and the supports of my reason and my sentiment, were drawing away incessantly, but the tree, the forest and my body nevertheless remained at the points they had occupied before the enchantment occurred, as

204

if a kind of sketch or phantom of their former presence was permitting them to reform incessantly out of new elements.

To summarize the incredible fact, everything was simultaneously stable and dispersing, fixed in a certain being, all of whose components were perpetually dissociating, relentlessly dismantled but continuously identical.

Now, the forms of the things, including myself, that were always going away and remaining in the same place, suddenly reappeared to me. On the moving screen of the indefinable light, initially confused, like the algae and the rocks to the diver, they became increasingly recognizable, resuming familiar aspects and characters. And now that I have said that, at the same time as I saw them all in their accustomed figures—the tree, my body, here ferns indolently fanning the pink air, a spider running along the edge of a blade of grass, there an elm whose leaves were fluttering in the wind—I saw them all as they still were, made of the same changing fulgurances as the river in which they bathed, and as such, going away in effluvia immediately melted into the endless cartage.

What was the reality of those forms, simultaneously fleeting and constant, absolutely certain to my returned senses, absolutely nonexistent to my other being, the one that was immersed in the traveling light, and for whom nothing existed any more, in himself, except that light? At present, now that I had rediscovered myself in my body, I could see myself going and coming, and I could touch beings and things. On contact with them—bark, plumage, fleeces—I reacquired the conviction of their reality. But what was that conviction worth, since the only instrument of experience that could guarantee the contours, densities and characters, averred its own illusoriness! Since my hands and my eyes, which testified to that reality, since my being of flesh, in sum, with all its batteries of perceptive apparatus, was only, like everything else, according the new sense that the arcandre had shared with me, a perpetual dissociation and reconstruction, a wave passing along a nameless river!

What, then, was real? And was not that mobile glitter it-self merely a more subtle aspect of the veritable substance of things, and the universe itself: a mere step, in a sense, toward the true structure of the universe, a step beyond which my gaze, prodigious as it had become, could doubtless never penetrate? A step beyond which, in sum, there was perhaps no longer even that light...and what could there be?

The arcandre, if he wished, could surely have resolved with a word the problems of the moment, at least: the order of that glittering; the mysterious operation by which I saw forms and character infinitely differentiated there, where everything was nothing but vagabond light. The arcandre had not left me. I looked at him, as always, standing in front of me, in the bos-om of the enigmatic pink daylight...

But as I extended my burning curiosity toward him, and just as I was about to question him, I suddenly saw him light up with a more ardent glare than that of the fantastic light that surrounded us, shining with an increasing scintillation, which became so intense, so various and so marvelous that even now, merely transcribing what was given to me then to con-template, I am obliged to lower my eyelids, as if the mere memory of the moment were dazzling me...

22

The gold of a diadem is pale compared with the jewels it supports, and the most noble of those jewels, whatever might be the warmth, purity and abundance of its fire, is extin-guished in the gaze that had just looked for a few seconds at the sun. And the supreme splendor of the star would be scarce-ly more than the scintillation of a lark-trap for anyone who was able to sustain the flamboyance of one of the gigantic stars that circle the confines of our sky, monsters before which the number that one assembles to evaluate their grandeur makes one think of Petit Poucet and his brothers catching sight of the Ogre.[15] There is a hierarchy of light. And such images can only assist me in representing the degrees of my contemplation, departing from the rosy light with which, at a sign from the arcandre, the night had been ornamented a little while ago, passing through the brilliance of the sheet of effluvia and from there to the successive resplendences by which the arcandre attained the state that I want to try to describe, the trenchant resplendence of an ever more magnificent glare, beyond the glare, so brilliant itself, of the effluvia...

Who has not admired in the circus one of those gymnasts, both acrobats and jugglers, molded in a leotard of vivid silk, spangled and tinseled? The lights of the theater, which refract a thousand times over the sparkling performer, at every move he makes, seems to fly from him in myriads of sparks of all colors. As much as the grace of the acrobatics, the eyes take pleasure in the iridescent arabesques that the gleams of the spangles trace. The man appears to be moving in a sheath of flame, to be a flame himself more capricious and more various than any true flame ever shows itself to be...

Let us suppose the man no longer speckled with precarious metallic facets, nor dancing in the light of a chandelier, but entirely transformed into a kind of living cluster of diamonds... Now that cluster is plunging into the fulgurant sheet... Only the imagination can represent to itself whose sheaves of rays would flow and blossom, what a hurricane of rutilances would launch forth at the slightest quiver of that fabulous fruit, every grain of which not only refracts the fulgurances that strike it from all directions, sending them forth a thousand times more ardent than when they arrived, but also marrying those exceedingly vivid fires with the radiations received from all the other diamonds...

Now, the light becomes even brighter. Every one of those marvelous nuclei is transformed into a living thing. Eve-

---

[15] In the remodeled folktale included in Charles Perrault's classic collection, usually known in English translation as "Hop-o'-my-Thumb."

ry diamond becomes a kind of minuscule sun, simultaneously rotating and radiating like a veritable star, animated by a pulse, an infinitesimal being all of whose organs must be made of light, as those of water-dwelling Monera, for example, seem to be made of the droplets among which the protozoan moves...

Such was the body of the arcandre after having been the multitude of scintillations that I have only been able to compare to a cluster of diamonds, made of myriads of tiny palpitating suns.

As I describe the light emanating from that tunic of suns, that torrent of stars, I seem to see the words dissolving, like moths falling as they approach a naked flame. You are nothing to me, ornaments of the Vedas, necklaces of Scheherazade, compared to that swarm of suns. You cannot better express the adorable conflagration of that body, vertiginous gleams by which the saints are intoxicated, the abode of angels, the Virgin's robes, ovum of triumphant flame around the head of the Son...

But I can go no further forward, seeking a comparison for a resplendence that nothing could equal, not even the primal light of the world that I had contemplated during the arcandre's initial enchantments. That one, in its terrible splendor, was entirely physical, while it was not possible that this one...

But now, scarcely had I glimpsed, scarcely had I entered into the delight of such a vision, than a new vision imposed itself. That light was populated by a host of individuals; the arcandre's miraculous body became the location of an inconceivable epic...

I remember having read, as a child, a tale in which a shipwrecked prince lands on a mysterious island. Wandering around, the prince discovers on that island three spinners, who are the Fates. One of them is sitting in front of a tapestry representing Destiny. The living creation is embroidered on one of those abbreviated frames that only fantastic tales can permit...

Now I affirm here that that the flamboyant body of the arcandre was the mirage of the universe. Those bodies became a sort of enormous carnival of worlds, beings, things and dramas...

I cannot say what arrangement of vibrations, what entanglement of reflections had made the innumerable figures and scenes that were narrowly amalgamated with one another, agitating in a kind of chaotic vortex, which was all contained within the measure of the body of fire; but what is certain is that every detail and every event was cut out of that chaos, perfectly clear and definite, as soon as I fixed my particular attention upon it. If my attention was prolonged, the object conserved its detachment from the amalgam, separated from the body, quit the turbulence and grew, attaining without delay the proportions of reality. Meanwhile, the ambience, the air and my own sensations immediately belonged to the ambience, the details and the time of the object...

I shall take an example.

I cannot take only one. If I attempted to enunciate what I saw passing and spinning in that race of living light, I would need...but what word could be more explicit here than a certain phrase of the arcandre's, among those that he had pronounced emphatically when revealing himself to me? "I shall not enumerate the countenance of my words," he said, "for it is not possible to state the number and the diversity of the outside and the inside of creation. And it is that number, and that diversity, which my words signify..."

23

For my example, something surprising is required—and the name of Savonarola, suddenly surges forth at this point in my adventure...

But let us get on, and continue the narration. It is only important to be a veracious narrator. And what is a brief start of surprise for whoever is following with me this tale in which one encounters a miracle on every page?

Among the images of the fantastic farandole that attracted my attention most keenly, one was the scene that the Michelets and the Taines have taken pleasure in painting for us. I saw the parvis of Santa Maria del Fiore in Florence, at a moment when Girolamo Savonarola was preaching in the open air on the piazza. Children were heaping up adornments—gold chains, carved combs, masks and boxes of make-up—in front of the Dominican. A passionate crowd was listening to the terrible monk, and I soon found myself mingled with that crowd.

Savonarola spoke about the imminent end of Rome, the legions of God ready to fall upon the city, on Alexander the Simoniac. He spoke about the necessity of a great penitence for Florence. I remember very clearly that the slightest details were clearly visible to me. A gesture of a weeper sculpted on the bronze door of the nearby baptistry...the sandal of a child hopping around the spoils of ostentation, which had become the heap of precious items assembled there by the monk's order, pillaged by the puerile hordes from noble homes, torn from the vestments of Tuscan ladies. A peasant woman was trembling both from covetousness of so many beautiful things and cruel anxiety at Savonarola's cries.

A milky atmosphere and a nacreous light enveloped the red dome of Santa Maria. The softness of Florence filtered through the prophet's maledictions like a languorous cat through the debris.

What thought pricked my mind, which suddenly caused me to draw away from the crowd and the basilica? Florence was real, since I could stroll idly through the streets. They were almost deserted because of the preaching. I wandered, simultaneously amazed to be there and savoring the seductive lightness of the air and the unparalleled delicacy of the city. I was walking slowly.

Suddenly, my gaze, full of delighted admiration, fell upon a tall bronze statue standing in a profound niche in the wall of a red stone church. That image summarized the finest grace allied with serene strength and masculine majesty. It was

Donatello's Saint George. I stood there, gripped by an ardent contemplation, in a kind of voluptuous and tender piety, forgetting the time.

A sound of footsteps broke my reverie. A man was crossing the street.

"What is this church?" I asked him.

"Your Lordship does not know Orsanmichele?" the man replied.

I suppose he expected other questions. My Lordship was too stupefied at first to continue the conversation, for I perceived that I had quite naturally interrogated the passer-by in his own language, in fifteenth-century Tuscan, and when he replied to me in the same tongue I had understood him. Undoubtedly, I was about to speak again, less to obtain more information than to hear myself express myself for a second time in a dialect of which I had not known the most elementary words until that moment...when a rumor became audible, which grew, coming toward us, becoming more precise.

The sermon had finished. Florence was quitting the parvis, about to spread out through the streets, resuming its multiple life. The sentiment of reality had gripped me so completely that a kind of frisson of involuntary anguish ran through my entire body. I was frightened by the idea that I was about to be cast into the midst of that coming-and-going of merchants, women and soldiers, among whom I would be a man fallen from five centuries in the future. A clawed impression of nightmare possessed me.

Assuredly, if I had reflected, remembering certain phases just as extraordinary of my voyages, that I had burned with the primal fire and battled with roots in the ground, I would not have yielded to that absurd fear. At any rate, that was what happened. A hectic desire to escape jangled my nerves. My thought twisted toward the memory of the arcandre as the hand of a drowning man clutches above the surface of the water.

It was sufficient. Immediately, I found myself extended once again, as peacefully as could be on the friendly mossy bank, in the clearing, where everything had resumed its normal appearance: the grass, the trees, the ferns, through which the fresh breeze was blowing, and where the same pale moon was shining as before I had asked the arcandre for more light and a little warmth.

But no! I was ashamed, I did not intend that the magical adventure should but cut short like that, so pitifully, nor that rotation of the universe around the radiant body of the arcandre...

I reprimanded myself harshly.

A burst of laughter rang in my ears, of the cherished timbre that had become so pleasant to hear...the arcandre forgave me. Everything was suddenly enchanted again. The forest became glittering again. The vision surged forth where I had left it. The farandole of countless images resumed its course.

24

I have said it. I will not try to enunciate all that I saw there. Imagine, rolling in the orbits of the vortex, a sabbat, a confusion of ever-new images succeeding one another pell-mell...

Pell-mell, the sublime, the horrible, the burlesque, the real and the mythological, the most tempestuous bustle, the most ludicrous and the most brutal transitions, the smallest detail of the most vulgar object, entire continents, centuries of history that a single glance embraces...

So that, in a thousandth of the time that it takes me to write it, appeared, coming after the Florence of Savonarola...an automobile spark-plug with its iron body, porcelain neck and copper head; a buckle of the doublet of one of Clotaire's pages; the statue of Sainte-Beuve in the Jardin du Luxembourg; two men dressed in animal skins fighting over the cadaver of a bear; Gabrielle d'Estrées, half naked, in the arms of the King of France; a locomotive emerging from the hall of a large railway station; crystal craters on a dead planet;

212

Pierre Corneille writing on the stone table in his garden at Petit-Couronne near Rouen; a drinking-den in Madrid where sailors were watching a gypsy dance...

I shall stop. To continue would be madness. Only a lunatic would be amused by stringing together the most varied figures in such a ludicrous succession—and yet, I am only describing honestly a scarcely-measurable instant of the chaotic saraband. In any case, dementia was perhaps involved in the affair, for fever and vertigo gradually invaded me. A host, a melee of covetousness, curiosity and avidity, burned me in turn. A gust of salacity drove me furiously toward two good-time girls going into a Montmartre dance-hall arm in arm—but that urge yielded to a profound thirst to approach Jacob Boehme, who, tapping soles in his cobbler's workshop, was meditating a chapter of *De signatura rerum*. My legs bounded of their own accord toward diaphanous dryads whose games would open up for me if I wished. My stomach swooned at fabulous pastries made for a snack for Semiramis...

As if my incessantly-whipped desires, all together and all entangled, had themselves formed one of the orbits of the cyclone of images, I gradually sensed myself carried away by the round, snatched from myself from all directions at once, as if torn apart in a thousand flames...

I was about to lose consciousness when I heard the arcandre's voice. "Look again," it said.

The flames were extinguished. My blood rediscovered its course; it was as if I were inundated by peace.

I looked.

Doubtless I was seeing with the mind's eye, for what gaze can contemplate with one vision four aspects of the same thing, four different states of the same form, not superimposed or delivering one another by transparency, but confounded and simultaneous?

25

This is what I saw:

The arcandre, in his person of flesh, dressed as I have said before, in garments fairly similar to mine, his body outlined against the foliage of the clearing, which had become a clearing again, as before.

The same arcandre, formed of effluvia; and while everything remained in its normal appearances around me, everything in his vicinity was dematerialized, unraveled, in a sense, degrading into effluvia at the extremities: the delicate tips of leaves, surfaces of bark, the heads of insects or nearby birds traversing that atmosphere, the air and light surrounding the body, the earth beneath it. The flow of fulgurance, incessantly renewed, that I have described elsewhere, recommenced in that space.

Now, as the effluvia were emanating from everything that was around the arcandre, the movement of the glittering was necessarily concentric; but I could not perceive or comprehend what became of those waves continuously springing forth, where they were going and how they vanished after having encountered one another at the hypothetical center on which they were converging. Were they rising upwards? Were they descending? Were they being reabsorbed in that center?

The zone occupied by that air, that light, that foliage, that bark and that dematerialized body presented itself as a kind of luminous column, the base of which was set I know not where, nor at what depth in the earth, and the summit of which terminated I know not where, nor at what altitude in the sky.

At the same time as I saw that column in which all forms were dissolved, however, I saw the arcandre resplendent in his body of suns, which rendered the electric fires in which he bathed wan and faint.

Fourthly, and finally, that same body, still unfurling the inexhaustible magma of the images of the universe.

Now, gazing at that quadruple figure of the same being, I heard the exceedingly harmonious voice again.

"This is my body," said the arcandre, "and this is my blood."

I shuddered. An extravagant thought agitated me.

"It is by design," he went on, "that I employ the same words proffered one day by another, at the terminus of pathetic adventures, still represented by a great many recent idolaters, the sweetest and most august story in the world. It pleases me to pronounce them, but in a sense entirely of delight, jubilation and pride."

26

He took a few steps forward. The luminous column was displaced with him—which is to say that everything from which he drew away resumed its normal appearance, and that what was now proximate dematerialized. And as he had advanced some way toward me, the corner of my bank, the extremity of my shoes, the tips of my fingers, crossed over on my knees—in sum, everything of me that was in the zone of dematerialization—became effluvia...with the consequence, and because the ground beneath the arcandre—to an indeterminable depth, as I have said—was no longer anything but a palpitation of fulgurances, that what remained visible of my legs seemed to be dangling over the edge of a well of light, while the tips of my toes were dipping into that well.

"Friend," I said then—and my voice, groaning with extreme passion, must have trembled as boiling water quivers, and I felt frantic, determined to interrupt the enchantment, resolved not merely to penetrate the meaning of the words that the arcandre had just pronounced but to comprehend, and finally to grasp the mechanism of many prodigies—"consent now to..."

The enigmatic smile that appeared on the magician's face exasperated me. But I did not have time to express my fury. How able my companion was in eluding the response! In the vortex of images, a face suddenly passed by that nailed my revolt in place, nimbly deflecting my excitement from its object

I cried: "Ascain!"

A Basque cowherd was slowly descending a path of red earth on the side of a mountain. A crespuscular sun draped violet sheets over the brown mountain slopes covered with grass and bushes, the paths of red humus and the ash-blue rocks. The man, his upper body braced, was marching at a regal pace, holding his staff in his two raised arms, resting it on the nape of his neck. He preceded a low cart with solid wooden wheels, sticky with red mud, drawn by a white ox whose feet and breast were spattered with the same blood-colored mud, splashed from the puddles on the path. At a corner of the descending route, the cowherd inclined his head, cordially saluting a young man sitting on a grassy bank, who must not have seen the greeting, because he made no response, his staring eyes seemingly lost in a heavy and dolorous reverie.

I recognized that young man. It was me.

It was me, a few years before that miraculous night. I shall step aside perilously from my present narrative to relate, as is appropriate, the strange and tragic adventure of the sojourn I had made, as an adolescent, in the village of Ascain, situated a few kilometers from Saint-Jean-de-Luz, at the foot of the mountain of the Rhune.

I had come to that village with the intention of composing, in calm and solitude, a theatrical work whose scenario seemed to me to respond to the philosophical ideas that populated my mind at the time. I can no longer undertake to describe minutely the nature of those ideas, nor the very singular psychological stages that had brought me to them, leading me to cherish them almost religiously, at least with a kind of mystical force.

To be brief, I can summarize the story thus: a certain event of a literary order having thrown me, when I was scarcely twenty years old, into a kind of extraordinary literary renown, the mirage was suddenly permitted to me to believe

216

myself a king. Positively, I suddenly held the superlative conditions of happiness, glory and all grandeurs. In terms of my
profession, a dazzling notoriety, abruptly arrived, flattened all
the ordinary obstacles. I was not unaware, having experienced
it when I tried to publish my first writings, of the rudeness of
the roads that a debutant must travel. I also knew how bitter
and cruel the ascension is to the heights at which the artist, if
he has not used up the best of his genius in the climb, finds the
freedom to express his art In accordance with his faith, able to
live on his work without having to take account of the murderous caprice of merchants. Thus, I savored in its full measure the unusual privilege of being immediately perched on the
very summit.

I was not any longer, and never would be again, reduced
to dressing an ideal with the forms and formulae that aid overly audacious conceptions to succeed in reaching the crowd,
and from which that process of disguise often amputates the
original generosity. On the other hand, I did not have to dread
ever knowing the bitter disdain that marks certain artists enclosed in the ivory tower of a genius too foreign to the general
sensibility of their time. For it would henceforth be the case
for me that I could say what I wanted, in the form that suited
me, and the world, turned toward me since the thunderclap
that had revealed me, would immediately give audience to my
words. Events duly fortified me a little more every day in that
incomparable certainty. Everything indicated that newspapers,
editors and theaters would snatch the golden egg, and, as urgent spokesmen, would keep the world attentive to my slightest productions.

As for what my state of mind was then, it is easily imaginable that in such circumstances. I shiver when I envisaged
the multiplicity and extent of what had become possible for
me. Everything for which youth can wish and contain was
well and truly offered to me: incalculable glory and gold. I
could, and I would always be able to, choose among the most
beautiful and most sumptuous that art, nature, science and
industry had engendered, to surround myself with the best

marvels, to be perpetually in the bosom of terrestrial enchantments, to adorn with those enchantments the woman I would love. I would have the inexhaustible joy of voyages, with their adventures. I would also know the exalted grace of being in communication, in friendship, with the most admirable men of my epoch. Everywhere I went, to the homes of painters, musicians, scientist, philosophers, and manipulators of men, I would be welcomed with warm benevolence, as a guest before whom the greatest was proud to allow his worth to shine.

In truth, the universe with all its spiritual and material riches was open to my twenty-year-old self. And the praise that had been lavished upon me authorized me to believe that I would have the virtue and the genius of singing that universe and those riches.

Now, one day, from the altitudes to which that idea that I had formed of my destiny had elevated me, I said to myself: *being so powerful, who am I?*

27

Seeking to know myself, and to grasp all my human possibilities, I was obliged, in meditating upon myself, to extend my meditation to human nature itself, to the laws that regulate it and the different reactions of its instincts, its miseries and its powers. It goes without saying that my discoveries were strongly influenced by the magnificence of the prodigious future that I accorded myself—which is to say that the sentiment of my fortune instinctively gave me a propensity to exalt myself to testimonies of human grandeur rather than to bemoan evidence of human weakness or ugliness. Thus, my idea of human nature was formed by the epic and creative feats that humans had accomplished in the course of the ages. And from the prestigious works with which they had enriched the world, and the new dominations that the world was assured by recent scientific discoveries, more astonishing every day, I inferred with boundless enthusiasm the sovereignties and delights that they could anticipate.

Now, as I was constructing my consciousness in that fashion, I did my military service. It was the ransom of my age. But the acclaim that had made my name illustrious had not crossed the threshold of the barracks. Only the senior officers knew that the trooper who was sweeping the courtyard or practicing the manipulation of weapons was, when he went on leave to Paris, called "Master" by reporters, that the newspapers published his portrait, and that the most celebrated actresses asked him to reserve a role for them in the next play he wrote. Thus, that young king, in everyday life, peeled potatoes, polished his equipment, learned the training manual side by side with worthy men of all classes, the majority of whom were massive, resigned peasants and grumbling city-dwellers, and who, under the coercions, the ennui and the coarseness of the military regime, laid bare the crude sentiments, the trivial appetites and the candid, elementary or imbecilic ideals of the bulk of humanity throughout the ages.

In my perpetual intellectual effervescence, my frenzy to learn the greatest beauty and to edify the most elevated Joy, it was inevitable that quasi-perpetual shocks should be produced in me, resounding in the utmost depths, caused by the disproportion that was blindingly evident, in every instant of my hours as a soldier, between the delightful objects of my meditation and the spectacles of the reality in which I was living. Quick to generalize, like all children, I most frequently gave these shocks the form of an immense bitterness, a tempestuous stupefaction at the fact that men—extrapolating from those I saw to all others—had remained almost identical to their brethren of prehistoric epochs in which eating, clothing oneself, fornicating and sleeping were the motive forces and the supreme goals, and that they had remained so on a planet which, in the meantime, I thought, human genius and great mechanical inventions had rendered well and truly propitious henceforth to actions and sensualities more grandiose, more liberated and more exquisite than had ever been accomplished, or even imagined, before.

I came to suffer with as much violence as I had had enthusiasm before, from the conviction that humans, in the main, were still content with their miserable semi-animal satisfactions, or resigned to a cramped or murderous life, when the times were realizing a magnificent royalty and that no more was necessary than to adapt themselves to live in the times, that they only had to look and understand to see that Paradises had arrived on earth, prodigiously more pleasant, splendid and various than those promised by the Bible.

It was, in the final analysis, and by virtue of the law of universal interdependence—the subtle and the liberated being weighed down and paralyzed by all the rest—that poor quality of the satisfaction of the mass of humans not disengaged from animality, and that blind resignation, which appeared to me to be largely responsible for the obscure and dolorous state in which humanity entire was still trailing.

If humans knew their veritable powers, I thought then, *and their right to veritable Joy, and what that Joy is, the light that would suddenly inundate them would instantly render them truly human and truly worthy of that marvelous name!*

Thus, by virtue of such relentless suffering excited by contact with a base and ugly reality, and by virtue of the sentiment that I, the fortunate, the victorious and the sapient, had a duty to reveal my luminous vision to the world, it is explicable that a tyrannical and resplendent notion of a mission—an apostolate, in sum—gradually expanded within me: before any other task, to sing, to proclaim, to affirm the new Joy that would recreate humankind!

And it was in that state of mind that, as soon as I had completed my military service, I departed for Ascain, in order to formulate, in the spacious serenity of solitude, the charter of terrestrial Joy.

28

At a bend in the zigzag road that goes from the foot of the Rhune to the village of Sarre, Ascain's neighbor, there is a large anfractuosity of black stone, an ancient slate quarry that was doubtless abandoned as soon as it was excavated. It rises about fifteen meters above the road. How many times, parading my tumultuous cogitation along that road, had I measured that abrupt black wall with my frightfully distressed gaze? *Tomorrow*, I told myself, *I'll climb up there.*

The opulent trees that bordered the road, the bushes, the wild flowers on the banks, the cheerful birds, the air and the sky of that winterless region all enveloped me with delicate salubrity, gracious and light colors. And yet I walked without seeing anything but my dream, and that black rock on which my dream was about to break.

I was carrying an infinite torment. How had it come about? A pitiful Prometheus, I had no idea how to manipulate or to guide the fire that I had stolen, and I was burning my fingers, my heart and my reason. A quotidian defeat was devouring me a little more before every evening: the shame and gehenna of a day used up vainly trying to express my thought.

My torture, banal in sum, was that which the majority of artists suffer at the genesis of their work. It is the enthusiasm brought by each of them to the affair that colors that tragedy, renders it more or less pathetic and biting, and sometimes terrible to the point of bringing the theater down and killing the protagonist.

I can honestly say that I was all the way there; my entire being was in the battle. In the same way that in the time when I had discovered and abstractly conceived Joy, my limbs and lungs had participated in the celebrations of my mind, gaining therein a livelier, more robust and richer blood, my body was now buckling beneath my excessively heavy head, wearied by an effort without issue. I could not give life to my thoughts, the life of words and form, but I did not know then that it was because I had not lived myself. The sparkling ideas that I had once attained, perfidious guests of an excessively youthful consciousness, now held me in their power. I was neither their king, nor their shepherd, nor their director, but their miserable serf, their prey.

I wandered, disabled, through their sabbat, toyed with, juggled, bullied and mocked by them. I could not consider one of them, trying to isolate it and fix it on the blank page, without it immediately summoning all the others. I was immediately surrounded, assailed and torn apart by the ferocious band. The precisions that seemed to me to be indispensable, the apparent contradictions, the metaphysical relationships, the criticisms and the counter-criticisms jostled one another, all trying to pass all at the same time into the first stroke of my pen. I left the page, I closed my eyes, in order to master the bacchanal, to chase away the intruders, the unnecessary, to prune, to eliminate, to simplify, to clarify, in order finally to grasp the elect...

Oh, well, yes! The furies multiplied their crowd. They beckoned to all systems, historical controversies, centuries-old disputes, ethics, articles of synods, dogmas, Kabbalahs and cosmogonies...all the corresponding human gesticulations, evolutions, crusades, miracles, fervors, deliria, massacres emerged from time and shoved me away. Bewildered, I fled the table and the house; I went to demand a diversion from the roads, the trees, the grass, the stones. I walked, I whistled, I sang, I forgot. Not having quit me, how they lay in wait for me! As soon as I resumed thinking, their chaotic carnival bounded toward me, trampling my plans, my sketches, my whims, sacking everything, soon rendering the poor point unrecognizable, incoherent and inextricable, however clear, precise and organized it had been when I glimpsed it...

What would have happened if I had not been recalled to Paris by the accomplishment of the literary event whose mere announcement had once made me famous? Perhaps I would have killed myself, so perpetually vain and odious did my life appear, if I could not inscribe my song of Joy radiantly upon it. All the dazzling perspectives opened to my young royalty, all the victories, delights and voluptuousness would be nothing to me if I could not set the seal upon them with the great word that would enchant the world. Already, on emerging from military service, at the moment when I could have begun to enjoy them, I had abdicated them in favor of that retreat to Ascain.

I reappeared to my fellows rich, in their eyes, with the most astonishing fortune that had ever been heaped upon a debutant; in my own eyes, I was impotent and miserable. All the windfalls that I had obtained, for which I was incalculably envied, had the effect on me of jewels colliding with an empty vase.

The event occurred. Announced, postponed, awaited for several years, it had aroused many preliminary jealousies, which had accumulated and strengthened with the aid of time. Those unleashed jealousies, the overexcitement of the wait, and the noise made round a work of which nothing was known except that the Academician director of the foremost French theater had accepted it, immediately after having read it, and whose author, complexly unknown the day before, was twenty years old at the moment of that reception—the very overexcitement that had pushed the public to prejudge of the work that it must be one of genius, whereas it possessed all the disappointing faults and awkwardness of an adolescent work—combined in a spicy ensemble to crush the object of so much agitation.

However, Paris is such that the racket made around the author, however wounded he might be by his resounding failure, was sufficient for all doors to remain open to his productions. I would then have been able to pursue my career with the rarest facility and, as they say, "find a home" for works almost everywhere. Furnished with a little money, which remained to me from the adventure, I fled, exiling myself to the mountains again with the illusion that I could finally realize the sole work that would make life worthwhile.

The money melted away before a hundred lines were written. Then I returned among people. It was expected that I would repair my fall. People were astonished that I appeared empty-handed after a long and silent absence. I could not explain that I thought, having attained one of the great truths capable of molding the world, that it had been necessary to

223

carry it for a long time and confront it with life in order to be able to pronounce it, and that the labor in question had not been as easy as writing a light comedy or a romantic novel. Many friendships had come to me once without knowing anything about me except the noise generated by the reception of my drama, and, as a flattering rumor had sufficed for some to call themselves my friends, it had only required the wind of failure to make them turn away from me. Others, who conserved some sincere sympathy for me, gradually drew away on seeing me remain sterile for several years. I found myself friendless, having lost any aureole, and obliged to earn my daily bread arduously. Then I began to live the same life as all men.

29

Scarcely had I cried "Ascain!" and recognized in the vortex of images the pensive young man sitting on a grassy bank on the pathway of red earth than the forest vanished and I found myself transported to the Rhune at the point where I had just seen the phantom of my youth. The latter had disappeared, but the same light of the violet dusk was floating over the slopes of the brown mountain. Broad mists were beginning to rise from the earth, slowly unfurling, spreading over the flanks of the massif, thickening, gradually hiding the villages down below. An immense peace dressed the silence.

I gazed with a strange emotion at the stones of the road, the little flowers on the bank. It seemed to me that every pebble, every blade of grass ought still to contain, fraternally, a little of the bitter confidences that my stifling soul had once allowed to escape every evening, here and in many similar places on the mountain, in serene and vaporous hours like this one.

Now, I saw the arcandre beside me. The malicious friend must have conjectured the emotion into which the bitterest of memories would cast me. The furious curiosity that I had experienced at his last words was extinct. That paraphrase of

Christ in which he had summarized the prodigy of his four bodies, if it still resonated in my ears, no longer held me in the same impetuous astonishment. So I listened to the arcandre calmly when he resumed speaking.

"Know," he said, "that everything I have enabled you to see before now was mere twittering. The illumination of the nocturnal sun, your immersion in the immaterial, the saraband of images, the suns composing my three bodies, the moment when you sensed yourself simultaneously fixed against your tree and carried away by the fulgurant river, were merely little games with which I was amusing myself while leading you to the light and warmth for which you had asked me. I count, when the time comes, on explaining everything. Amusements, I repeat, with regard to many other curiosities and prodigies that I have, by virtue of my nature, the faculty of engendering inexhaustibly. Now, because of the inexhaustibility that is possible for me, I beg you to give me credit, with respect to what you have seen, for the many other tricks of the same sort that I could show you. For I now have the intention of proceeding in a fashion other than I have done thus far.

"You complained of the coldness and darkness of an October night, and here we are in the soft light and perpetual summer of a blessed region. I have chosen this mountain, which was a place of servitude and defeat for you, and from which you shall depart victorious. It also pleases me that it should be on a mountain that you will hear the supreme words that I shall say to you. Oh, simple mischief! The one who, in handing out bread and pouring wine for his disciples, pronounced as I did a little while ago, to your great emotion: "This is my body and this is my blood," was taken one day by the devil, so the old books say, to a mountain, and was tempted. The evil one asked the messiah to choose between the felicities of the earth, which he showed him symbolically assembled at the foot of the mountain, and the problematic felicities of heaven. Jesus, as everyone knows, resisted the devil brilliantly. He opted for the spiritual wealth, and renounced the pleasures of the world."

Somewhat nonplussed, I stared at the arcandre. His bright smile poured out confidence toward me.

"There is," he went on, "a slight parallelism between that holy anecdote and where I am taking you. The correspondence is in the panorama of felicities that I count on unfurling before you. However, you are no messiah, and after all, I am not the devil; I am something much more extraordinary, more malign, more powerful and more original than the devil."

He laughed. I was very surprised by that speech. However, a bizarre and voluptuous impression of security and grandeur gripped me as the arcandre spoke.

"In the speech that I made at the beginning of our relationship," he continued, "I told you, I believe, that it was necessary to suspend, in my regard, any reminiscence of fable, for none of the names such as archangel, demon and others that one sees in religions and sorceries suits me. I also told you that you must also not expect to find in legends, bibles, and history figures, feats and ostentations, no matter how prestigious they might be, to compare with me..."

I found the precise words in my memory.

"It is those words," the arcandre went on, "for which I now want to furnish you with the proof. Let us take a few transcendent types from fable, the Bible and history, whether it be Hercules, who vanquished the hydra; Haroun-al-Raschid, named in the Thousand-and-One Nights as lord of the magnificences of Asia; Sindbad, who made voyages abundant in prodigies; Apollonius of Tyana, who walked on water and resuscitated the dead; Tristan, who knew the most beautiful amour; Lorenzo de Medici, who reigned in the time of Michelangelo; and many, many other individuals chosen as examples among all those who were the richest in power or materials of greatness and joy..."

The arcandre interrupted himself. "There is no question, for the moment, of considering these exemplary individuals in the employment they made of their advantages, nor the enjoyments that they were able to obtain from them, nor a few shadows or a few cares that might have might have balanced

226

their fortune. Nor is it a matter of seeing whether they were or bad, or whether they managed the beautiful materials of power, greatness or joy that were in their possession badly or well, but simply of examining, given a few superlative types of possessors, the proportion in which the possession that I have surpasses them."

He paused momentarily. Then he suddenly started laughing.

"Before then, let us consider a little more the temptation that was offered to Jesus. If one considers it closely, it is a very singular proposal that Satan made to the Lord, in asking him to choose between the joys of earth and those of heaven. He might as well, just as honestly and in the same language, have asked him whether, in order to walk, he preferred to abandon the left leg or the right. The fact of having to choose between two equally precious possessions, both equally necessary to life, is no less baroque than that which would consist, in truth, of having to abandon a leg in order to run better, a lung in order to breathe better, or an eye in order to see better."

I laughed in my turn, without understanding where the arcandre was trying to get to.

"I suppose," he went on, "that the felicities of the earth and those said to be celestial are, in reality, so tightly mingled, so harmoniously combined, that they only constitute a single species. Thus, the juice and the pulp of the orange form the fruit. One can swallow the flesh and the juice together; one can also press the former in order to drink the latter alone. Some are also pleased to savor the peel; but even in dividing the delights of the orange into two or three, it is one and the same fruit from which those delights are taken."

"Undoubtedly," I said.

"On the other hand," my companion continued, imperturbably, "the man who has drunk the juice does not believe that he is henceforth forbidden under the harshest of penalties to eat the pulp, and even the peel. If one can say that he has, at a given moment, opted for the for the flesh with the juice, or

227

the juice alone, or for the entire orange, his option has, in that case, only been one diversity of his hunger, and he conserves his full right to the complete enjoyment of all the oranges to come and all the parts of those oranges..."

"To be sure..."

"The impressive symbol of the option of Jesus is, therefore, worth exactly as much as some nonsense in the Tales of Mother Goose, if it is in the totality of life, known and knowable, terrestrial and celestial, temporal and spiritual, as with our orange, which forms a single fruit with various delights, and if, instead of having to deprive oneself severely of one thing in order to have something else, one has the leisure and the means to bite into everything that it contains of goodness..."

"Of goodness…," I began

"Now, everything in it is good," said the arcandre. "That which is called bad is that of which the goodness is unknown."

30

"Those premises," he went on, "of which God the Son furnishes us the substance—and consider that in our image of the orange we could have, without any great damage, and only changing a few terms here and there, used[16] instead of Jesus, Buddha and his Nirvana—can open the series of my comparisons. Indeed, let us take one of the prerogatives of my nature, and not the least considerable, that of finding in all things not only the goodness—which I mean here in the sense of flavor—but of also finding the beauty. Your epithets "bad" and "ugly" do not correspond to anything, or very little, for me, if there is, in my eyes, no object or state, no thing or person that

---

[16] One is tempted to suppose that a line has been accidentally omitted from the original text here, and that the object that might have been substituted for the orange (an apple?), creating an alternative to which the substitution of Buddha for Jesus would then have been compared, has vanished from the text.

does not always present some singularity or property that is capable in some measure of rendering the said thing, object, state or person, if not beautiful or good according to your canons, at least attractive, seductive in certain mysterious ways, and always in a disposition to deliver some precious confession.

"It is to that seduction, that attraction, that mystery that I go spontaneously, immediately and instinctively. As for the instinct that leads me directly, however poor or malign the appearances might be, to that which is the flavor, source of emotion or cargo of knowledge in any object, state or person, that instinct is properly that of Joy. It launches toward its aliment—flavor, emotion and knowledge being good nutriments of Joy—as air and light throw themselves into the slightest interstices of substances, no matter how hard and dense they might be.

"Thus, and by virtue of that instinct, I am protected from experiencing, before anything whatever, what you call disdain, disgust or indifference; and it therefore follows that everything that there is in the world will be immediately interesting, curious and attractive to me, and thus to some extent nutritious.

"In consequence, if we return to the example of Jesus, taking it for certain that everything that is in the world bears some source of joy, it is necessary for me to say, first of all, that, even at the price of paradisal bliss, I could not easily be turned away from such a world, and, secondly, that the question of option would not arise if I were to hold it as no less certain that the divine, the celestial and the spiritual that were shown to me on the far side of the clouds and outside my planet had no other true residence than in my sentiment and in my sense of things, with the consequence that, without having to renounce anything of this world, it is sufficient for me to savor the divine in all things, whatever they might be, with the fervor, bliss and delight particular to the celestial elect.

"And that is the first comparison that we can establish with that which was previous. If the pleasures of the world are for me exactly as numerous and diverse as the objects, things,

229

beings, elements and states composing the world, the glorious felicity of the God of the Christians appears very mediocre compared to mine. Firstly, since it is only made of half of the possession of that world, a half acquired by losing the countless advantages and perfections of the other half; and secondly because that God only has enjoyment in and by the spiritual side of things—to the extent that they have one—and in souls, and particularly the souls of celibate monks and nuns, old bigots, people in great fear or anxiety of dying, and all other wretches. Whereas, by virtue of the instinct of Joy that is nourished by the goodness and beauties, material as well as spiritual—and causing the former and the later to interpenetrate at will—I have the unlimited possession of the knowable world and the enjoyment of the best of all things concrete, comestible, caressable, odorous, and at the same time, the best of souls. With regard to that last enjoyment, understand that I can take without any prohibitive canons fixed in advance, with no restrictions or preliminary conditions, sniffing in every soul its specific perfume, whether it be similar to that of honey in the shepherd, that of the ocean or the forest in the artist, and thus, without reserve, of all things and without end...

"However, one point preoccupies you. We have prejudicially admitted that I have the prerogative of an unlimited possession, of everything beautiful, flavorsome and joyous, and that by the privilege of my nature. How dearly you would like to know where such a privilege comes from! It seems that I owe it partly to the particular constitution of my being—and that I shall explain when the moment comes—and partly to my instinct of Joy, which, in the final analysis, might well be the essential spring of that privilege.

"Thus, without being enlightened as to the genesis of the instinct, you can at least presume the mechanism of the privilege. The ever vaster possession of the world and the instinct of Joy are expressly interdependent. They nourish themselves in one another inexhaustibly. Is it the stammering sentiment of permissible possession that, in the beginning, gave birth to the first impulse of the instinct of Joy? Is it the latter that awoke the sentiment of that permissible possession? At any rate, whichever one was the initiator of the other, it is very easily conceivable that the nascent instinct, at the same time as it gave the nascent sentiment of possession its physical life—in a sense, its warmth, its basis of strength—gave it the ardor to know, to measure the extent of its power and its domain.

"The sentiment of possession immediately advancing into its literally infinite domain, in discovering extent and number, simultaneously assured and fortified the instinct of Joy. And thus, thereafter and forever, instinct fructifying and being fortified as the extent and number of possession was more fully discovered, the latter, under the ever more excited surges of instinct, progressed and advanced, extending proportionally and always multiplying its domain. Thus, by inexhaustible reciprocity, the instinct of Joy is endlessly enriched, which endlessly enriches the world..."

He fell silent then and extended his arm toward the mists that were covering the Rhune at our feet.

31

...Whereupon the mists opened, and unveiled a grim décor of black, gigantic rocks, looming up in a desert expanse.

"For a god," said the arcandre, "Hercules showed himself to be singularly stupid in cutting off the heads of the hydra. He had something much more genuinely Herculean, or simply cleverer, to accomplish with regard to the Lernean monster. I want to show you a very recreative spectacle, in which you will see featured nothing less than the hydra itself.

Having said that, he suddenly disappeared from my vicinity. A moment went by, and I perceived him digging in the ash-colored sand of a desolate location. He was naked. His flesh was gleaming with a gilded light similar to that with which Renaissance painters colored the bodies of angels. Svelte and robust, he walked toward the rocks. From afar, he raised his hands toward me, and showed me that they were empty. Then he went past the rocks. At that moment, a frightful roar, compounded from the sound of a hundred different but equally ferocious and furious cries, shook the air, and above the highest and most distant of the rocks, the heads of the hydra appeared, aspiring the winds and writhing toward the sky. Soon, the monster emerged between two other advanced rocks.

It loomed up, surpassing the vastest masses in height. I saw, standing on its tail, a formidable, frenetic trunk, covered in scales, dividing toward the summit into thick tentacular branches, each one terminated by a head that was howling and spitting fire from the mouth.

The arcandre continue advancing, and stopped, a gracious dwarf, a few paces away from the immense beast. There, without sketching the slightest gesture of attack or defense, he waited, contemplating the hydra. He smiled. His face expressed a curiosity that as simultaneously jovial and vigilant. The beast lashed the air with tongues of flame and convulsed its giant body, launching a storm of fire toward the visitor through all its mouths, with a multiple hiss...

As soon as they touched the gilded body, the flames vanished and the sand at the arcandre's feet was suddenly strewn with petals, as if a current of air had carried the flowers from some nearby garden and scattered them there.

The hydra redoubled its incendiary spitting. The arcandre fanned the air between himself and the monster with his hand, and now the flames curved back and returned to the body of the hydra, which they began to devour. The beast howled in surprise and pain, and the trunk and the heads, in hideous contortions all sought to escape the ardent bites and to attain the strangest of adversaries.

Now, as the hydra advanced, in these convulsions, the arcandre struck the ground with his foot. Then the earth opened up, and with a cataclysmic tremor, swallowed more than half the monster. The tentacles, left free, bristled and stretched, and their frightful heads rent the air with howls and flames. The arcandre stamped his foot again, and the earth was shaken, opened up again, vomited forth the monster and projected it bodily into the air, swinging it there. One might have thought it some apocalyptic balloon, struggling and writhing in an infernal tumult of whistles and roars, some of its tentacles reaching out in bewilderment toward the clouds, others folding back like hooks as if they wanted to grasp the void.

Having followed with an admiring eye the fantastic spectacle that the enormous gesticulations of the hydra created in mid-air, the arcandre raised and then lowered his arm. The beast abruptly fell, with all its weight and mass. It remained there, lying on the ground, as if flaccid, stunned. The arcandre considered it and did not move.

Gradually, slowly, with slow undulations like those of waves charged by a tempest, the hydra succeeded in getting up again, and came upright, swollen with hatred and rage, ready for further combat. Suddenly, the arcandre, with one bound, rose up and attained the height on one of its heads—and notwithstanding the roars, the fire and the fangs, he took hold of the underside of that head with both hands and transfixed with his eyes of light the enormous eyes of the monster.

This is what happened. The tentacle lashed the air violently, knotted itself around the body of the arcandre, forcing him to let go and swinging him in the void. Over the arcandre, held tightly in the curl that the squamous branch formed, the head of the branch leaned, avid with fury and voracity. The mouth opened with thunderous gasp, and the fangs touched the blond flesh—but as I was about to cry out in fear and anguish, the magician freed one of his arms from the colossal grip, raised it toward that head and began to caress it with the hand a little above the mouth that was, in a sense, the neck of the tentacle, as one might do with a pet cat stretching itself and purring among cushions.

And while doing that, my arcandre laughed in is childlike fashion, and while he flattered horrible head in that way, gradually, the roaring was strangled, the flames shortened, the hideous mask took on a character of stupefaction and pleasure that I cannot describe, so much did the ensemble seem burlesque, frightful and touching—and all the hydra's heads, flames extinct and whistling breathless, orbits dilated by bewilderment, leaned toward the one that the arcandre had bewitched.

"Ho ho ho! There!" said the latter. "That's better than our first duel...and it makes a change for you, beautiful monster, from the moans of horror and the maledictions that were until now the only concerts elevated toward you... Gently! Ho! Gently! And that's much more pleasant than the points of spears, the trenchant edges of blades, and the boulders with which certain individuals tried as hard as they could to kill you... Why kill you, eh, my hydra? Such a robust monument of flesh, such an ingenious adaptation of force, flexibility and impetuosity, such a generous source of flames! There, there! Is there nothing better to do with all that than annihilate it? Ho ho! As one can, by means of such a powerful apparatus, easily accomplish many rude tasks that the paltry muscles of humans renounce! But you have not, yourself, my poor monster, any other care than devouring... There! Of course! Is that your fault? Living in such a lugubrious décor, ennui must soon enrage you...and having nothing to chew but the roots and arid vegetation of this desert makes human flesh prodigiously tasty. So come on, then, graze these grassy meadows for me instead, dig these grasslands bright with flowers for me...."

A miracle burst forth. All around the rocks inside which that extraordinary combat was taking place, throughout the expanse, all the way to the horizon, the dull ground was covered with verdure. The desert was populated with trees and flowers. Nacreous springs flowed. Delightful birds fluttered from foliage to foliage. The leaden sky became blue. The hosanna of spring rose up from the earth, sung by every blade of grass, by every pistil, the light winds carrying it all the way to the vaults of the atmosphere, filing space with it.

Now, while the arcandre was speaking, the hydra had gradually loosened the knot of its tentacle. The curl broadened, as if languidly. And the arcandre might have fallen if he had not, while his body gradually resumed its freedom, while still talking and caressing the horrible throat, aiding himself with the scales, slowly climbed the living branch, which bewilderment was softening, in such a fashion that, still ascending, he perched upon the top of the head when spring surged forth beyond the rocks, his legs encircling the neck and his hands resting on the monstrous cranium.

And he continued.

"O voracious, famished, redoubtable utterly vigorous hydra, you only have to pass these rocks to reach that beautiful vegetation. There, perfumed winds flow, and an exquisite light shines. And beyond the meadows are regions without number, rich in all pastures appropriate to sustain you, much better than your desert, abundant in rivers where you can bathe, full of all sorts of delights superior to human flesh! Out there, what arenas for your strength and what goals for our ardor! Hup! There! The meadows, traversed, what voyages, what adventures! But my arms are too feeble to move on their own the rock that bars our route. It would be child's play for you to knock over the mass. Hup! Forward, beautiful hydra! Move that big stone out of the way for me, and let us wander in the charming meadow..."

And like a schoolboy stride a dog, the arcandre slaps and whips with one hand, laughing, and with the other caresses the giant mouth—and the hydra advances, prancing stupidly, extending all its heads together toward the miraculous spring, twisting its trunk as it advances toward the most enormous of the rocks, one thrust shoving you over and the other shoving you away like an ox shaking itself and chasing away a fly, and suddenly, on the threshold of the meadow, curving its trunk in monstrous serpentine movements toward the ground, and inclining its branches...and now the entire hydra, with all its heads, is crawling meekly through the grass, carrying the arcandre on its back.

32

A bird, intrigued, came to flutter around the monster. The beautiful bird! The plumage of its body shone with colored reflections of jade, like those that the foliage of forests produce in the light of the full moon. Its head shone with an ardent bronze glitter, like the fires of midday over the amber and of beaches. A tuft of opals danced on its vermilion head. It settled recklessly on one of the hydra's skulls.

The beast stopped crawling. Heads rose up from the grass, looking grimly at the radiant intruder, and attempting to seize it. Frightened, the bird flew away. Then it came back, and others followed—and they were all emboldened, playing and fleeing, brushing the hundred monstrous mouths with their multicolored sparkles.

The hydra, dazzled and exasperated, raised itself up entirely, its heads hissing, its mouths blowing out a mist, the precursor of flames. Now, a gust of wind agitated all the trees at that moment, shaking the flowery branches, and suddenly caused a downpour of white and pink spring blossom to rain down on the hydra.

The monster, momentarily blinded, fell back along its full length. The birds dispersed. Their songs and the music of their wings sounded in all directions. Whether it was the fraternal softness of the earth, the freshness of the young corollas, the soothing welcome of the grass or the limpid novelty of the dew, it seemed that an intoxication gripped the monster; it stretched, it grunted softly, it rubbed itself contentedly against the velvet of the ground...

33

I shall say no more about the enchantment of the hydra, for the book is thickening now, and I am far from having reached its capital point. Perhaps I shall report elsewhere the succession of further miracles produced by the arcandre, the vanquisher of the monster:

How the latter rose up from the baptismal spring, transfigured and stripped of its scales...

How it changed its form at the whim of the arcandre, and what astonishing forms it took...

How the magician produced different décors and, following the beast, accomplished all sorts of extraordinary labors before my eyes. At his signal, the hydra tunneled through mountains from one side to the other, deflected torrents and opened beds for them in sterile terrains that were covered with crops; stretched out toward the blackest clouds of the tempest, bursting and sweeping away the clouds and reopening the way for the sun; elongated itself all the way to the far side of the world, went to snatch the summer therefrom and transport it to regions sickened by winter...

I shall not say any more about the fantastic works of the hydra. I am in haste to arrive at a particularly solemn moment in my story. Because of that haste, I shall proceed more rapidly in the relation of prodigies, and doubtless even pass over in silence truly unimaginable scenes, or indicate them only in a few strokes...

34

The arcandre had returned to my side, and, having resumed his ordinary appearance, he said:

"To be sure, one sees, in legend, Marthe charming the Tarasque, and the beast following the saint obediently.[17] One also sees the dragon that murdered Saint George allowing itself to be attached and led away by a princess that it had hoped to eat...but in those fables the triumph over the monster is sufficient. The glory of God, thanks to whom the miracle is realized, is completed by the submission of the beast created by Hell. That is what the tales want to establish, and they go

---

[17] The Tarasque is a legendary chimerical monster of Provençal folklore. One of the stories accounting for its disappearance has Saint Martha of Bethany, the sister of Lazarus, who is mentioned in the gospel as having given hospitality to Jesus, coming with her sister Mary to live in Provence after the death of Christ and taming the Tarasque, in honor of which a church was built over her tomb in Tarascon.

no further. There is no question of making the beast of death serve the purposes of the living.

"Furthermore, fables of that species are rather rare. More generally, the monster is killed. For Hercules, there was no other way to vanquish the hydra than to annihilate it completely. Perseus killed the Gorgon, Theseus the Minotaur, Siegfried Fafner and the Archangel Michael, in trampling Lucifer underfoot, killed, as it were, his terrestrial power and consigned him to the empires of Evil. Now, is so much brutality truly admirable? Killing is the action of a butcher, not a victory of the gods.

"Those poor heroes shirked the most difficult, but most properly divine, aspect of their task. Perhaps they were not armed to do better, being too weak and too timorous to go beyond murder, fearing that if they did not slay the monster with the first blow, they would be vanquished themselves in the ensuing struggles...in brief, not being at all certain of still having the upper hand. In any case, they were too weak to attempt the great work: that which slowly transmutes darkness into light, lead into gold and Lucifer into a seraph. Trembling that they might be taken by the darkness, devoured by the inferno, burned in the athanor before the transmutation is achieved.

"Kill! Slay! Destroy! Such is the watchword of gods, angels and heroes. Siegfried would not have had the Ring if he had spared Fafner; Perseus only possessed Andromeda after having slain the Gorgon; Jesus only opened his heaven and Buddha his nirvana to those who kill their own terrestrial passions.

"These monsters that haunt all fables, whatever the ages and skies, are allied by the same sign, with is adapted to the unkind forces of the cosmos as well as the passions of human nature. In the same way that in the physical realm, a Franklin captures the incendiary lightning and utilizes it—for what works of power!—in the psychic realm, humans, within themselves, far from extinguishing those flames, that blood of the soul, those vital sources of force, can gaze at them, scrutinize them, proof themselves against their assaults, and learn to measure and manipulate their power.

"In the belief of fable, the heads of the hydra grow back apace if one cuts them off one at a time, and it is the same with all the passions, venomous flowers of a single stem, and their devouring danger remains the same, whichever one it is that is uprooted, until the moment when they are all scythed down at a single stroke—the virtuous method of the church! Effective, but too simple, and in the final analysis, disastrous.

"Is one any further forward for having ruined the treasure given, dried up the torrent, broken the irresistible lever of rude tasks that the muscles alone, too paltry, renounce? And it is in holding one of them that one can hold the others, not by means of the cutting blade, the consuming pyre or the stifling cilice, but proudly, by means of the audacious joy that raises them from their lairs, by means of charm, science, the lucid intelligence that assigns to each one, in accordance with its nature, delights other than and superior to those that it savors when served by instinct alone or blind heredities, making them, in the perpetual exaltation of all their resources and all their enthusiasm, the militias of the will of love and life...

"But enough preaching! We have better things to do, my friend."

35

Then, he resumed the game of comparisons by which he intended to specify for me the extent and the quality of his privileges. Apollonius of Tyana, by great efforts of fasting, incense and pentacles resuscitated the dead, or at least, it is said, caused a few phantoms to appear? The arcandre, by lifting his little finger, resuscitated not merely an individual but an entire city, an era, a sequence of centuries. Without any visible talisman, had he not transported me to the nebular age of the sun, to the planet in the time of the waters, and to the little family drawing room in an evening of my childhood?

I had strolled in Florence in the epoch of Savonarola. It had only required me to pause on the reflections of the vortex of images to share the intimacy of Corneille at Petit-Couronne or the meditations of Jacob Boehme in his shop, and eat Semiramis' pastries... In sum, I only had to report to any one of the prodigies that had been granted me to conclude without appeal that the slightest detail of such a confrontation sank all the spells of old Apollonius pitifully.

As for what was said about walking over water, again I was able—not without finesse, I thought—to make the observation to the arcandre that that was a miracle that humans operated continually with the greatest simplicity in the world, in that any one of them crossing a bridge was, in sum, doing neither more nor less than well and truly walking over water.

The arcandre having smiled at that quip, as I might have expected on the part of such a gracious individual, replied that even in taking the letter of the miracle as Jesus—or, in the case at hand, Apollonius—accomplished it, in stepping out of a boat at sea, he, the arcandre, could reply to the said miracle that he was not only able to walk on the water but in it: properly speaking, in the interior of rivers, seas and oceans, and at any depth; and that with as much liberty and ease as if he were walking along the path of some terrestrial garden. Even better, while walking in the waters, here and there, he was able to incorporate himself with the fish, the vegetation and fantastic minerals that populate them. In brief, that what we had once done in the soil, where I was a root, we could reproduce just as perfectly and picturesquely in the ocean or a river.

And as he finished that statement, we suddenly found ourselves on the edge of a real ocean. A boat was dancing, moored to the shore, into which the arcandre invited me to climb, and then climbed in with me. He raised the anchor and took the oars. We were soon out of sight of the coast. Then my companion abandoned the oars, stood up, took my hand, stepped over the side of the small vessel with no more ceremony than if he was passing over a doorstep; we traversed the empty space smoothly, entered into the ocean, and sank, continuing to walk and converse as if it were nothing.

36

Just as I did not relate the transfiguration and the endeavors of the beast of Lerne, I shall not describe at present my adventures in the interior of the sea. After having swooned by turns with pleasure, stupor and wonder at the revelation of a diversity of forms, lines and actions, so extraordinary that the craziest creations of the human imagination are by comparison as candle-flames are to the stars, I penetrated their internal attributes.

Immersed in the secrets of monsters without eyes, carnivorous plants and living gems, not only did I retain intact, as in previous proofs, my faculties of intelligence and sentiment, but I communicated them to the objects of that prodigious consubstantiation. The inorganic was animated, marine stones and vegetation acquired intellect and language. The ephemeral habitations that my curiosity chose revealed their aggregations or their fibers to me. Creatures of dream and nightmare told me their history, that of their species, the benefits and malevolence of neighboring species. In locations whose colors and arrangements have no expression in terrestrial language, I shared strange felicities and baroque tragedies or grandiose individuals that move beneath twelve thousand meters of water...

What I have depicted with some detail in the course of this narrative might have prejudiced what I could have said at length about the singularity of the diversions and dramas that I knew then. I can affirm that no tale of Armor[18] in which young fishermen are conducted by silvery sirens to the palace of the king of the Ocean, the loves of young fishermen with princesses with emerald eyes and algal hair, none of their nuptial

---

[18] Armor in the Celtic name of Brittany, which has a rich folklore of the kind indicated here.

feasts, no streams of diamonds in the treasures of the old sovereign of the Waters—no enchantments, ins sum, of those phantasmagorias that dazzle the infancy of maritime people—could equal in splendor or bizarrerie the spectacles and scenes of submarine reality to which the arcandre drew me...

One day, I will relate that enchantment, the most numerous and magnificent of all, and the emotions that I experienced there, by which my heart and my knowledge were permanently wonderstruck. Presently, I want to come to the moment when that new prodigy concluded, and I found myself back on my flowery bank on the Rhune.

The arcandre argued that the honorable Apollonius had undoubtedly been the pretext of the copious expedition that we had just accomplished, but that, all things considered, the disproportion seemed very great between the petty cause and its beautiful consequence. For that reason he wanted to benefit from the said expedition to pursue his work of comparison, enriching it by as much.

37

For if we cared to suppose the most privileged princes in the world, and all the great possessors of felicity, that he might take an example, and suppose them to be aboard the same boat from which we had just descended into the sea, would it not be slightly comical to contemplate, at that moment, resigned or furious, those to whom no whim was forbidden, and before whom the universe seemed to be enslaved...whether it be great Solomon, whose glory is sealed by the Bible, Caesar, the emperor of Rome, the Medicis surrounded by the most subtle ostentations of art and intellect, the king of France for whom the palace of Versailles was constructed...or any other that I care to imagine...?

"Draw," he said, "upon fable or history, and name the man who could have offered himself the strange pleasure that we have just taken, or, more simply, could have had a license merely to stroll, without risk of perishing, at a miserable pace at a depths beyond the length of his own body, through the marvelous would from which we have come? But would we not rather see each of our omnipotent and most fortunate individuals stop at the surface of the waters, and immobilize there, in his poor human condition, as a fly is imprisoned in the hollow of a child's hand?"

But that was only a small detail of their incapacity to accomplish the slightest of the gestures that we had made here and there in our enjoyment! Of their incapacity to be roots, to witness the genesis of worlds, etcetera, etcetera, as well as to transmute themselves, as we would have been able to do before, when my friend offered me the first enchantments, into a bird, a star, a ladybird, a butterfly, or pollen: in other words, into any object, any being, substance or element that my caprice had designated in the innumerable choice of the universe.

In brief, those princes, those fortunate individuals, those dazzling possessors were strangely limited to a very narrow category of possessions. If I had invoked the quality, the majesty and the abundance of the terrestrial wealth of which they disposed, to compensate in their own eyes for their defeat at the side of the boat or their impotence before any one of the extraordinary kingdoms to which the arcandre had opened the door to me, whether to their spiritual quality—in depth—or to their enjoyment the arcandre had the response that he had their possessions, their enjoyments and their happiness *as well*. What for them was splendid compensation for everything that they could not attain was for him merely a simple adjunction to what he had. Whatever, in fact, their victories, their voluptuousness and their ostentations were, he could recreate them; their palaces, their treasures, as many concrete and spiritual, were floating around his desire and he had only to reach out his hand to enjoy instantly whatever he wanted to enjoy. And all the powers and jubilations of those kings put together, in their unparalleled glory, only formed, in the final analysis, little more than a chord in the concert of his hours, a wave in the ocean of his joys.

And that said, could I believe, could I not take it as duly assured, that whatever individual I took as an example, the arcandre could always say in his regard: "I have all that he had, and I also have everything that he could not exploit or attain, in time and space, from the greatest density of the earth to the utmost depths of the sea and the detail of substances, in the stars and in souls..."

He added: "I have not brought you into the souls of human beings. The enchantments in which I guided you were all petty excursions into the curiosities of matter. But perhaps there is nothing in human souls but the refractions of matter...and the matter that is refracted there is not the matter I have shown you—which is only the matrix."

38

But at that moment, seized by I don't know what disturbance, without asking him immediately what he meant by that final remark. I questioned him thus:

"What about Tristan, the image of the most beautiful love? That love of Tristan, which you claim to surpass? Thus far you have said nothing, have accomplished nothing, in which there is love. What woman, thus far, has featured among your prodigies? What Helen? What Iseult? Of all the passions, delights and fevers with which you have caused me to burn, none was the desire for or the possession of adorable flesh. Nothing of the kiss, which is the veridical location of the greatest of prodigies, and the veritable athanor of all transmutations!

"As it seems that the summit of a mountain gathers, hoists, elevates and extends to the highest light the fields, the forests, the meadows and the individuals who live at its base and on its sides, so the kiss elevates toward the beloved lips the sum of the pride, dolors or crimes by which the soul is agitated. The flames of pride, dolors and crimes become honey in the mystery of joined lips. Then, all magic is possible. Pride, dolors or crimes, in the immense silence into which

244

consciousness sinks, can receive the sign that transmutes them...

"But let us leave that, and tell me, arcandre, what reign you assign to amour? In what way to you surpass Tristan, whom no lover equals in passion, in misfortune and in felicity? And if you are strong enough to grant all my prayers as soon as I ask you, at present, give me amour. What Helen, what Iseult, will rise up to my appeal?"

39

What happened then suspends my pen as a tremor in the hands of a hunter hinders the weapon if, from the thicket in which the prey is for which he is on the lookout, all the beasts of the forest, and, from the trees, all the birds, launch forth at the same time. How can I render in words the succession of fulgurance and unanimity that was, in an instant, simultaneously, produced in every part of me and outside of me?

It suddenly seemed to me that all the cells composing my body—its fibers, its blood, its nerves, its flesh, the billions of cells that are the body, from the extremities of the limbs to the tips of the hairs—that every one of those cells began to beat like a heart and light up, like those suns that once formed the third body of the arcandre, that every one of the billions of cells of my body was a heart and a sun.

And each of the particles of the earth, the grass, the flowers and the neighboring rocks, or the air and the mists, before, behind, beneath and above me, every particle of everything that I could embrace with my gaze seemed to beat to the rhythm of my cells, and shine with a similar light. A shining heart, that grain of sand; a strange undulation of palpitations and fires, that blade of grass; a thousand beating and sparkling hearts, the stem of that campanula; a dance of scintillating hearts that the wind sways, the corolla of that colchicum...and likewise every object and every substance...

And simultaneously, in, through and amongst the substances and objects, there was a similar unfurling of images of the universe, just as before, on the template of the arcandre, but this time whirling with all of space for a field, filing the expanse, from the mists of the Rhune to the depths of the sky.

At the hazard of the unfurling, women passed by: those that I had named, Helen and Iseult, Scheherazade and Broceliande,[19] and Melisande, and mingled with those fabulous women, saints, queens, courtesans, the heroines of noble amours, daughters of all races and all rejoicings, and unknown women, grave, languid, ardent, those who elevate dreams, those who stimulate pride...and like leaves around a tree, around them all, or reflected in them like the décor of the banks in a river, all that there is in the universe, always passing in the flux of images, everything that is, from the bed of the ocean to the confines of the ether, and from the Orient to the Occident of creation...

And me...

It seemed to me that I was, as well as the billions of hearts whose beats formed my being, simultaneously each of the forms and figures of that universal diversity, and the unique heart of everything...

I felt myself simultaneously dissolved in that enormous ensemble and containing it in its entirety. I grew all the way to the infinity of space; I was simultaneously vertigo, voluptuousness and immense possession, softly balanced above the ocean of forms and burning in each of my billons of hearts.

Now, I sought the arcandre in that innumerable enjoyment, and found him: as if all the palpitating gleams of my body were emanating a kind of arch of light above me, which occupied the total extent of space...as if the rhythm of the things whirling in that space were emanating a kind of arch palpitating with all the rhythms, as the song that rises from an organ forms a harmonious and invisible vault above the or-

---

[19] This reference is peculiar, given that Broceliande is the magical forest of Arthurian mythology, not a person. It cannot be a slip of the pen, because the name is repeated twice more in the context of the same list.

gan…as if the fire burning in every heart of millions of hearts were emanating and aren't sea that set space ablaze…that light, that fire, that rhythm were the arcandre. I saw him by way of the spiritual gaze, I knew that he was still in my presence, and his voice expressed itself as the light of the light, the face of the fire and the palpitation of the rhythm.

40

And I heard:

"Take, then. Choose. Fix your desire. Embrace. Possess. Al this is yours. Each of your billions of hearts has its pasture here. As many hearts as you see beating and shining, as many unions permitted for you with an object, a creature, a particle of creation."

The voice paused. I sensed myself floating and burning in an innumerable swoon, as various as if I were experiencing, at the same time, the passion and enjoyment of all the odors, tastes and voluptuousness contained in the passing images.

The arcandre's voice continued: "In addition to the hearts that you see here, which are merely your body of flesh, there are all those that beat in every vibration of your spiritual body and which correspond to the invisible things, flora, fauna, mountains and seas of planetary consciousness, immaterial kingdoms, secrets of souls…everything that cannot attain the physical senses alone."

There was a momentary silence.

"Thus, the number of your hearts is infinite, like the number of that which is in the visible universe and in the invisible universe."

Suddenly, a sort of laughter undulated through space, similar to a distant rumble of thunder in a summer sky, and which was prolonged in melodious resonances throughout the expanse.

"Are there enough women here for your liking?" the voice interrogated. "Choose, summon, cherish, embrace. But the one that you select will only ever be one crumb of the totality of these things that belong to you, and the pasture of a single one of your billions of hearts. Whether it is a matter of Helen, Iseult or Broceliande, it would be neither more nor less than if it were a matter of that grain of sand, that blade of grass, or that colchicum at your feet. As soon as one of your billions of hearts designates one of the particles of the universe, your consciousness comes running and accomplishes the nuptials. From that moment on, the couple can grow to infinite proportions, to be an ephemeral spectacle, an amusement of your intelligence, or an alliance requiring the totality of your being.

"It is your passion and our conscience that design the dimensions of your possession. Your passion and your consciousness can, at their whim, make any of those infimal hearts, any of those billionths of you, vast enough to contain the ensemble of all hearts, and the object vast and adorable enough for it to be worth all the resources of your being, the play of your members, your amour and all the warmth of our will to knowledge. It will no longer be an atom of you, but you, you, in our entirety, who will espouse and embrace.

"However, great as the passion might be, could you remain forever in a single one of your beings, after what you have seen here? Go, from voluptuousness to voluptuousness, always new. That fragment of flint, that blade of grass, that colchicum at our feet, might reserve for you as many surprises, caresses and mysteries as Helen, Iseult or Broceliande. Just because you cannot embrace them with the same organs, do not think that you cannot embrace them any less passionately or less magnificently."

And, while the voice of light spoke thus, the innumerable sensation that I was experiencing of possession and voluptuousness intensified and multiplied further. But I do not know how to describe something so astonishing in its prodigy and its quantity. Each of my billons of hearts was like an organism. I perceived that each heart had a mind, hearing and sight, lips with which to kiss and arms with which to embrace, and in the same way that the mind is double, able to project and receive, each of my hearts was both male and female, the calyx and what fecundates it.

And those gazes, those ears, those lips, those arms and those sex organs were alive and rejoicing. And they embraced, gave and received in the bosom of the ocean of images.

And then I heard the voice:

"You asked me for amour. This is the amour I give you. Not of one being for another being, but of the billons of beings that are you and are the prodigious population of your veins, your nerves, your blood, your flesh and the continents of your mind, the effusion of those billions of beings toward everything that is in the universe and time and space, and which they are able to conquer, cherish, embrace and possess, the union permitted to those billions of beings, and the marvelous nuptials permitted to them—that is what I call Amour. In each of our billions of beings, know the fevers of desire, the ardent or august intoxications of the embrace and the possession..."

Now, at that moment, rolled in the flames of the ineffable furnace, I was gripped by a desire that surpassed all others, and was suddenly like a man in chains trying to break his bonds. My being reached out in space and I wanted to be returned to my habitual face and body. And it was immediately done, and the arcandre reappeared beside me.

Then I stood up, and some unknown frenzy summarizing al the fevers that had excited me until that moment increased my strength and completed my audacity. I grabbed the arcandre by the arm, as if I wanted to wrestle him and throw him down, and, plunging my bewildered gaze into his eyes, I shouted: "Who are you?"

41

He loosened my grip gently. He looked at me in his turn and I was mastered in my delirium, like a docile child before the master, who is waiting for a word.

And he said: "I shall soon resolve that enigma. But first, I want to ask you a rather singular question."

A great curiosity immediately rose up within me. I was ready to listen.

He began, immediately.

"In the times when a few idlers marveled at locomotives, airplanes and large telescopes, rhetors, moralists, philosophers and predictors were unanimous, or nearly so, and rudely affirmed that no technology—nor, moreover, any other progress in science—could change or modify the profound nature of human beings, or of human passions, which, by the same token, they certified eternal. The amiable Anatole France in a chapter of his book about the Penguins, showed future times, as far as they could be imagined, automatically recommencing past times.

"Undoubtedly, those sages were telling the truth, for it is a fact that no great crowd rose up to protest, to proclaim some contrary assertion, and in response to the affirmations of the rhetors, allow the possibility to be glimpsed that absolutely new passions might emerge from locomotives, airplanes and large telescopes, capable of leading humans as profoundly, and with as much force and powers as either the primordial necessities of the human condition and the commandments of the viscera and muscles, or certain sentiments such as the will to survive, to possess women, or to obtain power or gold, had ever been able to do.

"And it is similarly a fact that in spite of locomotives, airplanes and large telescopes, the majority of musicians, poets, novelists, playwrights and other artists, who are the voice and the color of human passions, continue to sing and to paint the natural fatalities and sentiments of faith, love, hatred, lucre, ambition and dolor that their masters and colleagues have, throughout the ages, from writing on papyrus to printing by linotype, congruently and copiously sung and painted.

"The only modification that has taken place in mores is that the number of humans who aspired to enjoyment increased, and the plebeians have organized themselves in order that they too might attain the pleasures and sensualities of princes and great manipulators of gold. The most audacious of poets and musicians consecrated their songs to those aspirations, and to the evident notion of justice that animated them, but nothing in that seemed to indicate that the great passions would be other than they always had been, and that their goals might be transformed. Thus, just because more people climb a mountain in order to get closer to the sun, it does not follow that the sun must change

"Whatever humans might do, in fact, could it change the sun? Let us continue the examination by varying our term of comparison. To claim that locomotives, airplanes and any other machines might transmute in some way the ideals and passions emerging from the fundamental nature of humans would be as crazy as claiming that the sun that illuminates the earth might, by virtue of human invention, change into another sun!

"And yet, what if that were the case, my friend—*what if one could change the sun?*

"But let's be serious. So, one ought to take for decisive the affirmation of the sages; to hold that, no games that science, locomotives and telescopes might play can re-knead the fundamental dough of the human cake, a dough kneaded one and for all, and that is firmly set—if one is on this earth and not Saturn or Arcturus—with its acids and its honeys, its vices, its malevolences, its nobilities and its grandeurs. In the final analysis, the games of science are just caramel or orange-blossom, pistachios and pralines, fine layers of cream with which the pastry-cook Progress decorates the fundamental, essential and unalterable biscuit..."

"Arcandre...," I said.

"Nevertheless," he went on, "let's suppose that some of my prodigies were in the hands of those poor humans. I thus arrive at the question I want to put to you. Tell me, then: if humans had the privileges, a few of whose effects I have revealed to you...if the incalculable richness of amour that I have just rendered yours, and if the infinity of objects in which that infinity is dispensed were their common prerogative...if our casual displacements in time, space , substance and the elements were their resources...in sum, if all the prod-

251

igies to which you have been party, and all those you can infer therefrom, were in the human domain...tell me, do you believe that the mores of human beings would be as they ordinarily are, and do you believe that humans would remain similar to what they are?"

I let my arms drop, dazed. To ask me to answer such a question, in the state of overexcitement that I was I, appeared to me to be a strange challenge.

But the arcandre, placid and smiling, continued:

"Those poor humans have many maladies. Every great city, for each museum in which it honors the masterpieces that attest to the beauties and graces of life, possesses a good dozen hospitals in which the horrors of fevers and gangrenes are displayed, and a good thousand apothecaries' shops. The books describing those maladies, if one stacked them up, would doubtless realize the sky-piercing tower that the Hebrews attempted in vain to erect, and Nebuchadnezzar after them. The world is a kind of vast leprosarium. Whoever is not ill in never sure that he will not be before turning the next street corner or reaching the end of the field. Cotton wool, vials and unguents are in everyone's cupboards, and emerge therefrom more rapidly and more often than fortune, joy or amour.

"To judge human passions appropriately, I have to take account of human rheumatisms, fevers and abscesses. What would be the passions of a healthy humanity, devoid of cancers, gangrenes, crutches, without drugs, cataplasms and facemasks? Can I imagine that? Certainly not! But it is not reckless to suggest that the actions, the progress, of that humanity, its audacity in all things, its respirations and its appetite for life, would doubtless be more spacious, more vivacious and freer.

"Now, I would only have to lift a finger, as you have seen me do, to summon all remedies and accomplish all cures. Would you like to see that prodigy, after so many others? Would you like me to cause a hunchback to stand upright by looking at his hump, or render sight to a blind man by passing my hand over his eyes? Would you like me, more certainly than the baths at Lourdes, to give legs to cripples and enable paralytics to play tag? I have shown you finer and less easy miracles!

"So, if my resources were in human hands, would everything in their passions that stems from the hospital no longer be eternal, fundamental and unalterable?"

I looked at the arcandre in bewilderment. His clear visage radiated confidence and a kind of malicious gaiety. I hesitated to interrupt...

42

He went on:

"Those poor humans need to eat. *Primum vivere*. What efforts, for the hunk of bread and the glass of wine! What labors to acquire the right to sit down at table! What struggles, incessantly renewed, to conserve that essential right! How many furrowed brows, how many curbed backs, how many bitter calculi...

"Prehistoric man lay in wait for the bear, and was lacerated fighting it, and was lacerated again defending against other humans the quarter of meat that he was taking to his family, doing little a less or more than men do nowadays, in décor less bare, in a costume less primitive and with weapons and wounds less visible, if no less cruel, in order to succeed in paying every day the milkman, the butcher and the baker. Black men in the depths of mines, pale men in offices, men of traffic, thought or science devote the best, most energetic and most ingenious part of their mind and their muscles to that great quotidian victory over hunger.

"To pontificate honestly about human passions, I need to take account of human hunger. What would be the passions of a humanity for whom not only was the tithe of hunger abolished forever, but for whom, without there being any other trouble to take that that of eating, their table would always be abundantly supplied with the exquisite fare that as once only served to kings and the very fortunate? Can I imagine that? No, of course not! But I presume that if so many hours, so much strength, determination, calculation enslaved to the most brutal of needs were suddenly rendered free, that a singular freshness of the muscles and the mind would emerge from that peace and liberty! That so much impetus, diminished or totally subordinated to the conquest and the safeguarding of bread, suddenly disposable, would be a strange leisure to expend in satisfying other appetites...

"What appetites? Hungers of the soul? Those of mild interior joys? Those of intelligence? Certainly, those hungers. But those that I want to talk about are very different—except, of course, how can humans be made to hear them, since the objects of those other hungers, the nutriments that might be obtained from those objects, and the veridical delights and juices of those nutriments are obscured by concern for the hunger of the belly, ignored, unsuspected or rendered inaccessible by the exclusive and giant affair of gaining bread?

"But you, who have seen the entire history of the world emerge from a little stone taken at random from the soil, you would have been able, for as long as you pleased, and in the rare voluptuousness of new emotions, to enjoy in the most infinitesimal detail the fire, color and light of the prodigious combinations and innumerable splendors or the primal substance, and from there, with the slightest impulse of your desire, pass into no matter what epoch and no matter what domain—let us say hunting wolves and deer under Charlemagne, or strolling in one of the rings of Saturn—you, who, I think, ought to have understood by now that there is, in my company, an indescribable infinity of diversions, states, places, objects of emotions and possible sensualities, ought to be able to answer as to what hungers might be felt if humans could do what we have done.

"You would say that a lifetime would be very short to slake all the thirsts excited by so many marvelous territories opened and so many beautiful fevers permitted, and what feasts of the senses, the heart and the mind would be offered, far more various and enjoyable than the most copious repasts or the most subtle love-feasts! So, see then...

"Without asking you to abdicate anything of the extraordinary fêtes that I can deliver to you in space and in time, in history and in the cosmos, I can also give you all those of the belly! I would only have to stamp my foot on the ground like Riquet à la Houppe[20] to make succulent dishes without number, marvelous and ready-prepared. Would you like to see piled up here, this instant, more victuals and flagons than Gargantua could contemplate in a dream, than the Eddas can depict in Valhalla, where the gods stuff themselves relentlessly? Would you like to see baskets overflowing with fruits from the orchards of the five continents of the world, and plates on which are fuming, braised and jugged, the softest flesh of beasts of the meadows, the poultry-yard and the woods? Would you like to see the wines of the most illustrious vines streaming?

"Say the word and I can dispense a pleasant festival for your mouth and stomach! The elements themselves would bring you their guests, soon seasoned, roasted or friend, according to my own recipes. The ocean would cast fish at your feet in each of its unfurling waves. The forest would reach out toward you and dedicates it game to you, elegantly couched on beds of heather. Trees of America, Australia and India would make their fruits dance like milk-cows sounding their bells, extending their opulent branches through space and shaking them above you, who would only have to open your hands...

"But let us leave the enchantment that a tap of my foot could cause to rise from the ground or fly through the air. I have more precious things to show you! And yet, tell me: if such fare were the quotidian resource of all humans, and the hunger of their bellies was, so to speak, filled in forever, would everything of their passions that stems from their hunger, be eternal and immutable?"

---

[20] The eponymous hero of another of Perrault's tales, usually known in English as "Ricky with the Tuft."

43

Before I could utter a word in reply, he went on.

"As much by sense as by sentiment, men and women are terribly drawn to one another. Their frictions and enlacements occupy, lead and summarize all terrestrial lyricism. There are no august contemplations of nature, magics of science, ostentations of intelligence, that do not end in the triumphal duo of the sexes, the kiss of loins or souls, often both together, although not indispensably. Amour, that of woman and man for one another, is the great arcanum, the supreme hymn and the crown of all glory.

"Nothing can enter the lists with the erotic adventure. All human gesture testifies to that. Venture to sustain that an idea, a scientific research, the ambition of a power, the mystical apostolate or the worship of gold can provide an ardor and voluptuousness as keen as that of sexual conjunction, and springs as vigorous as the heat and impatience that precede the conjunction in question, and serious people will applaud you while laughing behind their hands. Let the woman come along who sits down in the visual field of the thinker, the ascetic, the scientist, the trader or the tribune, as you will see without delay the fevers of politics, trade, the gods, retorts and theories become more insipid than stems devoid of corollas, more extinct than a house devoid of windows.

"Amour sublimates genius and renders a hundredfold what it has first bowled over. Certainly, and there is no finer story than that of the exaltation of the higher faculties by its grace. It is the drama of human assumption. But the non-possession or the dolor of love flattens and scythes down all them most grandiose virtues. Thus the tyranny of amour proves itself dominant over any other, and the supreme motive force.

"Now, I am not denying its splendor at all. I salute its works and its gestures. I mean to enjoy such an amour—but while putting it in its place, let us say in the proportion of one to a billion. And its works, its gestures, its splendor, with a similar exultation of the senses and a similar warmth of the heart I want multiplied as many times as there are objects, states and places in the universe. Have you not felt the lips, the arms and the sex organs of every one of your hearts in your amorous hypostasis? If, instead of interrogating me so rudely and breaking the charm so suddenly, you had prolonged the proof, you would have been able, taking no matter what passing image of an object, and entity or a being, to live a grandiose and incalculable passion thereby, as emotional as by means of any of the individuals who enchant men and women.

"Do you remember the moments when you were a root? Tell me whether the triple sensation of struggling in the humus, of being the gracious tree and being the consciousness looking on, was not at least as strange and rare, and simultaneously and frenetic and delicious and cruel as one of those duels and one of those kisses that are the currency of amour, whose arena is the sempiternal bed and whose champions are the monotonous lips?

"When you felt yourself rolled by boiling oceans, in a décor surpassing those imagined by Dante, tell me whether your fear and the magnificent voluptuousness of knowing yourself the master of the moment, and that you could, with a gesture, scratch out the cosmic tragedy to find yourself...what do I know?...wherever you wished—let's say Praxiteles' studio, or Veronese's—tell me, my friend, if such games, in which sight and hearing, the flesh, emotion and intelligence have their part in the paroxysm, are not worth as much as one of the games of the amour that is the aliment of all human poetry and the major ideal of men and women?

"For those who know such games, for those who experience them, will the amour of men and women still be large enough to fill the entire realm of veridical amour? For will not that amour be the simultaneously timid and ardent palpitation toward a state, a place, or a mysterious and distant object, will not that amour be the tremulous and voluptuous possession of that state, that object or that place, many aspects of which will

257

escape at first, the mystery of which will grow as one perceives more of its details, and the graces and richness of which will multiply as the possession proceeds?

"Contemplate a hill or a sumptuous forest at a distance. At first it is an immense tuft of emerald and gold... Approach, enter, tread its paths, and there are a thousand species of trees, plants and small creatures...and every tree, every plant and every insect will be a monument to mystery, movement and elegance in itself. Fabre used up his entire life and composed twenty volumes on the mores of a few insects. Monet painted the same pool and its nympheas a hundred times without exhausting its splendors. Thus it is with any object, no matter how small. Dramas, fêtes, tournaments, revolutions and orgies pass in an instant in one of the particles of one of the petals of that colchicum at your feet. And I can enable you to witness it, if you wish, and enable to you take part in it, by magnifying it to human measure or by shrinking you to their atomic dimensions.

"There is not one object, not one instant, that is not charged, is not streaming, with events, adventures and endeavors. There is not an atom in you that does not have the power to involve you therein, and organs appropriate to give our enjoyment, emotion, sensuality. To someone who can do that, does not the amour of men and women, with its fevers and apotheoses, seem one simple aspect of possible fevers and apotheoses?

"Tristan and all the great lovers who are glorified were imprisoned in their passion like a fly in a drop of water in which it drowns. What Shakespeare, what Goethe, what Wagner of the fly race would sing the passion of the insect in the bosom of the droplet that slakes its thirst and kills it? Would it be a sublime poem for the fly race if the singer was great? Romeo, des Grieux and Werther, like Tristan, had only one heart. What if, around Iseult, there had been the rest of the universe, and if, around Tristan's heart, which contained Tristan's passion for Iseult, thousands of hearts had been beating, rich in the power of love? What if, around the hunger of a

Sade, had existed thousands of other sources of pleasures as voluptuous and strange as those with which he sought diversion?

"Do you, who have lived for a brief moment in the universal nuptials, not judge singularly primitive the exclusive love of a Tristan, the fastidious and very fragmentary curiosities of a Sade? And if what you know were the resource of men and women, do you not think that to subjugate to a single object all the riches of passion could only be the action of those who were unaware of all the other objects of amour? That to enclose the eternally new totality and diversity of the treasures and graces of the visible and invisible creation in a single being—whether it by Iseult for Tristan or Tristan for Iseult—and subordinating oneself to that single being to the extent of dying if it does, would be the archaic mathematics of lovers or poets blind to the number of their being, to the number of their hearts and that of permissible amours, an operation no less puerile and fallacious than to attempt to hide the barn under an ear of wheat, to enclose the forest in one of its leaves, to capture the infinity of spheres and systems in the flash of a mirror on which the sunlight plays, or to weave the immense tapestry of the universe with one of the threads of its weft?

"Now, tell me, if that were the case, if those billions of hearts that you felt beating were the bodies of all men and all women, and the delights and sensualities that it conferred were permitted, would the passions of human beings that stem from the itching of their loins, and the static ideal that they make of amour, be eternally fatal and forever irreducible?"

44

What was the arcandre's design? What response did he want me to make to that speech, entirely edified thus far on the hypothesis of an ensemble of perfectly phantasmagorical powers suddenly bestowed on human beings? I did not doubt the arcandre's own powers—those I had prestigiously used. But what was the objective of that tirade regarding their supposed application to old human rituals? But I dared not testify to him, yet again, my impatience...

"Humans," he continued, "love power—a very legitimate taste. In addition to the fact that they generally claim to acquire by virtue of it the means to do good on a more ample scale, that excellent pretention is not at all restrictive of pleasures of all kinds that one finds in elevated employments: wealth, elite society, the domination of others, the sweet intoxications procured to pride by the sensation of altitude and the sentiment of the importance of the actions one accomplishes, the vaster possession of the world's enjoyments and pleasures, within the limits fixed for humans by the resources of their epoch...and the resistance of the arteries, etcetera, etcetera...

"To attain that power, however, and to have its advantages, to acquire crowns, positions, promotions, how many battles, surreptitious crimes and treasons are required, how many duels with competing ambitions, how many pacts against hatred and perpetual ambushes...how much vital and strenuous force incessantly expended in such cruel obligations...?

"I possess a royalty, a power and a government compared with which those that humans exercise over other humans are negligible. As for the enjoyments and the brilliance that they dispense, nothing that the common run of humans possess, covet and adore can be compared with them. You smile at that exordium and think that a monk preaching will not say anything different when he wants to talk about the glory of the faith and the intimate delectations savored by the perfect congregation, who have been touched by the grace of heaven. Let us leave the monk there, my friend. The touch of God has nothing to do with this. The enjoyments and the brilliance of which I speak are of this world.

"What is that power? Of what elements is it made? On what objects is it exercised? What are the domains and the populations of that royalty?

"It is...but let us first consider one preliminary point. All those hearts that I have made you see, all those living suns in

260

our veins, your nerves, your blood, your flesh and the continents of your mind, those billions of lips extended toward the kisses of the universe, those millions of arms apt to embrace...when I have left you, how will you find them again?"

45

"If there were some magic in all that I have shown you, in you and outside you, that magic, to hasten your instruction, would only be in a certain contraction of objects and states— let us say a panoramic condensation similar to the abbreviations of immense countries whose image occupies a single page of an atlas, or those views of cities, palaces, buildings, crowds and passions in reality innumerable, but whose representation can be held entirely in a little photograph...

"As for the objects, the things that I condensed for you in that way, they were very real things, places and states, which exist, which I have attained, which I possess in the fashion that you have seen and ephemerally possessed, some of which, by virtue of your present human condition, will be for you, when I have left you, what gold still mixed with quartz is for the goldsmith.

"So, can you doubt any longer now that you are made of those billions of hearts with which you have momentarily burned? Can you doubt any longer, having seen them, and embraced some of them, the billions of objects of amour that creation sets before them? And to know that you have those hearts, to know what their objects are...is that not already a very precious information with which I shall leave you? And that is only a small part of my gift...

"But it will be necessary for you to rediscover those hearts. All these astonishing voyages, the prodigies that we have accomplished, and all the possibilities that I have sketched for you—those emotions, those contemplations, those intoxications— that you hold for real and certain, and that your memory will conserve, when I have left you, you must search for the paths that lead to them with only your human resources.

"There is, between what I have enabled you to see and feel and your present human condition, what there is between the page of the atlas and the actions it is necessary to accomplish to render the countries depicted there real. To know that those countries exist and that it is possible to go there—is that not an immense certainty?

"What epic stepping-stones the simple belief that paradise exists, and the hope of attaining that paradise, have been throughout the centuries! And yet nothing ever proved the existence of the paradise in a fashion that corroborated the faith, increasing the affirmation of that faith by evidence satisfactory to reason, and, in sum, to the science that might have enriched the ecstasies of seers, the *summas* of theologians and the delirium of crowds, with the incorruptible ratification of the meter, number and the balance...

"Now, as the certainty is established of the real existence of the America and the Australia depicted on the pages of the atlas, so, simultaneously, the science that your reason demands and the faith that moves your passion will perhaps compose your certainty of the prodigious countries to which I have brought you, the astonishing states that you have experienced and the miracles that I have performed for you or offered to you. As in proceeding from the images in the Atlas, there remains a route to follow, and it remains to find the money and the sandals necessary to make the journey.

"I shall not leave you without placing you at the entrance to the route. I shall leave you the money and the sandals. In any case you are already on that route, since you have encountered me. And you possess the money and the sandals, since you have the passion and the treasure of the will to Knowledge.

46

"And that is the power and the royalty that I mean.

"Just as a man who wants power encounters conspirators, poisoners, hypocrites, appeasers, delightful temptations that delay him or retain him in traps, redoubtable competitors, the envious, those who are moved to hatred and those who propose bloody or vile pacts, as soon as your first research toward your marvelous hearts, you will find within you powerful crowds and prejudices, learned beliefs, and the suggestions and commandments of your blood, your flesh and your mind, containing and carrying what was put into them before you thought of looking at them, of learning them and knowing them.

"Thus, when a man suddenly inherits a seigneurial domain, he arrives and finds fields lying fallow, forests full of game but all entangled, a park in which nettles mingle with the fruit trees and the flowers. If he questions the steward and the local people sagely, he will know why this has been neglected and that has been encouraged. He will know what flowers bloom in the park, what fruits grow in the orchard, what game runs in the forest, how solid the château is and how beautiful its rooms are, and what repair work is necessary. At the outset of his enterprise and his labors, the peasants will be astonished, the neighboring landowners will discourage him, the steward will protest in the name of habits that leave him in peace. The gardeners, the laborers, the foresters, the farmers and the masons in the château will need to be supervised continuously. It is the same for the good and bad things that are in your blood, your flesh and your mind, containing what was put into them before you thought of looking at them and taking an interest in them like that of the heir of a seigneurial domain in his inheritance.

"But the endeavors of the lord of the manor, and the struggles that must be sustained by the man who wants power, are only feeble comparisons with regard to the work that you will have to accomplish and the wars that you will have to undertake in your voyage through yourself and the discovery of your marvelous hearts. For your internal enemies are a thousand times more obscure, insidious, fleeting and ungraspable than the obstacles before the lord of the manor, who can pay, call upon judges and gendarmes, change his steward, the masons, the farmers, and see in broad daylight the brambles in the orchard and the cracks in the château's walls, and before the man in quest of power, who can buy consciences and weapons, employ swordsmen and pamphleteers for base endeavors, and has for lieutenants his eloquence, his seduction, his lies and his bluffing...

"You on the other hand, will not be able to trick, deceive or bluff your instincts, your beliefs, your habits and the influences of the environment, but will have to struggle face to face and in perpetual uncertainty, without any other weapons than the part of your will that, knowing those marvelous hearts, will reach toward them.

"I say 'perpetual uncertainty' because there is nothing anywhere in laws, canons, rules and bibles to enlighten such labor and such struggles, revealing exactly where in your instincts, your blood and your mind the good and the bad, the useful and the harmful are, but only a few items of information scattered here and there, unaggregated and drowned in the old gospels, kabbalas, philosophies and ordinary human disciplines. And there are no canons or rules for those profound investigations, because the majority of humans, in the turbulence of their cares, their amours and their wars, have too many other things to do than search themselves, and they consent, with the reserve of a few escapades, indiscretions and truancies, to a dogma, a bible, a science, a morality, a law, an ideal, a discipline, a good and evil, a useful and harmful, fabricated once and for all over several centuries of generations of humans, apt to satisfy general problems and responding to the principal itches of the blood, interests and consciousness.

"In a society, under ignorant codes and philosophies that cannot take account of the existence of those billions of marvelous hearts and the objects that correspond to them, and thus having nothing to conceive of or say to the labors that it is necessary to undertake in order to attain them, it will necessarily be you, simultaneously your explorer and your experimental field, your only guide and your only true disciple, who must gradually edify your own laws, gospels, rules and disciplines, as you discover what you ought to call your self, among all the influences before and around you that weigh upon you; as you discover your true wealth and poverties, searching honestly and intrepidly for any opportunity to test them, their true extent and their true strength.

"In that rude and virile task you will see rising within you delightful or genuinely prodigious powers of which humans are unaware or leave unutilized, ceding to the pitiful weaknesses that they adore or glorify. Each of your powers will be akin to a mine, of which you must be both the prospector and the miner, and afterwards the man who processes the mineral and who forms the gold into an ingot, and the touchstone, and the jeweler and, finally, the wearer of the jewel! And toward each of those miseries, it will be necessary for you to be the spectator and the judge, the flagellator and the one who offers half of his cloak, or the one, as you saw in the combat with the hydra, who charms and accomplishes the transmutation.

"Thus, from conquest to conquest of your interior truths, you will progress toward the light of your marvelous hearts. But what surprises, what recompenses in the very tribulations and vicissitudes of the route! In addition to the astonishment you will experience, the amusement you will obtain, sometimes piquant and sometimes grandiose, the strange things discovered in the innumerable domains of the body, in the savageries, the delicacies and the sapiences of instinct, in the thaumaturgies of the nerves, in the dark alleys, Pompeiis, cul-de-sacs, hovels and palaces of the mind; in addition to the sensuality of learning truths not veiled or painted by prejudice, fearful hypocrisies or the esotericism of dogmas; in addition to the fever of battle against the obscure, perfidious or stupid hordes of the blood, the flesh and atavism, and the delight of your victories; in addition to the pride of attaining in yourself physical and metaphysical justices and liberties, which will be the same ones for whose stifling or exaltation humans have, throughout the ages, murdered, burned and unleashed revolutions…in addition to all those escalations, diversions and beautiful endeavors of your voyage, you will encounter in the way, in that work—the pleasant adventure!—without having looked for them, the goods that humans seek at the summits, those that they expect of coups-d'états or social metamorphoses, and those that they snatch from one another in great troubles, by recourse to wars, ruses and rapes…

47

"You will encounter them because each of your victories over yourself has its repercussion in the external world. Because your richer consciousness, your more numerous intelligence and your more vivid sensibility have a clearer perception of the roads to human domains; because, your muscles more alert, your lunges enlarged by the winds of altitudes, your magnified gaze, which, having looked verities in the face, no longer blinks at the brightest lights and no longer avoids the most suspect darkness, but stares into them untroubled, having penetrated the worst in yourself; because your surer voice and, in sum, your entire being, more apt for the struggle and the calculation, lower the facile drawbridges for you beyond which lie the enjoyments and luxuries of human beings.

"But those enjoyments, luxuries and benefits you will contemplate then in their true light. The supreme goals of so much effort and furious and fratricidal gesticulations will only be, for you, reflections of what you will have found, held and possessed within you. Thus the man who returns from hunting eagles, descending the slopes heavy with the regal birds he bears on his shoulders, will find at the bottom marmots striving to catch lizards or snails…

"Crowns, positions, ranks, honors, dominations, worldly favors, will merely be the bagatelles of the threshold that you want to cross. Crowns you will wear when the roll-call of your will is answered by the strength of your muscles, your haulers, your gymnasts, your weavers and your forgers, the vessels and winches of your nerves, the battalions of your blood, enthusiasms, delights, temerities, fervors, and your passions with their wild beasts, mobs, debauches and courtiers, tendernesses, ardors, prides, and insatiable curiosities...

"The dominations, you have surpassed. There will be no crowd pressing around an apostle, a captain or an orator in which you will not recognize the human images of appetites, gross thirsts, muted revolts, cruelties, native obediences, hateful passivities that you have already known, numbered and regulated in your instincts and your atavistic beings...and the rest in accordance.

"As I say, they are the bagatelles of the threshold, since you will be well beyond those dominations and royalties, since the one and the other will merely be stages toward your marvelous hearts, which will open up to you, innumerably.

"Then you will be, among human riches—their feasts, their amours, their trafficking and their ambitions—like a voyager amusing himself at one of his ports of call with local games, sampling them, dabbling in them, informing yourself and then resuming your course toward other worlds and other beings...

"Except that the worlds where you are going, when you have had enough of your sojourn among humans, will not be in space, in the ether, on other planets, but in yourself and in other zones of the earth, those of which I have given you an idea, and which will be the places and pastures of your marvelous hearts attained...

"Now, tell me, if humans, before seeking power among and over humans, first attempted to obtain it over themselves, if those who demand liberty and justice, before federating and attempting revolutions against tyrants and oppressions, first made the same coalition of wills and efforts against their own interior injustices and slaveries—after which they might perhaps see that the revolution was accomplished and liberty acquired—in sum, if the zones of power and joy open to your marvelous hearts were, similarly, open to all humans, tell me, would the human passions that stem from the human hunger for power, or the bitterness of their subjugation, really be forever indelible?"

48

He remained silent for a few moments, but I did not think of speaking, only of meditating on what he had said. And I thought that in his hasty depiction of voyages through the domains and crowds that everyone bears within themselves, he had skirted a great deal of information—scattered, however, and almost in the form of charades—that I had read in many books of kabbalistic and theosophical sciences. Nevertheless, none of those books ended in concrete joys, corporeal as well as spiritual, of the kind that he had shown me, nor countries as extraordinary as the ones to which he had taken me.

Those works led humans, at the term of their mysticomagical labors, either to certain states luminous bliss similar to that promised by the Christian paradise, or to a kind of divine intelligence of the genre of the Hindu nirvana, a ravishing and static reintegration in the bosom of the "principle of things," with all terrestrial passions extinct. The arcandre intended to dwell solidly on earth, spoke of no renunciations of the goods of this world, but, on the contrary, calculated the enjoyment that one might obtain, after the subtraction of malady, hunger, the blinkers of overly-exclusive intersexual amour, the blinkers of particularly gross passions resulting from the state of slavery, and finally, the thirst for power; he augmented the motives and nourishment of the passions strangely, the number of locations and objects of diversion, knowledge and joy, and the number of means of obtaining them; and in every manner, he attributed to the senses, to the body and its organs, a place and an importance that many kabbalists and theosophists failed to give them, only deigning to interest themselves in the human machine and the formal

268

world in order to offer them as a holocaust to the soul and the divine spark that they inserted into them...

The arcandre casually interrupted my reflections at that point.

"I shall have finished soon," he said. "Equipped with what I have just told you, consider for a moment human wars. From territory to territory, boutique to boutique, rank to rank, people seek to devour one another neither more nor less than dogs contesting a bone. Perhaps the bone is an empire for two pretenders, a colony equally coveted by two great peoples, a sugar-cane plantation for two traffickers, a chair for two magisters, a stripe for two officers, a lady for two gentlemen, a wing for two eaters of a chicken, a piece of chocolate for two street-urchins.

"I sustain that it is the fault of the bone, whether it be an empire, a colony or a piece of chocolate. In fact, if there were not only one bone for every dog, but innumerably more bones than dogs, instead of snatching the desired treasure from one another, each one would appease his hunger, would eat a little more out of gluttony, and would then try to divert itself in other ways than watching ferociously over the remains of the bone, tomorrow's meal, or planning future conquests of bones necessary to future meals. And so much the better if the number of bones were such that one could be assured, even if one lived for a thousand years, that there would always be more than one could eat.

"I suggest, therefore, that the war for bones is the fault of the scant number of bones. I do not want to examine the question of whether the taste for war is natural to humans, and whether it corresponds as much to a deep-seated instinct of fighting for fighting's sake as to the regrettable but plausible necessity of fighting for something. Let us therefore accept, without going any further, that people make war because the number of empires, colonies, sugar-cane plantations, chairs, stripes, ladies, chicken-wings and pieces of chocolate is limited.

269

"Now—and this abridges my discourse—we have abundantly observed in the course of our excursions and displacements in time and space that the number of territories, domains and objects of joy, love, happiness and pleasure is actually infinite. It is all the more infinite because every territory, every domain and every object can be decomposed in its turn into an infinity of territories, domains and objects of possible joy and pleasure, as we can convince ourselves by means of the example of the forest, a few insects of which alimented the life and twenty volumes of a scientist, and that of the single pond that furnished a hundred paintings to an artist.

"That point admitted, if we suppose acquired by humans—and I mean fully and sumptuously acquired—all that corresponds to reasons for fighting, all the patrimony necessary for eating, for clothing, for lodgment in agreeable dwellings, for sleeping in good beds with as many mattresses and blankets as one wants, for ornamenting one's house and the woman one loves, for transporting oneself from one point of the globe to another, for sowing and harvesting wheat, for constructing bridges; in brief, the sumptuous acquisition of everything corresponding to the primordial necessities of life, and also the secondary necessities—which are, among others, musical instruments, earrings and bracelets, fishing rods. Bicycles and tennis rackets—and even tertiary necessities—which are, among others, paint-boxes, lace, stones and chisels for making statures of great men, carriages, pastries, comic operas and romantic novels...if, as I say, we suppose all the objects of necessity and all the elements of ordinary human happiness acquired, and so fully acquired that they are within arm's reach, so that they can be picked up with no more effort to accomplish than I need to pick up this little handful of and from our feet...then, would it not come about that thirsts, hungers, frenzies, itches, labors, activities and ambitions would turn toward the innumerable objects that the billions of arms, lips and sex-organs of your billions of marvelous hearts would succeed in holding, embracing and possessing everything, even if you lived for a thousand years?

"Will it not come about that when supply exceeds demand immeasurably, that instead of disputing miserly bones, all the humans endowed with those billion hearts, each one living for a thousand years, will occupy themselves, as soon as their appetites are sated, in running toward new pastures, in extracting all the juices therefrom, and enjoying themselves there, ever and ever newly?

"Will not so many new fields open to desire, to strength, to labor and to love transform before long the form of war and the fatally inexorable avidities that engender it? When everyone, in those new domains, can take all the goods and pleasures they want, always advancing without taking anything from their neighbors, who are themselves replete with objectives of joy and the means of obtaining them, will those frightful avidities not give way to a kind of competition...?

"But we shall return to that point. For the moment, let us agree that all that sparkling rhetoric, that supposition of an unlimited patrimony of objectives of joy, pleasure, happiness and love for all humans depends on the general preliminary possession of all the goods for which they fight, of empires and chicken-wings and pieces of chocolate...

"Now, my friend, no less quickly and no less easily than I have given you daylight in the middle of the night in the forest, taken you to the bottom of the sea, offered to cure you of paralyses and the gangrenes and invited you to dine on all the meats and fruits of the earth, I can cause to appear to you, by extending my little finger, all mines yielding their stones and minerals, iron, bronze and gold, all garments, all agricultural machinery, bridges before your feet, and locomotives, and all the apparatus primordially demanded by the human law of being and living, enduring, procuring and enjoying.

"If I were to extend my little finger, you would see your worn clothing become new, your house open before you, your meal prepared and your lamp lit, your pockets would be full of gold, you would see the plow laboring the fields on its own, the wheat scything itself down, storing itself in the barn, the grain milling itself, being flour and bread, an avenue opening

271

up inside that mountain from one side to the other, rails extending therein, a train traveling along them, and the carriages of that train carrying all useful goods and those of which you dream, flying along their route, all the way here, and emptying their cargoes at your feet.

"But spare me that miracle. I have sufficiently merited your confidence. Consider it accomplished. I want to come to something more important. And tell me, if such a harvest of materials essential to life, and such facility in their enjoyment, and my innumerable possessions were theirs, would not everything is human passions that stems from wars and trafficking between humans find itself somewhat, as I say, transformed?

49

"I am now on the threshold of the moment to which I wanted to bring you: the hour when I need to tell you who I am, the order and nature of my being and the substance of my prodigies.

"Let us summarize the recent proposals. We have looked at human passions, conditioned by human nature, their own structure and that of the earth that humans inhabit, and thus, it seems, immutable in their essential mechanisms, as immutable as the essential and the deep-rooted in that said nature, as the profound laws of the planet—immutable, in sum, as the fundamental form and structure of the human body.

"We have supposed many fatalities that weigh upon humans, leading their passions, dictating their actions and endeavors, inspiriting their morality and their metaphysics; we have supposed those fatalities vanished before powers of a veritably incalculable and unlimited extent, based on a possession of primordial material goods as complete and as immediate as air is for the lungs, light for the eyes. And I asked you whether, in such conditions the passions—I could as well say the actions, the endeavors and the metaphysics—of humans would remain as we see them. Can we imagine, conceive, seeing, as it were, through the prism of our hypotheses, what hu-

272

mans would be, by virtue of those powers and liberties, veritably delivered from their wounds, their crutches and the base cares that still hold them in the same rude physical fatalities as those of the first ages of the world?

"And I tell you this: humans would be like me, the arcandre. The enunciation of my excellences and my joys, the list of my privileges, such as I tabulated them for you at the moment when I appeared to you—those excellences and those privileges would by theirs. The few prodigies that we have accomplished would be, compared to what they might accomplish, what a few handfuls of dust on this bank would be to the soil of the entire earth. And the description I gave then of myself would apply to all humans. My movements and my liberty are to human movements and liberty what the course of the spring is to the compact waters that lie dormant in the calcareous subterrains and will only be able to flow after snaking slowly through the fissures of the interior silicates.

"Now, one point remains, at which we have not looked closely enough. That is the human body itself. It is that, and its fundamental structure, which we find behind everything. Progress, consciousness, domination of natural fatalities, the conquests of intellect and science—none of that, it seems, can make the human body other than what it is. No progress, no metaphysics, can change the location of the heart, or the double spasm of the lungs, or enable the species to reproduce other than by means of the organs and the act familiar to us...

"The great problem is that of the unalterability of the human viscera and the skeleton. Even if we change all the conditions of life, opening thousand of new fields to amour, labor and the will, so long as we cannot change the fatality of the viscera and the form of the human body, we will return to the fatality of their radical mechanisms and their unappealable commands, passions endeavors, labors and utopias.

"Now, what if the human body were other than the one we see, if its form was not immutable? If, to mortal fatalities, new realms opened, to new permissible amours, corresponding with other organs, other muscles, other tissues, other mechanisms of motion, of respiration and prehension, to other limbs and other hearts, and which would nevertheless still be the human body?

50

In the grottos of a village in the Dordogne, in the domain of Eyzies, primitive images, the works of prehistoric humans, were once discovered engraved on subterranean walls: depictions of individuals, reindeer and weapons. There was no artistry in the figures, no attention to detail; in brief they were drawings like those children scrawl on walls. The crudity of the forms, the depiction reduced to the essential exterior lines, were, self-evidently, due to the inexperience of those ancient sketchers, their awkwardness, their naïve lack of skill...

"What if it was also the case that they could *only* see those lines?

"What if their eyes, their senses, could only perceive the world in its general contours, if, where our exercised and educated gaze can perceive a thousand movements and a thousand signs, they could only perceive one?

"Take a child to a museum. He will perceive a confused mass of colors, here and there a horse, a fruit, a person. But you, you know the number of paintings, their differences, the subject of each scene, the detail of each image, and its psychology, and the detail of every detail. And the painter knew in even more detail, the colors of every fragment of color.

"We said the same once of the forest, simultaneously massive and singular, and innumerable.

"What if humans were, and still acted as if they were, before their own bodies and the formal world, similar to prehistoric humans before themselves, their fellows and the universe, and similar to the child in the museum, only perceiving the broad and general lines?

"What if the forms that humans see, their own bodies, the world and the universe, the laws that they discover there and with which they inspire themselves, and those that condi-

274

tion their passions, correspond to the crudity of their perceptions, and ought to become different as perceptions become refined and more numerous? What if that crudity of perception obliges them to consider as real and obligatory forms that have no other contours than the ones they design for them, and which would change their aspect, color and contours at the whim of their will, if they attained another reality of the universe, a reality less tyrannical, less rigorously designed, a reality in which that rock would be fluid and this entire mountain on which we are conversing more vaporous than the fine mists that cover it, as ethereal and diaphanous as the light that bathes it?

"Now, humans have attained that reality. Their senses are subtle enough to see it. Their passions and their gestures can be conditioned by it. But they live among the phantoms of their old fatalities, their prehistoric universe and their ancient body: phantoms that no longer depend on anything more than a burst of laughter and their consciousness, like the images of a nightmare when daylight comes.

"Do you remember the moment when you were immersed in the immaterial river? You could still feel tree standing behind you, and the bank of moss on which you were lying, at your back, and you could see the forest, with its plants and its small animals...and yet there was nothing but that strange light....

"It was you who designed in that river of light your body, the tree, the bank, the plants and the small animals, who saw them as real as well as vanished.

"I, the arcandre, to whom no form, including my own body and its organs, is any longer imposed by an excessively crude vision, but who has attained, in my gaze, the states of the universe in which form no longer exists, am the master of forms; I accept them or unmake them, and design the universe, my body and my organs at the whim of my caprice and my dilection.

"Now, that is possible to humans.

51

"And this is the mystery of the arcandre...

"I was born human. I was, to begin with, human in the sense that you give to the word. Once, I was in my mind as you were in yours at the moment when I appeared to you.

"How did the great rip occur in me similar to the one made in the cocoon when the chrysalid completes its metamorphosis? How did I arrive at the moment of my mind when my eyes opened on a new day, when my race was revealed to me, when I found myself on the threshold of that road that led me to the arcandrat?

"This is how: my intelligence was, at a certain moment, attracted to the veritably prodigious simultaneity that an instant can realize in human thought.

"Sitting, as you were, at the foot of a tree, I was savoring the odors of the air, the play of the light, the song of the birds. And suddenly, all the parts of my being that composed the quietude and pleasure of my body and the thoughts of my mind, became manifest and were numbered. It was as if a host appeared before me: the host of my distinct beings, the host of my perceptions, of my sensations and my distinct and simultaneous thoughts. I suddenly became conscious of the innumerable elements of an instant of my being and my thought.

"I sensed in my limbs the softness of the grass, the warmth of the sunlight, the placid circulation of my blood, the voluptuous languor of my nerves, caressed by the influx of light and all the ambient serenity. And I sensed through those same limbs the rise of saps in the trees and stems, and the running of beasts, their frolics, their hungers, their ruts; because I KNEW that there were in my veins and my arteries movements of blood similar to those of sap in trees and stems, and that there were in my limbs and my organs the possibilities of the running, the hungers and the ruts of animals, and that I was similar to them in certain elements of my physical being. And my thoughts were, at the same time, as numerous as the things I saw, forms, actions, colors, and what my other senses perceived: air, light, warmth, softness, peace, birdsong, murmurs of wind, and that thoughts were born simultaneously of the spectacle of each thing and the consciousness of each sensation.

"In addition, the science that I had learned permitted me to represent certain things that were interior to what I saw and felt, the processes and the elements of the rising of the sap in the tree, the circulation of the blood within me, the life of that bark, the tenacity of that lichen, the functioning of the cells of that blade of grass, the parturition of that small animal, the nature of the strata of the earth beneath my feet, the atomic duels of the gulps of air that I breathed in, the vibrations of the light that was dancing on my hand, and many of the laws and invisible planetary energies present in the space surrounding me, and those which presided over the aggregation of my own being—and thus, because I KNEW that, and I could represent it to myself, I shared, in a sense, mentally, in the internal movements and modalities, if it was a matter of things and forces, springs and the mores, if it was a matter of beasts, and I was thus, in a sense, simultaneously exterior and interior to bodies and substances, mingled with movements and things.

"And by virtue of what I had learned and knew, I could also think and represent to myself the past and the evolution of that fern, or that ant I could see in the present, and I could evoke by looking at that oak the time when it had been an acorn, and the oak itself broken by the tempest or ravaged by age, and so, in sum with regard to anything which was momentarily before my eyes...

"And from each object, and my own sensations, I could extract the different images of what I saw and what I sensed, the stripes of shadow and light on bark making me think of a tiger in some jungle, and the chirping of a bird causing to pass through my memory a succession of chords from the Pastoral Symphony, and before my visual memory the hall of the last concert in which I had heard that concert, with its musicians and the audience.

"And no matter how far, and into what baroque places my memory or my imagination took me, that concert, the jungle, the time when the oak was still an acorn, and the seigneurial hunts that had once taken place in the forest where I could hear the whistle of a nearby train...I nevertheless retained the present perception of real things and the consciousness of my sensations...

"And none of those sensations, those perceptions, those thoughts, those images, those evocations in time and space, or those representations of the interior of substances and things, was exclusive of any of the others, but all of them, corresponded to a perceptive, sensitive, knowing, imagining and remembering part of my being; and the host and ensemble of those distinct parts, each of which had its own nature and character, was held entirely within an instant of my consciousness.

"And that which is extremely ordinary and perpetually common to all humans, so common that none of them ever thinks of being astonished by it, suddenly astonished me nevertheless, and I suddenly marveled at that apparatus and the entity that I was, which held thus, in a single instant, the forest and the exterior spectacle of its trees, its vegetation and its insects, and the past and future of objects, the science of the interior of objects, substances and elements, and the sensation of being in some sense inside the things, the substances and the elements, and the images in time and space of other things, and the memory, and my own sensations and the choice and direction of those sensations and thoughts, and the delectation of those spectacles, that science, those sensations, those images and those thoughts.

52

"Now, my wonderment at that simultaneity immediately drew me to think that if I wanted to, I had an unlimited license REALLY to go to the objects of my sensations, my evocations, my thoughts and their images. The history of that forest,

278

the relation of the seigneurial hunts that had taken place there, the evidence of the times when it had been haunted by wolves, and long before them by aurochs, and those of the primitive times when animal life had not yet been born—that history and that evidence were the inhabitants of a kind of universe coexistent with the one that I could call contemporary, a universe that humans have constructed in its entirety and which is the book.

"Are libraries anything other than the Memory of the species, and do they not constitute a spiritual atmosphere around humankind akin to the atmosphere of air around the globe, so that in the same way that the lungs drink in the air that becomes the blood, the springboard of the succession and renewal of action, the mind breathes the planetary memory that becomes knowledge, the springboard of the succession and progression of thought?

"Railways, ships and airplanes could really take me, with promptitude, to the jungle that a pattern of shadow and light on a piece of tree-bark evoked for me. The phonograph could reconstitute the concert for me, a photograph the audience. The microscope could really deliver to me the cells of the blade of grass, the spectroscope the prisms of light. And geology and cosmology could really permit me to reconstitute the history of a pebble in the humus at my feet...

"Human knowledge, the machines and apparatus of science, were as many means that were offered to me, innumerably, to attain, to sense, to penetrate and possess the places, objects and states evoked by my thought, my sensations, my imagination and my memory, in substance time and space...

"And then I thought:

"The mind has always been able to go wandering through objects, substance and time. Any man sitting where I am, against this same tree, centuries ago, had the leisure and scope, by means of thought, to evoke and imagine and to surrender himself to the charms of the reverie. But there would always come a moment when he bumped into the insurmountable walls of matter. In addition to those walls, limiting his universe to that which his senses alone could perceive—and I mean his animal senses, those given to him by nature—the mind, in rebounding from the insurmountable, then formed fictions and hypotheses, empirical systems of gods, which the slightest atom of reality sometimes shores up, but often pulverizes more surely than a ton of dynamite causes a citadel to collapse.

"What that man could not do, I can do *now*. I can go corporeally, I can *really* go, with the batteries of my sensibility, my passion and my consciousness still armed with my mind's powers of knowledge, to the objects, places and states of the universe, and into the inexhaustible detail of those place objects and states. And with that sensibility, that passion and that consciousness always present permit myself as much as the ancient man of centuries ago to dream and to imagine, but with bases of emotion, dream and imagination much richer and more numerous than his!

"And I am fully entitled to say 'inexhaustible,' for the merest laboratory apparatus multiplies for me the components of the smallest object by numbers that reason cannot contain and human calculations still renounce. The study of the elements of a molecule and the movements of its constituent atoms lead to figures comparable to those that one heaps up when it is a matter of solar systems. And furthermore, if, even so, I cannot yet go to all these places, objects and states it is really and reasonably permissible for me to think that it is only a question of days, years and apparatus—in sum, of temporary and apparent modalities, not of the fatality of the supposedly impotent and paltry human condition but of reparable stupidities, such as the squandering of money on the maintenance of military forces and a hundred others of similar quality, or under the jurisdiction of the precarious use made of human genius by a society still ignorant of its path...

And I thought;

"There is *now*, by means of the instruments of locomotion, introspection and knowledge that are within human power, the possibility of an incalculable spiritual life, but, no longer outside life, in dream, phantasmagoria or the heavens, no longer severed from the real, but, on the contrary, nourished entirely by the real, having the real for its base, its roads, its springs, its flowers, its summits and its horizon: a spiritual life able to grow and to be enriched incessantly, and also to react incessantly upon the corporeal organism as on the social organism, permitting new faculties in the one and ever more profound and audacious inventions in the other.

53

"The influence of the spiritual life on material organisms, social and corporeal, will only appear to begin within humans of veritable measure. A man in the routine of life does not think about the role of the mind in the flow of the blood, the play of the muscles or the stomach, the respiration or the varying agility of the nerves. In the daily routine, it is quotidian life that leads him, a life mounted on very precise mechanisms: job, family, the care of earning a living, the automatic functioning of the organism; honest distractions from the interior of the laws and policing of the collective. The influence of the spiritual life is only apparent to him in certain well-delimited cases, when he thinks about a monk imprisoned in the monastery and subordinating all his actions to his faith, or when he thinks, in the social domain, about great revolutions, led by and for his ideas.

"What is the faith that regulates and transforms the organism of the monk? What are those great revolutions that subordinate peoples, their essential interests, and even their life, to ideas?

"What is that force of which one only sees the rare spiritual effects fulgurating in the somnolence of current human life, the force that, in rare circumstances—mystical faith or revolutions—subordinates the corporeal or social organism to the spiritual life?

"Its name is the arcanum of arcana, the secret of supreme magical authority. The faith that uplifts worlds, the revolutions that precipitate peoples, and the amorous frenzy that leads humans, are only facets of that force. It is the interior sun, the inextinguishable incandescence; it is the fiery wheel, the horse of flame of which deeds and actions are the chariots.

"It is at the core of human being. It is the blood of the blood. Nothing can do what it cannot. It waits to be summoned. It is indifferent to good and evil, laws and dogmas, to what is useful and what is harmful. As soon as it is awakened, the blood flows, the muscles are excited, the nerves tense, the mind crackles under its whip and its alcohols, in its squalls. What does the appeal that awakens it matter? Whether it comes from the crypts of instinct or the summits of intelligence, it will serve the instinct as well as the thought; it will expend itself in murder as in the construction of a grandiose work.

"If humans are led by primordial tyrannies, those that we considered a little while ago—maladies, hunger, intersexual amour, thirst for power, wars, trafficking, the slavery of the plebeian—it will be the instrument of their material desires. It will animate all their resources, those of the body and those of the spirit, for their bitter goals. It will transport the mind in the endeavors of hunger, fornication or war. If humans are suddenly led by the mind, they will give to the mind the resources of the blood, the muscles and the nerves that it stimulates indifferently with its own heat.

55

"Thus, the spiritual life awakening the interior sun to its goals, the fiery wheel of PASSION can be for the organism what life as we still live it, the life conditioned by sovereign fatalities, for the organism.

"Thus, by passion, the innumerable realms of a marvelous reality, suddenly open before the human mind, might be to human beings and their organism what hunger and the viscera clawed by the implacable laws and all the goals conditioned by such hunger were.

"It is sufficient for passion to be involved in the affair. The passion, led by the mind, which moves the body of the monk on behalf of illusory paradise, the passion led by idea, the passionate moment of peoples that overturns the social body... Those rare examples of the regency and the influence of the mind on the organism via passion would become the common law of human being if the mind were suddenly passionately attracted to goals more powerful than ever before in the history of humankind, if the mind were led passionately by hungers more imperious than those that guide the viscera.

"And can one foresee the adventure of the human body, its blood, its muscles and its nerves, regulated and alimented by a spiritual life that no longer avoids reality, but attains it, but means of the science and instruments that humans invent, the inexhaustible nourishment and ever-renewed wellsprings of an ever-vaster science, power and liberty?

"One philosopher has represented the world as will and idea; another has represented human being as the will to power. I shall represent the world as passion. *I shall represent human being and mind as passion in the possession of reality.*

56

"Then, in a moment of my consciousness, I seemed to hold the totality of human possession, the totality of the reality that is in human possession:

"The human body, washed clean of its wounds, delivered from bandages of fear and hypocrisy, the body of the self, with its resources and its enjoyments, its ability to know, receive, absorb, embrace, via its physical, psychic and spiritual organs all the forms of the earth, the colors, the spectacles, the juices, the aromas, the effluvia, the works of nature and human works, exterior beauties and internal treasures; the human body, with the countless host of its cells, which are as many lives, gazes and memories, and each of which, somewhere, in the universal material, has a relationship, a correspondence, with the salt of the seas, the gold of minerals, the honey of fruits and the pollen of flowers, with the bodies of other beings and the matter of the stars; the body, with the innumerable keyboard of sensations, with the host of spiritual vibrations, each of which will, in time, find a relationship with everything that was, is and will be.

"Human inventions, science, books and prodigious apparatus, which attain the secrets of the stars, the extreme depths of the sea, the densest part of the earth, weighing space, manipulating light, delving into substance, fixing time; apparatus that makes desire, thought and commands run from one pole to the other instantly; and the machines that bring goods from all over the world, marching across the waters, through the air, on the ground, recreating day for humans in the middle of the night, taking them to summer if they are tired of winter, lending to their works the fluids of the ether and the forces that move suns...

"And the possession of the materials of the life of the body and the viscera, everything that gives the body and the viscera alimentation and the satisfaction of their primary necessities, everything that corresponds to what humans signify by the name of 'material concerns,' everything for which they have to struggle before living their psychic or spiritual life for a moment, roads, vehicles, textiles, victuals, agricultural implements and those with which houses are built and those within houses, everything acquired forever and profusely but is merely poorly divided and whose profusion needs to be organized...

"Thus I held and contemplated in a moment of my consciousness, in a kind of burning aspiration of my mind, the totality of the authentic wealth of humanity—and it was that moment which produced in me the great rip, like that made in a cocoon when the chrysalid has completed its metamorphosis.

"The state that represented the word 'human' according to the meaning that you give it then represented for me my chrysalid. When I was human, in your sense, there was a co-coon around me in which I was enclosed, with all humans, but when the rip was effected in me, I saw that the cocoon was woven and fixed with humans inside it in the midst of what has been called the garden of Eden.

"And it was that moment when I recognized in my thought that nothing subsisted of the great Poverty that had been behind the essential laws, works and passions of humans since the commencement of the ages, like the rope that attach-es a vessel to the shore and retains it before the expanse of the sea. The rope has been slowly corroded by the salt of the ma-rine air and the salt of the waves, pricking and biting its hemp relentlessly. A more impetuous wave rising from the depths of the sea encircles the rope and it gives way, to the point at which the hemp has been more intimately corroded—and now the vessel is free to go across the entire extent of the sea, drawing behind it a stump of the cable that is no longer any-thing but the image of an abolished coercion...

"Thus had I recognized that humans could henceforth go freely throughout the extent of creation, but it was as if the cable had not been broken. In other words, they remained im-prisoned and lamenting their Poverty in the cocoon of their laws and passions, and had no sense of the garden called Eden around their cocoon.

"I had, therefore, recognized that nothing subsisted of that Poverty, and that Joy could henceforth be around human laws and actions like space, light and the immensity of the sea around the detached vessel. And I was like that vessel, and no longer felt the presence of Poverty either in the limbs of my body or the thoughts of my mind.

"However, the humans that I called my brothers and my fellows continued to lament, and to sing, laugh, love, dream, worship, construct and add laws to their laws and works to their works, while continuing to lament—for whatever their songs, works and laws were, there was always the certainty of their Poverty beneath them, and even if they did not state that certainty, if they covered it with decorations, if they strove to forget it or deny it in sensuality, beauty or love, a moment always came when, in the most delicious fruit, the tooth or the knife would encounter the hard stone. Thus I saw humans living in accordance with the obsolete verity of Poverty, while I could not renounce living in accordance with the fresh verity of Joy.

"I could no longer go back into the cocoon by reclosing the rip, or tear out of my eyes the vision with which my gaze had been permanently struck, blow out every last flicker of my memory. I could no longer fold back the wings that I sensed henceforth attached to every fiber of my body, every one of the palpitations of my thought, since the moment I had recognized that the extent of creation was freely open, and that creation was for humans similar to the one celebrated of old under the name of Eden. I could not, even if I had folded back those innumerable wings and climbed back into the cocoon, resume the state and the posture of the larva, immobile in a meager light, the slights quivers of which immediately ran into walls.

"Then I began to go forth and live in accordance with the verity of Joy. I was similar in appearance to other humans, and yet I was no longer human in the sense that you give to the word. And my new name and race were revealed to me when I encountered the arcandres, and realized that I was similar to them.

58

"Do you remember the legend of the sphinx of Thebes? The monster with the human head that stood at the threshold of the fabulous city was made, it was said, of the passions of Thebes. It was the emanation of the passions of the City. It was the spirit of those passions made flesh, having taken form:

286

that particular concrete and living form. Elsewhere, certain authors and demonologists claim that the Devil, such as he appeared to the people of a region, to troubled nuns and many visionaries, was similarly the concretized sum of terrestrial sins—which is to say, not a creature pre-existing the sins, but an emanation of those very sins themselves—or, more exactly, the sins themselves manifest in a plastic, synthetic and living form.

"That is to aid you to understand what the arcandres are: a race of beings proceeding from the major power of human beings, emanations, living syntheses, incarnations of the superlative human spirit. To assist you further in understanding, know that in that sort of aspiration of my mind, during which the instant of my consciousness in which I held the totality of human possession was 'objectivized,' I was making, in that knowledge, the first gesture of the arcandrat, the initiating gesture of the marvelous race.

"That is all that I can tell you in that regard. Don't expect me to enlighten you any further, beyond the revelation of that spiritual aspiration, as to the mystery of the formation of the arcandres. That mystery is not communicable in words. Its possession can only come from yourself, your desire, your labor. The Mystery is within you and in regions of you that it is necessary for you to discover and that you alone can attain, in order to know them in the force and irradiation of a verity that has no influence.

59

"Having joined the arcandres, I penetrated and shared the miracle of their synthetic nature. That miracle was that I hold within myself, everything that a man can do with the aid of his books, his instruments and his apparatus. The displacements that humans effectuate by means of railways, ships and airplanes; the places they penetrate with submarines, microscopes, telescopes and light-bulbs; the apparatus by means of which they transmit their will, telephones, telegraphs and airwaves; those by which they open mines, enter stones, melt minerals, forge iron; the machines used for cultivation, in factories, and engines…all that is within the power and means of humans… I can realize in my body and with my body.

"Thus, I have a license to shrink myself to atomic size, and to elongate myself to the stars, to cross the earth from one pole to the other in an instant, to dilute myself in forces and ambient energies, to move in the ground, in the sea, in the ether. Thus are explained some of the games with which I have amused myself in your presence.

"Thus, in the forest, I made a beam of light emerge from my finger which suddenly illuminated a foraging ant—the same beam that you produce from an electric bulb costing a few sous. And when I made the light rosy that filled all the nocturnal space, I was accomplishing nothing more by extending my arm than men do whose electric bulbs light up an expanse of darkness as vast as they wish…

"You perhaps understand now of what those little music pills are made, and your parents' little drawing room, a form as convenient as I gave to that wax, and those impressionable coatings by which the phonograph and photography fix subtle sound and fleeting images.

"The battle of the roots, that condensation of several months into a few minutes, any cinematographer can succeed in producing, and other miracles more complicated…

"But the explanation of those paltry material games does not suffice to enlighten another aspect of the prodigies through which I enabled you to live. Books of geology and cosmology, and photographic or electric machines, would not have excited the emotion and sensuality you felt when you saw the root, burned in the original fire and found yourself in your parents' drawing room or on the Rhume, The book would only have given you the science and the image of primordial times; the wax pill only retains for you the image of the familial décor, the cinematograph only offers you the image of roots. Their real life is the mystery of PASSION.

"Similarly, I could have explained to you, for example, that the moment a little while ago that we spent under the sea and when you swooned with admiration and amazement before some extraordinary madrepore, combined, condensed and literally synthesized the material means offered to you by the submarine, submarine photography and the soundings carried out by certain oceanographers at extreme depths, and the spiritual introspection that permitted you the data acquired by Science...

"Or I could have explained to you that the coexistence on which you interrogated me so furiously once, asking me about its mechanisms and in what antechamber of the real it resided, was entirely in your brain, in the book, in photography, in planetary memory, in our subjective faculties, in certain material modes that we have enumerated—whether as a matter of a displacement in space, like Bayreuth, or a contraction of time, as among the roots—in brief, that it resided in an ensemble, in a synthesis of images, zones, places and means that were all in my arcandre's body, and which I made yours momentarily...

"But, in explaining everything like that, I would not have said anything, if we did not add PASSION to the prodigies. That is what, by exciting your blood, precipitating the rhythm of your heart, alcoholizing your muscles and flagellating your nerves, gave you those prodigies—those images, rather—for real...in sum, permitted you to live them in plastic and sensible reality, as if you had seen, touched, smelled, felt and embraced the objects and the things that stood out from what you normally call the real...the fruit that you pick from the tree, the familiar ground on which your feet tread, the table in front of which you sit down every evening, your garments, the houses in your street, the passers-by, the people...

"But are that fruit, the ground, the table, your garments, the houses of stone and iron and the people, and everything else that you see, touch and know ordinarily by virtue of your actions and your days, any more real, in the final analysis, than what I have given you by means of prodigy?

60

"I shall not return to the discussion of philosophies or mysticisms regarding the unreality of the formal world. I have other paths to tread.

"It is necessary for us to return to the moment when you were submerged in the immaterial river, after having seen the forest decompose and dissolve. Although your plunge into the bosom of a universe without forms was merely one of my amusements, the comprehension of that plunge, and the spectacles that followed it, the reappearance of forms, the simultaneity of my four bodies, necessitate for you a few improvements of your customary notions.

"Here is a drop of water. To your normal gaze, it is a small colorless and diaphanous mass in which the surrounding light is reflected. Observe that same drop under a microscope: a thousand hallucinatory animals populate it. The two aspects of that drop are rigorously real, one as much as the other, corresponding to your two gazes, your natural gaze and your microscopic gaze.

"While you gaze at the drop through the microscope it is perfectly real, as is the tiny world of infusoria revealed to you by the lens. If, leaving the apparatus momentarily, abandoning your microscopic gaze for an instant, you resume your natural gaze, you see, no less real, the little colorless mass, diaphanous, and devoid of the population that you have just seen there.

"So, moving your gaze from the drop seen through the apparatus to the same drop seen with the naked eye, you can consider two realities, prodigiously different, of one thing, and exist yourself, in a manner of speaking, alternately, in the reality of the universe corresponding to what your natural gaze sees, and in the reality of the universe corresponding to what the microscope reveals in the water drop.

"Now, knowing that what you have seen in the microscope, without the aid of it, your memory, and your science of what you have seen, can henceforth transpose into the normal drop, the microscopic reality of that same drop—or, to put it otherwise, accomplish the transposition of the subjective into the objective, the simultaneity of that which you know and that which you see.

"Consider where such an operation takes us. Knowing the two realities of the drop of water, you can subjectively see them, or at least think them, at the same time; and that is, in a sense, as if you were yourself, in relation to that drop, simultaneously in the different states of reality corresponding to those different states of the same thing.

"Now, if I lend you the privileges of my being, for which the notions of subjectivity and objectivity, of the concrete and the abstract, no longer have the meaning that you give them, no longer being modes, one of direct perception and the other of thought, but different states of the entire being; and, on the other hand, if the devices that attain the different states of an object are no longer—for you, on whom I have conferred my faculties—exterior things, but correspond to faculties of your own being, then, in the same object and in the same moment, you will see different states of those objects simultaneously and *you will be in the different corresponding states of the universe yourself.*

"I have only taken the example of the drop of water to bring you to a more complex comprehension. Think, to begin with, that such a perception of a more intimate reality of things will immediately begin to overturn, in a fashion, your ordinary notions of space and time...from which will necessarily follow *the disappearance of all substance.*

By ordinary notions of space and time I mean that of physical space and that of the honest everyday time that clocks and calendars divide: entirely archaic and fallacious notions, as everyone knows, and as the ABC of philosophy informs us, at least with regard to the fallacious, which is a function of the archaic.

With regard to that archaic I will go a little way into the margin of philosophy. I call those nations archaic because they go back to ages when humans were unaware of the reality that what is delivered to them by animal sensibility—which is to say, the produce of bare sensation, by virtue of seeing, smelling, touching solely with the resources provide by nature, without the enrichment of any of the apparatus thanks to which the constituent states of matter are revealed and multiplied, the revelations of which are now definitely acquired by the knowledge and intelligence humans have of that matter, and thus of their conception and vision of the world.

"The order of my proposals demands that I assume momentarily the aspect of magister. Between one of the leaves of that fern near your hand and your hand, which could pluck that leaf, your normal gaze certainly perceives space. That is to say that between the leaf and you there is a kind of relative void, a milieu furnished with elements so scantly resistant that they do not exist for your eye, for your hand and for the muscular effort you would need to make in order to reach out from where you are to the leaf: vapors of air, reflections of daylight.

"That notion of space, the issue of your sentiment of quasi-void, a sentiment itself tributary to your impression of non-resistance, is based on the givens of your eye, your hand and the muscular effort required—givens that it is not inexact to call animal. Now, if, by virtue of a sudden sharper and finer sensibility your impression received for bases the other veritably innumerable elements that fill the short extent that extends between the leaf and you, your notion of that extent would be transformed, henceforth founded on far more subtle givens, which are no less true, demonstrable and as conclusive as those formed by the animal notion of space.

"Now, you are not unaware that your gaze and your hands, such as nature has made them, perceive here what you know and what you can presume that there is of the real, of the imperiously existent, between the leaf and you, about as much as could be seen of a procession by two idiots enclosed in a cellar looking through a ventilation shaft.

"Thus, I suddenly confer on you a certain immediate visual acuity, representing, in a sense, the sum of possibilities of vision and the knowledge that results synthetically from the employment of all the instruments of physical and chemical introspection presently in the service of humans, The consequence of such a vision would be, as I said, the momentary perturbation, and then the annihilation, of your normal notion—your archaic notion—of space.

"Firstly, for a clear-sighted gaze of such acuity, forms would no longer be anything but molecules, some of them closer than others, those which constitute bodies, bathed or traversed by more distant molecules, which are juices or vapors; around both, and similarly traversing them in many places, swarm the bacilli of the air, the living dust, the organic individuals that agitated in myriads in the smallest parcel of the atmosphere; those molecules and dust particles would be everywhere enveloped by the gases whose vehement embraces form the air, and those gases and their furies, having become visible, would be furrowed themselves by the sparkling fluids whose endless flux constitutes light...

"In addition, all of that being only the grosser part of our space, also visible would be the electricities and all the energies that science can name resolutely, that it can weigh, measure and manipulate, those that are based on speculation rather than experience, and those apparatus can detect without our being able to name them yet; the great magnetisms would be visible, those suns registering and remaining associated with the atoms of that leaf; emanations, affinities and projections would be visible. Finally, as vast as infinity and as constant as eternity, all the laws of being, or movement and order, which play, turn and agitate here, have their part in the presence of that fraction of the universe, and influence over it...

"In truth, my friend, when those hosts of forces, fluids, fires and infinitesimal organisms are made suddenly visible, what significance, what reality, would your anterior notion of space retain? At what point in that fantastic world in which all things appear not only linked but aggregated together by those dusts, those rays, those magnetisms and those laws, and in which you would no longer see yourself, in its new modalities, mingled and confounded, as anything but dances and struggles of molecules and currents, would the slightest interstice corresponding to what you call space be retained?

63 [21]

"All that is only said for space, and we have said nothing yet. That somewhat chaotic face of matter could only endure momentarily. Scarcely had your notion of space been abolished before a more numerous representation of reality than your notion of time would, in its turn, be fundamentally surprised. The everyday notion of time having for materials, for its only materials, the different aspects and successions of events, before the suddenly complicated world that we sketched just now, you can imagine what a riposte that notion of time would receive, after that of space.

"That world being offered in much more intimate appearances, you would, as I said, become momentarily a phantasmagoria of swarming particles, ephemeral arabesques, entangled gases, incessantly changing colors, magnetic undertows, currents colliding, absorbing one another and interpenetrating…but I said 'momentarily,' because that spectacle could only be transitory. That world, multiplying its figures and its moments, would by the same token have multiplied the reference points of time.

"At whatever point your miraculous vision might try to pause upon, in every part of that ensemble, the transformations, the exchanges, the disjunctions and the developments make time so numerous, so laden, so active—in sum, so animated-that it becomes…indivisible. The sum of events and metamorphoses being effected everywhere and simultaneously would be no more fractionable into moments for you than the ocean is divisible into droplets for a diver.

"You can no longer count. You can no longer see anything but an immense total and perpetual trepidation, in which

---

[21] *Sic.* The original text omits chapters 61 and 62 and jumps directly to 63.

the prismatic cascades of light, the conflagrations of electricities and the revolutions of forces fulgurate, matter in a universal frenzy of alliances and transfigurations—and infinite glittering, in sum, with neither up nor down, left or right, devoid of horizons and limits, which, renouncing space and refusing time, is simply be the world seen at slightly closer range.

64

"Thus, that immaterial river in which you saw yourself plunged was the universe, momentarily rid of your animal notions of space and time. And it was your memory that designed the resurgent forms, those of the forest and your own body...we shall come back to that detail.

"As for the river of a matter devoid of space and time, it was only an amusement. Such a state of the universe, although the mind can be diverted in conceiving it, cannot be accepted by the estates of the mind. Although it was real, everything that permits thought being dissolved there, how and by what could it be thought? I have told you how I was able to make you see it, by rendering you my faculty of rendering the metaphysical plastic and sensible, and in a sense corporeal, but was it really only to divert ourselves? Was it merely an amusement in the course of the journey? Was it not, rather, to enable to you estimate whether, between two extreme states of the universe, that one and the lumpen material universe in which humans still agitate, and the only one from which they extract their knowledge, their subsistence and their passions, there is not some other state of the universe accessible and habitable?

"To return to our glittering universe, let us posit, then, that it was it was only an amusement, for the impossibility of numeration that the succession of phenomena and indivisible aspects rendered to you is not produced in a reality.

"In a reality, one can conceive that the states of consciousness march in step with the perceptions and sensations of a new modality, whatever it might be. Thus, if a human being could exist entirely on the planes of the universe corresponding to those that apparatus reveal to him in a drop of water or an atom, he would succeed, just as on the plane of the universe where he still lives, in perceiving, sensing and enumerating the variation of events and appearances. Then, what he presently calls a minute would be charged with more events and spectacles than could be accomplished in a century of present time. What he calls an instant would be divided into millionths of millionths...but nothing would be changed except the number..."

"And forms!" I said.

"Undoubtedly. All forms, including his own, would become the seat, at every instant, of myriads of metamorphoses. And yet, that fulgurant world would still be REAL before his new consciousness...but wait. That perpetual fulgurance of events and spectacles in all things, including his own body and consciousness, that frantic trepidation of transformations, would be even further accentuated as his sensibility became increasingly subtle, and his means of knowledge and prospection more ingenious and more adequate to the new modes of the universe. And thus, via trepidations within trepidations, he would arrive at a state of the world and of intelligence so perpetually changing and mobile that there would no longer be anything durable, no longer anything from which the sentiments—amour, art, tenderness—could draw satisfaction. Scarcely has he grasped an object, having only held the object for a billionth of a second when it has become something else, as he has too...

"Then, in that frightful torrent of frenetic and myriad renewals, and while knowing that the torrent in question is a real state of the world, could that which the man would then be construct from the torrentiality of those renewals images and ensembles of some sort? Would he invent forms—relatively static forms—which he would know to be arbitrary but which would be, so to speak, willed and designed by him, imposing stages, halts and reposes, first of his consciousness, and then of his entire being, on the universal mobility. Meanwhile, science, the increasingly perfect knowledge of the mechanisms, rhythms and forces of life, and the experience of number, would make those forms and those constructions increasingly better adapted to the true rhythms and forces...

"On the unstable screen of the universe the man would project his harmonious inventions, to remake, to *redesign* a formal universe...

"But I shall come back to that hypothesis of the man re-constructing the universe freely. A detour is useful, which will perhaps make it apparent to us that without plunging into a future so strangely distant and paradoxically chimerical, that reconstruction of the world and that unusual liberty over forms are in human hands now, since everything that seems to us to be in the future *is in the present*.

65

"For is it really *at this moment* that that fern-leaf is both as you see it with your natural daze and the seat of the perpetual metamorphoses that we have talked about. And your body, the world and the universe are like that leaf. So, if that is the case, what is it that gives that leaf, your body, this mountain, the sun and the world these appearances, these fixed and constant contours that you know to be illusory as soon as you think beyond your immediate, natural perceptions, which we have called animal? It cannot be those perceptions themselves, since their physical bases, your gaze, your senses, your nervous system and your brain are not what they seem to be, but are themselves in perpetual movement and metamorphosis.

"In that discontinuous succession of differences, in that flux, that incessant unfurling of transformations of everything, including yourself and all your parts, what is it, then, that perceives, and why, among the innumerable combinations that have your being as a theater—or, more precisely, the entire universe comprising your being—why are you, and why do you see, a certain arrangement of those combinations that you call 'me' (and the universe) rather than the following ar-

297

rangement, which is also 'you' (and the universe), but which you do not see and no longer count, as if it did not exist?

"In fact, you do not see yourself existing, between all these innumerable states of yourself, and you do not see the world between its innumerable dispositions, you do not distinguish a certain aspect of the universe and differentiate yourself from the totality of universal movement, you are not 'you,' properly speaking, you only exist insofar as your consciousness enters into contact with something. But what corresponds to what is said to be 'your' consciousness? In reality, the consciousness that lights up at that contact is that which is at the moment, 'you'—and already, because the thing—object, spectacle, sentiment or idea—is already no longer what it was a millionth of an instant before, your consciousness is no longer the same. From which it follows that what you call your consciousness of something is a halt, an arbitrary fixation, a fallacious constancy, a *memory* in which in enclosed an indeterminate sum of the states or faces of the thing...whether it is a matter of that fern, your body or the universe.

"However, how can we conceive of the formation of the consciousness of something, or the first spark of the succession of consciousnesses that you call the consciousness of something, if we deny the perceptive system and any reality of the formal world? It is necessary for us to leave the perceptive system, however, and speak momentarily as if we held it to be real. Nevertheless, the words that we employ here will only be representations of things that are familiar to you, without which reasoning would be impossible. We are free to come back to those words and the things they signify later, enriched by our reasoning, and more apt in consequence to specify the true nature of things and the words in question. We shall therefore take for real, momentarily, the world of phenomena such as it is commonly observed.

"What is perception? Physiologists consider it, in their harsh idiom, to be a centripetal nervous activity proceeding from the peripheral agitation of the sensori-motor centers, which is then centrifugally reflected in movement or a tendency to nervous or muscular movement.

"How does that nervous activity become consciousness? Let us posit as certain that the activity in question, in its influx and reflux, agitates, awakens, stimulates, or, more precisely, provokes a kind of nebular mass, made of latent cellular memories—memories that are, properly speaking, medullary traces similar to curves imparted to grass by a storm, meanders imposed on a river by the terrain, or a pleat left in a fabric by friction. Memories, traces of anterior movements or tendencies to movement, almost of the same order as the movement presently necessitated, memories, traces, pleats perhaps originating from the most indecisive gropings of instinct, the most obscure reflexes of substance...

"Around those memories, those suddenly affected traces rise up, grouping together and colliding, the affinities, associations and antagonisms of possibilities of the immediate moment. Every vibration of those traces, every one of those affinities, and every one of those antagonisms summons and attracts images, which flow through a psychic world similar for the individual to the one we have attributed to the species, that planetary memory, that spiritual atmosphere of which the book is the concrete sign.

"The concrete sign of the memory of each human individual is the human individual himself. The images that respond to the appeal of the aforesaid associations, antagonisms and affinities will be those of events, spectacles and objects recorded, experiences, habits, sensations and thoughts accomplished, experienced on occasions of more-or-less similar movements. Those images themselves associate with one another or conflict with one another, precipitate, entangle, seeking to engulf themselves in the movement that is about to be effectuated, or to tend to be effectuated...

"The awakening of memories, their magnetisms, groupings and conflicts of tendencies, the surges and mingling of images—all of that generation, all those vicissitudes—are unfurled and resolved in a time that words cannot translate. The

299

alarm that one experiences before the quantity of figures necessary to express superlative dimensions—the distances between solar systems, the masses of suns, the years or centuries taken by the light of certain suns to reach human beings— would seem slight by comparison with what one would experience before the decimal quantity of numbers fractioning the duration of what you call a second to the point of obtaining a time corresponding to the rapidity of the multitudinous work of the psychic nebula.

"From the impetuous encounters, impacts and frictions of all those whims, all those larval ardors thirsty for being, rushing to the possibility of being, tending to insert themselves into being by muscular or nervous movement, surges the primal explosion, the initial fulgurance of the series of consciousnesses whose sum is conscious perception of the impression received by the nervous system. That enormous drama with a thousand scenes and countless characters unfurls in the duration contained between the moment when the retina receives the impression of that tree and the moment when you see it—or, more precisely, when your retina receives a certain impression that your consciousness and the selected images make of that tree..."

Now, personally, at that moment—was it the image of that sabbatesque nebulosity elaborating the fire and light of consciousness from the seething of its tendencies and its affinities?—I sensed my memory tremble. For my thought, as if of its own accord, recovered the terms in which, at the beginning of the prodigies, my vision of another fire springing from another nebula had been described:

"That light was the light of a fire that had just been born in the surf of stellar dust... in the silent fields of time its particles had assembled. From their duels and their alliances, the shock of their gyrations, the innumerable labor of electricities, fire, the first visible face of forces, had surged..."

66

The arcandre continued, interrupting the strange parallel into which my memory had been drawn:

"I once tried," he said, "to render these illuminations of consciousness visible and objective. That was my body of suns. The same play of illusion that limited the subjective phantasmagoria of the glittering of a word devoid of space and time to that luminous column what your eyes formed of the second aspect of my being and, similarly, the vortex of the images of the Memory of the species that my fourth body designed, limited the template of my physical appearance to that silhouette sparkling with a flamboyance that, in reality, developed and shone infinitely in number and without limits in extent. Which is to say that if I had not circumscribed the spectacle to that figure of fire, you would have seen those suns everywhere, innumerable, scattered in the great quiver of substance, much as the constellations are seen, unequally spaced or grouped in the ether. And in the same way that vagabond stars glide through the sky, while stars are born and others are extinguished, similarly and incessantly, those spiritual suns move, illuminate and go out—but what in stellar events is counted in centuries by your measurements must, according to the same measurements, be counted here in fractions of millionths of millionths of a second.

"Thus, each of those suns shining in the universe substance was one of my consciences rendered visible, consciousnesses of one thing, one sentiment, one thought...and each of those consciences was 'me.' Which is to say that among the images summoned and, as we have seen, collaborating in the formation and the luminous explosion of each consciousness, were certain images, certain memories, certain circumstances, an enormous contingent of images of that which I call 'me' and among which dominated in each consciousness the image, the memory of the 'me' that best corresponded to each new perception.

"And thus, in a way, if the abstract and the psychic were made visible, were possible to contemplate under the aspect of such a swarm of suns spread throughout an expanse like constellations in the physical sky, every human being would be as numerous in perceptions, sensations and thoughts. The number and the frequency of those suns, and the extent that they would occupy, would be in direct proportion to the frequency of sensations and thoughts, and that frequency would be a direct function of the subtlety of the perceptive system, the diversity of the sensitive system, and the vivacity of the spiritual system.

"But we have now returned to the nervous system, the brain, the senses, the physical bases of all perceptions, sensations and thoughts. And now I say this to you: why do I need matter such as you see it to explain perception and the thing that is perceived? Taking as fundamental the perpetual instability of all things, I cannot conceive the nervous system, nor the brain, nor any physical base, as you represent them, nor in any other fashion in the formal world. There is, therefore, only one phenomenon that I need any longer to take into account: that is the contact between something that perceives and something that is perceived. The form that perceives, and the form of that which is perceived are, like the rest, the resultants not of perception but of images—they are what gives the perception its form.

"But where are those images themselves situated? Where do they come from? Agree that words are inapt to localize what I only made visible to you by prodigy. Where can the images the situated other than, as we said, in the spiritual atmosphere of the earth, an atmosphere that humans can only see, concretely, in books, monuments, traditions and mores? Where can they be situated other than in the psychic atmosphere of the individual, an atmosphere that humans can only see concretely in the individual himself, and in his eternal gestures?

"But then...books, monuments, traditions, mores, and the individual, and the universe, in sum, such as you see them, are only images themselves: images, specifically, taken and formed from the moving and inconstant reality, or, rather, the inconstant and moving state of the reality that we obtain in the ultimate analysis. Where do those images come from? Why are what I call the nervous system, the brain, the human being and the universe such as I see them those images rather than others, incessant combinations of substance? Whatever images and notions I acquire of things, via them, it is necessary that those notions and images have emerged from somewhere.

"What gives to the something that perceives, to the primary perception, the first form from which all the others will be issued, such as we know them—or, more exactly, receive them? What differentiates itself from the universal mobility, and differentiates that mobility into a primary image?

"Now, I cannot name that which perceives something or other the foundation of being, the something or other that triggers the primary perception. We have run into the great initial enigma. The mystery of the notion of forms leads us to the problem of Being itself. I shall not attempt to elucidate certain aspects of that problem, to which humans seem very attached—knowing, among others, whether the first cause of everything was, as some say, the desire that whatever was had to know itself, to attain self-consciousness, or whether the primordial desire to be triggered the genesis of things...if there is only time in human measurement, one cannot say 'that which was.' How can the 'beginning' of anything whatsoever be conceived, or what was 'first,' outside the strictly objective notion of material phenomena? It would therefore be necessary to conceive of that desire, that quiver, in an eternal and perpetual present—or, to put it better, in an eternal being...you can imagine where that leads us.

"Now, it is not a matter, for the moment, of such vast problems; it is only a matter here of seeing whether the image of the universe in which humans live might be tidied up somewhat. We shall not stray from that modest but precise objective. And we shall only attempt to suppose the formation of the consciousness that humans have acquired of the universe that they see, including themselves. It is solely the formation of the consciousness in question that ought to occupy us, since all the rest flows from it and that we cannot conceive of anything outside the notion that consciousness has on what it is. It is that notion which interests us, and it is, as I say, necessary to see whether that can be tidied up somewhat...

"So, being left in a mystery—the attempt to penetrate which still remains an excellent exercise for the mind, and which there is no reason to think, piteously, that intelligence will never attain—being left in the original tremulous shadow, let us content ourselves with supposing how the something that perceives gives a form to its perception.

67

"Let us imagine, then, a state of substance that is not yet the formal world, since that which will give a form to that which does not exist as yet in something that is not yet what you call time, that which commences to perceive only perceiving in a manner that one might call nebular. What you will one day call actions are like the as-yet-blind encounters of forces, nebulae and vortices.

"That which commences to perceive confusedly constructs that which is not yet images, but constancies: vague, vaporous, indescribable reference-points in the perpetual gusts of the unstable. These points are the indecisive substrate of primary forms—which is to say, if the word can be applied to anything, *memories* to which that which wants to be will attach itself, memories in which to enclose itself and disguise in constancy the real movement around which the perpetual metamorphosis of substance will flow, like the sea around an errant hull; nebulous memories of enormous confused ensembles; fleecy memories, immense images, gigantic reference-points, which will be as gigantic as the perception is massive, and as durable as the perception is slow, less frequent in renewing the acquired image.

"What you will one day call humans cannot see themselves as yet, and thus do not exist, and nothing therefore exists of the world as you will one day represent it with the aid of the formidable accumulation of images consequent to these obscure gropings. Something commences to exist, made of those memories, those groping fixities, those giant and soft contours. That which commences to exist gradually designates day and night, the ground, water and the air, which are far from being what you know them to be, since you know that even now you perceive them other than they are, the air being inhabited by billions of bodies, gases and forces that your present eyes cannot see and that you would never have supposed if science and your apparatus had not revealed them to you.

"Now, gradually, humans see themselves, but such as they draw themselves in the grottos of Eyzies, and the universe that they see—beings, things elements—corresponds to the coarseness of their vision. Have they a nervous system? You will know one day that they have one, and you will designate it as science attains it, but how can they receive it by their means of perception, which can scarcely see their own general contours and those of the world? All the same, your nervous system, such as you see it, is, for you who that which perceives; for them, it was their hands, it would be their eyes, their mouth...

"The form of that which perceives cannot, therefore, be any more definitive for you than it was under the gaze of that obscure being.

"But the memory having expanded, the world has become an immense reservoir of images. Every new perception, scientific, sentimental or metaphysical discovery immediately receives the influx of the innumerable mass of those images on which humans live, and from which they take their form.

"I should like to revise the old Cartesian apothegm and enunciate it thus: 'I think, therefore I am; but thanks to the thought that permits me to conceive that I am, I arrive at seeing myself so perpetually changing and unstable in all my parts, in a universe in perpetual conversion of all its parts, that

I shall end up no longer being able to think of myself, and thus ceasing to be, if I do not enclose in an image, a fixity, a constancy, that infinitely mobile being and that fleeting universe.' Now, are that image of me and that of the universe necessarily those I see? 'Yes,' said Descartes, *who had no means of attaining another image.*

"But you can perhaps make a different response. For apparatus has discovered the veritable world, or, at least, a more subtle state of reality. It has revealed the filiation of forms since the massive notions of the original gestures, and that those forms, such as human still see them are suffered and not real in themselves. Human perceptions, renewed by apparatus, multiplied by machines, permit them now no longer to suffer the aspects of reality emerged from the darkness of the first hours, but to choose new aspects from the innumerable metamorphoses of a better known substance, to recreate via them new images in conformity with their more profound and more intimate intelligence of reality. Humans can form a *new memory* with their science, their possessions, redesign their body and the universe on the basis of new givens—the givens of their lucid desire, of their power, of their liberty, of their WILL TO JOY...

68

"These items of information, I have done my best to sketch for you in the course of our adventure. I have told you enough for new light to shine through your thoughts and your habits. I have only touched superficially on points that would be good and profound subjects of meditation. I would have liked to reveal to you how the arcandres live, in the knowledge of these sources of liberty and joy, the holders of powers that attest to the superlative verity of these facts and assure to whomever lives in accordance with them, the incalculable and radiant possession of the world that I conferred upon you momentarily. But it is appropriate that you, by the labor of your thoughts, regarding all that I have told you and showed you, attain the comprehension of the secret of the effective life of the arcandres, the games of delectations that compose their hours and their actions.

"Remember that these games have for lists not merely the universe such as you know it, where their physical bodies sport, but the different simultaneous planes of that universe, to which their other bodies have access at the same time, and where they can linger on those planes selected by their caprice. Remember too, as I have enabled you to experience, that their psychic and spiritual movements, and the corresponding worlds, can assume a character of concrete and plastic reality similar to the one—but how much more extensive and numerous!—that humans only know via their physical actions and the corresponding plane of the world...

"In any case, these separations of the physical, psychic and spiritual are all in human vocabulary. Thus, for us, our bodies, our limbs and the material world are, if we wish, if we look at them from the other planes of our being, images and vaporous abstractions, as thoughts are for humans. In the same way, the most subtle and most fluid aspects of our minds can be transferred into the simplest actions of our fleshy bodies, or the meanest object in the world.

"It is passion, as I have told you, that is the great agent of these transfers of life and reality into the different planes of being and the world. What I have called passion, for humans and for arcandres, is amour. The marvelous hearts that you have seen, in each of your cells, in each of the vibrations of your mind, the palpitations of the suns that you saw in my body of consciousness, are merely the transfusion of that amour into all the particles and all the tremors of being. It is your passion, as I have said, that was magnified to the point that you could see in reality the passing images of my four bodies; it is amour that gives us the real possession of things, contact with which ignites our consciousness.

"We love; we are nothing but love. Humans promulgate the thesis that combats for the enjoyment of the primordial rights of life, the inexorable necessities of the viscera, thirst for gold, the love of women, ambition for greatness or power, are the stimulants of action, the motors of all will, and suppose that without them, unspurred desire would languish or become extinct, and that would be the end of action and all life...a fine story! We, who have surpassed the fog of fatalities whose phantoms still weigh upon humans, exempt from all combats in order to eat, drink, clothe oneself and sleep, have an infinite supply of all the concrete goods for possession of which humans still devour one another, and we direct our labors, our efforts and our action towards more subtler goods. Do you reckon as nothing the uninterrupted desire to KNOW, and to embrace or possess more fully by virtue of knowledge a world that is magnified and multiplied as one penetrates it further?

"Do you think, in spite of our privileges, that we hold the entire reality of Being? What we know and possess is still very little by comparison with what there is to know and grasp in that reality! We are incessantly discovering new curiosities and delights, by means of our bodies of flesh in the world of forms, by means of our spiritual bodies in the abstract world. The innumerable multiplication of the elements and aspects of all things opens before our incessantly stimulated desire an infinity of goals, perpetually renewed. And in going into that innumerable world, under the influence of environments, spectacles, décors, under the influence of our joys and sensualities, we discover incessantly new, unforeseen and unsuspected faculties in ourselves, new beings awakening in our being, which lead us toward new goals, and other joys. The former and the latter react upon the faculties, which are refreshed and arm themselves for further voyages toward more discoveries.

"Now, there is no lassitude if we renew ourselves relentlessly, no satiation if the world is always new.

"We live and love in the perennial fortune of being innumerable in the bosom of an innumerable universe. Masters of forms, we do not limit ourselves to the sex that emerges from a single physical disposition. We are male and female by turns, at our whim, according to whether it pleases us to embrace or to be embraced. Our sexes are as numerous as our consciousnesses. The consciousness that illuminates when I hear a great symphony gives my entire being more profound sensualities than those that a woman in love knows in the arms of her lover. The consciousnesses that are illuminated in the course of my meditations are sometimes male, sometimes female, and my entire being that is devoted to them experiences by means of ideas caresses, languors and embraces that sometimes swoon and sometimes rise up in its ultimate molecules.

"There are no shadows over our joy. Your decrepit dualisms cannot conceive of anything without its contrary. Your excellent Anatole France, already named, and who counts among your most jovial sages, has said expressly: 'We are only happy because we are unhappy... Evil is necessary. Like good it has its profound source in nature, and one would dry up without the other... Moral evil and physical evil incessantly share the empire of the earth with happiness and joy, as night succeeds day therein... Suffering is the sister of joy and their twin breaths, in passing over our fibers, make them resonate harmoniously. The breath of happiness alone would render a monotonous and tedious sound similar to silence.'[22]

"But your dogmas of duality, that old law of contraries, that practical joke of necessary oppositions, Ormuzd and Ahriman, good and evil, happiness and unhappiness, suffering and joy, are as solidly founded as the contrast of black and white, massive colors that are only the play of your retinas. Dualism is, it is said, as real as the two eyes, the two arms or the two legs. Having attained a reality in which the states interpenetrate, in which forms are only images over which our passion or our amour has absolute power, I do not see any necessity in contraries, but rather perpetual ascendant transitions, the highest of which is the springboard and the contrast of one even higher, and so on.

"Undoubtedly, in order to think like that, it is first necessary to escape from the notion of a limited world and a human

---

[22] The quotation is from Anatole France's *Monsieur Bergeret à Paris* (1901).

condition to which it was said: *You shall go no further, and who ever attempts to do so is locked forever in a closed circle.* It is necessary to conceive of the world as innumerable everywhere and in all its parts, and to believe that it is possible to accede to it, to know it and to possess it without limits. My present joy has for its springboard and contrast the greater joy that I shall obtain. I have no need of suffering to savor joy; it is sufficient for me to think that the joy I am savoring is less than the one I shall savor. I have no need of unhappiness. It is sufficient to want an ever more gracious happiness, and to know that I have the resource to attain it, to find in that thought and that determination the contrast demanded by your philosophers and the springboard commanded by your moralists.

"Everything for us is a source of joy and magnification. The resistance of things is a springboard of efforts that enables us to know the quality and extent of our strength more fully. In the same way that the power to pierce any physical darkness relieves us of the terrors of the night, the sentiment of the power of knowledge, the sentiment of having the resource within us to learn and to know relieves us of the terrors of ignorance and doubt in so much suffering. Every ignorance is a springboard, the joyous opportunity for new knowledge

"Finally, we are safe from the worst suffering of all, which is that of losing the person one loves. You groan when an item of your property succumbs, because you believe it to be irreplaceable, and because you know that no matter how happy and rich you believe yourselves to be, how precarious is the patrimony of happiness and wealth that anyone possesses, and that any loss is a part of that patrimony that is gone forever. Would it be thus if you knew that you were rich with all calculable wealth, and knew that in the hour of your worst distress, or whenever you wished, every loss could be compensated by a new prebend? We have that knowledge, knowing our number, and the number infinite and incessantly increasing, of that which is pleasant. And as we know at the same time that inexhaustible profusion, the moving reality of the universe, and the superlative instability of everything, if one of those wisdoms gives us the sense and the intelligence of perpetual fragility, the other corresponds to the instinct and the consciousness of the unlimited abundance of life. The result is that the sense of immense generation abolishes in the arcandre the sentiment of the catastrophe."

69

At that moment, the voice of my friend was transformed. It became strangely melodious, as if increasingly fluid, similar to the chords that a harpist draws momentarily and then allows to die down of their own accord.

"So," he continued, "provided with everything for which humans still labor in dolor, nourished on all terrestrial nutrients, what tasks are our tasks? What are the ends that you would call the objectives of our powers and our being?

"Our works emerge naturally from our movements and our actions, in which the joy of being circulates as blood circulates in the limbs of humans. In Being, we give, we emanate, we radiate. We are similar to the light that accomplishes its work in shining, similar to the river that, without doing anything but flowing, carries vessels and fecundates its banks. Our cares, our labors and our duties are, for us, being in the eyes of others incessantly more beautiful, more radiant, more odorous, freer, more worthy of our status and our prerogatives..."

As he spoke thus it seemed that the arcandre became less and less real; it seemed that his body gradually became diaphanous and allowed the daylight and the spectacle of the surrounding things to pass through him. And his voice was so tenuous that one might have thought it the rustling of the grass.

"My friend," said that voice, still, "I have shown you nothing, told you nothing about our rhythms and our laws, our joys and our powers, which are merely the class and the pre-

311

rogative of all humans…the wheat is ripe that they have arduously sown, and the sickle is in their hands…"

He finished speaking, and there was a kind of dazzling
fulguration *behind* my eyes. I put my hands to my forehead
and lost sight of him momentarily, but I mastered that surprise
and opened my eyes again.

And now I was at the foot of the tree in the clearing
where the arcandre had appeared to me. I was alone, and nothing in the familiar décor had changed.

How had the arcandre vanished? Would I ever know…?

However, and extraordinary sensation suddenly gripped
me. It seemed to me that I was not the same person as I had
been before the marvelous visitation. Something was within
me that made me, now—I experienced the certainty of it—
stronger, more assured and more lucid.

Something…I dared not think, I dare not say and I dare
not write *someone*.

I stood up, simultaneously heavy with astonishing things
and radiant with a light to which I was not able at that moment
to give a name.

I left the clearing and headed toward the city.

70

My darling, my beloved, I wanted to tell you about that
adventure in case I was killed And now that the war is over
and I have come back to you, and the Ark that I resolved to
construct in which our dreams, our desires and our treasures
were assembled was not necessary, for each of us has retained
them intact within us, and we found them, on the day of our
reunion, as joyful, certain and familiar as the flowers that you
had arranged that day, as of old, on my work-table. My darling, where have I allowed myself to be led by the story of my
strange adventure? And how far that story has taken us away
from the goal I traced at first! But how else would I have been
able to tell you the marvelous story of my certainty of Joy, of
that certainty suddenly awakened in the midst of the war, by

the very words that I was writing to you, by the certainty that enabled me to get through the most sordid and the bitterest hours of that war, aided me to live, enabled me to live, in those execrable moments when the tree of life shed incessantly more human fruits than it seemed the crows of Death would ever be able to collect!

My darling, you would like to know what is authentic in that apparition of the arcandre, whether the long dictation is not a parable, whether it is true that arcandres really exist...

Does it not seem to you that the adventure was entirely true, and that the words spoken to me were true, in considering the bright joy of our life? And does it not seem that the visitation and the words have, with a singular force—the very force of reality—directed both my thoughts and my actions, and the destiny that set you in my path?

Have you not come, really, my beloved, like the miracle of my faith, to crown my certainty...?

But I will add that it ought not to go any further than the two of us, who are of the domains where the secrets of great happiness ought still to be kept.

15 November 1914-21 September 1919

SF & FANTASY

Adolphe Alhaiza. *Cybele*

Alphonse Allais. *The Adventures of Captain Cap*

Henri Allorge. *The Great Cataclysm*

Guy d'Armen. *Doc Ardan: The City of Gold and Lepers*

G.-J. Arnaud. *The Ice Company*

Charles Asselineau. *The Double Life*

Henri Austruy. *The Eupantophone; The Olotelepan; The Petitpaon Era*

Barillet-Lagargousse. *The Final War*

Cyprien Bérard. *The Vampire Lord Ruthwen*

S. Henry Berthoud. *Martyrs of Science*

Aloysius Bertrand. *Gaspard de la Nuit*

Richard Bessière. *The Gardens of the Apocalypse; The Masters of Silence*

Albert Bleunard. *Ever Smaller*

Félix Bodin. *The Novel of the Future*

Louis Boussenard. *Monsieur Synthesis*

Alphonse Brown. *City of Glass; The Conquest of the Air*

Émile Calvet. *In a Thousand Years*

André Caroff. *The Terror of Madame Atomos; Miss Atomos; The Return of Madame Atomos; The Mistake of Madame Atomos; The Monsters of Madame Atomos; The Revenge of Madame Atomos; The Resurrection of Madame Atomos; The Mark of Madame Atomos; The Spheres of Madame Atomos; The Wrath of Madame Atomos* (w/M. & Sylvie Stéphan)

Félicien Champsaur. *The Human Arrow; Ouha, King of the Apes; Pharaoh's Wife; Homo-Deus; Nora, The Ape-Woman*

Didier de Chousy. *Ignis*

Jules Clarétie. *Obsession*

Michel Corday. *The Eternal Flame*

André Couvreur. *The Necessary Evil*; *Caresco, Superman; The Exploits of Professor Tornada* (3 vols.)

Camille Debans. *The Misfortunes of John Bull*

Captain Danrit. *Undersea Odyssey*

C. I. Defontenay. *Star (Psi Cassiopeia)*

Charles Derennes. *The People of the Pole*

Chevalier de Béthune. *The World of Mercury*

Georges Dodds (anthologist). *The Missing Link*

Charles Dodeman. *The Silent Bomb*
Harry Dickson. *The Heir of Dracula; Harry Dickson vs. The Spider*
Jules Dornay. *Lord Ruthven Begins*
Alfred Driou. *The Adventures of a Parisian Aeronaut*
Sâr Dubnotal *vs. Jack the Ripper*
Odette Dulac. *The War of the Sexes*
Alexandre Dumas. *The Return of Lord Ruthven*
Renée Dunan. *Baal; The Ultimate Pleasure*
J.-C. Dunyach. *The Night Orchid; The Thieves of Silence*
Henri Duvernois. *The Man Who Found Himself*
Achille Eyraud. *Voyage to Venus*
Henri Falk. *The Age of Lead*
Paul Féval. *Anne of the Isles; Knightshade; Revenants; Vampire City; The Vampire Countess; The Wandering Jew's Daughter*
Paul Féval, *fils. Felifax, the Tiger-Man*
Charles de Fieux. *Lamékis*
Louis Forest. *Someone is Stealing Children in Paris*
Arnould Galopin. *Doctor Omega*; *Doctor Omega and the Shadowmen* (anthology)
Judith Gautier. *Isoline and the Serpent-Flower*
H. Gayar. *The Marvelous Adventures of Serge Myrandhal on Mars*
G.L. Gick. *Harry Dickson and the Werewolf of Rutherford Grange*
Delphine de Girardin. *Balzac's Cane*
Léon Gozlan. *The Vampire of the Val-de-Grâce*
Jules Gros. *The Fossil Man*
Edmond Haraucourt. *Illusions of Immortality; Daah, the First Human*
Nathalie Henneberg. *The Green Gods*
Eugène Hennebert. *The Enchanted City*
Jules Hoche. *The Maker of Men and His Formula*
V. Hugo, P. Foucher & P. Meurice. *The Hunchback of Notre-Dame*
Romain d'Huissier. *Hexagon: Dark Matter*
Jules Janin. *The Magnetized Corpse*
Michel Jeury. *Chronolysis*
Gustave Kahn. *The Tale of Gold and Silence*
Gérard Klein. *The Mote in Time's Eye*
Fernand Kolney. *Love in 5000 Years*
Paul Lacroix. *Danse Macabre*
Louis-Guillaume de La Follie. *The Unpretentious Philosopher*
Jean de La Hire. *Enter the Nyctalope; The Nyctalope on Mars; The Nyctalope vs. Lucifer; The Nyctalope Steps In; Night of the Nyctalope; Return of the Nyctalope; The Fiery Wheel*

Etienne-Léon de Lamothe-Langon. *The Virgin Vampire*
André Laurie. *Spiridon*
Gabriel de Lautrec. *The Vengeance of the Oval Portrait*
Alain le Drimeur. *The Future City*
Georges Le Faure & Henri de Graffigny. *The Extraordinary Adventures of a Russian Scientist Across the Solar System* (2 vols.)
Gustave Le Rouge. *The Mysterious Doctor Cornelius* (3 vols.); *The Vampires of Mars; The Dominion of the World* (w/Gustave Guitton) (4 vols.)
Jules Lermina. *Mysteryville; Panic in Paris; To-Ho and the Gold Destroyers; The Secret of Zippelius; The Battle of Strasbourg*
André Lichtenberger. *The Centaurs; The Children of the Crab*
Listonai. *The Philosophical Voyager*
Jean-Marc & Randy Lofficier. *Edgar Allan Poe on Mars; The Katrina Protocol; Pacifica; Robonocchio; Return of the Nyctalope;* (anthologists) *Tales of the Shadowmen 1-11; The Vampire Almanac* (2 vols.)
Xavier Mauméjean. *The League of Heroes*
Joseph Méry. *The Tower of Destiny*
Hippolyte Mettais. *The Year 5865; Paris Before the Deluge*
Louise Michel. *The Human Microbes; The New World*
Tony Moilin. *Paris in the Year 2000*
José Moselli. *Illa's End*
John-Antoine Nau. *Enemy Force*
Marie Nizet. *Captain Vampire*
C. Nodier, A. Beraud & Toussaint-Merle. *Frankenstein*
Henri de Parville. *An Inhabitant of the Planet Mars*
Gaston de Pawlowski. *Journey to the Land of the 4th Dimension*
Georges Pellerin. *The World in 2000 Years*
Ernest Pérochon. *The Frenetic People*
Pierre Pelot. *The Child Who Walked on the Sky*
J. Polidori, C. Nodier, E. Scribe. *Lord Ruthven the Vampire*
P.-A. Ponson du Terrail. *The Vampire and the Devil's Son; The Immortal Woman*
Georges Price. *The Missing Men of the Sirius*
Edgar Quinet. *Ahasuerus; The Enchanter Merlin*
Henri de Régnier. *A Surfeit of Mirrors*
Maurice Renard. *The Blue Peril; Doctor Lerne; The Doctored Man; A Man Among the Microbes; The Master of Light*
Jean Richepin. *The Wing; The Crazy Corner*

Albert Robida. *The Adventures of Saturnin Farandoul; The Clock of the Centuries; Chalet in the Sky; The Electric Life; The Engineer Von Satanas*

J.-H. Rosny Aîné. *Helgvor of the Blue River; The Givreuse Enigma; The Mysterious Force; The Navigators of Space; Vamireh; The World of the Variants; The Young Vampire*

Marcel Rouff. *Journey to the Inverted World*

Léonie Rouzade. *The World Turned Upside Down*

Han Ryner. *The Superhumans; The Human Ant*

Pierre de Selenes: *An Unknown World*

Angelo de Sorr. *The Vampires of London*

Brian Stableford. *The New Faust at the Tragicomique;The Empire of the Necromancers (The Shadow of Frankenstein; Frankenstein and the Vampire Countess; Frankenstein in London); Sherlock Holmes & The Vampires of Eternity; The Stones of Camelot; The Wayward Muse.* (anthologist) *News from the Moon; The Germans on Venus; The Supreme Progress; The World Above the World; Nemoville; Investigations of the Future; The Conqueror of Death; The Revolt of the Machines; The Man With the Blue Face*

Jacques Spitz. *The Eye of Purgatory*

Kurt Steiner. *Ortog*

Eugène Thébault. *Radio-Terror*

C.-F. Tiphaigne de La Roche. *Amilec*

Simon Tyssot de Patot. *The Strange Voyages of Jacques Massé and Pierre de Mésange*

Louis Ulbach. *Prince Bonifacio*

Théo Varlet. *The Golden Rock. The Xenobiotic Invasion; The Castaways of Eros; Timeslip Troopers* (w/André Blandin); *The Martian Epic* (w/Octave Joncquel)

Pierre Véron. *The Merchants of Health*

Paul Vibert. *The Mysterious Fluid*

Villiers de l'Isle-Adam. *The Scaffold; The Vampire Soul*

Gaston de Wailly. *The Murderer of the World*

Philippe Ward. *Artahe ; The Song of Montségur* (w/Sylvie Miller) *Manhattan Ghost* (w/Mickael Laguerre)

MYSTERIES & THRILLERS

M. Allain & P. Souvestre. *The Daughter of Fantômas*

A. Anicet-Bourgeois, Lucien Dabril. *Rocambole*

A. Bernède. *Belphegor; Judex* (w/Louis Feuillade); *The Return of Judex* (w/Louis Feuillade); *The Shadow of Judex*

A. Bisson & G. Livet. *Nick Carter vs. Fantômas*

V. Darlay & H. de Gorsse. *Arsène Lupin vs. Sherlock Holmes: The Stage Play*

Séamas Duffy. *Sherlock Holmes in Paris*

Paul Féval. *Gentlemen of the Night; John Devil; The Black Coats ('Salem Street; The Invisible Weapon; The Parisian Jungle; The Companions of the Treasure; Heart of Steel; The Cadet Gang; The Sword-Swallower)*

Émile Gaboriau. *Monsieur Lecoq*

Goron & Émile Gautier. *Spawn of the Penitentiary*

Paul d'Ivoi. *Around the World on Five Sous* (w/Henri Chabrillat)

Rick Lai. *Shadows of the Opera: Retribution in Blood; Sisters of the Shadows: The Curse of Cagliostro*

Steve Leadley. *Sherlock Holmes: The Circle of Blood*

Maurice Leblanc. *Arsène Lupin vs. Countess Cagliostro; Arsène Lupin vs. Sherlock Holmes (The Blonde Phantom; The Hollow Needle); The Many Faces of Arsène Lupin; The Island of the Thirty Coffin; 813*

Gaston Leroux. *Chéri-Bibi; The Phantom of the Opera; Rouletabille & the Mystery of the Yellow Room; Rouletabille at Krupp's*

Richard Marsh. *The Complete Adventures of Judith Lee*

William Patrick Maynard. *The Terror of Fu Manchu; The Destiny of Fu Manchu*

Frank J. Morlok. *Sherlock Holmes: The Grand Horizontals; Sherlock Holmes vs Jack the Ripper*

Jean Petithuguenin. *The Adventures of Ethel King*

Antonin Reschal. *The Adventures of Miss Boston*

Frank Schildiner. *The Quest of Frankenstein*

P. de Wattyne & Y. Walter. *Sherlock Holmes vs. Fantômas*

David White. *Fantômas in America*

Pierre Yrondy. *The Adventures of Thérèse Arnaud*

Victor Margueritte. *The Bacheloress; The Companion; The Couple*

SCREENPLAYS

Mike Baron. *The Iron Triangle*
Emma Bull & Will Shetterly. *Nightspeeder; War for the Oaks*
Gerry Conway & Roy Thomas. *Doc Dynamo*

Steve Englehart. *Majorca*
James Hudnall. *The Devastator*
Jean-Marc & Randy Lofficier. *Royal Flush*
J.-M. & R. Lofficier & Marc Agapit. *Despair*
J.-M. & R. Lofficier & Joël Houssin. *City*
Andrew Paquette. *Peripheral Vision*
Robert L. Robinson, Jr. *Judex*
R. Thomas, J. Hendler & L. Sprague de Camp. *Rivers of Time*

NON-FICTION

Stephen R. Bissette. *Blur 1-5. Green Mountain Cinema 1; Teen Angels*
Win Scott Eckert. *Crossovers* (2 vols.)
Jean-Marc & Randy Lofficier. *Shadowmen* (2 vols.)
Randy Lofficier. *Over Here*

ART BOOKS

Jean-Pierre Normand. *Science Fiction Illustrations*
Raven Okeefe. *Raven's L'il Critters; Rave's Faves*
Randy Lofficier & Raven Okeefe. *If Your Possum Go Daylight...*
Daniele Serra. *Illusions*
Randy Lofficier. *Over Here*

HEXAGON COMICS

Franco Frescura & Luciano Bernasconi. *Wampus*
Franco Frescura & Giorgio Trevisan. *CLASH*
L. Bernasconi, J.-M. Lofficier & Juan Roncagliolo. *Phenix*
Claude Legrand, J.-M. Lofficier & L. Bernasconi. *Kabur*
Franco Oneta. *Zembla*
L. Buffolente, Lofficier & J.-J. Dzialowski. *Strangers: Homicron*
Danilo Grossi. *Strangers: Jaydee*
Claude Legrand & Luciano Bernasconi. *Strangers: Starlock*
Thierry Mornet & Juan Roncagliolo. *Guardian of the Republic*
J.-M. Lofficier & others. *Strangers 0: Omens & Origins*
J.-M. Lofficier, M. Garcia, F. Blanco & J. Pima. *Strangers 1: Strangers in a Strange Land*